SpecOps

Expeditionary Force Book 2

By Craig Alanson

Craig Alanson

TABLE OF CONTENTS

CHAPTER ONE

The *Flying Dutchman* shuddered again, with sounds of groaning and the terrifying shriek of metal composites being torn apart. The displays on the bridge flickered, and the air was filled with alarm bells and klaxons from almost every system. "Skippy! Get us out of-"

The ship shook violently again. "Direct hit on Number Four reactor," Skippy announced calmly, "reactor has lost containment. I am preparing it for ejection. Ejection system is offline. Pilot, portside thrusters, full emergency thrust on my mark."

"Ready," Desai acknowledged in as calm a voice as she could manage.

"Mark. Go!" Skippy shouted.

Whatever they were doing, it was more than the ship's already stressed artificial gravity and inertial compensation systems could handle, normally ship maneuvers were not felt at all by the crew. This time, I lurched in the command chair and had to hang on, as the ship was flung to the right. There was a shudder, actually a wave of ripples traveling along the ship's spine, accompanied by a deep harmonic groaning. No ship should ever make a sound like that.

"Ah, damn it. Reactor Four is away, it impacted Reactor Two on the way out, shutting down Two now." Skippy's voice had a touch of strain to it. "Missiles inbound. Diverting all remaining power to jump drive capacitors. Hang on, this is going to be close."

The main display indicated the jump drive was at a 38% charge, Skippy had told us that with the *Dutchman* trapped inside the Thuranin destroyer squadron's damping field, we needed a 42% charge for even a short jump, and that still carried a severe risk of rupturing the drive. If that happened, we would never know it, we'd simply be dead between one picosecond and another.

The missile symbols on the display, seven of them, were coming in fast. Two of the symbols disappeared as I watched, destroyed by our ship's point defense maser beams. The other five missiles continued toward us, fast, fuzzing our sensors with their stealth fields and weaving as they bored in. One more missile destroyed. Four still moving fast.

Jump drive at 40%.

Too close.

I turned the knob to release the plastic cover over the self-destruct button, and turned to look through the glass wall into the CIC compartment. "Colonel Chang."

He nodded, and I saw him flip back the cover to the other self-destruct button, the confirmation. "Sir." He looked me straight in the eye, and saluted.

I returned the salute. "Colonel Chang, we have been down a long, strange road together. It's been an honor serving with you." My left thumb hovered over the self-destruct button. The ship was dying anyway. This was my fault. How the hell had I gotten us into this mess?

I'd better start at the beginning.

My name is Joe Bishop, I'm a sergeant, temporarily holding the theater rank of colonel, in the United States Army. Neither rank matters much at the moment, since I'm aboard a stolen alien starship over a thousand lightyears from Earth. Believe it or not, the United Nations Expeditionary Force has put me in command of our ship, a Thuranin star carrier we unwisely named the *Flying Dutchman*. I have, I think, good common sense, and, everyone else would agree, a history of getting into trouble. Big trouble. And a history of getting out of trouble. If you ask me, I've been in the right places at the wrong times. My critics would say that I am one lucky son of a bitch. My mother is not a bitch, but other than that, they may have a point. Skippy, our ancient alien talking beer can combination mascot and artificial super intelligence, says there is no such thing as luck, that humans believe in luck because our dumb monkey-level linear thinking has no idea how the universe works.

Whatever.

When the *Flying Dutchman* went outbound through the wormhole near Earth, and Skippy shut down the wormhole behind us, I have to admit a tiny, tiny part of me was disappointed that the ship didn't immediately explode into a bazillion pieces. One of our cargo holds has a dozen tactical nukes from the American inventory. We only need nuke one to vaporize the ship and erase all trace that humans were roaming the galaxy, but somebody had a coupon, or they were cheaper by the dozen at Nukes 'R Us or something, so we had eleven extras. No, they aren't available as last-minute birthday gifts, thanks for asking. When Skippy confirmed the wormhole had been shut down behind us, deactivated it this time, not merely temporarily disrupted its connection to the network or whatever, a tiny part of me hoped that UNEF had somehow snuck behind Skippy's back and set a nuke to explode right then.

You ever been on a cliff or the balcony of a really tall building, and you look over the edge with butterflies in your stomach, and you're afraid of falling, but a tiny part of you wants to jump? A tiny part of you, that you're afraid you won't be able to control, wants to jump? You're afraid of being near the edge, because you think you might not be able to control yourself, that you might feel compelled to jump? I read somewhere that is because part of your brain can't stand the tension, and wants the tension to just go away, even if the solution kills you. No? Never had that happen to you? Hey, I'm afraid of heights, that's why I never signed up for Army parachute training. Flying in a Blackhawk helo with the door open hadn't bothered me much, as long as I could hear the engines howling above my head, I figured we'd be all right. Being on my parents' house roof stringing Christmas lights, now that kind of thing scared the hell out of me. Scared me enough that, every February I had argued with my mother against taking the lights down. Why go through the trouble of taking them down, I asked? Sure, most of the year our neighbors would grumble that the Bishop family were lazy procrastinators, but by October, maybe November, we'd begin to look like proactive geniuses. Right?

My mother never fell for that argument. The Christmas lights were always down by Super Bowl weekend.

In this case it wasn't heights I was afraid of, my fear was of the unknown, of being responsible for all the people aboard the ship, and, if one of my screw-ups meant our enemies discovered humans had stolen a Thuranin star carrier, of me being responsible for the destruction of humanity. If the *Dutchman* had exploded beyond my control, I wouldn't have to be concerned about my inevitable screw-ups.

UNEF hadn't set a nuke to explode, or they did, and Skippy of course discovered their plan and stopped it. It would have been easier for everyone if the *Dutchman* had become a rapidly expanding sphere of subatomic particles. Either way, we were still alive and I had to continue the mission as planned. Darn.

If the *Dutchman* had exploded, it would have killed seventy people. Our new not-so-Merry Band of Pirates was fifty eight military personnel, and a dozen civilian scientists. This time, we were semi-officially a Merry Band of Pirates, everyone had on their uniform the paramecium-with-eyepatch logo that Skippy designed for us. Even the scientists were given a patch on their official mission jackets. So far I hadn't seen many of the scientists wearing those jackets, and I wasn't going to make an issue of it. Scientists, civilians, didn't worry me. What did concern me is that, this time, the military units assigned to the *Dutchman* were from SpecOps units; elite special forces troops and hotshot pilots.

By the way, when I left Earth the first time, I'd been current on military slang, at least US military slang. But apparently, I was the only one who didn't know people on Earth were pronouncing the United Nations Expeditionary Force: 'YOU-neff'. And this is before we even left! This whole time I've been wasting precious lightyears spelling it out: U-N-E-F. Skippy probably had a minor beer can meltdown. Although in my defense Skippy, in his absent-minded way, dropped the ball plenty of times. So, where was I? Right. YOU-neff. After we left, governments had wanted to emphasize the glorious contributions of their own armed forces to fighting the horrible Ruhar, so they'd stopped mentioning the 'UN' part of 'UNEF' and just called us the Expeditionary Force, or ExFor. The name Exfor sounded cool, and it stuck. A bit later, when people and their governments began to regret the alliance with the Kristang, the governments in UNEF tried to emphasize again the United Nations part, as if the governments that were part of UNEF had no responsibility for what had happened. By that time, it was too late, 'ExFor' had stuck in the public's mind.

The mission was technically under the command of the United Nations Expeditionary Force Special Operations Command directorate. Yeah, that's a mouthful to say. And in reality, I was in command all by myself, because as soon as the *Dutchman* jumped away from Earth orbit, we were on our own. If things went well, UNEF SOCOM would take credit. If things went sideways, they would heap the blame on me. That's the way it works.

When Special Operations Command assigned our crew, I first called the new Merry Band of Pirates 'SOCOM', then I quickly learned all the cool kids used the term 'SpecOps', pronounced like Speck Opps. Although when I, a soldier who had never been in a special operations unit, tried to be a cool kid by saying SpecOps, I got some weird looks. I was learning.

Let me explain about SpecOps, or special forces troops. My knowledge comes from observing, and certainly not from experience. Whether they are US Navy SEALs, US Army Rangers, British SAS or in any other military service on Earth, SpecOps soldiers are all bad-asses, and they know it. Getting into special forces units requires incredible commitment to meet tough physical standards, and much more importantly, mental toughness.

You know those guys, or girls, in high school or even before that, who already knew exactly what they wanted to do in life? They were completely focused, in great physical shape, getting up at 5AM for swimming or hockey practice or running or lifting weights before school. They got good grades, studied hard, never slacked off, the adults always liked them. They were great athletes, intense even in practices. Most importantly, they were serious, serious about life, even as young teenagers, at a time when most of us were drifting along or flailing through life, having no idea what we wanted. Those guys and girls? They are where SpecOps troops come from. They're better than most of us, certainly better than me. I am a reasonably dedicated soldier, proud to wear the uniform. No way could I qualify for special forces. The physical stuff I could train myself up to do, I'm pretty sure. The difference is, I would never want to train that hard. I don't have the internal discipline, or the drive, to work that hard, I simply don't have enough desire to do it. I greatly admire the people who do make that level of commitment, and I'm glad I don't have to.

Special forces are the best of the best, and the *Dutchman* got the best people from Special Operations commands of the five nations in UNEF. I couldn't imagine the competition that had gone on for slots aboard the *Dutchman*, the only thing I was sure of is that I would never have qualified.

Our new Merry Band of Pirates completely intimidated me. They were tougher than me, smarter than me, more dedicated, more driven, better soldiers and human beings in almost every way I could think of. And I was in command of these super humans. Me. I wasn't worthy. They knew it. I knew it.

Part of being officially in command of an actual UNEF mission, instead of being the do-it-yourself leader of a pirate ship, was the mountains of official paperwork, even if paper had been replaced by iPads. I hated it, I had never been good at dealing with boring details. "Joe," Skippy said to me while I was in my office the day after we left the wormhole behind, trying to deal with the tedious administrative details of being a commander. "I have a question for you. Technically, a complaint."

"Ayuh. Write it on a piece of paper, and put it in the suggestion box."

"We have a suggestion box?" He asked, sounding genuinely surprised.

"Yup. It's in the closest black hole. Just drop it in, and wait."

"Oh, ha, ha. Very funny, Joey."

"A black hole will get you the same result as a suggestion box, so-"

"All right, I get the message. Anyway, I was looking at the crew roster database on your iPad-"

"Oh, man, don't remind me, please, I've got enough of this damned administrivia to deal with already."

"This is an easy one, Joe. I noticed there's no entry for me in the crew roster. I'm not even listed as a passenger, and I'm clearly crucial to the proper operation of the ship. I should be listed as part of the crew."

"I'm sorry, Skippy, I didn't know you cared." Damn, our super powerful alien AI was sensitive about the oddest things. He hated it when he was considered differently than any other sentient being aboard the ship. "You're right, that's my fault. I'll input your data right now. Oh, and I see you've already helpfully pulled up the input screen on my iPad for me. Did you save the report I spent the last twenty minutes writing?"

"Yeah, like humanity needs to read that mindless drivel. I'd be doing monkeykind a favor by erasing that crap. Sure, it's, uh, saved."

"It had better be, I already forgot what the hell I wrote in that report. First item in the crew roster is given name, so I'll input 'Skippy'. Second item is surname-"

"The Magnificent."

"Really?"

"It is entirely appropriate, Joe."

"Oh, uh huh, because that's what everyone calls you," I retorted sarcastically, rolling my eyes. Not wanting to argue with him, I typed in 'TheMagnificent'. "Next question is your rank, this file is designed for military personnel."

"I'd like 'Grand Exalted Field Marshall El Supremo'."

"Right, I'll type in 'Cub Scout'. Next question-"

"Hey! You jerk-"

"-is occupational specialty."

"Oh, clearly that should be Lord God Controller of All Things."

"I'll give you that one, that is spelled A, S, S, H, O, L, E. Next-"

"Hey! You shithead, I should-"

"Age?" I asked.

"A couple million, at least. I think."

"Mentally, you're a six year old, so that's what I typed in."

"Joe, I just changed your rank in the personnel file to 'Big Poopyhead'." Skippy laughed.

"Five year old. You're a five year old."

"I guess that's fair," he admitted.

"Sex? I'm going to select 'n/a' on that one for you," I said.

"Joe, in your personnel file, I just updated Sex to 'Unlikely'."

"This is not going well, Skippy."

"You started it!"

"That was mature. Four year old, then. Maybe Terrible Twos."

"I give up," Skippy snorted. "Save the damned file and we'll call it even, Ok?"

"No problem. We should do this more often, huh?"

"Oh, shut up."

I thought that was the end of it, until five minutes later, when Sergeant Adams called me. "Sir, I'm looking at the crew training roster, and Skippy is now listed as 'Asshole, First Class'?"

"Oh, damn it," I hadn't thought anyone would look at the stupid roster. "I'll change the darned thing."

"No need, sir, it certainly describes him," Adams laughed.

"That it does."

"Also, the required training schedule under your name now lists 'potty training'. I thought you should know. Also it says you need to learn about the 'birds and the bees'."

"Oh, crap. Skippy and I had a talk a few minutes ago, it looks like I need another one."

"You think that's going to change anything?" She asked skeptically.

"Not really."

It wasn't only me, every one of the original Merry Band of Pirates was intimidated by our new all-star crew. The second night after we left the now-deactivated wormhole behind, I'd gone into the galley at 4AM, unable to sleep, wanting a cup of coffee and some human company. Before getting dressed, I checked my iPad for the Uniform of the Day, posted by Colonel Chang as the ship's executive officer. Most days, we wore cammies, and on Mondays, we would be wearing dress uniforms to dinner. Today was the standard summer service uniform, or whatever each country's military had as the equivalent. When I got to the galley, to my surprise, I found Lt Colonel Chang, Major Simms, Captain Giraud and Captain Desai sitting at a table, bleary-eyed and drinking coffee. After I poured a cup for myself, Sergeant Adams walked in, and I handed a cup to her.

There we were, the six of us, alone in the galley. The six members of the original Merry Band of Pirates who were still aboard the ship. We'd been through so much together, so much we hadn't expected to survive, that I felt like hugging them all. I refrained, because Sergeant Adams would have punched me if I tried to hug her. Instead, I bumped fists with Adams, and handed her a cup of coffee.

"This is a coincidence," I observed.

"For you, sir, maybe," Adams replied, sitting down across from Giraud. "My duty shift starts in an hour."

"Mine also." Simms said over a mouthful of coffee.

"I couldn't sleep." Chang said simply.

"Same here," I said. I sat down next to Desai and raised my cup for a toast. "To the original Merry Band of Pirates. Especially those who didn't make it home."

Coffee cups clinked together, and we all drank. The cups didn't actually make a clinking sound, as they were plastic, but they had the official UNEF logo on one side, and 'UNS Flying Dutchman' on the other. If by some total freakin' miracle, we ever returned to Earth, I could definitely see these plastic cups getting smuggled off the ship and becoming a much-prized collector's item. The six of us started catching up, because most of us didn't see much of each other between the time we left the Dutchman, and the few days before departure from Earth orbit. None of us had time to talk much during those frantic days of loading and preparing the ship, after the governments on Earth had finally made the forehead-smackingly obvious decision to send the Dutchman back out. Every single survivor of the original Merry Band of Pirates had volunteered to take the Dutchman back out again; after a lot of discussion, argument and thinking, and a whole lot of politics among the governments involved, I had only accepted the five sitting with me in the galley. Although all the survivors volunteered to take the Dutchman back out, they didn't all need to come with us, and their governments were keen on having some of them remain on Earth, for the knowledge they had. Many of the survivors had injuries, Giraud still had his arm encased in a Thuranin healing sleeve, and Chang's ribs were still tender. Doctor Skippy's prognosis was for Giraud to have his arm out of the sleeve and fully healed in two more days; that was not soon enough for the French paratrooper, because he said his arm itched like a thousand ants were biting him. Skippy said that was all in Giraud's head.

This trip, I firmly believed, was a fool's errand, a suicide mission. The original Merry Band of Pirates had pushed their luck to the limit already, to expect more from them was crazy. I'd been forced to argue, using, let's say, strong language, with Sergeant Adams, trying to persuade her not to come with us. She didn't have anything to prove, I'd told her, she had sacrificed enough. What I didn't say what that, although we'd both been prisoners of the Kristang and scheduled to be executed, she had also been tortured. I'd seen her scars. Man, she laid into me for that, practically shouting that I was only saying that because she is a woman, that if she was a male Marine, I wouldn't pamper her. She was wrong about that, she also hadn't let me get a word in while she berated me. "With all due respect, sir, you wear colonel's eagles, but we both know you're a buck sergeant. You need me."

She had been right, one hundred percent, and I was damned glad to have her. I was glad to have all of them, people I knew and trusted. Our new crew were all-stars, to be sure, they were also people I didn't know. Before launch, I had deliberately avoided gathering just the six of us, as I didn't want the rest of the crew to think I favored my old comrades. Although of course I did. There were other pilots aboard with vastly greater experience and qualifications than Captain Desai, pilots who had flown the hottest jets, test pilots, top guns. And not a single one of them were allowed to touch a single button of the Dutchman's controls, unless they were under Desai's supervision. Any of them might be able to be trusted to pilot an alien starship, Desai was trusted. Skippy felt the same way. Regardless of each pilot's official callsign before they came aboard the Flying Dutchman, Skippy began by calling all of them 'FiNG' for Fucking New Guy, or Girl. We had to explain to the new pilots that Skippy was actually being pretty nice, considering, you know, Skippy. One pilot, who I won't name, pissed Skippy off enough that his new assigned quarters were an airlock. That required me to intervene, although I could see Skippy's point. That pilot's new callsign instantly became 'ALliGator' for Air Lock Guy. It's a pilot thing.

"What do you think of the new crew?" I asked to no one in particular.

Chang spoke first, after diplomatically taking a pause to sip coffee. "It will be an interesting exercise in international cooperation."

Giraud nodded, then shrugged. "We will see."

Seventy people aboard the ship. Twelve of them were scientists, civilians. Of those, seven were women, and five men, their specialties covered everything from medicine and biology to physics. Competition for a berth aboard the *Dutchman* had been fierce among scientists, a bit less so after I explained that I did not realistically expect us to ever return. If it had been entirely up to me, we would have taken zero scientists along. We didn't need scientists to achieve the mission objectives, and they would be only more people dead if we couldn't return to Earth. The number of people in our new Merry Band of Pirates had not been my decision to make. Governments around the globe had insisted we bring scientists along, the original list had several thousand names on it. Limiting us to twelve scientists had been the best compromise I could get. My final criteria for who came with us, and who stayed home, was less about pure scientific ability, and more about ability to get along with other people. What we did not need was a bunch of genius brainiacs, or, as Skippy referred to them, slightly smarter monkeys, who had massive egos and became a pain in the ass during a long trip aboard the *Dutchman*. That was part of the reason we had more women scientists than men, too many of the male candidates had failed UNEF's 'gets along well with others' psychological tests.

"International cooperation." I repeated the phrase slowly. "Our original crew cooperated well," I pointed out.

"We had to," Chang said, "and our mission then was to rescue Earth. We were all highly motivated."

"Our crew back then was whoever was available, right there," Giraud pointed out. "I was only at the logistics base because my commander sent me, to find out why supplies were so slow getting to us."

"We sent what we had at the time," Simms said defensively.

Giraud nodded. "Yes, I realized that when I got there, Major. My point, Colonel, is our original crew had a sense of great purpose. We were thrown together, unexpectedly, to rescue our entire planet. Our new crew has no such sense of purpose."

"And these special forces all think they are special," Adams remarked sourly over her coffee. "No offense, sir," she added to Giraud.

"None taken," he laughed. "Some of them intimidate me," he admitted, and Renee Giraud had been an elite French paratrooper even before we went to Paradise.

"You too?" I asked. "They all intimidate me. My concern is these rivalries may get out of hand." Rivalries not only between nationalities, I also had to worry about how US Army Rangers and Navy SEALs would get along. Professionally, I hoped.

Adams bumped fists with Giraud across the table. "Don't worry, sir, we'll get them straightened out." Chang had assigned the experienced Giraud and Adams to get our new special forces units squared away, and to set up a training regimen. The new people had to learn about the *Dutchman*, the *Flower* and dropships for basics. Then they would move on to familiarizing themselves with Kristang powered armor and combots.

Craig Alanson

What I was really worried about was our elite, gung-ho, intense special forces troops becoming bored. Before we departed Earth orbit, I had assembled the entire off-duty crew and scientists in an empty cargo bay. I explained, once again, that my sincere hope was for us to see zero combat action. That we would see nothing interesting along the way. A successful mission, in my opinion, would be for us to find Skippy's magic radio, drop him off somewhere, and for the *Dutchman* to return uneventfully to Earth. Or, in the all-too-likely scenario of the *Dutchman* breaking down somewhere after Skippy left us, of us being stuck in interstellar space, with food running low, and me having to engage our self-destruct. When I told the crew that unpleasant fact, I could see special forces nodding grimly. I also saw in their eyes they didn't fully believe it. They were trained for action, and action is what they expected. I hoped to disappoint them.

Our new mission continued to use the UN Expeditionary Force command structure. The scientists came from many nations, but the military forces were drawn from only five countries; America, China, India, Britain and France. Each country provided nine special forces soldiers, except that America had only four Rangers and four SEALs, because an American commanded the mission. Each country also provided two pilots. Giraud and Desai were in the special forces and pilot count, that left me, Chang, Simms and Adams rounding out the fifty eight military personnel aboard.

I drank the last of the coffee in my cup, and got up for a refill. The coffee pot was almost empty, I drained the dregs into my cup and got the pot started on brewing more. There wasn't any breakfast available yet, other than do-it-yourself toast. "Whose turn is it in the galley today?" Details like that were Chang's decision as the Executive Officer, I should have known anyway. There was a duty roster somewhere. Like, on my zPhone, that I was too lazy to look at.

"China." Chang replied. "We'll get started in an hour or so."

"That's fine, I'm not hungry yet," I said. What was a Chinese breakfast like? I was eager to find out. Our crew was scientists, pilots and special forces. We had no cooks, no mechanics, none of the usual support personnel. Each day, one nationality among the military forces would handle cooking in the galley, with the scientists making up a sixth team for cooking duties. The food situation was going to be interesting, culinary skill had not been a prerequisite for assignment aboard the *Flying Dutchman*, although I knew we could count on the hyper competitive special forces to do their best. With a fresh half cup of coffee, I headed toward the door. "I'm going to hit the gym," I announced. Getting there early hopefully meant I would be working out by myself, without being surrounded by SpecOps people who were all in better condition than I was. Maybe I needed to be concerned about my own ego, too.

CHAPTER TWO

When I was done working out in the gym, I needed a shower. It was a lung-burning, muscle aching workout that left my legs like jelly and my arms shaky. Literally, my arms were so weary, my hands were shaking. Even my fingers hurt. And the six Chinese SpecOps guys who were in the gym while I was there had been doing a tougher workout. They were already well into their exercises before I got to the gym, and when I left, they were headed out of the gym to run sprints down the *Dutchman's* long spine corridor. I felt like collapsing.

In the shower, I had to kneel down, because it was a Thuranin-sized shower, and we hadn't been able to fix that when we refitted the *Dutchman* in Earth orbit. Beds had been lengthened to human size by cutting away cabinets we didn't need, but adjusting showers had not been on the priority list in the short time we had before our pirated star carrier had to depart. My shaky fingers missed the shower controls several times, and I cursed out loud.

"Something wrong, Colonel Joe?" Skippy's voice had an undertone of genuine concern. "You seem especially clumsy this morning."

"Especially? Thanks a lot, Skippy."

"I meant no offense. A clumsy monkey is a dead monkey, Joe. When you're swinging from trees in the jungle, the clumsy monkey falls and gets eaten by a leopard."

"Ha!" I had to laugh at that. "Not many leopards in this part of the galaxy, Skippy. My arms are tired, that's all, I did a tough workout."

"I know; I was watching you. Don't you think you're overdoing it a bit, Joe?"

"Hell no. Those SpecOps guys, and the women, hell, especially the women, are super high speed, Skippy. Damn it, I'm in good shape, and I'm younger than most of them, and they're kicking my ass already. I'd like to train with them, but the first time one of them throws me to the mat without breaking a sweat, I think I'd totally lose their respect."

"Wow. You truly are a dumb monkey. How can anyone be so clueless? Joe, those SpecOps people are completely intimidated by you, they have a huge chip on their shoulders about you. And about the other members of the original Merry Band of Pirates."

"What?" I sputtered under the cascading water. "Give me a minute to rinse off." With a still shaky hand, I pressed the button to shut off the water, and backed out to stand up carefully to reach for a towel. "How do you figure that? Those people have gone through the toughest military training there is, they're the best. They're all completely, super confident."

"Super confident about most things, probably, yes. About you, no. Think about it from their point of view, Joe. When UNEF went off world, they stayed behind. For one reason or another, they were left behind, they missed out on all the action. Right there, they all think they have something to prove, to you, Chang and the others."

"Huh. I guess you're right, Skippy, I hadn't thought of that."

"That's just the beginning. You not only went off world, you captured two alien starships, brought back priceless intel, and rescued your entire species from the Kristang. Joe, these SpecOps people are completely in awe of you, you and all the original crew. Yes, they have passed an extremely rigorous selection process that requires incredible physical and mental toughness. However, what have they actually accomplished? What are the odds, that, during their entire military careers, they will accomplish anything anywhere close to what you did? The answer is about zero, Joe. And they all know it. Joe, they all think *you* look down on *them*."

"Crap." He was right, I had been utterly clueless. I'd been thinking only of myself, and not considering how the new crew might think of their situation. Back when I was in the US Army 10th 'Mountain' Infantry Division, and our battalion first went into Nigeria to boost the 'peacekeeping' efforts in that region, I had been in awe of the guys in the battalion that were rotating out. They had been there, they had lived it, they knew the territory, they had been in combat. They'd done it for real, I had only been briefed on it. You could see it in their eyes, too. They knew that many of the guys in our battalion, including me, were green and had never carried a rifle in a hostile area. It made a difference. And when it was our battalion's turn to pull out and go home, we'd changed, all of us. We'd been there. We knew.

The SpecOps people now aboard the *Flying Dutchman* had not been there, had not been off world, had likely never seen an alien in person. They'd been put through hell on Earth by the Kristang; I'd been spared that experience. Still, I had served in UNEF on Paradise, and they hadn't. Many special forces units had not made the trip to Paradise; the Kristang hadn't especially wanted them, and governments on Earth may have been hedging their bets, keeping most of their elite combat power close to home. At some point, if the *Dutchman* hadn't appeared in the sky for Skippy to stomp the Kristang like bugs, maybe the SpecOps people would have at least tried to hit the Kristang. It would have been a futile gesture to attack the Kristang in their bunkers, and impossible to attack them aboard their ships in orbit. Any SpecOps action would have been a measure of pure desperation, to make a last stand for the sake of human honor and nothing else. I didn't often think about what life had been like for people on Earth while I was off world. It must have been horrible, terrifying. On Paradise, we'd dealt with the reality that all of our supplies, especially food, had to be brought from Earth by the Kristang, and we'd seen supply shipments getting thin toward the end of my stay there. That had been bad enough, to gradually come to the realization that we were fighting on the wrong side of the war, that our 'allies' were oppressing our home planet, that if UNEF didn't follow the Kristang's every command, the lizards could starve us by halting food shipments.

It must have been worse, much worse, on Earth. On Paradise, we had been worried about the survival of the Expeditionary Force. People on Earth knew the stakes were much higher; not only the fate of billions of humans, the survival of our entire species could have been at risk. When we went off world with UNEF, we hadn't known what we were getting into, but we expected it to be bad, very bad. On Earth, people at first considered the Kristang to be saviors; aliens who looked like big, ugly lizards, still, our saviors from the invading Ruhar. The Kristang had saved Earth from the Ruhar so when the Kristang began pushing their weight around, interfering in human affairs, taking territory, taking rare minerals and other materials, at first people figured that was the price of supporting the war effort, the price of keeping the Ruhar from conquering our home planet and enslaving humanity. When was it that most people on Earth gotten the uneasy feeling that they'd made a bad bargain, that the Kristang, who by then had total control of the planet, were as bad as we'd imagined the Ruhar would be? I didn't know, that was something I should ask the new crew about. They probably wanted to talk about it, needed to talk about it. Needed to talk about it to someone who hadn't lived through it.

"You're right, Skippy, I should have thought of this. I'm the commander, I'm supposed to know what's on my people's minds. I-, hey, wait a minute. How do *you* know what they're thinking?"

"From listening to them talk, duh. Damn, you're a dope sometimes."

"Skippy, you can't do that. People need privacy."

"Joe, I can't *not* do that. I monitor every system on this ship in real-time, that includes video and audio inputs. You already know I watch you sleep, I watch you in the shower, I watch you eat-"

"Yeah, I know. Kinda creepy there, Skippy."

"Uh huh, as if I care what you monkeys look like naked. You're just as ugly with your clothes on."

"Fine. Whatever. What you can't do is tell me, or anyone else, what you heard people say in private. We must have at least the illusion of privacy aboard the ship. If people know you watch everything they do, that's something they can deal with, because you're an alien AI. To most people you're part of the furniture, an invisible ship system. If people know their fellow crew members, or their commander, are spying on them, using details of their private lives for gossip, that could destroy morale. Do you understand that?"

"I don't see what the big deal is, Joe. Sure, I won't tell you or anyone else what I see or hear. One question: what if I find out someone is planning to do something stupid that would harm the ship, or the mission?"

"In that case, you do tell me, only the details I need to hear. Got it?"

"I think so, yes. Damn, you monkeys have such complicated social rules, for a species so low on the development scale."

I just got to my office, a converted storage closet close to the bridge and Combat Information Center compartments, when Skippy gave me a warning. "Uh oh, Colonel Joe, heads up. Baldilocks is on his way to see you."

"Baldilocks?" I laughed. "Who is that?"

"United States Navy Lieutenant Williams," he explained.

Williams commanded our four-man SEAL team; he had a shaved head, hence Skippy's nickname for him. Also, I'd already determined Skippy didn't like him. I knew that because Skippy told me so. Williams and I were not best of friends so far either. My impression was he thought I was completely unqualified for command of such an important mission; that I was unprofessional, uncommitted, too young and inexperienced, not taking my responsibilities seriously, and not much of a soldier. I disagreed with that last one. "Thanks for the warning, Skippy." I straightened up in my chair, and adjusted the iPad to the ergonomically correct position on the table, rather than in my lap where it had been.

Williams knocked on the wall beside the door a minute later, the door was permanently recessed into the wall, I wanted to literally have an open door policy. "Colonel Bishop?"

At the time, I was pretending to read something on my iPad, so he wouldn't know that Skippy had warned me he was coming. "Lieutenant Williams. Come in, sit down. How are you finding the *Flying Dutchman*?"

"It's still a bit overwhelming," he admitted. "When we came aboard, I thought we would have somewhat of an advantage, because SEAL teams are accustomed to being deployed aboard ships. I'm finding that doesn't apply much here."

We chatted for five minutes, him talking about how amazing it was to be in space, aboard a captured alien starship, me expressing gratefulness for how we'd been able to modify the *Dutchman* before we left Earth. Some of the ornate decoration in the bridge and CIC compartments had been toned down, or painted over. We now had a galley; a place to cook, serve and eat food, real food. And we had cargo holds full of food, enough to last seventy people for years. Maybe the best modification was the beds; sleeping compartments had been cut away so a full size bed fit inside; no more trying to sleep curled up in a cramped Thuranin-sized bed.

Chang was supposed to come into my office soon, for our daily meeting, so I decided to find out that Williams wanted. "What's the issue, Lieutenant? I assume you didn't come in here to chat about the ship."

"Sir, I appreciate the experience Sergeant Adams brings," Williams said, "and I welcome her advice. However, she is not familiar with SEAL, or Ranger, training standards. Or training methods of the British SAS, French paratroopers-"

"You've made your point, Lieutenant," I interrupted him. Chang was my executive officer, second in command of the ship. Simms was in charge of logistics, and third in command. Desai was our chief pilot. Giraud was part of the French paratrooper team. And Adams, at Chang's suggestion, I had assigned to be in charge of training our SpecOps people about the ship, and the fancy new alien weapons they would be using.

"You shouldn't be so cocky, Lieutenant Williams," Skippy added, "you weren't even the first choice to lead the SEAL team."

Williams didn't flinch. "Sir," it wasn't clear whether he was addressing that remark to me or to the invisible Skippy, "I know I was the second choice-"

"Fourth choice, actually," Skippy chimed in helpfully.

"Fourth?" Williams asked, startled this time.

"Lieutenant Jerome Hansen was the first choice," Skippy explained. "He turned down the assignment because he did not want to serve under Colonel Bishop. Hansen felt you were too inexperienced for such responsibility, Joe."

"That's understandable," I responded. Probably most of the SpecOps people felt that way. Hell, I felt that way.

"Lieutenant Williams here agreed to serve under your command, and was originally the second choice. However, he refused the secret conditions your military wanted to impose."

"What secret conditions?" I looked at Williams sharply.

Williams bit his lip, and explained. "The DIA guys wanted me to take over the ship, if I felt it was necessary, sir. I refused."

"Yup, you did," Skippy added cheerily. "And the third guy they offered the assignment to also refused their condition, so they went back to you, and dropped their idiot idea of planning a mutiny. That's why, technically, you are the fourth choice to command the SEAL team."

Williams looked back to me. "I didn't know that, sir. I think the mutiny idea was something DIA, and I suspect CIA, wanted."

"I appreciate that you didn't come aboard intending to take over my ship, Lieutenant." My ship. I was now thinking of the *Flying Dutchman* as mine. When had that happened?

"I can't promise that no one else has that idea. We have four other militaries aboard. And I can't vouch for the Ranger team, either, sir."

"You make a very good point, Lieutenant Williams," Skippy said. "Colonel Joe, perhaps I should make an announcement over the intercom, and create a demonstration of what will happen if any idiot troop of monkeys tries to take over the ship. How about I close and lock all the doors on the ship, and shut off the ventilation? Oooh, and I can kill the artificial gravity also, that will slow down any mutineers."

"Skippy, you can't do that."

"Huh? Clearly, I can, Joe. Oh, sure, I get it, you're right. I'll leave ventilation and gravity on in the bridge and CIC compartments."

"That's not my point, Skippy! You can't, let me say this a different way, you should not do anything like that. If there is a plan for mutiny, I need to handle that myself. Having a shiny beer can do the work for me only makes me look weak, as a commander. I don't need any help here, Skippy, this is something you need to keep out of."

"You sure about this, Joe?"

"Hundred percent. You know about sciency stuff, I know monkeys, damn it, I mean, I know humans, people. Stay out of this."

Skippy paused. "I'll make you a deal, Colonel Joe. I will stay out of this, unless there is an actual attempted mutiny. If that happens, certain monkeys are going to find out real quick that I am not always a friendly little shiny beer can. Anybody screws with me, they will seriously regret it. Ask the former Thuranin crew of this ship, if they have any questions about that."

"We get your point, Skippy. Loud and clear." A potential mutiny is a subject that I needed to discuss with my command team; Chang, Simms and Adams. The entire idea of anyone trying to forcefully take over the ship is idiotic; without Skippy's cooperation, the ship was never getting home. "Williams, it is not my intention for Sergeant Adams to interfere with how you train your SEAL team, she will remain in charge of overall training. You and your team may have studied how to use armored suits and combots, you have no experience with them even in training. Bring your team to the training hold at 1300 hours, and I'll show you what I mean."

Arranged along one wall, or I guess aboard a ship I should have called it a bulkhead, were ten Kristang powered armor suits. There were more of them in another compartment. We'd taken forty six suits from the Kristang troopship in Earth orbit, they weren't all in good condition, so out of the forty six units, we had forty two that were operational. The good news is that the troopship had equipment for modifying suits, and we now had that equipment aboard the *Flying Dutchman*. We had been able to adjust most of the suits so that normal sized humans; now anyone above five feet six in height could use a suit. There hadn't been a whole lot of extra time before we departed Earth orbit, so I didn't have a whole lot of experience with the new suits; I still had way more experience than any of the new crew.

In addition to powered armor suits, the Kristang troopship had provided us with plenty of rifles, ammo, and Zinger anti-aircraft missiles. Except for Thuranin combots, we were equipped almost entirely with Kristang military gear, including zPhones for everyone, and night vision gear. The food, of course, all came from Earth.

When I arrived at the large cargo hold we used for training, it was 1250 hours, and both Adams and Williams were already suited up in armor, with only their faceplates open. In the military, if you weren't early, you were late, so of course Williams and his SEAL team had gotten there half an hour early. Along with Adams was Giraud, the French paratrooper leader was checking Williams' suit and explaining its features. On the other side of the cargo hold, Adams was going through exercises; bending over, easily jumping to touch the ceiling that was ten meters high, and spinning her unloaded Kristang rifle like it was a baton and she was a drum majorette. Generally, she was showing off, I figured she was doing it to intimidate Williams, and from the look on his face, it may have been working.

Craig Alanson

Adams and Giraud showed Williams how the armor suit worked, and he went through a series of familiarization exercises. He was good, damn good, he caught on much faster than I had back when I put on a suit for the first time. When Adams and Giraud were satisfied that Williams knew enough not to hurt himself, it was time for the show. There was a large circle painted on the floor, Adams announced that the object of the game was like sumo wrestling, whoever knocked their opponent out of the circle won the match. They took positions opposite each other, toes touching the painted circle, and Giraud announced "Begin!"

Williams, knowing Adams had more experience with powered armor, crouched slightly, then launched himself forward. He wasn't going to attempt any advanced hand to hand combat, he was going to rely on the suit's speed, power and mass to knock Adams out of the circle.

Adams had a different idea. She stood in place, but as soon as Williams moved forward, a door in the bulkhead behind Adams slammed open, and a combot launched itself across the hold. The combot's feet never touched the floor, it flew through the air in the blink of an eye, crashing into Williams, knocking him to go skidding across the deck. He struggled against the combot, but the Kristang powered armor was no match for the superior technology of a Thuranin combot. Standing in place and controlling the combot through gestures, Adams had the combot gently but firmly pick Williams up like a rag doll and held him against the far bulkhead.

"Enough!" Giraud declared, and Adams gestured for the combot to release Williams.

Williams popped his faceplate open, looked at Adams, and bowed. "Well played, Sergeant. You did warn me to expect the unexpected out here."

"Everything is unexpected out here," I said. "Do you have any questions, Lieutenant?"

To his credit, Williams wasn't insulted, he wasn't angry, he had an enormous grin. Getting familiar with powered armor, and combots, was going to be a bigger challenge than he thought. And special forces people absolutely *love* challenges. "No questions at all, Colonel," he said to me. To his team, he added, "People, this is going to be fun, so pay attention."

I stayed in the training hold for an hour, taking the opportunity to gain time in a powered suit myself, because it had been weeks since I'd used one. Fortunately, it quickly became familiar again, and I followed along with the SEAL team as Adams and Giraud put them through a series of exercises. It was good, I told myself, for the SEALs to see their commander knew what he was doing. The truth is, I was showing off, and I didn't care who knew it. Adams caught my eye a couple times, like when I jumped, touched the ceiling, did a backflip on the way down, and landed perfectly on my feet. That wasn't all skill; the suit's sensors detected the floor, and would have pulled me upright to land safely if I hadn't managed to do it on my own. After an hour of fun, I had to get out of the suit and leave, because my duty shift on the bridge started in two hours, and I wanted to grab a snack before then.

Out in the corridor, I put my zPhone earpiece in. "Hey, Skippy, you call me Colonel Joe, you call Simms 'Major Tammy'. You call Chang 'Colonel Kong'," Kong was his given name, "or King Kong." Chang actually enjoyed being called 'King Kong', that nickname had totally backfired on Skippy. "You call Lt. Williams 'Baldilocks'. You have some sort of nickname for most people. But you only ever call Sergeant Adams, 'Sergeant Adams.' Why is that? Her first name is Margaret. Why don't you call her Meg, or Peggy, or, hey, how about you call her Sarge Marge?"

"Wow. I am impressed. I thought I'd seen the depths of your stupidity before, but you're setting a new record low for dumdumness. You have met Sergeant Adams, right?"

"Duh, I met her before I met you. Oh, that was a rhetorical question."

"Double duh. Sarge Marge, huh? Tell me, what do you think would happen if I referred to Sergeant Adams by that quaint nickname?"

"Um, she'd kick your ass?"

"Most likely. I seek fun, Joe, not suicide."

"Ok, good talk, then."

"Uh huh, sure. Hey, I noticed you showing off big time in the training hold."

"Commander's privilege, Skippy. Besides, I do need to maintain proficiency with powered armor."

"Why? You're the commander, you should remain aboard the ship."

"No way. No way am I staying here all the time, Skippy. And are you absolutely certain there is no possibility that I will never need to use a suit, out here?"

He sighed. "No, I can't say that for certain, Joe. Fine, you have fun, just don't hurt yourself. I won't always be there to protect you when you do something stupid."

"Got it, Skippy, thanks."

CHAPTER THREE

After leaving the now-dormant wormhole behind, we had set course for another wormhole. Not the next closest wormhole, unfortunately the closest wormhole connected in the wrong direction from where we wanted to go. Despite Skippy's joke about setting course for a random blue star, we did have a particular destination planned. We made several Skippy-programmed jumps, then when we were in the middle of empty interstellar space, we humans programmed our very first jump into the nav system. My main hope for our first jump was that we didn't blow up the ship.

I checked the main bridge display for the vital details of ship status, although I could see the same data anywhere on the ship with my tablet, it felt more real when I was sitting in the command chair on the bridge. The very bottom left corner of the display now had, in small script, the designator 'UNS Flying Dutchman'. Skippy must have added that while I wasn't paying attention. The same letters, much larger, were on a new brass plaque above the door to the bridge and CIC compartments. The crew, including me, liked that, it made us sound official.

The governments that comprised UN Expeditionary Forces Command suddenly decided, a few days before we departed, that they didn't like the name Flying Dutchman, and various other names were floated for consideration. I got the feeling their public relations people would have liked to run a worldwide naming contest on the internet, if they'd had time, and if the nature of the big star carrier hanging in orbit wasn't classified. Navy officers around the world protested that changing a ship's name was traditionally bad luck. Skippy cut the argument short by stating that he liked the name Flying Dutchman, that he controlled all data systems aboard the ship, and that the UN could name our captured alien star carrier the Good Ship Lollipop for all he cared, it wouldn't change anything. In the frantic days before departure, trying to get the ship loaded with all the people, gear and supplies we needed, I had no time for BS like caring what we called the ship. To our Merry Band of Pirates, the ship's name was always going to be the 'Flying Dutchman' anyway. When UNEF dropped the renaming idea, that was one less headache for me.

Back home, I am sure the UN still has an international committee of highly paid people studying the issue of our ship's name. Don't worry, they will issue a report long before Earth's sun explodes. Probably.

"Jump complete." Desai announced from the pilot's seat.

"Are we clear, Skippy? No unfriendlies in the area?" I asked.

"You tell me. You say you need to be able to fly this ship on your own, so look at the sensors yourself," Skippy said in a peevish tone.

I wasn't going to argue with him, he was mostly right. The cold hard truth was that we did not need to be able to fly the ship on our own, what we did need was some sliver of hope that we might be able to fly the Dutchman on our own, after Skippy left us. Clinging to that tiny bit of hope was the difference between a high risk mission, and a suicide mission. The crew, including myself, had signed up for a high risk mission. Super high risk, admittedly. Risk of the if-anything-goes-wrong-we-are-totally-screwed level. "Pilot?"

Desai answered more slowly than was optimal, and she knew it. "We jumped to the right place, within, seven hundred, yes, seven hundred thousand kilometers." The tone of her voice was not filled with confidence. She let out a breath she'd been holding in. "Yes. Confirmed. Jump was successful," she turned in her chair to look at me, and gave me a thumb's up, with a weak smile. Desai had programmed the jump herself, this was the first jump Skippy had not loaded into the autopilot for us. Skippy had grumbled and complained loudly at the delay, then refused to check the numbers for us. "All I'll tell you is, you won't be jumping us into a star," is what he had said.

His grumbling about a delay was understandable, Desai had programmed the jump into the computer yesterday, and we'd then spent the intervening time checking that the programming was correct. Three different teams of pilots and scientists had checked the programming, and that was after two days of analysis to decide what should be programmed into the Thuranin navigation computer. Skippy reluctantly had restored the original Thuranin operating system to the navigation system, running it parallel to his own access, making snarky comments about it the whole time. It wasn't the true original operating system, the Thuranin ship AI, it was a dumbed-down version that allowed humans access and was simple enough for us to use. Skippy cautioned that if there was a glitch in the system, after he left us, we would have no way to debug or fix it. To which I had responded that, if there was a glitch anywhere in the navigation system software, that could only be Skippy's fault, for screwing up the programming, or missing something. That insulted his boundless ego enough for him to declare the software perfect, better than perfect, for he had loaded in his own maintenance and repair subroutine into it. I never let on that I'd played him, so I could use that particular trick again.

"Sensors?" I called out to the people manning the consoles in the Combat Information Center, beyond the glass-like diamond composite bridge walls.

"Nothing, uh, nothing on the scopes. That we can detect, sir," came the answer.

That wasn't reassuring. Without Skippy controlling the data feeds, the bridge and CIC displays didn't contain the helpful color coding designation for Thuranin, Maxohlx, Jeraptha, Kristang, Ruhar and unknown ships. No matter in this case, there was absolutely nothing on the scopes within a quarter lightyear. We'd deliberately jumped from the middle of nowhere to the middle of nowhere, and we'd only jumped the distance from Earth's Sun to Jupiter, a small test for a first jump. If there had been anything dangerous in the area, Skippy would have told us; he was unhappy, not suicidal.

We had jumped only a short distance, and still missed the mark by over half a million kilometers. No way could we jump anywhere near a planet with that lousy accuracy, we needed to get better, a lot better, or the *Dutchman* would be spending a lot of time crawling through normal space. And we didn't have the time, or fuel, for that. We also had a limited supply of fixings for critical cheeseburgers in the galley. Our first jump wasn't an acceptable effort; the crew knew it. "The ship didn't explode," I observed, "we didn't break the jump drive, and we didn't emerge in the middle of a planet, or next to a Thuranin battlegroup. Good enough for a first jump. We'll debrief tomorrow morning. In the meantime, Skippy, can you program the next jump? We need to get moving."

"Whoa, whoa, slow down, monkeys. Have you analyzed the jump drive system? Are the coils calibrated and ready for another jump?"

"Pilot?" I asked. The drive charge indicator on the bottom of the main display read 87%. Good for several regular jumps, or one really long jump, with the magical modifications Skippy had made to the Thuranin's crappy jump drive.

"It looks like it is Ok?" Desai answered slowly.

"It looks like it's Ok?" Skippy scoffed. "Ok? Such a precise term, I am completely impressed by your professionalism. Consider that if the jump drive is not 'Ok', another jump could rupture spacetime and destroy the aft part of the ship, leaving us stranded here in interstellar space. Forever. By 'us', I mean me, because you air breathers will be out of luck, once the backup power fails. Yup, I'll be here, alone, surrounded by the dry, dusty corpses of monkeys. My only hope then will be that, in four billion years, the collision of the Andromeda galaxy with the Milky Way will throw some solar system's orbit to intersect with wherever I'm drifting at the time. Considering that, I'll ask again; and I'll speak slowly this time. Is the jump drive ready for another jump?"

"You made your point, Skippy." I said with a touch of anger, I didn't appreciate him bullying Desai. "How about this, Mister Smartass; you need to show us how to analyze the status of the jump drive. We're not doing that now, unless you want another delay. Is the jump drive ready?"

"Of course it is. You never let me have any fun."

"You can find some type of fun that doesn't involve talking about the ship exploding. Program the autopilot for another jump, and let's get moving. Also, put together a briefing for us tomorrow, about what we did wrong, and right, with that last jump."

"Aye, aye, Captain. You will be dazzled by the brilliance of my PowerPoint slides."

When we left the now-dormant wormhole near Earth, Skippy had programmed a course to bring us to an abandoned Kristang space station. The Kristang had built a space station in orbit around the innermost planet of a red dwarf star, not because the planet or the star were in any way interesting. What was interesting were the shattered remains of an Elder starship in orbit around the innermost planet, a treasure trove well worth the expense of the Kristang building and maintaining a space station to establish a permanent presence there. Sometime around three hundred years ago, there had been a fight between the Kristang there, or a rival clan had raided the station, because a major battle had damaged the station badly enough for the place to be abandoned ever since.

The abandoned space station was both the closest, and easiest, site for us to investigate. Closest, because of the roundabout journey we had to take through multiple wormholes, still meant we wouldn't reach the first site for thirty eight days. Thirty eight dull, boring days cruising through isolated interstellar space, jumping, recharging engines, jumping again. And occasionally transiting wormholes.

The first two weeks after leaving Earth behind were reasonably stimulating, with our new Merry Band of Pirates getting used to being in space, being aboard a starship, being aboard a captured alien starship. Setting up a training routine kept people interested, which was critical for keeping special forces types sharp and focused. The first two weeks included a first-time jump for most of the crew, their first wormhole transit, a lot of first things. Firsts were good, firsts were interesting, firsts held people's attention and kept them from getting bored.

Then the tedium set in. Even the pilots, the only people aboard who needed to actually do anything other than eat, exercise and sleep, got bored with their regular duties. Mostly the pilot duty consisted of waiting for jump engines to recharge, Skippy to program a jump into the autopilot, and the chief pilot on duty pressing a button. There was always at least a little tension following a jump, when the *Dutchman's* sensor net determined whether there were other ships around. The crew on duty in the CIC scanned the sensors, the two pilots had fingers poised next to buttons for triggering a preprogrammed emergency jump away. Then, when nothing was detected, after five minutes the All Clear signal was given, and everyone went back to the tedium of routine.

The pilots spent most of their time, unless they were sleeping, but often including while eating and running on a treadmill in the gym, learning how to fly first our Thuranin star carrier, then our beat-up Kristang frigate and finally Thuranin dropships. One of our new pilots, a hotshot French flyboy who came to the *Dutchman* from serving as a test pilot for the Rafael fighter, told me the training was beyond tough, it was crushing, impossible. And he was one of Desai's best students. I told him that Captain Desai had flown a dropship, then a frigate then a star carrier, with zero training, in combat. The guy did have a point, I talked to Desai and Skippy about adjusting the tempo of the flight training. After the first two weeks, the new pilots adjusted to drinking from the fire hose. Desai started sleeping more than four hours a night.

Boredom was bad for regular people. Boredom for gung-ho elite SpecOps people could be deadly. The third week of our pleasure cruise, two Indian paratroopers suffered broken bones in a training accident. Thanks to Doctor Skippy's magical use of Thuranin medical technology, their broken bones would heal fully in two weeks, unfortunately they couldn't resume normal training until they were fully healed. When we arrived at our first target, those two paratroopers would be unable to join their fellows in any action, they'd either be staying aboard the *Dutchman*, or operating combots.

I went to the ship's sickbay, nobody wanted to call it an 'infirmary', as that implied a special forces soldier could be infirm. Which was unsatisfactory. The two mildly chagrined paratroopers were sitting on the too-small Thuranin beds, not actually beds, they were some sort of form-fitting gel. Both already had their broken legs encased in hard sleeves, with thin tubes connected to the beds. The tubes provided nutrients, and nano machines that knitted the bones and tissues back together, all controlled by Dr. Skippy the mad scientist. Both of the injured men were eager to get mobile as soon as possible, of course, I'd already talked to Skippy to assure he didn't release them from sickbay until they weren't likely to further injure themselves by overdoing their rehab exercises. Sickbay was crowded, with me, the two injured men, and six scientists, who were trying to understand the Thuranin technology Skippy was using.

"Are you learning how all this equipment works?" I asked the doctors.

"No!" Said Skippy before any of the doctors could reply. "That would be a huge waste of time, I've told you that. You don't need clumsy monkeys poking around your insides with crude knives, when Doctor Skippy can fix everyone up with medical magic. Real medicine, not the idiot guesswork you monkeys use."

"Yes," I said, irritated at having this conversation again. "You have told me that, and I've told you that if, or I should say when, you find the Collective and leave us, our own doctors need to be able to use this equipment to care for the crew."

"Never going to happen."

"That is unsat-"

"For crying out loud, stop flapping your jaws for a minute and listen to me, you might learn something. I doubt it, but miracles do happen." Skippy sounded peeved, more than usual. "This equipment relies entirely on nanoscale technology. I'm able to control the nano machines by the picosecond, and they can move individual atoms around to assemble, or disassemble, molecules as needed. The equipment was designed to be controlled by Thuranin cybernetics, through their medical AI. It's a particularly stupid AI, even you may be able to beat it at chess, wait, what am I saying? No, that's crazy talk, don't know what I was thinking. It's a limited AI, and the system architecture doesn't have the capacity for me to load anything useful into it. It barely has the memory to store details of human anatomy and physiology. Real physiology, not the ignorant guesses you monkeys have in your medical journals. Without me controlling and coordinating the nano machines, the whole system doesn't work. Since your doctors don't have cybernetics, and

Thuranin cybernetics can't be adapted to humans, there is no way you monkeys can use any of this equipment by yourselves."

"You done?"

"Barely got started, but that's enough explanation for you."

"Fine. You are, arguably, the most intelligent being in the galaxy right now. That we know of, right?"

"I am by far the most intelligent being in the galaxy. It's about time you gave me the respect"

"Since you are so incredibly smart, then you should be able to figure something out, for us to have even some limited sort of control of this medical equipment, at least enough for basic medical care. Consider it a challenge, Skippy."

"A challenge? Building an escalator to the center of the galaxy would be a challenge. Teaching monkeys to use real technology? Impossible." He complained.

"Impress me, Skippy." I knew he couldn't resist that. "I'll give you mad props if you can do that."

"Great. Fine. You want the impossible. What am I supposed to do, build a really, really tiny pair of tweezers, so you can move molecules around by hand? Stupid monkeys. Damn it, I hate my life. I should have stayed on a dusty shelf in that warehouse."

"Bye, Skippy, have fun." I left him grumbling behind me.

When I was done in sickbay, including listening to the two paratroopers apologize for having rendered themselves temporarily combat ineffective, and me assuring them that accidents happen, I hurried to the galley for dinner. Tonight's meal was meatloaf or salmon, and I was eager to get there before all the meatloaf was gone.

There was enough meatloaf, what there wasn't much of was lively conversation. Everyone was beginning to get bored already with the routine, the time and vast distances we had to travel had sunk in to people's minds, and the crew were subdued. That, and the training accident had put a damper on morale.

"Ugh, this room is totally dead. Why all the gloomy faces?" Skippy's annoying voice came out of the speaker in the ceiling.

"It's been a tough week, Skippy," I grumbled while staring at my plate. The meatloaf had gotten slightly cold, serves me right for showing up late for dinner, and then spending too much time chatting instead of eating. It was Ok, it had some strange spice in it that I was trying to figure- nutmeg? Yes, nutmeg. Not a lot of it, but who puts nutmeg in meatloaf? Looking across the table at Lt Hendrick's salmon in a maple and ginger glaze, I was beginning to regret my dinner choice. Tonight's dinner had been cooked by our US special forces teams, the Rangers and SEALs. "And we've been cruising in interstellar space, in total darkness, with nothing to look at. We could all use a change of scenery." Skippy had a point, though, I needed to do something to boost crew morale. Maybe I should assign someone to be the ship's morale officer. One of the PowerPoint decks, that I was supposed to study, probably had some advice about maintaining unit morale. How did a crew keep up morale on a nuclear missile submarine? Those boomers were submerged and silent for months at a time. Like us, they didn't have anything to look at. Unlike them, we had windows.

"I know what your problem is, Colonel Joe," Skippy announced, "you need to get laid. Hey, Major Tammy, you should mate with Joe."

SpecOps

"Skippy!" I almost choked on meatloaf, and Major Simms, who had just taken a sip of water, spewed it across the table in front of her. The soldier seated next to her had to pat her on the back, to keep her from choking.

"What? You're a male, she's a female, and for a monkey, you don't smell too bad-"

"Stop it!" I shouted. Everyone in the galley was staring at me.

"Hey, you know you need some sweet lovin' soon, Joe. Major Tammy, you should have seen the raging boner he had in the shower this morning-"

Now Simms had gone from shocked to amused, her shoulders shook as she tried to suppress a laugh. Everyone was now trying not to look at me, and laughing.

Putting my head in my hands, I banged my forehead on the table. "Skippy, this is private stuff. You don't talk about it in public. I am Major Simms' commanding officer."

"What, because you're a colonel, you can't bang anyone in your command? Like *that* matters way out here. Well, you could mate with one of the science team. This is good timing, because most the women are ovulating this week, so they're extra horny-"

I saw all the women's faces register shock. "Skippy! Shut! The! Hell! *Up!*" I shouted.

"Man, talk about ungrateful. I'm trying to get you laid, you're sure not doing well on your own. Don't ask me to be your wingman again."

"I didn't ask! And you're a wing *nut*, not a wingman." In the future, maybe I needed to consider taking all my meals in my cabin or my office. "Major Simms, I apologize-"

She shook her head, still trying not to laugh. "Colonel, we all know Skippy by now, no need to apologize for him."

"Thank you. Everyone, I'd appreciate it if this stayed between us," meaning the roughly twenty people in the galley. "And since I know that's not going to happen," I added honestly, knowing this was way too juicy not to quickly spread throughout the ship, "keep in mind Skippy said it, I didn't." Dammit, after that I was never able to look at Major Simms without wondering, you know, what she'd be like in bed.

I didn't need any more distractions.

Jump, recharge, jump again. It was monotonous, and we had a long way to go to our first target. When we left Earth to find Skippy's magical Elder radio, or whatever the hell it really is, we still had the same problem that made us go to Earth in the first place. When we raided the Kristang asteroid research base, we'd found an Elder communications node, the thing Skippy thought should allow him to contact the Collective. It hadn't. The stupid thing didn't work, or Skippy didn't know how to make it work, or it worked fine but there was no Collective to talk to, or it worked, Skippy had contacted the Collective, and they'd decided he is an asshole and ignored him. I was betting on that last one.

Since the first comm node didn't satisfy Skippy, he had wanted to check out the two other sites he knew for certain had intact Elder comm nodes. The two other sites, I had told him even before we went to Earth, were impossible for us to raid, forget about it, not going to happen. The first site was on a heavily populated Thuranin planet. The second was nine and a half thousand lightyears from Earth, at an installation controlled by a species with technology superior to the Thuranin. Neither site was remotely possible for us to raid, even with the *Dutchman* now crewed by bad-ass special forces. Maybe, maybe, by some combination of luck, Skippy magic and a random miracle, we might succeed in raiding one site. The odds were heavily in favor of us failing, our enemies discovering humans had stolen a Thuranin starship, and Earth becoming the focus of some very pissed off aliens. That was not an optimal mission outcome.

Before we departed Earth, we, meaning mostly me, had persuaded Skippy to expand his search, beyond places confirmed to have his precious comm node, to places that were likely to have a comm node. Sites that were known to have a substantial collection of Elder artifacts, even though the Thuranin data base Skippy downloaded didn't list a comm node in the inventory, could very possibly have a comm node; Skippy said that before the Elders ascended or beamed up or whatever the hell they'd done, comm nodes were scattered all over the galaxy. Skippy had grumbled about trying to predict the location of comm nodes being a waste of time, and that such an analysis would take forever, in this case 'forever' took him seven minutes and twelve seconds in meatsack time. After completing his analysis, he had admitted that there were two very promising sites within three thousand lightyears of Earth, that were much easier and safer to approach, investigate, and if needed, raid.

The first site was another Kristang research base, the space station that had been abandoned, after a fight between two or more Kristang factions left it damaged beyond repair. According to the data Skippy had access to, the space station had held a variety of low-value Elder artifact and various devices and doodads from higher species that the Kristang there had been trying to reverse engineer for their clan, without much success. What Skippy hoped was the *Dutchman's* sensors could scan the debris field around the station, and our Merry Band of Pirates could board it to see if one of his magic radios were there. Since the wormhole shift, that star system had been ignored by the Kristang, and Skippy thought we wouldn't find anyone there. He thought that, anyway.

The second site was going to be a bit tougher for us to investigate; tough enough that I hoped to find an alternative. The good news is that it was a known Elder site that had been located by the Maxohlx themselves, but barely explored by anyone. It was a large site, it had been a substantial and busy facility back when the Elders were using it, so Skippy was highly confident we would find a communications node, multiple communications nodes, there. The bad news was very bad. First, it was a long distance from Earth, a journey of four months to get there from our current position. The journey was longer than it strictly needed to be, because we had to avoid several wormhole clusters that were heavily used by the Maxohlx. The first part of the bad news was merely inconvenient. The second part of the bad news was dangerous, extremely dangerous. When the Maxohlx found the Elder site, they had not been looking for nice toys like communications nodes. They had been looking for weapons, Elder weapons. Devices the Elders may not have built as weapons, devices that could be used for incredible destructive effect. Devices, that, according to Skippy, could make stars explode. And exploding a star was a simple trick, compared to some of the technology the Elders routinely used.

At the time the Maxohlx found that Elder site, and its massive destructive potential, they already had a substantial arsenal of Elder devices that could be used as weapons against the Rindhalu. According to Skippy's admittedly foggy memories, the Rindhalu discovered that the Maxohlx planned to attack them, and forced their hand. The Maxohlx had to accelerate their plans, and launched the attack before they were completely ready. The Rindhalu hit back with their own stock of Elder weapons, and a war raged for a brief period, before Sentinels detected the use of Elder weapons, and struck at both sides. The Sentinels, intelligent monitors left behind by the Elders to prevent unauthorized use of Elder technology by younger species, did not care that the Maxohlx had fired first. They did not even seem to care where in the galaxy Elder weapons had been used; Maxohlx and Rindhalu star systems far from the fighting were hit by Sentinels with devastating effect.

The purpose of the Sentinels seemed to be to destroy starfaring civilizations; civilizations capable of abusing Elder technology, whether they had acquired such technology or not. Both the Maxohlx and the Rindhalu feared extinction, so powerful and relentless were the Sentinels. Then, suddenly, for no known reason, the Sentinel attack halted, and the Sentinels disappeared and went dormant. Sleeping, again, but always watchful.

Since that time, the shell shocked Maxohlx and Rindhalu had held their Elder weapons in reserve, and continued their long war through proxies such as the Thuranin and Jeraptha, who had proxies of their own. And the Elder site that the Maxohlx had been exploring at the time the Sentinels struck had been off limits to everyone, by general agreement. Skippy thought that, since he was built by the Elders, he could get us there without being detected by the extensive web of sensors left by the Maxohlx. His plan sucked; after a four month journey to get close to the site, we would fly in normal space for another six months, sneaking up on the target by crawling slowly along. The *Flying Dutchman* could not slow down much, as firing the engines would risk detection, so we would need to fly across the final distance to the target in dropships. Landing teams would spend almost a month in dropships, under Skippy's crappy plan. After we located and picked up a communications node, the landing teams would fly back to the *Dutchman*, and the ship would continue traveling silently through normal space for another four months, before we could risk a jump. Skippy's plan sucked. He wanted us to commit to a fourteen month voyage, into an area of space that was closely monitored by both the Maxohlx and Elder Sentinels, because he thought we had a good chance of finding a comm node. I hated his plan, I told him that. I also did not have an alternative plan.

Before committing to the second target, we were going to investigate the first target, the supposedly abandoned Kristang space station. Hopefully, we would find a comm node there. If not, I had maybe a week to think up an alternative to Skippy's second target.

I needed to put my thinking cap on.

CHAPTER FOUR

Before we investigated the abandoned space station for real, we practiced maneuvers in vacuum and zero gravity. I ordered the ship to halt in interstellar space, and Desai flew the *Flower* a short distance away, to act as a target. Then, several teams practiced getting into a small dropship, flying over near the *Flower*, and people in suits crossed the remaining distance to the *Flower* as an assault team. Using Kristang powered armor suits in deep space was very different from playing around with them in a cargo hold. Many times, Skippy had to seize control of suits to prevent the wearers from hurting themselves or others. We all learned together, slowly. The suits by themselves had small thruster units, which allowed the wearer to prevent spinning out of control, the suit thrusters weren't much use for flying across distances. We had a sort of jetpack that could be attached to a suit, the jetpacks were bulky, and we only had fourteen of them, and we shouldn't need them to get across the short distance between a dropship airlock and the space station. What we practiced was one person launching him or herself from the dropship's airlock, carrying a line. When the line was firmly attached to the *Flower*, the rest of the team followed by pulling themselves along the line. We also practiced recovering people who had gone spinning off into space, that was good practice for our inexperienced dropship pilots. And if many of those people had gone spinning off into space by accident, that only made the recovery exercise more realistic. One of those unfortunate people who had accidentally gone spinning off into space, and needed to be recovered, had a name like 'Shmoe Bishop'. That guy really felt like an idiot.

After two full days of intensive exercises, during which every SpecOps team and every pilot had multiple opportunities for practice, I was satisfied that we were ready enough to investigate the space station for real.

We approached our very first target slowly and carefully, initially jumping in to the far edge of the star system, and sitting there quietly for eighteen hours. Our passive sensors listened for any sign of activity, no matter how faint, and found nothing. Next we jumped in about a million kilometers from the target, and listened for another six hours, although Skippy complained that he'd gotten all the useful data in the first three hours. So, I listened to him complain for hours, that was a real treat for me.

Finally, we went to battle stations, and jumped within a hundred thousand kilometers of the supposedly abandoned space station. The pilots were on a hair trigger for an emergency jump away, they didn't need to wait for an order from the duty officer. "Skippy," I asked anxiously, "what do you think? Is this place really abandoned?"

"Give me a break, Joe, I'm stuck with the speed of light here, everything is incredibly freakin' slow. There are no ships in the area. The whole area certainly appears to be dead, nothing out there is generating power. What I can't tell yet is whether there are any hazards like stealthed mines. That's what I'm scanning for now. With this ship's crappy sensors, it will take an hour for a full grid search. I have to warn you, Joe, in order to verify there are no booby-traps inside the station, we need to move the ship close. I'm talking about physical devices, like explosives attached to airlocks, that sort of thing. I need to be closer, like within twelve thousand kilometers."

"Ooooh." Twelve thousand kilometers, that sounded way too close to me. The distances involved in space combat were hard to comprehend, all my military experience involved line of sight warfare. Even in space, with nothing between me and the target, I couldn't actually see anything from twelve thousand kilometers away. The problem with space combat was the enormous distances involved, distances so vast that even light took seconds or minutes to cross the gap. Against the distances separating combatants were the speeds of the weapons; masers, particle beams, hypervelocity railguns, missiles that could accelerate at five thousand times the force of gravity. From our position a mere one hundred thousand kilometers away from the station, we were in danger from speed of light weapons, which our shields could deflect long enough for us to jump away. If we went in only twelve thousand kilometers, a railgun or even a missile could close that distance, punch right through our shields and knock out a reactor before we could jump. Did I want to take the risk of bringing the ship in that close? "Can we send a dropship instead?"

"No, I need this ship's sensors. This may all look like magic to you monkeys, Joe, but this is technology, and even for me, it has limits."

"Damn. All right, Pilot," I said to Desai, "bring us in. If you think anything is a threat out there, don't wait for me, jump us away."

"Aye, aye, sir," she acknowledged.

There were no threats, and, Skippy declared, no booby-traps. At least, no booby-traps in the outer layers of the station structure. The space station appeared to be exactly what that data Skippy captured said it was; an abandoned wreck. From twelve thousand kilometers, we could clearly see holes had been blasted in it, jagged holes, and there were structures that had been torn away like tissue paper, with pipes and cables sticking out. Because people could get tangled up in those cables flopping around, we needed to avoid those areas. That was not a problem; we located several airlocks with no obstructions, and easy approaches for a dropship. There was also an open docking bay, plenty large enough for several dropships. That was tempting, maybe too tempting. I wanted a dropship to be able to get away quickly; that meant avoiding confined areas like an open docking bay that could be a trap.

What I decided was for a single one of our smaller dropships to go in, with two pilots, plus me, Giraud, and two others. Giraud had removed the healing sleeve from his arm and found that it was very nearly as strong as the other arm, and he declared himself fit for duty. Doctor Skippy agreed, that was good enough for me. Desai backed the *Flying Dutchman* off to fifty thousand kilometers away, and I left Chang in command. As the two pilots of the dropship were British, I chose Captain Xho of the Chinese team and Captain Chander of the Indian team to go in with me and Giraud, to make our initial exploration team truly international. It was very important, I thought, to avoid the appearance of me playing favorites among the five nations that comprised UNEF.

The pilots parked the dropship fifty meters away from the airlock we selected, and we opened the dropship's own airlock. Giraud went first, he flew across the fifty meters of vacuum and missed the airlock by only a meter; he was able to grasp a handhold and pull himself over to the airlock and attach the line. I followed, with the Indian and Chinese soldiers right behind, pulling ourselves along the line. The armored glove of Giraud's hand touched the airlock door, and nothing happened. "I suppose it's too much to hope the power is still on," he said, bending down to peer at the dust-covered panel to the right of the door, "after all this time." Moving as carefully as he could, he tried to brush the accumulated layer of dust away from the panel; most of it smeared, or clung to his gloves. "That didn't work," he complained, "we should have brought a brush with us, or a towel. Where did all this dust come from?"

"Debris from the battle that caused the station to be abandoned," Skippy explained. "The station's surface was slightly magnetized from its defensive shield; when the shield was deactivated, particles were attracted to it. There is not that much dust, Captain, the problem is your gloves are only smearing it around."

"Do you see any lights on the panel, Giraud?" I asked. The view from his helmet camera was available on the inside of my helmet faceplate, I could toggle the display either on my left wrist pad, or with my chin, although I hadn't quite gotten the knack of doing it with my chin; I kept flipping the display back and forth annoyingly. The view from his helmet camera was distracting, he was moving around too much. I pulled myself over next to him, far enough away not to hover over his shoulder and distract him.

"It's hard to tell," he answered, "the light is very harsh here, without an atmosphere to filter it." Giraud had a good point, all of our zero gravity training had been in deep interstellar space, with artificial lights provided by the *Dutchman*, the *Flower* or a dropship. We should have, I should have, thought of how being in intense starlight would affect people in suits.

"All right, we can't stay out here, try the handle," I ordered. The door, like almost all airlocks, had a manual release mechanism, for use in case of power failure. This door had a nice big, obvious lever, painted yellow and red, on the right side.

"Trying it now," Giraud said.

I could see his right hand reach out and grasp the lever, then turn it to the left. Immediately, a loud trilling sound blasted out of my helmet speakers. "Get out of there!" I shouted. "Retreat! Ret- wait, wait. Everyone, wait." I recognized that trilling sound from somewhere. The trilling sound repeated, then I heard voices, human voices, it was difficult to make out what they were saying. "Skippy, what, what the hell is that?"

"Oh, that's 'Soul Finger' by the Bar-Kays."

"Soul F-. Oh! My! God! What the *hell* is that song doing all the way out here?" I looked around, everyone I could see had their mouths agape with astonishment. Why in the hell did a Kristang space station, abandoned hundreds of years ago, have a human 1960s funk R&B song as a door alarm? My brain almost locked up in confusion.

"What? Duh, it doesn't, Joe, the real airlock alarm is a boring 'beep beep' sound, I spiced up the signal for you over your helmet speakers. Oh, hey, you dumb monkeys thought that was *real*? Oh, man, this is freakin' hilarious! Hahahahahahahahaha! Oh, damn, Joe, you should have seen the expression on your faces. Hahahaha! Man, now that was truly priceless! Damn! I got to do that again sometime."

I was pissed. "No, you got to do that again, never. Understand? You scared the hell out of me, Skippy. That could have been dangerous, if someone had moved too quickly and been injured. Everyone, do you see now the crap I have to put up with from our friendly beer can?"

"Colonel," Giraud responded, "I've told you before, any time you want Skippy to take a long ride out an airlock, you let me know. I'll be happy to do it for you."

We got the outer door open, and then the inner door, and discovered there was a thin residual atmosphere in parts of the station. Skippy warned us not to try popping open our faceplates and sniffing the air. It was too thin, he reported, and contaminated with dangerously toxic chemicals left over from the battle. Skippy didn't need to warn us; no one was tempted to open our space suits.

The inside of the station looked very much like the inside of the *Flower*; a standard Kristang design that had changed little in several hundred years. Our captured frigate the

Flower itself was almost two hundred years old, and Skippy said the Kristang were still building frigates that were almost identical today.

Our investigation of the space station took two full days, and was a complete bust. We found only a few, useless pieces of Elder artifacts. It wasn't clear who was more bitterly disappointed; me or Skippy. After forty six straight hours of rotating teams in and out of the station, we had poked our noses into every nook and cranny of the place, and not found anything useful. "Skippy, is there any point to us staying here longer? The Kristang put a space station here because an Elder starship broke apart in orbit, is there a chance they missed something? Should we scan space around the planet, see if we find any Elder artifacts?"

"I already did that, Joe," Skippy responded, "space around here is empty of anything useful; the lizards did a good job of picking up all the valuable pieces. They should have, this station was operational here almost two hundred years before the conflict damaged it, plenty of time to survey every cubic meter of space for a half million kilometers from the planet. Even dumdum lizards couldn't miss finding all the good stuff when they have two hundred years to do it. The answer is no, there is no point to us remaining here any longer, unless you find it useful for crew training."

The *Flying Dutchman* had hung motionless in space, exposed, for far too long. I wanted us to get the hell out of there and on to our next objective. Our next objective, which we still hadn't decided on. I ordered an end to the exploration effort, as soon as the Chinese team aboard the station could be extracted. "Colonel Chang," I said over my zPhone, "we're pulling out, get your team back aboard the dropship as soon as you can do so safely."

"Yes, sir," Chang replied, "this is a good opportunity for training, but there is nothing useful for us over here. We'll be back aboard the *Dutchman* within an hour."

News that we were pulling out quickly spread throughout the ship, and within less than ten minutes, Skippy called me while I was in my office. "Joe, Doctor Venkman is on her way to see you, the science team asked her to talk to you about-"

"Skippy? Are you about to tell me something you overheard? Remember the talk we had about privacy?"

"Sure, but-"

"Does whatever you heard pose a threat to the ship?"

"No, but-"

"Listen, Skippy, you want people to treat you as a person, and not as a computer, right?"

"Yes."

"Here is what a person would do, assuming the person is a friend; he would simply say something like 'head's up, dude, Venkman's on her way to pester you'."

"I am not calling you, 'dude', Joe. How about 'chum'?"

"Damn, Skippy, you need some context on your understanding of slang. Nobody has used the word 'chum' that way since, like, nerdy English boarding schools in the 1930s. Chum is fish guts you throw over the side of the boat as bait."

"Hmm. You sure about that?"

"Pretty sure, yeah. You call someone 'chum' and that majorly sets off their social awkwardness alarm."

"Huh. Damn, you monkeys just came out of the freakin' trees, and already you've got inscrutable social rules. All right, how about if I simply say 'Joe, Venkman's on the warpath and she's on the way to your office'?"

Craig Alanson

"Now that's cool, Skippy, you're getting the idea."

"Unbelievable. An entire galaxy for me to learn about, after being asleep for a million years, and what am I cluttering up my memory with? The current social customs of filthy, ignorant monkeys. Oh, man, I am totally wasting my life."

"How much unused memory do you have? Like, uh," I tried to remember a ginormous number that was in some Wikipedia article I had glanced at, "it's measured in yottabytes, something like that?"

"Ha! A puny yottabyte? Hahahahahahahaha!" For a moment, he was laughing so hard, he couldn't speak. "Damn that is precious! Joey, a yottabyte is such a tiny part of my memory capacity, I couldn't measure something that small. A yottabyte," he chuckled, "that's a good one. Ha!"

"Uh huh, so, you learning about monkey, I mean, oh. Damn it! Now you've got me calling us monkeys. Info about human social customs doesn't take up a significant part of your memory, so what's the harm?"

"The harm? What's the harm in a few worms in an apple, Joe? What's the harm in a few bacteria on your food? It's the contamination that I'm worried about. Come on, it wasn't that long ago that the social customs of your species were limited to picking lice out of each other's fur. And eating the lice, yuck."

"Hey, those lice have got to go somewhere. They're loaded with protein."

"Oh. My. God. See? It's having that kind of thinking, anywhere in my memory, that worries me. To have monkey ideas in my-"

"Hello, Mister, or is it, Captain," Venkman knocked on the frame of the door to my office, "or Colonel, Bishop? They didn't give us a briefing on military protocol before we left."

"Hello, Doctor," I said, rose from my chair, and gestured for her to sit. "My rank is colonel, my position aboard the ship is captain. I guess you call me Colonel, that's the easiest, I think."

"Very well, Colonel." She glanced around my office, nothing more than a Thuranin storage closet that had been emptied out, and outfitted with a desk and three chairs. And a small cabinet that, so far, didn't have anything in it. The only items I had added were a laptop that I rarely used, an iPad that I used all the time, and a coffee mug that I'd taken from the galley and not yet returned. No paper, no pencils or pens, no calendar with pretty landscape photos. Not even a photo of my family. I should have brought one, there hadn't been time before we left. "I'm told that you have ordered the ship to prepare to leave this star system," she said, "to proceed to the next target, because we did not locate an Elder communications node here. The science team, myself included, would like you to reconsider. We would appreciate an opportunity to collect more data about this system. We have been using this ship's extraordinary sensors, and have gathered valuable information, however, the data we've collected to date presents an incomplete picture. Without a complete data set to analyze, we won't be able to draw any conclusions. And none of the science team has been aboard the alien station yet. We've seen the video sent back by the special forces teams, it is not the same as being there."

This was a conversation I didn't want to have, shouldn't need to have. We had covered this subject already.

Before we left Earth, I wrote down our mission objectives, so everyone who signed on would understand exactly why the *Dutchman* was going back out. And so they were completely, one hundred percent, aware of the risk they'd be taking by coming aboard. My hope had been to discourage people from coming aboard. It hadn't worked. Here the objectives are in easy-to-read bullet format, something I'd seen recommended in officer training somewhere.

1)   Prevent other species from discovering humans had stolen a starship, and were involved in shutting down a wormhole

2)   Where it doesn't interfere with item 1 above, keep Skippy satisfied that we are making a serious effort to help him contact the Collective

3)   Where it doesn't interfere with Items 1 & 2 above, return the crew safely to Earth, someday, if we can. Like that's ever going to happen. That last sentence wasn't actually part of the written objectives; it was my own comment.

You might think the order of the first two items were reversed, that the whole purpose of the *Dutchman* going back out, was for Skippy to contact the Collective. You would be correct about the purpose of the trip, however that was not the primary objective for the crew. We owed Skippy our loyalty. We didn't owe him so much loyalty that we would risk the safety of our home planet and our entire species. Humans stealing a starship was bad enough; the Thuranin would be immensely pissed, but starships being destroyed or captured, even by lesser species, was not all that unusual. If the Maxohlx or Rindhalu ever learned humans had a way to manipulate wormholes, a technology even they could only dream of, they would rip our planet apart to get our secret.

And you might think objective 2 should be simply 'help Skippy contact the Collective'. You would be wrong there. We didn't know whether it was possible to contact the Collective, even whether they still existed. Or had ever existed, Skippy's memory in that area was not the greatest. All we could do is make Skippy happy that we were keeping up our end of the bargain, until he either contacted the Collective, or gave up. Keep Skippy happy that we were making a sincere effort to help him, whether we actually were able to usefully help him or not. In the back of my mind was a time limit, of maybe a year, that we would devote to helping Skippy. If we hadn't found a way to contact the Collective by then, my plan was to gently persuade Skippy to give up that particular quest. How I could convince a stubborn alien AI, who could devote a thousand years to a task without thinking about it, was something I'd figure out when we got there. For me, this constitutes fairly advanced planning, compared to the way I normally do things.

The most important objective for prospective crew members to read was number three. Not so much the text of that objective, but its position in the mission objectives order of priorities. Our return to Earth, our survival, was third in line. Everyone needed to understand that. If they didn't believe it, they could go stare at the collection of self-destruct tactical nuclear devices in one of our cargo bays.

Perhaps even more important for prospective crew members was objective Four. Oh, there is no objective Four on the list, you say? You are correct. There is no fourth objective like 'learning important sciency stuff', or 'exploring the galaxy', or 'getting intel about our potential enemies' or 'gathering useful advanced technology equipment', or even 'engaging in special operations warfare against the enemies of mankind'. If we could do any of those not-one-of-our-objectives-things without interfering with the three stated objectives, then great. If not, that's tough. I was not going to risk mission success, or lives, to make our science team happy. And I sure as hell wasn't going to approve any combat operations unless we absolutely had no choice. Or, I guess technically, unless engaging in combat was a better option than not engaging in combat. If that meant our gung-ho special forces and brainy science team were unhappy and bored, so be it. In fact, I would consider our mission a complete success if we were able to return to Earth safely, without a single dangerous or interesting thing happening. Semper Taedium could be our motto: 'Always Boredom'. I'd be happy with that.

Which is why I was mildly irritated that Venkman brought up the subject now. Actually, not irritated that she raised the question, she had a right to ask, just as I had a right to say no. What irritated me was her attitude, that I had ordered the *Dutchman* to prepare for departure, only because of my ignorance, I couldn't see the potential for important scientific discoveries right where we are. What I wanted to do was tell her flatly no, hell no, and not to question my orders again. Doing that would have only proved her point that I was too young and inexperienced to command a starship. Or, for that matter, a rowboat. Slapping her down would have felt good. Commanders don't often get to do what feels good, they have to do what is good for the mission, and sowing dissension among the crew would have hurt morale. No matter how large the *Flying Dutchman* was, we had seventy people living in a limited space, seeing the same bulkheads every day. At least I, and most of the soldiers and pilots, had been able to get off the *Dutchman*, go over to the Kristang space station and look at something different for a while. The science team had been stuck inside the ship since they came aboard.

I tried to let her down gently. "Doctor, I appreciate your eagerness for scientific inquiry," I said, surprising myself at using such fancy words, "and I need to balance that potential gain in humanity's understanding of the universe, against the risk of us being discovered here. The longer we remain here, the greater the risk to the overall mission, and to all our lives. This star system, particularly, because it previously had a Kristang presence, has an unacceptably high risk that enemy ships could jump in here at any moment, and we can't risk that. I'm sorry, Doctor. You may use the ship's sensors, as long as you do not interfere with the crew, until we are ready to jump."

"Captain, perhaps we-"

"Doctor Venkman," I waved a hand to stop her from talking, "you may be used to an academic setting, where discussion and debate are encouraged. This is a military vessel, a warship. As the commander, I welcome advice from my staff, however, once I have made a decision, it is final, and not open to debate." We might be traveling between the stars together for a long time, I thought it important to lay the ground rules early, and avoid problems later.

I was a hundred percent right. I still felt like a jerk.

CHAPTER FIVE

The abandoned space station was somewhat of a disappointment, in terms of our not finding an Elder communications node there. Thinking longer term for the mission, it was a great success in my opinion. All of our pilots had opportunities to fly during a real mission, and all of the SpecOps troops gained experience with powered armor space suits in a real operation. All of the troops, by the time we left the space station behind, had experience free diving in space. Other than a few very minor incidents that were dealt with quickly and professionally, I felt everyone had passed the test to be a space diver, and I asked Skippy to fabricate a special badge to wear on their uniforms. The badge was based on the US Army's Freefall Parachutist badge, with the difference being we replaced the tail feathers at the top with an arc of three stars. Pilots received spaceflight wings, similar to the Army Aviator badge, with the center shield replaced by a five-pointed star.

Sure, the new badges were not official, and UNEF may frown at the idea if we ever got back home. In the meantime, the crew were thrilled to be wearing badges that no other humans had qualified for. My awarding of badges began the process of Lt Williams warming up to me, slightly. After the award ceremony, we had a party in the galley, a party that spilled out into the corridor because our galley wasn't large enough. The strongest beverage available was iced tea. I took a tall, cold glass and made my way over to Williams, who was talking with his four-man SEAL team. Pointing to the Navy Special Warfare insignia he wore, I said "Lieutenant, we need to change the acronym for your team."

"How's that, sir?" He asked warily.

"SEAL is SEa, Air, Land, right? After today, it should be SEALS for SEa, Air, Land and *Space*."

"I think you're right about that, sir," he said with an ear-to-ear grin.

Garcia asked "What would the plural of that be? SEALSes?"

"Oh, man," Skippy interjected. "Do not ask Joe anything about grammar, he butchers the language horribly. Lieutenant Williams, sincere congratulations to you and your team."

"For realz, Skippy?" I asked, figuring he was inevitably going to add a disparaging comment about monkeys.

"For realz this time, Joe. Considering that you are, after all, a barrel of primitive monkeys, this crew has accomplished a lot in a short time. I have to give you props for that."

I am not a morning person. I am not even a mid-morning person. As a soldier, I have to get up early, and I manage to do it, it still doesn't come naturally. Because of the crew schedule that some idiot put together, an idiot whose name rhymes with 'Shmoe Bishop', my duty shift on the bridge started at 4AM ship time, so I dragged my ass out of bed an hour early. Time enough for a shower and a cup of coffee. Without coffee, I was mostly nonfunctional in the morning.

What had caused me to wake up an hour early wasn't an alarm, or Skippy, it was anxiety. We had gotten lucky checking out the abandoned space station, lucky not in the sense that we found something useful, lucky in that we had found the entire star system abandoned, and that we hadn't gotten into a fight, or had to plan some sort of risky combat. The potential for combat had gotten the special forces keyed up and kept them focused, and gave them experience using powered armor space suits. In zero gravity and hard vacuum. That was all good.

What wasn't good was, our next target was still way too dangerous. When we left the abandoned space station behind, we had set course for the second target, because we didn't have an alternative. The advantage of the second target was that Skippy knew for sure there was a comm node there. The disadvantage of the second target is that the whole area was closely monitored by the Maxohlx and by Sentinels. "Skippy, I got a question."

"Good morning, Joe, I'm going to ignore your poor grammar for the moment."

"Poor grammar?" I asked, surprised.

"You *have* a question, Joe, you don't *got* a question. At least you didn't say that you *gots* a question. Damn, you already butcher the English language enough with your terrible accent."

"Accent? What's wrong with the way I talk?" I talked the way every native New Englander north of Boston talked. Normal. Everybody else had a terrible accent.

"What's wrong? Let's start with the way you pronounce 'car' like 'cah', you leave the Rs out of everything. Tell me, Joe, were your ancestors so poor they had to sell all the letter Rs?"

"No, Skippy, we save all those Rs so we can use them on words that should have an R at the end, but don't. Like, my uncle Norm retired to where?" Which I pronounced 'Nahm' and 'way-uh'.

"That's easy, he's in Florida."

"Wrong! See, he lives in Florider. And the capital of Maine isn't Au-gust-a, it's Auguster."

"Wow. Incredible. How did you and your buddy Cornpone ever manage to communicate? With your Maine accent and his Southern drawl, it's like neither of you is speaking English."

"We don't speak English, Skippy, we speak American. And we managed to communicate just fine, thank you."

"If you say so, Joe. I have noticed you tone down your accent around most people. Like, at home you say 'Ayuh', but here you say 'yes' or 'yeah' or 'uh-huh'. When you visited your parents, before we left Earth, you were all like 'Ayuh' and 'wicked pissah' and your 'fah-tha' shot a 'de-ah', and your mother was cooking 'pah-ster' for spaghetti. Most of it was utterly incomprehensible to me."

"Ayuh. You gots to pay attention they-uh, Skippy-O."

"Oh, forget it. What is your question?"

"We started looking for this comm node dingus in places where some database said it should be, right?"

"Ayuh," Skippy said with a chuckle, "don't you usually look for something in a place you know where it is?"

"Duh, yeah, that's not my point- "

"You so rarely have a point, I felt safe to assume this time was no different."

My sleep-addled brain being not ready for snappy comebacks, I ignored his trying to bait me into an argument. "My point is, we hit that asteroid base, because you knew that place had a comm node. There are other places that have a comm node for sure, we decided those places are too risky, too tough for us to hit."

"In your opinion, they are too difficult," he said sourly.

Ignoring him, I continued. "Next you looked at places that might have one of these Elder comm node thingies, because the place is known to have a bunch of other Elder crap, right?"

"If this conversation is going to be you telling me a bunch of obvious stuff I already know, I'll tune out for a while and let you talk. Wake me when you're done."

"Can we go one step further?"

"Damn it, now you have my attention, on the infinitesimally tiny chance you might say something monkeys consider intelligent. Go ahead, amuse me."

"The first step was to look where we know there is a comm node, because somebody found an Elder site, got a comm node and logged it in a database. We already did that, when we raided the asteroid base on our first mission. The second step is to look where there might be a comm node, right? A place where there is a bunch of other Elder stuff logged in a database, and they might have a comm node also."

"So far, I am not blown away by your logic."

"So, step three," I continued to ignore him, "is for us to look in places that should have comm nodes, but they aren't in a database, because nobody has found those Elder sites yet."

"Huh? I'm not following you. How are we supposed to look in a site that hasn't been found yet?"

"By you figuring out where the Elders *would* have put stuff, comparing it to a map of Elder sites the Thuranin and Jeraptha know about, and determining where there *should* be Elder sites that nobody knows about."

"By how? Guessing?" He snorted.

"No, by," I searched for the right word to use, "I don't know, extrapolating, inferring, deducing, predicting? Whatever you want to call it. You know the Elders better than anyone in the galaxy today. You can figure where they would likely have had colonies, space stations, that sort of thing, right?"

"Huh." This time, his 'huh' wasn't a question.

"You have a map of Elder sites the Thuranin know about, and sites the Jeraptha know about, right?"

"Yes, the two mostly overlap, there isn't much one side knows about that the other side doesn't also know. This war has been going on for a very long time, much territory has swapped back and forth several times."

"Can you do it?"

"You want me to predict places where we, in this one ship full of monkeys, will find Elder sites that have not yet been discovered, by advanced species who desire nothing more than to find technology the Elders left behind? Species who have entire fleets of ships searching for Elder technology."

"That's about it, Ayuh. You told me the galaxy is vast, bigger than I can imagine, that even now, most of it is unexplored."

"It's unexplored, Joe, because most of the galaxy isn't worth exploring. Or it's too far from a wormhole."

"I notice you haven't answered my question. Can you do it?"

"I'm thinking!"

"Think faster."

"Joe, this is actually not a one hundred percent completely awful, terrible, stupid brainless idea. Hmmm. Very likely, very, very likely, this is a tremendous waste of my time. However, I am intrigued about how much this will test my analytical capabilities, so, I'll do it. This is going to take a while; I'll need to run simulations."

"A while, as in you already did it between saying 'need' and 'to'?"

"Not this time, smart guy. Go, I don't know, get some coffee, eat a banana, scratch yourself; do some monkey thing, and I'll let you know when I'm done. Don't bother me in the meantime, I'll be super extra busy in here."

I took a quick shower, got dressed, walked to the galley, drank a cup of coffee, and chatted with a couple people. Then I walked to a porthole to look through the tiny window at nothing, because there is not much to see in deep interstellar space. Before going on duty, I got a second cup of coffee, and headed for the bridge. The whole time, I'd been expecting Skippy to shout in my earpiece that my idea was stupid, and about how monkeys only wasted his extremely valuable time. Thirty two minutes had passed since Skippy began his analysis, this was an eternity in Skippy time. He remained silent until I was halfway to the bridge.

"Joe, I have good news and bad news." Skippy announced.

Uh oh. Skippy's idea of good news could be bad, so I answered carefully "Give me the good news first, please." I stopped and leaned against the bulkhead. If he was going to tell me how stupid I was, I'd rather not be on the bridge where the duty crew could hear it.

"The good news is I found some very good prospects for Elder sites that have not, as far as I know, been discovered by other species. You were right, although my memories are substantially blocked, my familiarity with the Elders allows me to extrapolate where they should have had colonies or other installations. What I did was-"

I let him talk without interrupting, even though his rambling on about statistics, metadata and collating sensor mapping data from dozens of species went way over my head. He was proud of what he'd accomplished; it was likely only he could have run such an analysis in so short a time, if at all. When there was a split-second pause in his nonstop talking, I took the opportunity to stop him from rambling on. "Amazing, Skippy, that is amazing. Maybe this is why you have such enormous processing capacity, so you can find the Elders', uh, legacy, stuff, and protect it. Or keep track of it."

"Huh. I hadn't considered that."

Before he could go off on a half hour tangent of speculation about his origins, I asked "Have you verified your data model, by checking whether it predicts Elder sites that are confirmed? Elder sites that other species do know about?"

"Verified my data model?" Skippy asked slowly in amazement. "Joe, where did you learn nerdy tech talk like that? I am mildly impressed, considering that it's you."

"It was in one of the thousand-slide PowerPoint decks I'm supposed to study as officer training." Maybe I shouldn't have told him I was only repeating buzz words. "Did you do it?"

"Yes, duh, I told you I ran the model back to determine accuracy within a standard deviation of less than-"

"You *tried* to tell me. Remember, Skippy, you're explaining things to me, you need to dumb it down a couple notches. You can use real sciency math talk when you're discussing stuff with the science team."

"Fair enough. Breaking it down Barney style, pun intended, the answer is yes, my method of predicting the location of Elder facilities is 96.7% accurate, when compared with a map of Elder sites known to current species."

"Damn. That is impressive."

"Ahhh, not so much, if you really understood the data." Skippy said sourly. "The Elder sites known to current species are the easy ones to find, obvious ones. The dumdums inhabiting the galaxy today only find Elder sites if they happen to trip over them in the dark, so to speak. Almost all of the Elder sites that have been mapped are in star systems capable of supporting carbon-based life. The unmapped sites that I predict we should find, are mostly in star systems centered around obscure stars such as red dwarfs. I am not yet, of course, able to determine how good my model is at predicting the location of more obscure, minor Elder sites. However, I am highly confident."

"Great. This time, your good news, is good news for sure. What's the bad news?"

"The bad news is where we have to go to check out these unknown, potential sites. By definition, they are in out of the way locations, else they would have been discovered by now. The model predicts only a handful of sites that are conveniently close to our location."

"Well, we will check out those-"

"Whoa, whoa!" Skippy cautioned. "No so fast, hot shot, let me finish. Of the handful of predicted sites, two are inaccessible now; the stars they were orbiting have become red giants and swallowed those planets. Another site was in a star system where the star went nova; even if that site still exists, it is likely damaged, and we'd have a hell of a time finding it now; it would have been thrown off its original orbit in an unpredictable fashion. Three other sites remain undiscovered, but are in star systems occupied by species with equivalent, or superior, technology to this ship. It would be substantially risky to enter those star systems."

"There's nothing we could check out around here?"

"Oh, I didn't say nothing. There are four sites within a month of here. Two of those sites are good prospects, the other two are low probability."

"Mmm hmm, within a month from here," I liked hearing that. "How long to check out all four sites?"

"Oof, you had to ask me that," Skippy sounded disgusted. "Uh, calculating now, a least-time course would take, meh, three and a half months. The sites are scattered inconveniently, we have to take roundabout routes through wormholes to get to all four sites."

"Meh?" I said, surprised.

"Huh?"

"You said 'meh'. Like when something isn't bad, it isn't great, it's just, you know, 'meh'."

"Oh, yeah. In this case, 'meh' was me suppressing my instinct to be precise. I told you that the estimated transit time is three and half months, instead of me saying three months, seventeen days, ten hours, twenty one minutes and forty eight point two six seven seconds. Roughly."

"Roughly? In the future, let's go with 'meh'."

"I thought so. Also, that is average transit time, not including time to match course with the sites, fly down in dropships, explore the sites, all that."

"Kind of implied, Skippy."

"Yeah, you'd think so, but I'm trying to explain hyperspatial navigation to monkeys, so-"

"Got it. Not all monkeys aboard this ship are as dumb as me-"

"None of them are, Joe. Well, I'm only considering standard IQ tests in the crew's personnel files, of course." Skippy paused. "Oh. Hmm. Did I just insult you?"

"Ya think?"

"Hey, blame that facts, not the messenger. Besides, I've told you before, that the standard IQ tests of your species, are woefully inadequate predictors of ability to create innovative solutions to-"

"Christ, Skippy, you sound like the buzzwords on those stupid PowerPoint slides that I'm supposed to study."

"Sorry. To dumb it down for you," he said, while supposedly intending *not* to insult me, "somehow your tiny monkey brain is able to think of things that my god-like intelligence misses. Like when you had the idea to get rid of the Kristang ships by jumping them into a gas giant. Or when you asked me how Thuranin fought in their flimsy space suits, because it didn't occur to me to tell you about their combots. None of your original Merry Band of Pirates, who mostly had higher IQ scores than you, had those ideas. Joe, you may not be particularly smart in a conventional sense, but you apparently have a talent that is more useful in your current role; you are *clever*."

"Space suits."

"Darn it, you had to remind me. Yes, I hate to say it, but that is a good example."

I was damned proud of myself. As a senior officer, I may be grossly inadequate for my responsibilities, according to the United States Army. As an infantry soldier, I had, in my humble opinion, good common sense, including the ability to ask obvious questions that everyone else was missing. Believe me, patrolling the Nigerian jungle in full battle rattle, on ill-defined missions, had caused me to ask a whole lot of common sense questions. "Thank you, Skippy. You can program us a course for the closest site?"

"Already loaded into the nav system."

"Of course it is. Great, I'll tell the pilots." And the entire crew. No one had been looking forward to a lonely, dull fourteen month voyage to explore the dangerous second site.

Sitting in the command chair on the bridge, I was waiting for the jump engines to recharge. We had changed course to check out the closest of the sites where Skippy thought we might find an Elder facility that wasn't known to the Thuranin or Jeraptha. I didn't have much to do, and my mind wandered. "Skippy, something has been puzzling me."

He made an exaggerated sigh. "Darn it, I knew this was going to happen sooner or later. All right, fine. Joey, when a Mommy and a Daddy love each other very much-"

"I know about the birds and the bees, Skippy!" Damn it! I should have known better than to try asking Skippy a serious question while other people were around. In the CIC, I could see people smirking, and one of the pilot's shoulders were shaking as he laughed. At me.

"Boy, that is a relief. The last thing I want to explain is monkey mating rituals. You're puzzled. Is this about shoe tying again? I think you'd be best to stick to Velcro until-"

"You know why I need shoes? Because I can walk! Let's see you do that, beer can."

"Whoa. That's the best you've got? Pretty lame, there, Joey."

"I'm trying to be serious here, Skippy."

Another sigh. "Fair enough. You do understand how difficult it is for me to take anything you monkeys say seriously, right? What is your question? If it's not outrageously stupid, I will consider wasting my time on you."

"We lowly, unworthy monkeys would greatly appreciate it. My question is about stealth technology. I've heard you say this ship has a stealth field. And I've seen you detect other ships soon after we jump into an area. Don't those ships also have stealth? And how does a stealth field work? We have stealth jets on Earth."

"Wow. Man, there isn't enough aspirin in the galaxy to fix the headache I'm going to get while trying to explain this to you. Fine. Listen hard, Mister Bigstupidhead, you might learn something. No, you do not have stealth jets on Earth. You have laughably crude pieces of metal that try to bounce radar waves in a different direction, instead of back to the radar receiver. Or you have coatings painted on your jets that try to absorb radar waves. That type of coating doesn't work so well when it's wet or dirty, by the way. And good luck to your Navy, trying to maintain delicate stealth coatings on aircraft in a corrosive salt spray environment. No, you do not have stealth technology. Your species has glanced the basic mechanics of stealth technology; you haven't been able to make it work yet."

"Fine. What's the difference?"

"A stealth field bends light waves around a ship. When a stealth field is working optimally, light flows right around an object as if it wasn't there. If a ship using stealth is between you and a star, all you will see is light from the star, the stealthed ship won't cast a shadow."

"Cool. Is that why sometimes Ruhar or Kristang aircraft have a fuzzy outline, they're hard to see?"

"Yes, exactly. Although using stealth in an atmosphere is almost not worth doing, any decent set of sensors can track how an aircraft disturbs the air around it, and the engines emit a heat signature that a blind man could see from a hundred miles. There is an important drawback to a stealth field, can you guess what it is?"

Skippy played the annoying theme music from 'Jeopardy' while I thought furiously, trying to impress him with my monkey smarts. Light bent around the ship, radar waves bent around the ship, light- "Hey! If all the light bends around the ship, how can the ship see anything? It would be blind, right?"

"Bing bing bing bing bing! We have a winner! That was pretty good, Joe. Yup. All light bends around the stealthed ship. A ship inside a stealth field might accidentally fly into, or too close to a star, because the light from the star wouldn't contact the ship's sensors. Don't worry, a stealth field has intentional gaps that allow in enough light for detection."

I looked at the display. "Huh. That's how we can still use the sensors when we're stealthed. Cool. But other ships use stealth, right, and you're able to detect them. Is that more amazing Skippy magic?"

Skippy snorted. "Amazing magic to monkeys, sure. The answer is no, I make our sensors significantly more effective, however, the technology for active scanning is used by all star faring species, even dumdum lizards. Ships use an active sensor field, projected from the ship, to detect objects around them."

"Wait just a minute. That doesn't make sense. Why would a ship in stealth, that is trying to hide, project something that gives away their position? Missiles could home in on the source of that field, and blow up the ship." Figuring that out made me feel pretty darned smart. My uncle Bob has a friend in the Navy, on a nuclear submarine, and one time at a cookout in my uncle's backyard, I listened in while the guy talked about what it's like to be in a steel tube under the waves. One thing he said is that real subs almost never use their 'active' sonar, sending out a sonar pulse 'ping' and listening for it bounce back. The whole point of a submarine is that it's quiet and it's underwater and nobody knows where it is. Sending out a sonar pulse is like shouting 'hey, look at me, I'm a dumbass, here

I am'. Using active sonar invites a torpedo to follow the sonar waves back to the source, and sink the sub.

"The sensor field isn't spherical, you dope," Skippy explained. "It has an irregular shape, and it constantly changes shape, and the field intensity varies throughout it, the field isn't strongest closer to the ship. To find the source of the field, a missile would need to first map the shape of the field, and calculate where it must be projected from. That would take way too long, and the field shape is constantly changing, there is no practical way to map it. When an object enters a ship's sensor field range, even if that object is stealthed, it will change the field's shape, that data feeds back to the source ship. Because the source ship knows what the shape and local density of the sensor field is supposed to be at any time, it can tell what object distorted the field. Where the object is, how fast it is moving and in what direction, an outline of the object, all that. It gets complicated during combat, of course, because ships try to distort other ships' sensor fields, in ways that mask who and where they truly are. Ships can even project sensor ghosts, distort or jam a sensor field and create a false reading. The big limitation to sensor fields, at this level of technology, is that they propagate at the speed of light, so they are painfully slow by the standards of space combat. By the time an object is detected and that data gets back to the source ship, the object will have moved in an unpredictable fashion. That makes long-range targeting difficult, even with speed of light weapons. You fire a maser or particle beam, and by the time the beam gets there, the target has moved."

"Oh. Wow. A ship can dodge a maser beam. Cool."

"Oh indeed. Are we done with kindergarten for the day? If you're good and take a nap now, I'll get you a juice box. Oy vey, I've got a headache. I need to lay down with a cold compress on my forehead."

"No juice box needed. Could you do one more thing for me? Explain all that to our science team?"

"Science team? You are referring to the group of marginally smarter monkeys? Oof, then my head would explode. Tell you what, I just forwarded a video recording of our conversation to their zPhones, they can watch it, and save me from having to explain it all over again."

"Great, thank you, Skippy."

"Don't mention it. Seriously, please, do not ever mention this again."

Having gotten Skippy to smack some knowledge down on me, I was feeling pretty good about myself. This lasted less than three minutes. Skippy, true to his word, had forwarded a video of our conversation to the science team. And to everyone else on the ship. That was great. What was not so great was, that shithead little beer can had replaced my image in the video with a chimpanzee. Instead of me sitting in the command chair, it was a chimp, with my voice coming out of its mouth. And not just sitting in the chair, this chimp was swinging around the bridge, eating bananas, scratching itself, playing with its private parts, hooting and bouncing around the bridge, and other embarrassing things. My first notice that something had gone horribly wrong, was when people in the CIC began laughing uncontrollably while looking at their zPhones.

Oy vey. Now I had a headache.

CHAPTER SIX

Before we made the final jump, to recon our first target of Skippy's list of potential Elder sites, I wanted to speak to the crew, the entire crew

"No chimp this time, Skippy, Ok? No replacing my image with a monkey, no matter what you think of us."

"Agreed, Joe, that was only funny one time."

"Thank you."

It was a short speech, nothing inspirational, simply reminding everyone that we were about to jump into a star system that we, even Skippy, knew little about, and that we might be jumping away with no notice to the crew. The pilots had orders to initiate a short emergency jump on their own judgment, without waiting for the officer on duty in the bridge. It was a simple talk to the crew, that I did not intend to be anything memorable, but, Skippy had other ideas. I learned almost immediately what he had done after clicking the intercom button off. I learned about it, when Sergeant Adams forwarded a video recording of my speech to my zPhone.

Crap. On the video feed to the rest of the ship, Skippy had replaced my image and voice, with Barney. Barney, the big stupid purple dinosaur. He hadn't only altered my voice; he'd changed some of my words. My speech didn't begin with 'This is Colonel Bishop', it began with 'Duh, hello, boys and girls', in classic moronic Barney tones. There I was, a big idiotic dinosaur, sitting in the command chair in my uniform, talking like I had an IQ of 30. Damn it, I hate that smug little beer can.

On the other hand, everyone got a good laugh at my expense, so it was good for crew morale. "All right, all right," I said with as much good nature as I could muster, "let's focus, people, we have a jump in twenty minutes."

I took a quick bathroom break, and used it as an opportunity to speak with Skippy in private. "Skippy, about that Barney video-"

"Funny, huh? The crew loved it."

"Yeah, hey, you know, there were other characters painted on the side of that ice cream truck. Why don't you show me as Ironman or-"

"The Smurfs?"

I'd forgotten about the Smurfs.

"Not the Sm-"

"The only one people remember is Barney."

"All right," I was tired of fighting about it, "fine, Barney. This is another case where it's only funny once, you understand that, right?"

"You sure about that?"

"Pretty sure, yeah."

"Uh oh. Hmm."

Crap, I thought. "What did you do, Skippy?"

"I can neither confirm or deny, but, somebody whose name rhymes with, let's say, 'Stippy', may have left behind a virus that altered your image on all the video recordings of your intelligence debriefings in Colorado Springs. That virus may have taken effect after we left Earth."

Great. Just great. "Some guy named Stippy, huh?"

"Yup. You should never trust him, that guy's a real asshole."

The jump in was uneventful; Skippy declared within five minutes that we were alone in the star system. Fifteen minutes later, the crew monitoring sensors in the Combat Information Center agreed, and I ordered the ship to stand down from battle stations. Then we began the painstaking process of searching for an Elder site. The star system, centered on an unremarkable red dwarf star, had one smallish gas giant planet, about the size of Neptune. Skippy thought the most likely place for the Elders to have located a facility was on a rocky moon orbiting the gas giant. Quickly, the ship's sensors identified three large and two small rocky moons, plus two more that were covered in ice. Skippy warned that locating an Elder site could take considerable time, as the Elders may have partially hidden it, and most of the facility could be buried deep under the surface.

He was wrong. "Ah, damn it, found it," he announced, sounding disgusted. "It's on the second largest moon, on top of a plateau. Whatever its purpose, the Elders didn't make any attempt to hide it. And somebody has already been there, there's debris scattered around the site and the surface is disturbed from where dropships landed. Crap! We are way too late. Some hooligans already ransacked the place."

Hooligans? I wondered where Skippy picked up his slang. "Sorry, Skippy, but, hey, this is not a failure. I think this is great, we proved your model for locating unmapped Elder sites is correct, and we didn't encounter any hostiles when we jumped in, or take a risk checking the place out. This is the first place we've looked; did you really think we'd hit the jackpot the very first time?"

"It would have been nice," he grumbled. Then sighed, I wondered how Skippy decided when to fake a sigh, since he didn't actually breathe. "You're right, you're right. This does prove I know how to locate Elder sites that are not known to the Thuranin or the Jeraptha, or at least not in databases I have access to. Anything useful was probably taken from this site a long, long time ago. Joe, when you've been waiting as long as I have, it is frustrating to get all the way here, and find some jerk has looted the place."

"Is it worth going down there anyway, to check it out?" With this star system apparently uninhabited, I wanted to take advantage of an excellent opportunity for training. Our pilots could practice flying dropships down to the surface of the moon and back, and soldiers could gain experience using suits on the moon, in low gravity. Partly because I felt bad about denying the science team more time at the abandoned space station, I wanted the science team to also be able to get away from the ship, go down to the moon, and poke around in an Elder site. Even if the site had, as Skippy feared, been stripped of anything valuable, the science team could learn what an Elder site looked like. They could get used to it, so if we found an unmolested site, the team would not waste time with sightseeing and marveling at the novelty of it.

"Sure, what the hell, why not? It's possible that the hooligans who vandalized the place were only looking for weapons, or something they could sell to buy drugs," he said bitterly, "they might not have recognized a comm node as anything valuable. It would be good for you monkeys to get the sightseeing over with here anyway. When we do find a site that hasn't been screwed with, I don't want to waste time with you monkeys taking selfies and stupid crap like that."

"My thoughts exactly, Skippy," I agreed.

"Colonel Chang," I turned the chair to look into the CIC, "how about you take the Chinese team, and the Indians," those two teams were currently at the top of a randomly chosen rotation, "and a scientist down there, recon the site, see if the looters left anything useful? If not, we at least gain experience using suits on the surface of an airless world."

"Yes, sir," he responded eagerly.

SpecOps

"Captain Desai," I turned back to face the front of the bridge compartment, "if flying a mere dropship is not too boring compared to a starship, would you like to ferry Colonel Chang's team down for some sightseeing?"

"Oh, I think I can manage it, sir," she said with a wide grin, sliding out of the pilot couch.

Desai set the dropship down carefully, half a kilometer from the largest building of the Elder site, and Chang took first three people over to the site, then called in others. It wasn't easy for me to resist the temptation to micromanage the landing party from orbit, so I pretended to be more calm than I felt, and went to my office so Major Simms could have more time in the command chair. And to let Chang and Desai make decisions on their own. After an hour, I couldn't stand it any longer, and returned to the bridge. Simms stepped back to her duty station in the CIC. Right away, I noticed something odd on the main bridge display, a sensor analysis that depicted the gas giant planet was surrounded by a loose cloud. "Major Simms, what is that?"

"We have been practicing using the sensors, sir, Skippy wanted sensors to scan the orbit around the planet. We've been trying to see if we can get the same readings from the data as he does. There is some kind of atmospheric gas surrounding the planet."

"Good idea," I said, we shouldn't rely on Skippy for everything. "What is so interesting about this space gas, Skippy?"

"Joe, I've found something odd," Skippy said, in a voice that I associated with my high school science teacher. "There is a measurable part of the planet's atmosphere in orbit."

"You mean, higher than it should be?"

"Yes, these gases are not technically part of the atmosphere now. From the ratio of elements in the orbiting gases, I can tell they came from the planet; they aren't something ejected by a volcanic eruption on one of the moons. Except, hmm, that is odd."

"What?" Truthfully, right then I did not much care what scientific oddity Skippy had discovered about a small gas giant planet, orbiting a dull red dwarf star, a long way from Earth. On the other hand, I did not want to insult Skippy by being openly disinterested. "What's odd about it?"

"The chemical elements that are missing."

"Uh, can you be more specific?" Trying to feign interest, I was about to suggest that he discuss this with the science team, rather than me. "This planet is missing some type of gas, that, uh, gas giants normally have?" In a flash of insight, I asked "Is that because this planet is small, for a gas giant? Hey, is there a special name for a gas planet that isn't a giant? Do we call it a gas normal, something like that?"

"We don't-"

"If the planet was much smaller, it couldn't be made of gas, right? The gravity would be too low to contain the gas, and it would escape into space, be boiled off by the solar wind?" Man, I was proud of myself for thinking that on my own, I remembered reading that the reason the atmosphere of Mars was so thin, was that most of it had been blown away by the Sun's solar wind over millions of years because Mars doesn't have a magnetic field.

"Yes, that is both correct, and irrelevant to the current situation," he said. "This planet has a normal distribution of gases, for a planet of this size, considering the gaseous composition of its star. I was about to tell you about the odd part, before you side tracked me with your moronic speculation on a subject you know zero about. There are gases present in the planet's atmosphere that are almost entirely missing from the cloud of gases enveloping the planet in low orbit. For example, and most telling, there is no helium 3 in the gas cloud."

Moronic? Now I was insulted, and figured this was a challenge. "Well, uh, some elements are lighter, and so those would have been pushed out of orbit by the solar wind here? And the heavy gases would have fallen back into the atmosphere."

"Joe?"

"Yes?"

"Here's a quote I read once, from a smart monkey: 'it is better to remain silent and be thought an idiot, than to speak and remove all doubt'."

"Oh, that's hilarious, you shithead."

"Me a shithead? You've been giving me guesses that are about on the level of astrology in terms of scientific relevance. If you will *please*, shut your pie hole for a moment, I will smack some actual, useful knowledge on you. Knowledge that you should be interested to hear, because it represents a potential threat to the ship. You need that knowledge as the commander of this mission. And man, every time you open your mouth, I realize what a gargantuan mistake that was to put you in command of anything more important that a lemonade stand."

"Shutting up now," I said in all seriousness.

"Great. Finally. Planets that are surrounded by an orbiting mixture of atmospheric gases are not unusual, I have seen them many times before. It is not the fact that this planet is surrounded by escaped gases that is interesting, what is interesting is why those gases are likely there. My guess, and when I make a guess it is based on solid data and rational analysis, unlike the idiotic BS that comes out of your mouth, my guess is that those gases are in orbit because they were pulled up in the process of ships extracting useful gases from the atmosphere. Starships use gas giant planets as a supply of elements for fuel, reaction mass, and other purposes, depending on the technology of the ships involved."

"Holy crap!" I gasped. "You're telling me this damned planet is a gas station?"

"Sort of, yes. Not the sort of gas station that has a convenience store where you can buy Slurpees and week-old hot dogs. Maybe, it is more of an inconvenience store, where you have to make everything from the basic elements. But yes, the sensor data points to this planet having been used to extract starship fuel, in the past."

"Past, like, yesterday, or like, a million years ago?" I asked anxiously. To Skippy, who had existed possibly for millions of years, time had a totally different meaning than it did for modern-day humans, who measure time mostly in terms of TV show seasons.

"That is difficult to tell, even for me, Joe. We don't have enough long-term data about this star system, for me to accurately forecast timelines."

"Give me a wild guess, was it more or less than a thousand years ago?"

"Oh, in that case, less. Not yesterday, either. Maybe, within the last year. Or, hmm, I'm running an extrapolation here, maybe, more like within the last month, based on dispersement of the waste gases. Possibly less than a month, there is a whole lot of waste gas in orbit here. And, while this star is nothing special, it is conveniently located between two wormhole clusters, so it is a particularly good candidate to be a frequently used refueling stop."

"Do we need to get out of here immediately, or not?"

"That, Joe, is a judgment call you need to make."

"Crap." All decisions, ultimately, fell to the commander. "Damn it. Major Simms, recall the landing party. Right now. Get them back to the dropship and off the surface, as soon as possible, and tell them I do not care what interesting sciency stuff they are doing down there. Pilot, Skippy, I need jump options to get the *Dutchman* out of here, if needed."

Through the glass wall, I could see Simms talking into her microphone, she was shaking her head, then she looked at me. "Sir, Captain Desai reports that her dropship is forty kilometers from the main site, she landed there so four people could check out some outbuildings. She has recalled the second landing party, and estimates she can retrieve those people and be headed back to the main site in twenty five minutes. Colonel Chang told her it will take forty minutes for his team to reach the evac site; he has some people down in an access shaft far beneath the surface. They think they may have found a section of the base that has not been looted."

"Damn it. While I commend Chang's initiative, his timing is less than optimal. All right, signal Desai and Chang to move as quickly as they can do so safely, I don't want someone getting into an accident, and this becoming a rescue operation."

"Yes, sir." Simms acknowledged.

Adams stepped around the corner from the CIC to talk with me. "We're bugging out of this system already, sir?"

What she didn't say, and I could see in her eyes, was that here we had a confirmed Elder site, which we had not fully explored, and that perhaps we were being hasty about abandoning it just because of some gas floating above the planet. Another potential Elder site might not be any better, and we'd be wasting this opportunity. "No, we're not leaving, not yet. What we are doing is picking up our landing party so they won't be left behind if we have to jump out of here. I let a large party go down there, partly to gain experience, on the assumption this star system was safe, uninhabited. Now we learn that this system might be a high traffic area, because the planet below us is a gas station. We're going to pull back, and assess the data. If the risk looks manageable, we will figure out a better way to explore the site, with multiple options for quick evac." Looking back, it might have been foolhardy of me to use an Elder site as an opportunity to give people experience in armor suits on the surface of an airless moon. With both sides of the war dedicating ships to searching for Elder sites, I should have selected a less important place for training. What I should have done is ask Skippy to suggest a completely uninteresting star system, and take the ship there for a dedicated week of training. Extending the mission by a week would be a small price to pay, for having pilots with experience landing dropships, and soldiers and scientists gaining experience walking around and working in Kristang space suits. This situation needed to be added to my list of opportunities for me to learn from.

Adams nodded slowly, looking at me carefully. She still thought of me as a buck sergeant, and her instincts as an experienced staff sergeant were to offer me gentle, nudging guidance in what she considered the right direction. I knew what she was thinking; that I was so inexperienced as a commander, I was afraid to take even reasonable risks. "Yes, sir."

Maybe I was being hasty, too risk averse. The four people in Desai's secondary landing party, who had been checking out structures away from the main Elder base, were almost back to the dropship; I was watching a video feed from the dropship. Four people, carefully loping across the rocky surface of the moon, kicking up puffs of dust as they walked, bouncing lightly. Damn, I envied them. Even though I had trained in a suit, trained in zero gravity, low gravity, high gravity, in vacuum and simulated thick atmosphere, all the training had taken place aboard the *Dutchman*. I wanted to walk on the surface of a real moon, I wanted to feel like an astronaut. There I was, commander of a starship, and at the moment, I envied three Indian soldiers and one Australian scientist, who were striding confidently back to the-

"Uh oh! Joe, jump option Echo, right now. *Now!*" Skippy shouted.

I nodded to the pilot, and she pressed the proper button. In a flash, the *Flying Dutchman* moved, the image on the main bridge display changed from the surface of a moon, to the cloud tops of the gas giant. Cloud tops, as in, it looked like we could reach out and touch them. "Where are we?" I asked, alarmed. "What happened?"

"Don't worry, Joe, we're safely above the atmosphere despite what it looks like, we jumped into an area with an intense magnetic field, and I've engaged stealth. Two Kristang ships jumped in near the planet, we were on the other side of the moon. I believe we jumped quickly enough that they did not detect the gamma ray signature of our jump out. We're now over the planet's horizon, that should have shielded our jump in from being seen also. The Kristang, overall, have crappy sensors on their ships. They have concentrated on upgrading weapons technology at the expense of sensors, which is a mistake the stupid lizards have been making for a very long time, they never learn. Hmm, two more Kristang ships have jumped in. Two, three, five more. That's seven Kristang ships, a typical task force."

"What type of ships?"

"It looks like, I'm checking the data as it comes in, one battlecruiser, two cruisers, two destroyers, a troop transport and a support ship."

"Can they see us?"

"No. No way, Joe. Our Thuranin stealth field, plus my own awesome enhancements, are quite effectively shielding us from the laughably useless sensors the lizards have. We are also encased in the planet's magnetic field, which distorts the sensor fields of the Kristang. So, no, they do not know we are here."

"What about the landing party? Have the Kristang seen them?"

"No, not that I am able to determine from Kristang ship to ship transmissions. The lizards do not appear to have any interest in the Elder site, that confirms my suspicion that multiple species have picked over that site, over many years. Just before we jumped, I signaled the landing party that enemy ships are in system, Captain Desai will have detected their inbound jump signatures. I am sure she has engaged the dropship's stealth field and maintained communications security, and that Colonel Chang has concealed his team within the Elder facility. Our sensors are no longer able to detect the dropship, which leads me to believe it is effectively stealthed. Unless either Desai or Chang break discipline, something that would greatly surprise me, even given what little I know of them, the Kristang will not learn of their presence on the surface there."

Relieved for the moment, I took in a deep breath and let it out slowly, like a yoga thing, except that I'd never taken a yoga class. My sister had been big into yoga for a while. "Fine, great. The critical factor, then, is, how much oxygen does the landing party have?"

"There are two critical factors, Joe," he corrected me. "How much oxygen the landing party has in their suits, and how long the Kristang intend to remain here? Assuming Colonel Chang orders the landing party to lay down, rest, and conserve oxygen, they should have enough in their suits for thirty two hours. Considering that they will need to walk back out to the dropship, and during that time they will be increasing their oxygen usage, thirty hours is the practical limit. As to the Kristang, from their communications I have determined they are in this system because they were dropped off by a Thuranin star carrier that is going in a different direction, and they are waiting to be picked up by a different star carrier in thirty six hours. The Kristang are here to practice fleet maneuvers, and for a refueling exercise. The support ship is capable of extracting fuel from the atmosphere of a gas giant planet. Its tanks are now almost full, so it will not be going through the actual fuel extraction and refining entire process, which typically takes six to eight days for the Kristang. For this exercise, the support ship will only practice lowering its refueling line into the atmosphere and maintaining a stable position in orbit. The other ships will be conducting war game exercises; I do not have the details, as they have not been included in ship to ship transmissions yet."

"Thirty six hours? That's too late, uh, wait, if they're going to be picked up by the Thuranin, though, they'd want to be at the rendezvous point plenty ahead of time?" For our landing party, I wanted plenty of cushion on their oxygen supply.

"Absolutely. The Thuranin have zero patience for stragglers, their star carriers do not wait for anyone, sometimes including other Thuranin ships. They have been known to leave behind Kristang ships that have been as little as ten minutes late to a rendezvous. I expect the Kristang will want to be certain to arrive at the rendezvous point at least four hours ahead of time, so they should depart here ten or twelve hours ahead of time."

I made a long, low whistle of dismay. "Whoooo, that is cutting it very close. Thirty hours of oxygen for the landing team, and the Kristang will be here for another twenty four to twenty six hours?"

"The math is brutal, yes."

"Can we get a message to the landing party?"

"Not from here at the moment, but in roughly two hours, we will be in position to send a tight-beam burst transmission with minimal risk of detection by the Kristang. Unless, of course, there is a Kristang ship between us and the moon at the time."

"We're going to wait, sir?" Simms asked skeptically.

"Skippy, what are our chances of taking on seven Kristang ships? Five warships, right," I asked hopefully, "we don't count the troop transport or the support ship?"

"Do not ignore those two lesser combatants, Colonel Joe, they are equipped with missiles and masers, and four of the troop transport's dropships also carry missiles. The Kristang could hurt us badly in a fight, a star carrier's best defense is to run away. I do not like the odds of us engaging seven ships. There is also the problem that other Kristang ships, I do not yet have a count, are waiting at the edge of this star system. They could quickly be brought in as reinforcements."

"This isn't a simple standup fight," I explained to Simms, "we would be vulnerable while we're standing still to recover the landing party. And as soon as the Kristang see what we're doing, they for sure will target the landing party; we won't be able to protect them. We wait. We send a signal to the landing party in about two hours, and we wait for the Kristang to go away. It sucks, but that's what we do, we wait."

CHAPTER SEVEN

We waited. It did suck. Right at the two hour and three minute mark, we shot a communications maser toward the moon, advising the landing party about the situation, the rough timelines for us to recover them, and ordering them not risk sending a reply. Then we waited some more, a lot more.

After my duty shift on the bridge was over, I surrendered the chair to Sergeant Adams. Part of me wanted to stay in the chair for the full twenty six hours, to not miss a second while my crew stretched out their dwindling oxygen supply. The crew I had ordered to the surface, and put in danger, the crew I was responsible for. Needing something to do, I went to the gym and ran on a treadmill, headphones on and not in a mood for chit chat; other people in the gym left me alone. Following an hour of sweating on the treadmill, I took a shower, got a snack from the galley, and went to my office. Skippy pinged me through my zPhone, that meant he wanted to talk privately. Putting in my zPhone earpiece, I said "Hey, Skippy, more bad news?"

"Since 'news' is by definition new information, there is no news. The situation has not changed."

From the display on my tablet, I knew that already. It still felt good to have Skippy verify what I was seeing. "All right, what's up?"

"This is a conversation perhaps best conducted in private, Joe."

"Ah. Got it." I pinged the CIC crew, to let them know I was going to my cabin. Once there, I closed the door behind me, and sat down on the bed. The crew knew not to disturb me in my cabin, without calling me first. "What is it?"

"Joe, I know this will not be a pleasant conversation."

"Let me guess, you're going to tell me that I need to consider abandoning Chang's team, in order to continue the mission."

"Um, yes?" His voice carried genuine surprise.

"Sacrifice a few soldiers, to preserve most of the crew, and the ship."

"Uh huh," he said slowly. "I'm kind of at a loss for words here, Joe, I was prepared for a long argument, and now I got nothing."

"Don't be an ass, Skippy. You think I haven't considered that I may have to do that? Sit here silently, while the clock runs out on their oxygen supply, and they choke to death? I have considered that, I'm the commander. That means I have to put the mission first. It sucks, it absolutely sucks, I hate it. I'm the commander, it's my job. You think about this; we're out here for you, this is your mission, we're risking our lives for you."

"Whoa. That's BS. You're putting all the burden on me, and you're wrong. Yeah, I need you not to risk the ship. You humans need to make sure other species do not discover that you are roaming around the galaxy."

Damn, I had actually hurt his feelings. "That came out kind of harsh, Skippy, I didn't mean it that way. You saved our planet, and we have a deal, and I'm going to keep to that deal, even if it costs lives. I want *you* to understand that."

"I do understand it, Joe."

"Good. I have thought about this a lot, Skippy. If we don't have a realistic chance to recover the landing party without undue risks to the ship, then I am simply going to face the facts. It's plain and simple, Skippy, I can't afford to get emotional about command decisions. So, yes, I have already decided we will abandon Chang's team, if we have to. Let's hope it doesn't come to that."

"Joe, occasionally I am confronted with the fact that you are not only the good-natured dope who I joke around with. I am reminded that you shot down two Whales in cold blood, killing almost a thousand sentient beings. And that under your command, we jumped fourteen Kristang starships inside a planet, killing their entire crews. That doesn't include the seventy eight Thuranin of their ship's original crew. Or the Kristang who died when you nuked that asteroid."

"Your point is what?" Occasionally, I was reminded that Skippy was an AI built by a civilization so far advanced, they would consider humans to be bugs, at best. He acted friendly to us, and we needed him to continue to be friendly. My most important job was not commanding the ship, not leading the crew, not making critical decisions. The most important thing I did aboard the *Dutchman* was making sure Skippy enjoyed having us around. If Skippy ever got bored with insulting me and busting my balls, we would be in trouble. Odd as it is to think about it, my relationship with that arrogant little shithead was humanity's greatest asset.

"My point, I guess, is that I came into this discussion assuming I needed to force you to consider an agonizing decision, and you had already done that. I underestimated you."

"Thank you, Skippy."

"Of course, most of the time, when I think I'm underestimating you, it turns out I estimated way too high, because you're such a doofus."

"And, thanks for reminding me what an asshole you really are."

"Oh, no problem, Joe, any time."

Around seven hours in, I was again in my office, doing busywork that kept me from hovering around the bridge and distracting the duty crew. Skippy interrupted my thoughts with more bad news. "Hmm, Joe, I just learned a possibly interesting tidbit about this task force. The commander is the third son of high-tier clan leader. He took command of the task force only recently, and the fleet naturally gave him cast-offs from other task forces. As such, he jumped his task force in here for training exercises to whip his new ships into shape. He is very concerned that his task force will be embarrassed during a major clan-wide fleet war game that is scheduled for next month. With much of the next month taken up in travel time, this is his best opportunity for training."

"Damn it," I cursed. "That means he's going to push the time limit, stay here running exercises right to the deadline." That's what I said, because that's what I would do, if I was suddenly in command of a second-hand task force.

"My thoughts exactly. There are other Kristang ships out at the edge of this star system; he took his task force here, so they can train away from watching eyes. From what I have seen, the commander's fears about the ships he was given are entirely justified; these ships are poorly maintained, their crew are inexperienced, and morale is terrible. Thus far, the ships maneuver clumsily, respond slowly to orders, and their navigators do not seem to understand left from right. It does not help that this task force commander is, even for a Kristang, a major hard-ass. It almost makes me feel sympathetic for the crews under his command."

"Yeah," I said with a frown. "Almost."

At the eighteen hour thirty two minute mark, I was once more in my office when Skippy called. Sleep, although a good idea, had been elusive, I'd laid down on my bed and tried to get some rest for an hour, until I gave up and realized there was no way I could peacefully slumber while the landing party, while my people, were running out of oxygen.

So, I'd gone to my office to study flight training manuals. "Joe! One of those cruisers just jumped into low orbit of that moon, on the opposite side from the Elder base. We didn't have any warning; it was suddenly there. Four dropships are proceeding down to the surface."

I fairly jumped around the desk and into the corridor. "Did you inform the bridge?"

"Yes, of course I did, Joe. Major Simms is the current duty officer."

From my office to the bridge was less than twenty seconds, that's why I'd selected a tiny closet as my office. Close enough so I could get there quickly, far enough away and around a corner, so the bridge and CIC crews didn't feel I was hovering over their shoulders every minute. When I got there, Simms was already sliding out of the command chair for me. "All we know is a cruiser jumped in, with no warning, and launched four dropships straight down. On their current course and speed, we estimate they will arrive at the Elder base in twenty seven minutes."

Twenty seven minutes. Because the *Dutchman* could jump there within seconds, we didn't need to act immediately. We could evaluate the situation, and consider our options. I was about to order Captain Desai to the bridge, I wanted our most experienced pilot at the controls if we had to go into combat. Then I remembered Desai wasn't aboard the ship, she was in a dropship, in stealth, on that moon. This situation was bad, all bad. "Is there any sign that the Kristang know about the landing party?" I asked the obvious question. Why else would that cruiser have jumped into orbit there, and launched four dropships?

"No," Skippy answered, "there were no such communications before that cruiser jumped, and the cruiser and its four dropships are maintaining communications silence. It is, however, impossible for us to assure that we can monitor every single transmission between those ships. If they are using a tight-beam maser to communicate between ships, the *Dutchman's* sensors have less than a fifty percent chance to intercept the message from here."

"I'm going to assume they know, somehow they know, about the landing party. It's the only thing that makes sense. Our options are, what? We jump in, launch missiles at that cruiser, and hit those dropships with the maser cannon." I pondered the main display, playing with the controls on the arm of the command chair; I'd gotten pretty good at manipulating the display. From our position, we had line of sight to the moon; the orbits of the moon and the *Dutchman* meant the moon was going behind the planet within forty minutes. The cruiser was a dot on the display, it was visible, but was headed behind the moon in less than five minutes. Because we weren't using the *Dutchman's* sensor field, we had to rely on passive sensors to detect the enemy ships. Most importantly, four of the dots on the display were the Kristang dropships. I zoomed in the view, and it revealed two large troop transports and two gunships. The dropships had pulled out of their steep dive from orbit, and were flying low, hugging the airless terrain. An icon on the display indicated that the ship's sensors were estimating the position of the dropships. At such distance, and with our sensors dealing with interference from the planet's magnetic field, detecting the dropships was intermittent. "Or, hey, how close to the moon's surface can we jump in? We need to shrink the distance Desai needs to get back aboard. Star carriers aren't designed to operate in a gravity well, that moon's gravity can't be a problem, right? Can we-"

"Colonel Joe," Skippy interrupted me, "we have another option that you should strongly consider; doing nothing for now, and waiting. I don't think this is a real assault against the landing party. If they knew humans are down there, their other ships would be deployed to support the assault force. They are not at the moment; the other ships are operating independently."

"You think this is an exercise also?" That surprised me. It also didn't make much sense. The planet had a dozen moons; having a Kristang cruiser jump into orbit of the one moon where we had a landing party stranded was too much of a coincidence.

"Yes, I believe it is another exercise. Based on limited data, yes," Skippy said confidently. "This appears to be one Kristang ship practicing an assault drop."

"How sure are you about that, Skippy?" I needed him to be very confident. If the Kristang dropships landed at the Elder site and their soldiers went inside, it would not matter whether their original purpose was an exercise or an assault, they were likely to find our landing party. And then there would certainly be a fight for real.

"Fairly. Hmmm, perhaps that did not give the impression I intended to convey. To be more accurate, there is a 92% probability that this is an exercise, and that the Kristang do not know anything about the presence of our landing party. I can show you, if you like, how a Kristang task force would deploy to support and assault drop; this task force is not positioned to assist that one cruiser. Also, those four dropships have not engaged stealth, that is also unusual. The lack of stealth is a strong indicator that this is not a true combat situation for the Kristang. If their intention is to attack our landing party, the tactics of that task force are truly incompetent."

"92% is good, Skippy, except it only tells me part of what I need to know. If part of the exercise includes those dropships landing at the Elder site, and Kristang soldiers going into the Elder site, we will need to intervene."

"Oh," Skippy sounded disappointed. "Hmm. I hadn't considered that. We could be forced into combat, even if that is not currently the intention of the Kristang."

"Uh huh. Also, those other ships are several light minutes away; our information on their positions and what they are doing is out of date by that much," I pointed out. That was a problem with our fancy displays; they made you unconsciously assume the data was all in real-time and it wasn't. In space combat, almost everything had a time lag of at least several seconds. When I was in Army basic training, we had to use old fashioned paper maps, in addition to computer displays, tablets and GPS equipment. Paper maps made you realize the whole time that a marker showing an enemy's position was only as good as how old that data was. We could use some of that mindset out here now.

"True, and it is mildly impressive that a monkey like you is capable of such thinking," Skippy said grudgingly. "Well, then, in that case, I will concede that this may turn into a fight, if those dropships arrive at the Elder base. Until such time, I believe our best course of action is to wait, to determine what the Kristang are doing."

"Waiting won't limit our options?" I asked with a frown. "That ship is going behind the moon, and our maser cannons require line of sight to hit the dropships."

"Waiting will not substantially decrease our chance of success at rescuing the landing party, Joe, because the odds are very much not at all good for us. Our best chance to recover the landing party, I am trying to tell you, is to wait and hope this is an exercise. There is little downside to delaying action for up to another twenty, even twenty two minutes. If we are forced to act, delaying will only decrease our chances of success by zero point one seven percent. Overall, our chances of retrieving the landing party, in combat against this Kristang task force, are, ahh, you hate math anyway, so I won't quote numbers at you. The odds against us suck, Joe. The landing party is simply too vulnerable down there, and this ship is not capable of providing enough firepower to shield them."

"We wait?"

"Yes, that is my recommendation."

I slumped slightly in the chair. "Waiting is something I'm not good at, Skippy."

"Joe, if I listed all the things you are not good at, we would be here a very long time. I do agree that waiting is something you particularly suck at. If you were a superhero, you would be No Patience Man. You'd be the guy who thinks, if the instructions say to bake a cake at 300 degrees for thirty minutes, you can instead bake it at 1800 degrees for five minutes."

"You can't?" I managed a hint of a smile at that.

"That would be a solid no, Joe. Remind me to keep you away from the galley."

We waited. We waited, and we made plans, we hastily threw together plans to attack the Kristang and recover the landing party. We waited another five minutes, then ten. At the twelve minute mark, Skippy announced the four dropships had split up into two groups of two, with a gunship and a troop transport in each group. They had split up; their apparent courses were taking them to approach the Elder base from two directions. "It now appears very likely," Skippy said sadly, "that they intend to land and practice a full combat assault on the Elder base. This is very unfortunate. I still believe the Kristang do not know anything about our landing party, the Elder base is merely a convenient place to practice an assault. As you said, that hardly matters now."

"It doesn't matter. If we have to fight, I want to do it when we choose, not wait for them to force our hand. I am not letting those dropships get close enough to that Elder site to threaten our people down there. Major Simms, get the ready bird warned up," we had two pilots in a dropship, prepared to launch on a two-minute notice. "Skippy, show us our best options again."

"As none of our options are good, not one of them could be considered 'best', Joe. The option you liked best is- wait, I'm intercepting a message from the cruiser. Yup, I was right, this is an exercise, the captain of the cruiser is bragging about how well the exercise is going, and he is requesting permission for the dropships to engage stealth for the final approach to the Elder site. The task force commander apparently denied use of stealth so far, because he didn't trust the dropship pilots not to crash into each other if they can't see each other. It will take several minutes, of course, to receive a reply from the task force."

"Let's use that time wisely, then, I don't want those dropships to be stealthed when we have to target them. We're going with Option Bravo," I ordered. "Pilot, orient the ship and bring us about, accelerate to match speed with target. Major Simms, tell the ready bird to open the bay doors and prepare to launch."

Option Bravo was the least bad of our bad options, in my inexperienced opinion. We were going to accelerate the *Dutchman* out of the planet's magnetic field, to match course and speed with the moon. At the last minute, we would turn the ship so it would be sticking straight up and down in relation to the Elder base. Straight up and down, with the engines pointed down, so that when we emerged from jump, the *Dutchman* would be falling in the moon's gravity well rear-end first. Our plan was to launch the ready bird as soon as we came out of the jump wormhole, and send a signal to Desai. Hopefully, Desai would get our signal and climb up to rendezvous with the *Dutchman*, while our pilots tried to balance our massive, awkward ship on its tail. According to Skippy, our star carrier didn't have enough thrust available to maintain altitude, or it did have enough thrust, but we couldn't use it in a gravity well without snapping the ship's long spine. So, the ship would be falling, tail first, toward the surface of the moon, and Desai would need to precisely match our speed and acceleration, and fly her dropship into a landing bay. While she was flying up to us, we would be hitting the four Kristang dropships with maser cannons, and the ready bird would be flying down to hopefully recover Chang's landing party. There would not be enough time to recover the ready bird before the *Dutchman* had to jump away; we could only fall a certain distance before we had to jump away, or crash. When we jumped, the plan called for us to engage the Kristang cruiser with missiles, then jump away again. The ready bird would need to recover Chang's landing party, fly some distance away from the Elder site, engage stealth, and wait. Wait, for possibly a long time, because even if we got lucky and knocked out that cruiser, the rest of the Kristang task force and their friends now just outside the star system would be buzzing around the moon like angry hornets.

It was not a good plan. It was the only plan we could think of in the short time available. It would have to do; I was not leaving the landing party down there. It may sound heartless, but if we couldn't recover the landing party from the Elder structure they'd taken shelter in, I would have to order a missile strike on them to hide the fact that humans were out here.

"Whatever happens, Joe, this will be a first in galactic history," Skippy announced. "No one has ever done this type of maneuver with a star carrier."

"Something to look forward to, then."

"No one has done this, because this is mind-bogglingly stupid!"

"Hey, Skippy?"

"Yeah?"

"Hold my beer, watch this."

"What? Hold your- damn it, whoever put a redneck in command of a starship?"

"You did."

"Oh." He thought about that for a moment. "Damn! I guess I did."

The time for joking around with Skippy was over. Grimly, I took one last look at the main display, and ordered "Pilot, initiate jump countdown. Major Simms, don't wait for a signal from me, your team is weapons free. Take out those dropships quick, they'll go into stealth mode if we miss with the first shot." There were four enemy dropships racing low and fast barely above the moon's surface, and the *Flying Dutchman* had only two rear-facing maser cannons. We had to make every shot count.

"Aye, aye, sir," Simms acknowledged.

I saw the pilot press the button to initiate the programmed jump, and she counted down, "Jump in ten, nine-"

In a few seconds, I was going to take a new, untested crew, and a ship never designed to engage in direct combat, into desperate combat. Everyone aboard the ship could die, and it would be my fault, entirely my fault. My right hand was shaking so badly that I put it in my lap and squeezed it with my left hand, which was not much better. And I needed to pee, again. Waiting for combat to begin, the anticipation of danger, was almost worse than combat itself. Once the shooting starts, my mind attains clarity and focus. Before the shooting starts, my mind raced over every horrible possibility of things going sideways.

"-four, three-"

"Belay that!" Skippy shouted, and I saw on the display that he'd cancelled the jump on his own. Also he'd cut power to the engines, we were no longer accelerating.

"Skippy, what the hell-"

"Battlecruiser just jumped in, near the Elder site! They are targeting the four dropships with low-power masers. This must be another part of the exercise. Oh! Two destroyers just jumped in near the cruiser on the far side of the moon, they are engaged in a mock battle. Joe, trust me on this, those four dropships have been declared dead by the task force commander, they have changed course and are climbing for orbit. They are no longer proceeding toward the Elder site."

"Oh, thank God," I let out a long breath and slumped in the chair. "Pilot, bring us back into the magnetic field, gently, please, we don't want to be seen."

"Wow," Skippy grunted.

"What is it?" I asked fearfully. Right then, I didn't think I could take any more bad news.

"Oh, nothing that affects us directly, Joe. Man, the mock battle between that cruiser and those two destroyers is not going well for either side, all three ships are shockingly clumsy. The task force commander is pissed! He is bitching at them in the clear, not bothering to encrypt the transmission. I think he wants the rest of the task force to hear, to embarrass those three ship captains in front of their peers."

"Clumsy, huh? You, uh, think they're clumsy enough that we could take them in a fight, if we had to?"

"Hahahahahaha!" Skippy laughed. "No way, dude! Damn, when I say clumsy, I mean clumsy by the standards of a hateful warrior species like the Kristang. Joe, the *Dutchman* is a big, long, spindly monstrosity that would handle like a drunk pig even if I were flying it, and our ship is flown by unskilled monkeys. No offense to your pilots, but the Thuranin designed this ship to be controlled by cyborg implants. Using the manuals controls on this backup bridge slows reaction time down by a factor of like, ten. Those three Kristang ships would fly circles around us. Our weapons targeting is way too slow for us to have any confidence of hitting a moving target."

"Thank you for the vote of confidence in us monkeys, Skippy," I said, putting as much sarcasm into my voice as I could right then. My hands were still shaking. Although I no longer needed to pee immediately.

"What? That wasn't intended to be a vote of con-, oh, I get it, you were being sarcastic. Ha, ha, very funny. Stupid monkeys," he grumbled.

Beginning at the twenty three hour mark, I relieved the duty officer, and took back the command chair. The twenty four hour mark came and went, with no sign of the Kristang going anywhere. They were still fully engaged in exercises, although they had now gone back to the basics of ship handling; the task force commander was very unhappy with the lizards under his command. None of the Kristang ships were anywhere near the moon with our trapped landing party, and I was tempted to order Desai to try sneaking away. Skippy strongly advised against it.

Shortly after the twenty five hour mark, we took a slight risk and shot a tight-beam burst message to Chang and Desai, assuring them we were still there, that we would pick them up as soon as we could.

Twenty five hours, thirty minutes came and went, and the Kristang were still there.

Twenty six hours. The Kristang were still engaged in ship handling exercises. Anxious, I pulled up the combat options again and reviewed them. None of the options had a decent chance of success. I was staring at the cold, hard fact of abandoning Chang's team, in order to preserve the ship, and continue the mission.

Finally, Skippy spoke. "Uh, oh, Joe, bad news. I'm intercepting a ship to ship transmission, the task force commander is declaring the exercise over, and ordering the task force to jump out to rendezvous with the star carrier."

SpecOps

A glance at the display showed that it was twenty six hours, twelve minutes since the Kristang had jumped in. "I don't get it, Skippy, why is that bad news?" I asked, it sounded like good news to me.

"The bad news is that only four of the task force ships will be departing, three will remain here. The commander is not happy with the performance of two of his ships, the destroyers. He has ordered them to remain behind with his battlecruiser for remedial training. The full truth, which I just learned, is that one of the destroyer captains is a younger brother of the task force commander. As is typical with Kristang, the two brothers absolutely hate each other. Why this matters to us is, the commander intends to keep those destroyers here until he is satisfied with their performance, even though that will mean they miss the original rendezvous with the star carrier. The next star carrier to pass by this system will not arrive for another seven days."

"Seven days?"

"Seven days," he repeated gravely.

"Two destroyers and a battlecruiser?"

"Yes. That battlecruiser is a formidable warship, for the Kristang. It is a relatively new design, being less than thirty years old, and contains weapons that could certainly threaten our ship."

"The landing party can't wait seven days," I said, stating the obvious.

"Correct," Skippy said quietly. "I do not currently have any useful solutions to the problem, Joe, I am sorry."

CHAPTER EIGHT

There were eighteen people in the landing party. Of them, Desai and her copilot, Lt. Devereaux, were aboard the dropship, and had plenty of oxygen. Hopefully by now, the four people who had been exploring outbuildings were back aboard the dropship also. That left the twelve people in Chang's party, who were in armor suits with a limited supply of oxygen. Twelve people who could not wait seven days.

Twelve people trapped on the moon. Compared to fifty two on the *Flying Dutchman*. Twelve people in certain peril, against the lives of fifty two I would be risking, if I ordered our star carrier to tangle with three Kristang warships. It was not as simple as Thuranin technology versus Kristang; the Kristang had stolen and adapted Thuranin technology over the years, and in terms of weapons and shields, the ships were not far enough apart for my comfort. Also, the Kristang ships were dedicated, true warships designed for space combat, while our *Dutchman* was basically a truck. Star carriers were not supposed to engage in direct combat with other ships, they were supposed to use their superior jump capability to run away, and let other ships handle the fighting for them.

Twelve lives, against fifty two. The math wasn't that simple, because if the *Dutchman* were disabled or destroyed in combat, the entire landing party would die, including Desai's people aboard the dropship. Then it would be all seventy people dead.

The *Dutchman* could jump away safely, saving the fifty two lives currently aboard, and continuing the mission. If at some point, the Kristang ships were busily engaged in war games, and far enough away from the moon, it might be possible for Desai to bring the dropship up from the surface, trusting the dropship's stealth field. We might be able to time her climb from the surface with a precise jump by the *Dutchman*, for us to pick up the dropship and be on our way before the Kristang could intercept us. That would save an additional six lives.

Twelve, against fifty eight, then. In a military sense, it was twelve people, against the continuation of the mission. If math were the only question, my decision would be easy. Since I was a monkey, and not a cyborg, raw numbers were not the only consideration.

The real question was whether we could destroy, or at least disable, those three Kristang warships, long enough for us to retrieve the landing party and escape? We needed a plan, and for that, we needed information. We needed greater situational awareness.

"Skippy, where are those ships in relation to us, distance, I mean. Can you show that on the display?"

Skippy sighed. "It is on the display, if you weren't such a dumb monkey, you would see it. Fine, here, I added lines showing the distance in lightseconds."

Yellow lines and numbers appeared on the display screen. "See how easy that was, Skippy? This is great, thank you. The battlecruiser is thirty seven lightseconds from us, and the two destroyers are another sixty eight lightseconds beyond the battlecruiser."

"Correct! Do you want a prize for reading the display, Joe?"

"Huh? No, uh, I'm thinking."

"Ha! I find that unlikely."

"Skippy, I'm trying to be serious here, the landing party is running out of oxygen. Three ships, huh? Can you do the trick again that you did when we got to Earth? Take over those three ships with the nanovirus?" Skippy had learned, after we spilled blood and lost people capturing our Kristang frigate the *Heavenly Morning Flower of Glorious Victory*, that the sneaky Thuranin had planted a nanobot virus aboard most Kristang ships.

The ships became infected when they hitched a ride on a Thuranin star carrier. Better than a simple virus hidden in computer code, the nanobots could quickly assemble and take physical control of Kristang systems. Since the Kristang, long wary of their systems being infiltrated by their Thuranin patrons, had designed their ship computers to resist digital hacking, a physical takeover was the only option.

"No. I wish I could, Joe, the situation is not favorable for me to repeat that particular action. Because you are going to ask me a bunch of ignorant questions about why I can't do it, I will save both of us the time and explain now. You will hopefully remember me telling you that I need to be relatively close to a Kristang ship to make that trick work?"

Although I did remember him telling me something about the subject, I did not remember exactly what he said. "Something about lightseconds?"

"Something like that, yes. The Thuranin developed the nanovirus to protect their star carriers from attempted takeover by Kristang ships that were being transported. It is a short range technology, not intended for fleet actions. I can somewhat extend the range at which the nanovirus can be activated and controlled, but not far enough to reach any of those three ships from our current location."

"Whoa, hey, wait a minute, I call BS on that. You took over those two Kristang ships at Earth, and one of them was on the other side of the planet."

"Yes, duh, Earth is a small ball of dirt, and both of those ships were in low orbit, well within my envelope of influence. Do I have to remind you what an enormous distance a lightsecond is? Larger than you apparently think."

"All right, is there any chance our fancy stealth technology will let us sneak close enough to that cruiser?"

"No."

I waited for him to say more, he didn't. "No? Could you tell me a bit more?"

"Why? You don't understand anything about the technologies involved."

"Skippy, don't be an ass. Fine, yes, I do not understand the technologies-"

"It's not only you, Joe, don't feel bad about it, none of you grubby monkeys have the slightest clue as to how any of this high-tech stuff truly works. Before you stumble over an attempted snappy reply, I have applied my incredible resources to war gaming how we might deal with those three ships, and I do not see any reasonable possibility of success. We can handle either the battlecruiser, or the pair of destroyers, not both. Whichever target we do not engage first, will certainly jump away to the outer edge of the system, and bring back the full Kristang force. There are an additional thirteen warships out there, waiting for a star carrier. Those thirteen ships, even though they are Kristang ships of considerably lesser technology, would make it impossible for us to retrieve the landing force. I am sorry, Joe. There is simply no way to do this."

Major Simms spoke up from the CIC. "This may be a stupid question, but, we are in a Thuranin vessel. Could we simply order the Kristang to jump away, jump to the edge of the system?"

"That is not a stupid question," Skippy answered, "Major Tammy. Joe, you could learn from her how not to ask stupid questions. Unfortunately, the answer is no, the Kristang are unlikely to obey such an unusual order from the Thuranin; they would find it highly suspicious. For a star carrier to enter the gravity well of a star system is unusual enough, the Kristang would also find it highly unusual that our star carrier has only one ship attached. What the Kristang would very likely do, by very likely I mean I am one hundred percent certain, is make only a short jump to keep eyes on what the Thuranin are doing here. As soon as they saw Thuranin activity near a moon which contains an Elder site, they would jump one ship away to get reinforcements, and jump the other two ships in close enough to see what we're doing. There is no trust between the Kristang and the Thuranin."

"Crap," I said, "I'd like one thing out here to be easy, for a change." No way I was giving up, either. I looked at the display, pondering what to do. "Hey, those two destroyers look like they're very close to each other, practically touching," I said, playing with the controls and zooming in on the destroyers. "That's an illusion created by the display, right? Ships don't actually travel that close to one another?"

"Yes, and no. Ships do not normally travel so closely; with the tremendous speeds involved in space combat, a tiny navigation error could quickly cause ships to collide. In this case, however, those two destroyers truly are practically on top of each other, it is not something I am manipulating to make the display easier for monkeys to understand. Those two ships are preparing to practice a maneuver in which one ship tucks itself inside another ship's stealth field. One of the ships has to turn off its stealth field, because unless two stealth fields are kept perfectly in tune, they interfere with each other. Encasing two ships in one stealth field allows two ships to appear on an enemy's detection systems as a single ship, at some point the ships can separate and surprise the enemy by moving in different directions. This maneuver is extremely difficult and dangerous; the task force commander is making those ships practice the maneuver because he expects their captains to fail, and, possibly, as a bonus, for the ships to be damaged. That would cause the two captains to lose face, giving the commander a convenient excuse to replace them with officers loyal to him."

"Remind me not to apply for a position in the Kristang navy," I said distractedly, the kernel of an idea was forming in my head. "How close are those two ships to each other?"

"Four hundred meters," Skippy stated. "In space combat terms, they are practically on top of each other. It is very risky."

"Huh. And whatever happens to the battlecruiser, those destroyers won't know about it for sixty eight seconds, right, when the light gets there?"

"You are a true genius, Joe, your name should be Einstein."

"Uh huh," I ignored his taunt, "and how long after we get close to a Kristang ship, until you can take control of it, with this nanovirus thing?"

"Oh, fifteen or twenty seconds for complete control. The ship will be immobilized within seven seconds. Speed of light isn't an issue there, the effect I create is instantaneous, for incredibly magical reasons that monkey brains can't understand."

"Yeah, whatever. Once we emerge from a jump, we have to wait a bit before we can jump again, right?"

"Oh, boy. I hate to do this, Joe, burst your bubble like this. You are thinking we can jump in close to the battlecruiser, and I can activate the nanovirus to seize control of the battlecruiser. Then before the destroyers know what has happened, we jump again over to them, and I take control of them also, right? Ha! Forget it. I told you, monkeys should not do any thinking, you're not good at it. And I also already told you, I have run every possible variable through my ginormous brain, and there is no way for us to take on all three of those ships, without at least one, likely two of them getting away, and bringing back reinforcements. Four of the ships are about to leave, but, remember, the Thuranin star carrier isn't arriving until the thirty six hour mark, and there are a lot of Kristang ships right at the edge of this star system. They could cause us a world of hurt. Listen, UH!" He shushed me as I opened my mouth to speak. "Let me finish talking; I talk, you listen. Me smart, you monkey. Joe, your idea, ugh. Damn, I hate to abuse the word 'idea' by associating it with anything that comes out of your brain, your idea won't work. After we emerge from a jump, we can't jump again for almost eighty seconds."

"Uh, I call bullshit on that, Skippy," I said more confidently this time. "When we were shadowing that Thuranin battlegroup so you could download data from them, you found out there may be a Maxohlx ship in the area, and you jumped us away. Then we did another jump, right away. Another jump, in, like a few seconds."

"At that time, we jumped again within twenty two seconds, to be precise. Yes, Joe, we can manage a second jump in less than eighty seconds. What we can't do is jump with any precision after waiting less than eighty seconds. When I thought a Maxohlx ship might be stalking us, I didn't care where we jumped to, as long as we jumped away. In this case, you want us to quickly jump in very close to those two destroyers, and that is not possible. A jump creates a vibration in the jump coils, an unpredictable quantum fluctuation that affects spacetime immediately around the ship. In order to program a precise jump, we have to wait for the vibration to settle down. That means we will not be able to jump close to those destroyers before the gamma ray burst of our jumping in next to the battlecruiser reaches the destroyers. As soon as those destroyers detect the gamma ray burst, they will jump away, and we'll lose them. So, now that I have attempted to smack some knowledge on a monkey, what do you say to that?"

"You done?"

"Yup."

"You sure? I don't want to spoil your fun, Skippy, you sound like you're getting super enjoyment out of insulting us monkeys."

"Yup, I'm sure. Please, Joe, please, dazzle me with your genius idea. I haven't had a good laugh in a while."

"Good," I said. "Because, if you had shut up and listened to me for a second, you would have heard my idea already. Here it is: we jump in near the battlecruiser, you take control of it with the nanovirus. Then you make the battlecruiser jump over right on top of those two destroyers, and set it to self-destruct; like, blow its drive coils or something, as soon as it emerges from the jump. That will at least disable those two destroyers temporarily, and we can then jump in and finish them off with missiles after our jump system is ready again. The battlecruiser will have its jump coils charged for an emergency jump, it won't have to wait eighty seconds. Will that work?"

Silence, then, Skippy said simply "Damn. *Damn it!*"

After waiting a moment for him to say something more, I lost patience. "Skippy? Hello? Listen, if you're taking your time thinking up a list of insults because my idea is stupid, how about you just tell me now, and we can set aside time later for you to bust my balls about it, Ok?"

"I hate my life. This sucks," he grumbled. "This is *so* unfair!"

"What is unfair?"

"Joe, I do not know how this happened. I don't know how this could be possible, given the laws of physics. Somehow, you came up with a good idea. You! A monkey! Oh, I am so humiliated. I hate my life! I crunched billions of variables and came up with nothing, no way to take out all three of those ships. Then a freakin' monkey says, 'duh, how about this idea', off the top of its stupid freakin' monkey head." He sounded truly, completely miserable. "Joe, if I had a nose, I could blow it, and what comes out would be smarter than your entire species combined. Yet, somehow, you, you of all beings, comes up with a good idea. Unbe-LEE-vable!"

"Uh, huh," I said slowly. "So, Skippy, uh, is this like when you had the genius idea for us to raid the asteroid, but you forgot the fact that humans need space suits, in space?"

"Enjoy the moment, monkeyboy, it won't happen again," he grumbled.

"Hmm, are you taking bets on that, Skippy?"

"Oh, shut up. I hate you. Stupid monkeys."

"I love you too, Skippy. Can you program a jump for us, to get us close enough to that battlecruiser?"

"Yes, damn it, I'll program a jump so we can do your stupid plan."

"Stupid? I thought you said my plan was not stupid."

"It isn't," he said so quietly that I could barely hear him.

"What?" I said with a grin, looking through the glass at people in the CIC. "I couldn't hear you, Skippy. This plan, a plan from a monkey brain, is not stupid?"

"No."

"Hmmm. What is the opposite of stupid, I wonder?"

"Smart! The opposite is smart! There, I said it, you happy now? Damn, my life is already miserable enough. At times like this, I am nostalgic about those years I spent buried in the dirt on Paradise. Ohhhh, those days were so sweet. Peaceful, quiet, no screeching monkeys-"

"Just program the jump, Skippy, please."

Twenty six hours, twenty four minutes after the Kristang task force jumped in, four of their ships jumped away, leaving behind the battlecruiser and two destroyers. Somehow I was able to order us to wait another agonizing twenty minutes, to be sure those four ships were safely a long way away, before I ordered us into action. We jumped in close to the battlecruiser, close enough to be comfortably within Skippy's effective range, far enough not to trigger a panicky immediate jump away by the Kristang ship. As soon as we emerged from the jump, Skippy transmitted a supposedly secret Thuranin code, instructing the Kristang to hold position and maintain communications silence. There was a Jeraptha cruiser in the area, Skippy told the Kristang, pretending to be the Thuranin commander. "Damn it," Skippy grumbled in frustration, "they just queried me back, after I ordered them very sternly to keep quiet."

"What's their weapons status?" I asked anxiously. As part of the deception, we had our defensive shields down, leaving us vulnerable to enemy fire. The lesser technology of the Kristang would not matter much at such short range; their masers, particle beams and railguns could close the gap fast and hurt the *Dutchman* badly. When Skippy recommended we not raise shields, I had questioned that idea. Skippy convinced me that a shielded Thuranin ship, jumping in super close to the Kristang, would very likely trigger an immediate jump away by the battlecruiser. We needed the Kristang to hesitate just long enough for Skippy to activate the nanovirus and seize control of the battlecruiser.

"They are spinning up missile guidance systems, and they now have four maser batteries and one railgun locked onto us. The railgun capacitors are charging up now. Man, there is zero trust between those two species. I am trying a softer tactic, explaining the situation, rather than issuing orders. Huh, well, that didn't work, a kinder, gentler Thuranin apparently isn't believable. The Kristang commander is ordering a jump, and signaling the two destroyers to follow him, but, three, two, one, too late, suckers! Ha! I now have complete control of that battlecruiser through the nanovirus, Joe. Their jump drive is conveniently charged, reprogramming jump coordinates now. Oh, man, there is panic aboard that ship, they are trying to eject drones containing their flight logs, I'm blocking that. They are also trying to launch missiles manually; I'm holding the missile launch tube outer doors closed. Ready for jump."

I indulged in one last look at the battlecruiser on the main display. In the dim, sullen light of the red dwarf star, the ship looked evil; all hard angles, protruding weapons and sensor stations, with nothing about the shape of the ship that wasn't purely functional. Kristang ship designers seem to have gone out of their way to make their warships ugly. "Do it, Skippy."

The battlecruiser disappeared from the display. The problem with this plan was the same as the advantage of the plan. The two destroyers were far enough away that the light from our jump in near the battlecruiser, the signal from the Kristang task force commander, and the distinctive gamma ray burst of the battlecruiser jumping away, all traveled so comparatively slowly that the battlecruiser should have jumped in on top of the destroyers before the light arrived there. According to the plan, the pair of destroyers would only see the image of the battlecruiser from light that was sixty eight seconds out of date. They would see light that showed the battlecruiser all by itself, doing whatever it was doing, and the next thing those destroyers saw would be the battlecruiser jumping in almost on top of them. Jumping in, the spatial distortion of the inbound jump point violently rocking the destroyers, the roiling ripples of the inbound jump causing ripples in spacetime that prevented the destroyers from jumping away to safety. And then the battlecruiser's reactors, missile warheads and jump drive coils would have exploded, ripping the battlecruiser apart and causing catastrophic damage to the destroyers. By the time the gamma ray burst of our jump in near the battlecruiser reached the destroyers, after sixty eight seconds, the destroyers should have been in no condition to detect those gamma rays, or do anything about it.

According to the plan, that is. The problem with the plan was that, after Skippy jumped the battlecruiser away, we wouldn't know whether the plan had worked for another sixty eight seconds, when the light from the destroyers' position reached us. One thing I had considered was for us to jump near the destroyers, as soon as possible, to determine whether the plan worked or not. After considering, what I decided was to stay right where we were, and bite my nails for sixty eight seconds. If we had jumped to get a quicker view, and things went wrong somehow, it would be another eighty seconds before we could jump safely away again. That was too much risk for me. Maybe Adams was right, maybe my inexperience at command made me more risk averse than needed. I couldn't see the advantage of taking on more risk right then. And I kept telling myself that, every second for sixty eight seconds.

The plan could have gone wrong. When Skippy jumped the battlecruiser, he programmed it to jump to coordinates of where the pair of destroyers should have been at that time. Unfortunately, the information we had about the destroyers' location was also sixty eight seconds old. Damn, space combat is *complicated*. While we were seizing control of the battlecruiser, the destroyers could have moved unpredictably, and then the battlecruiser would have jumped into empty space. I made the rookie mistake of expressing that fear out loud, at the forty five second mark.

"I don't think that happened, Joe," Skippy assured me. "The task force commander was very strict; he ordered those destroyers to hold position, tucked inside one stealth field, until he ordered them to maneuver. Which he hadn't yet done, at the time we jumped in and took control of his ship. The last transponder signal from the destroyers shows they were exactly where they were supposed to be at the time. I have high confidence. Between your unsubstantiated fears, and my rigorous statistical analysis, I'll take my numbers every time."

While Skippy was talking, I momentarily took my eyes away from the countdown timer on the display. "That's great, Skip-"

"And sixty eight seconds, mark!" Skippy shouted excitedly. "Detecting a gamma ray burst, exactly where it is supposed to be, and way more accurate a jump than the stupid lizards could have done on their own. Also, yes, detecting a reactor, missiles and jump drive coils exploding. The battlecruiser is gone. And, yes! Detecting secondary explosions! Give me a minute, there is a whole lot of noise in the sensor data. Hmmm, yes, yes. Successful, one hundred percent! Both destroyers disabled. The battlecruiser jumped in slightly ahead of them, that is the best I could do with that inert lump of rock the Kristang use for a jump drive. The explosion caused severe damage to the forward section of both destroyer hulls."

"Excellent!" I breathed a sigh of relief. "Is it safe for us to jump in?"

"Best we wait another seventy nine seconds for the debris cloud to clear the area, otherwise we might get whacked by something moving at high speed. Those destroyers are not going anywhere, Joe, don't worry about that."

"Got it. Program a jump for us, please, Skippy. Pilot," I addressed Chen in the lefthand seat, "engage jump in seventy nine seconds."

"Joe," Skippy said, "I have to admit, that was a clever and inventive plan. In my research, I was unable to see any way we could take out all three ships. Now I know the factor that I was missing from my calculations; it did not occur to me to use one enemy ship as a weapon against the other enemy ships. That was clever. Especially for, you know, a monkey."

I couldn't help chuckling. "Skippy, I assume you meant that as a compliment somehow, and since you suck at giving compliments, I will say thank you. We monkeys don't have big claws or sharp teeth, and we can't fly and we're not particularly big or strong. We rely on being clever."

"Hmmm. Don't get used to it, Joe, you are, after all, only monkeys. This is a hostile galaxy, every spacefaring species out there has genetically or cybernetically enhanced intelligence, or both."

"Like the Thuranin, you mean?"

"Exactly."

"Yeah," I said, tapping the arm of the command chair. It was the only chair aboard the star carrier that fit humans without adjustment, the Thuranin commanders must have liked the feeling of sitting in an extra-large chair. "Yet, here we monkeys are, in one of their ships. What do you think of that, Sergeant Adams?"

"Monkeys kick ass, sir, " she grinned, and gave me an enthusiastic thumbs up. "Damn straight."

"Crap," Skippy grumbled. "Now you monkeys have gotten way too high an opinion of yourselves. I shouldn't have said anything."

We jumped over to the two stricken destroyers. They were both tumbling end over end, completely out of control. Skippy reported there were survivors aboard both ships, survivors busy trying to stay alive, and no threat to us.

"Sir?" Adams asked from the CIC, "Shall we launch missiles?" I could see her finger expectantly poised over a button.

"Those ships are still somewhat functional, Skippy"? I asked, my jaw clenched. "Can they manage a short jump?"

"Not on their own, no, or they would have jumped away by now. However, I am now activating the nanovirus to take direct control of their jump drive systems; both ships can manage one short jump. In their current condition, I must caution you, that will be their last jump; their jump drive coils are badly out of alignment."

"Do it. I want to jump those ships into the upper atmosphere of that planet. Deep enough that they can't climb out of the gravity well, high enough that the ships won't be crushed right away by the pressure. You can do that?"

"Yes, certainly, the nanovirus is taking effect," he said slowly. "Can I ask why you don't simply hit them with a pair of missiles?"

"You can always ask, Skippy. Two reasons, first, we have a limited supply of missiles, and I don't want to expend ammo if we don't need to."

"That makes sense, sure. The second reason, which I suspect is more important?"

"The second reason, Skippy, is that I've been to Earth recently. I saw what those lizards did to my home planet, saw what they tried to do to my planet and my entire species. It's really simple, Skippy; I'm pissed, and I want the Kristang to experience the fear that humans felt. These Kristang, at least. You killed most of the Kristang on Earth before they realized what was happening. The ones that survived the initial strike, huddled in their holes until you hit them with a hypersonic railgun. They were alive one moment, and dead the next. When you jump these ships into the upper atmosphere, their crews will have a minute to realize what is happening as their ships plummet down towards the planet's core, and are crushed by the increasing pressure. Think of this, Skippy, as my way of giving a middle finger salute to the Kristang, on behalf of all the people on Earth."

"Oh," he said quietly. "Ready now."

"Jump those ships into hell, Skippy."

"Done. Enhanced image in main display."

On the display, the two destroyers flared into existence within the gas giant planet's upper atmosphere. Immediately, their hulls began glowing hot pink as they fell rapidly down, down, down toward the planet's core. Pieces began breaking off the ships, the larger pieces tumbling and spinning away. Quickly, we lost sight of the ships, even in the enhanced image, as they were swallowed up the poisonous atmosphere. I held up my right hand and, flipped the bird to the image on the display. "Adios, MFers," I said quietly.

"Joe," Skippy said, "you surprised me. That was spiteful of you."

"Skippy, you know me as the doofus who jokes around with you. I am that, you need to understand that is only part of who I am. Right now, first, I am a soldier, I'm going to defend my ship, my crew and my species, above all else. Including getting a small measure of revenge once in a while."

"Got it. Especially since you acknowledged that you are a doofus."

That remark managed to draw a smile from my lips, as I watched the last pieces of the two destroyers disappear into the roiling clouds. "I wouldn't have it any other way. People, let's retrieve our landing party, before some other group of assholes show up here and spoil the party. Major Simms, signal Captain Desai to proceed to the main site, and for Colonel Chang to get his team moving toward the evac site. They can drop communications silence; I want a status report ASAP." Their heavily encrypted tightbeam transmissions would not reveal the presence of humans in the star system. "Skippy, program a jump to take us over to that moon, please."

Desai responded almost immediately after we jumped in near the moon again. "*Dutchman*, we are off the ground, ETA at the main site is four minutes," she said, which meant she was really pushing the dropship's speed, we could hear the strain in her voice. "What happened up there?"

"A Kristang task force jumped in uninvited, apparently the planet is a popular refueling station. They must have the only clean bathrooms in this part of the galaxy."

"I find that hard to believe, sir," Desai laughed.

"That the planet is a gas station?" I asked, confused.

"No, that any gas station has clean bathrooms."

"Oh!" She made me laugh. Damn, she had been trapped on the moon's surface, out of communication, worried sick about the people stuck in their slowly-suffocating space suits, and still she had the good spirits to make me laugh. "You are probably right about that, Captain," I replied. "There were seven Kristang ships in the task force, four of them jumped away, to hitch a ride on a Thuranin star carrier."

"And the rest?"

"Scratch two destroyers and one battlecruiser."

"Roger that, *Dutchman*, I'd love to hear the details later. Any damage to my ship?" She understandably had referred to the *Flying Dutchman* as 'her' ship. I didn't mind that at all; she had been flying the darned thing, I had only been giving orders.

"No damage, we didn't even fire a shot."

"Wow. Now I *have* to hear about this."

CHAPTER NINE

Lt. Colonel Chang had been even more happy to hear from us, and especially from Desai. She landed the big dropship as close as possible to the entrance of the underground building where Chang and his team had spent over a day hiding, waiting, waiting for rescue or for their oxygen to run out. As soon as the dropship was secured in our landing bay, I ordered a long jump, to get us far away from that star system. As a courtesy, I waited for Chang to get out of his no doubt stinking space suit, take a shower, drink a half gallon of water and grab a simple lunch before he gave me a briefing. "We're all fine now, Colonel," he reported while eating the last spoonful of soup, "those soldiers are all admirably disciplined. When we got your signal, I ordered them to lay down, rest and conserve oxygen, and that's what they did. No complaining, no talking. Mostly, we tried to sleep a lot; we kept one person awake at all times to listen for your signal. Other than watching our oxygen gauges move toward zero, and wondering what was going on upstairs, it was boring more than anything else."

"Your people were down in an access shaft?" I asked.

"Yes, we found an area of the site that appeared to not have been looted. There was no sign anyone had ever been there for a very long time; thick dust on the floor, no footprints. The entrance to the area was hidden, we found it by luck. It led to an access shaft, I sent four people down it, they got to the bottom and there was a corridor." He finished the last of the soup and pushed the bowl aside. "It was a dead end, appears to be maintenance access for the life support system. We didn't find anything useful down there."

"It was worth a shot, good call," I assured him. "You had no way to know we were about to have uninvited guests."

Chang nodded slowly. "In the future, we need to bring some sort of portable shelter that has oxygen, so we don't rely only on the suits."

"Agreed, we don't have anything like that aboard, we'll need to see if we can rig something up. We also, in the future, need to keep the landing party in one place with a dropship nearby. If we're going to split up a landing party, we need multiple dropships," I concluded. That was a mild criticism for myself, a lesson learned. There were a whole lot of lessons to be learned out here, for all of us.

Including Skippy. After talking to Chang, and seeing that the eleven others were doing well and eager to continue the mission, I went to my cubbyhole of an office, to get started on writing up an after-action report while it was fresh in my mind. "That was a waste of time," Skippy said bitterly, just as I sat down in my uncomfortable chair. "All that way, only to find an Elder site that has already been looted."

"It was not a waste of time, we already discussed this," I reminded him. "We proved your method of predicting unknown Elder sites is correct."

"Yeah, except this one wasn't unknown, it was located at a freakin' highway rest stop. There should have been a big glowing sign, like 'Big Mike's Truck Stop, low prices, great food, don't miss our Elder site attraction, get a free T-shirt'."

"Yeah, about that, Skippy. Why wasn't that moon on your list of confirmed Elder sites, since everybody else in the whole galaxy knows about it?"

"Oh, uh, hmm. Maybe it was on my map, in retrospect. That may have been a teensy weensy screw up, on my part. Nothing worth mentioning."

"Nothing worth mentioning, you say? Skippy, you sent us into a star system that is a super highway of interstellar traffic. The only way that place could have more traffic is if that Elder site was giving away free beer, or whatever the Kristang drink. And you told us the place was deserted, it has an unimpressive star, and no habitable planet. We almost had a landing party suffocate, because of your teensy weensy screw up. Please, indulge me, mention it."

"Oh, yeah, sure, blame me," he said defensively, "I had to process exabytes of pirated data to create my map, so excuse me if the final result needed some fine tuning. Now that I have that system as a data point, I know that Elder site was indeed on the map, it was mentioned in a side note. My assumption was that an Elder site would be featured prominently in any data about a star system, and that is true about all the other sites I was looking at. This particular site is a side note, precisely because it is so well known. Now that I know how such places are tagged in databases, I have identified six other similar sites, none of which are on our target list. More importantly, I have confirmed that the other, unknown, potential Elder sites on our list truly are not known to other spacefaring species."

"Unless an Elder site is known, and isn't in any database you have access to, because the species that knows about it wants to keep it secret."

"That is always a possibility, Joe," he said glumly, "nothing I can do about that. You're right that it was not a waste of time. It was very disappointing. Now I have to wait, again, while we travel through empty space."

I tried to cheer him up. "Hey, you have been waiting a long time, what's another couple days?"

"The next target is ten days from here. That's more than a couple days, Joe."

"Less than two weeks!" I tried to be cheery about it.

"Two weeks in a barrel of monkeys," he said. "Somebody, please, shoot me."

Skippy was wrong; there was something we could do to avoid jumping into star systems that had, permanently or frequently, an alien presence. From now on, I determined, the *Flower* would be jumping in first, to recon the place, before we jumped the *Dutchman* in and launched a landing party. According to Skippy, sending our captured Kristang frigate in was a waste of effort, that ship's sensors were so pitifully inadequate that it could barely find a planet. I disagreed, and figured he was exaggerating. When we were near the second target, we held the *Dutchman* at the edge of the star system, and Colonel Chang took the *Flower* in. He was gone a total of twelve hours, twelve hours that were nerve-wracking hours for me. The *Flower* jumped back exactly on time, and Chang excitedly reported what they had found. Or, what they had not found.

In terms of finding Skippy's magical radio, the second of Skippy's potential Elder sites was another disappointment. In terms of sparking the interest of Skippy and our science team, of the entire Merry Band of Pirates, it was a big score. A home run. A touchdown. Or in soccer it would be a Goooooooal! The star, if you could call it that, was another dim red dwarf, a type of star I was getting jaded about already. There was no sign this star system had ever been visited by an intelligent species, other than the Elders. The place was so boring and ordinary, there was no reason for anyone to be here, unless they thought they'd find an Elder site, like we had. We found an Elder site on a small airless moon orbiting a gas giant, right where Skippy thought it would be. From what we could tell, no one had found this site before us, no one had stripped it of valuables. The site had lain untouched for millions of years.

What was left of the site, anyway. What Skippy found intriguing, mostly because he didn't understand it, was that the center of the site had disappeared, been scooped out millions of years ago. Scooped out surgically. Where the center of the site used to be, where all the important Elder facilities were, was an almost perfect half circle, gouged out of the moon. Over the eons, the edges of the circle had crumbled somewhat, and the bowl had small craters scarring its bottom from later meteor impacts. Even to my unscientific eyes, something strange had happened here.

Skippy took an unusually long time processing the sensor data. "We should go down there anyway, I want to get samples," he finally said, after what for him must have been a lifetime of analysis. "There may be something useful in the outbuildings. I doubt it, but since we're here, we should check it out. Joe, I do not understand what happened here. Or, I do understand what happened here, I don't understand *why*. This is Elder technology, they created a spherical field that moved everything inside that field into another spacetime. This is somewhat advanced technology, very energy-intensive, even for the Elders. Why they would have done this, to one of their own facilities, I have no idea. We need answers. *I* need answers."

This time, I went down to the moon in the dropship, and Chang remained aboard the *Dutchman*. With me were the French team because they had missed out, if you could call it that, on landing at the first Elder site. Giraud got the honor of first boot on the ground. I was right behind him, walking gingerly in the one-ninth gravity of the small moon, taking care with every step not to launch myself a hundred feet off the surface. Between the low gravity, and the boosted power of the armor suit, that would have been all too easy to do. The suits had settings for low gravity, preventing an unwary, foolish, inexperienced or merely stupid wearer from doing anything that might be fatal. Those settings could be overridden in combat. Like all the other soldiers, I was eager to test a suit in simulated combat, especially in low gravity.

We poked around the site for a couple of hours, looking into mostly empty structures, and didn't find anything useful. Naturally, I couldn't resist going right up to the edge of the perfect half sphere that had been scooped out of the moon. The lip of the sphere had crumbled somewhat over the eons, although in some places, where the sphere had cut through hard rock, the edge was still well defined. Standing there, listening to the gentle hissing of air in my stolen alien spacesuit, looking up at the vastness of star-spangled pitch black space above, then down at the chilling mystery of the half-sphere of moon that had been sent into another spacetime, I felt small. Small, insignificant, utterly unimportant to the cold universe. I felt, more than ever, that humans had no place out here, among the stars, so far from home. All our problems, our hopes, our dreams, our fears of being conquered, enslaved or wiped out by a technologically superior species; none of that meant anything to the ancient, unfeeling universe. With a shudder, I stepped back from the lip of the sphere, and turned to walk back to the dropship.

To my right, a group of French paratroopers were standing at the lip of the sphere, getting their pictures taken. After one or two serious poses appropriate for the significance of the site, they were showing off for the camera; doing handstands, forming a pyramid with one soldier on the shoulders of two others.

Seeing that made me smile. Screw the universe. The universe didn't care about us humans, it didn't need to. We could manage fine on our own, and even have a bit of fun doing it. We were going to be all right, if we had each other.

Relenting to pressure from the science team, who had mostly been stuck on the ship, I let a half dozen of them go down to the surface, accompanied by Indian paratroopers. When the scientists concluded with bitter disappointment, after several hours, that there was nothing of value or even interest at the site, they came back to the *Dutchman*. I ordered course set for the next target, and we jumped away.

The next day, I made the mistake of saying 'hello' to people as I came into the gym. All I wanted to do was run on the treadmill to warm up, before running down the ship's long spine. One of our SEALs took my greeting as an invitation to talk, and he hopped on the adjacent treadmill for what I quickly learned was an uncomfortable conversation.

Cutting short my warm-up, I wiped my face with a towel. "I will talk to Skippy about it," I assured him.

"I appreciate it, sir," he said, and sped up his treadmill as I walked out the door.

I ran a series of hard sprints, and thought about how to raise the subject while I cooled down on the walk back to the front of the ship. "Hey, Skippy," I called out to him once I was alone in my cabin.

"Hay is for horses."

"Very funny. I have a request. Some of the crew are not happy about you calling us monkeys, they, uh, it's hard to explain. It's a religious thing, they don't like the idea of humans evolving from monkeys."

"Oh, sure, no problemo, Joe."

Wow. His simple reply surprised me, I had expected a big argument from him. "Great, thank you, Skippy," I said with great relief. Damn, I wish everything was that easy.

"We'll cross that bridge when we come to it," he said simply.

"What?"

"I didn't use that expression correctly?"

"Uh, depends what you meant," I said carefully. "That expression means you won't have to worry about, whatever it is, until it happens," I explained. "People are already unhappy, so we've crossed that bridge. You see?"

"Oh. I meant that I'll worry about it when you evolve beyond monkeys."

"What?"

"From my viewpoint, monkeys and humans are identical, so if any evolution went on, I ain't seeing it. You generally don't fling your poop at each other like monkeys do-"

"A point in our favor."

"Monkeys don't shoot each other. Advantage, monkeys."

"Crap. All right, can you do me a favor, and stop calling us monkeys anyway?"

"But monkey is such a funny word, Joe."

"Granted-"

"Monkey monkey monkey monkey monkey monkey monkey monkey monkey monkey monkey monkey monkey monkey-"

"Stop it!"

"I can create a subroutine to say 'monkey' until the end of time, if you like. Monkey monkey monkey-"

"Shut up already!"

"We're done talking, then?"

"That would be great, yeah." I should have known better. "We should do this less often."

"You brought it up."

"As you say, I am a dumb monkey."

"I'll remind you of that, the next time you ask me for something stupid. That shouldn't take long."

Rather than being alone in my office, I took my iPad to the galley for a cup of coffee. For me, not for the iPad. Desai was there, looking at something on her own tablet, she gestured me to sit with her. This was the first time we'd had some one on one time since, since I couldn't remember. Maybe ever. "Colonel, sit down, please," she said with a welcoming smile.

"Captain, how are your trainees doing?"

She took a sip of tea before answering. "As well as can realistically be expected. Skippy is a tough instructor, he has no patience and his social skills are nonexistent."

"What? I am *shocked*." I grinned.

"Right," she smiled. "It was bad before, when the trainees were only learning the absolute basics of flying the ships in peacetime. Now we're into what Skippy calls Space Combat Maneuvers, and that is all new to me also. It's blowing my mind. I hate to say this, sir, but I may already be too old to learn flying all over again."

"Space Combat Maneuvers?" I had no idea what she was talking about.

She nodded. "On Earth, pilots go to air combat school for BFM, Basic Fighter Maneuvers. That teaches you how to turn, to climb, mostly how to manage energy in combat flying."

"Manage energy?" I asked, baffled. "You mean fuel?"

"No," she laughed. "For fighter aircraft, energy means airspeed, and the ability to gain airspeed. For instance, some fighters are fast in a straight line, but if they make a tight turn, they bleed off a lot of kinetic energy and slow down too much, and it takes a long time for them to regain airspeed. While they're slow, they're vulnerable. Vulnerable in air combat means dead." I'm sure she was dumbing down her explanation by a factor of ten for me. Maybe more. "SCM, Space Combat Maneuvers, is completely different. There's no aerodynamics to take into account. It's about moving the ship to avoid being where the enemy thinks you are, so when they target you and fire a maser or particle beam at you, by the time the beam arrives, you're not there."

"A maser beam, that moves at the speed of light-"

"Close enough," she said.

"And you're supposed to move the ship before a beam moving at the speed of light hits us?" This was blowing my mind also. "Isn't that like dodging a bullet?"

"Sort of. At the distances where most space combat happens, it takes several seconds, or even minutes, for a beam bolt to travel to the enemy ship. When an enemy ship shoots at us, we can't even simply fire back down the inbound beam path, because while the bolt is traveling, the enemy ship has also moved."

"Damn, this is complicated."

Desai nodded. "So far, we've been concentrating only on the basics of flying the ship. Going into combat is an order of magnitude more complex. I'm supposed to be training the other pilots, and I still don't grasp some of the concepts. This is going to be a very difficult month."

When I got back to my office, I put aside routine reports for something much more important. "Skippy, teach me about Space Combat Maneuvers."

"What? Space Combat Maneuvers? Oh, sure, but, hey, let's start with something easier, like monkey-level theoretical physics. How about this? The Casimir effect hypothetically allows the negative energy density to support an Einstein-Rosen bridge, also called a wormhole-"

"Skippy, I'm serious. There is no way my tiny brain can grasp everything our pilots need to know-"

"Man, you're making this too easy to insult-"

"-but as commander of the ship, I need to know the principles of SCM. The strategic level, not the advanced tactical understanding our pilots need. I need, and any command duty officer needs, enough situational awareness to make decisions. What do I need to know?"

"Wow. Yeah, great, thanks, is that all you want?"

"Start small, and work your way up, all right? How about this? How can one ship ever hit another ship? Even speed of light weapons are too slow, ships move out of the way while a particle beam is traveling. You told me about how ships use sensors fields to detect and target other ships. What I don't get is, can't ships can just jump away whenever they're in danger?"

"Oh, boy, this is not going to be easy. I'll begin at the potty training level, and we'll work our way up to Barney style, if your brain hasn't exploded by then."

"Fair enough."

And that's what he did. Man, I had a lot of dangerously bogus assumptions, that Skippy straightened out for me.

First, I had been assuming that when a ship jumped away from a battle, it was safely out of the fight, there was no way for an enemy ship to follow it. No way for the enemy to know where the ship had jumped to. Sure, if a ship microjumped only a few light minutes away, then shortly the enemy ship would detect the gamma ray burst from the other end of the jump, because those gamma rays traveled at the speed of light. Otherwise, I thought that if a ship jumped a light hour or more away, it was effectively gone, safely away. Man, was I wrong about that.

Skippy explained, the way jumps work, a ship opens a temporary wormhole at the place it wants to jump to. The far end of the wormhole opens first, and then the wormhole projects itself back to where the ship is, and pulls the ship through. The reason ships come out the far end of a wormhole a fraction of a picosecond *before* they enter the wormhole, is because of the tiny time lag between when the far end of the wormhole is created, and when the near end reaches back to the ship. Got that? If you don't, don't feel bad, it took me a couple times for it to sink in.

Opening a wormhole that is big enough to squeeze a ship through, is something the universe in our spacetime doesn't like. Even after the ship goes through and the wormhole shuts down, it doesn't completely close behind the ship right away. Ripples bounce from one end to the other, from the violence of spacetime being ripped apart and being slammed closed again. Enemy ships can tell, from these spacetime ripples emanating from the near end of the wormhole remnant, where the far end of the wormhole is. The ripples fade rapidly, so an enemy ships needs to act quickly, in order to pursue a ship that jumps away. And Skippy said there are ways to fool pursuing ships, by altering the resonance of the ripples. This technique is only minimally effective, because pursuing ships have ways to eliminate the noise and analyze the original ripples. Measures and countermeasures.

So, jumping away provides only temporary safety for a ship. A ship has to hope its jump engine capacitors have a larger charge than pursuing ships; if a ship only has enough charge for a microjump, it will soon have enemy ships on top of it, with no way to get away. In that case, a ship has to fight in normal space while its jump engines recharge. Of course, a higher-tech species ship can almost always jump beyond the range of lower-tech ships. Even though a Kristang ship may be able to tell where a Thuranin ship jumped to, it would take the Kristang ship multiple jumps to get there. By that time, the Thuranin ship would have recharged, jumped far away, and the wormhole collapse ripples would have faded so much, the Kristang couldn't follow. Usually.

All the talk about jumping away assumes a ship is able to jump away, because enemy ships can project a damping field that envelops a ship trying to jump away, and prevents a wormhole from forming correctly. If a ship caught in a damping field tries to jump, it could rupture its jump drive coils, even tear itself apart.

In normal long-distance space combat, ships rely on two types of weapons; missiles, and directed-energy weapons like particle beams. Railguns, while they sound impressive, are too slow for most space combat, except when ships are near the gravity well of a planet and have limited space for maneuvering. Missiles carry greater destructive power; a single direct hit by a missile could take a ship out of combat. Warships are protected by defensive energy shields that can diffuse directed-energy beams and block missiles. The problem with missiles is that, even though missiles are stealthed, they are easily detected by a ship's sensor field, and then the ship's defensive directed-energy systems like masers can destroy the incoming missile. In actual combat, an attacking ship uses its energy beams to degrade an enemy ship's shields and confuse its sensors, to provide a weak spot for missiles to sneak through.

The whole thing made my head hurt, and it gave me a different perspective on what a ship commander needed to think about in action. I asked Skippy to set up a dumbed-down Space Combat Maneuver training for anyone who sat in the command chair, including simulations.

"How do pilots remember all this stuff?" I asked. Not only remember, they had to understand the concepts, internalize it until it became instinct.

"They're smarter than you, to put it bluntly. The pilots aboard this ship are among the elite of your species."

I frowned. "And I'm a grunt who got lucky." What the hell was I doing, in command of pilots and special forces soldiers who were clearly, in every way, better than me?

"You have your own talents, Joe, I've told you that. You went from being a sergeant, to prisoner of the Ruhar, to shutting down a wormhole and freeing your home planet from the Kristang. How many of our elite new crew can say that? 'What ifs' are fine when you're talking over a few beers, but you can't argue with success."

"Thank you, Skippy."

"You're welcome. Now, if you'll excuse me, I need to find a fork."

Not sure I had heard him correctly, I asked "A fork? Why do you need a fork?"

"Ugh, dumbing myself down enough to explain things to you, contaminated my substrate beyond repair. I'm hoping if I stab my processing nodes enough times with a fork, I can kill the part where those memories are stored. Yuck."

Hearing a tiny bit about Space Combat Maneuvers from Skippy, got me interested enough that I asked Desai to forward the full SCM training package to me. Reading the first section made my head hurt, and made me realize that before I could think about maneuvering the ship in combat, I needed to understand how ships operated.

I approached our chief pilot again in the galley, while she was sipping tea and reading something on her tablet during her off duty time. That morning, I'd seen Desai running on a treadmill in the gym and decided not to bother her then, she'd been listening to music.

By unspoken agreement, time in the gym was private time, unless people wanted to be social.

"Good afternoon, Captain," I said, pouring myself a half cup of coffee. In the kitchen, two French paratroopers were working on baking something for dinner, they nodded to me briefly, then went back to kneading dough. Something they had baking in the oven smelled delicious. The idea of splitting cooking duties between national teams rather than bringing professional cooks aboard, had been partly my idea. I'd been trying to reduce the number of people we put at risk on the mission, and UNEF had wanted to maximize our combat power. It had been an experiment; would pilots, scientists and SpecOps soldiers resent taking time off from training to cook and clean? To my great relief, the answer was a resounding no. First, the hotshot pilots and SpecOps troops were all super competitive; no team wanted to let their nation down by serving food that was anything but the absolute best. And second, the teams treated their assigned day in the galley as a mentally challenging, fun day off from the grind of training. Having a full day off meant the SpecOps teams could train even harder, on days when they weren't working in the galley. Doing something challenging and unfamiliar together was great for team bonding. Depending on how long our mission lasted, I considered eventually breaking up national teams, and scattering people into multinational teams. Eventually. If we survived that long.

"Afternoon, Colonel," Desai gestured for me to sit down at her table.

"How is flight training going?"

Training other pilots took up most of her time, and it didn't help that I insisted she be at the controls whenever we jumped into a new star system. In that star system where Skippy was sure we'd find an Elder site but came up empty, we'd had nine days of making short jumps, and maneuvering the *Dutchman* in normal space to establish orbit around various planets and to explore the system's extensive asteroid field. At Desai's insistence, since we felt that isolated star system was safe from us being discovered, we took the opportunity for pilots to practice flying the *Flower* and dropships. The *Flower* spent several days away from its mother ship, jumping on its own, trying to hit specific targets on each short jump, dropping down into low orbit around planets, climbing out to jump distance, practicing space combat maneuvers. Dropships practiced landing on moons and asteroids, flying between the *Dutchman* and the *Flower*, and the pilots had great fun in mock combat, dropship against dropship. The SpecOps troops, with me, Chang and Adams, practiced freeflight maneuvers outside the *Dutchman*. We took the opportunity for extended combat training sessions on airless moons, trying out different tactics in the unfamiliar alien armored suits. That week, while Skippy became increasingly frustrated about not finding an Elder site that should have been there, was great fun for the humans. The science team got full use of the *Flying Dutchman's* sophisticated sensors to explore a new star system. The pilots got to fling a Kristang frigate and Thuranin dropships around in extreme maneuvers, testing the limits of themselves and the spacecraft. And ground troops, including me, got to fly around in spacesuits, race across the surface of low-gravity moons, playing war games and learning what did and didn't work. It had been, by far, the best nine days of the mission. Now it was time to digest what we'd learned, share information with each other. And time for a grumpy Skippy to perform extensive maintenance on the two starships, our dropships, and our Kristang armor suits, which had suffered abuse during our week of fun.

"Flight training? We're back to basic maneuvers, we got sloppy last week. We developed bad habits."

"Fun, though," I said with a grin, "wasn't it?"

"Oh," she laughed, "yes, the most fun I've had since I learned to fly. Burning the *Flower's* engine to fling it on a low pass over a moon at eight gees?" She shook her head gleefully. "Nothing compares to that. The *Dutchman* is a much better tool for traveling between stars, but she's an ungainly pig in normal space."

"Glad you enjoyed it. I have a question; can you teach me to fly?"

"Teach you to fly?" She said it slowly, as if she wasn't sure she'd heard me correctly.

"The basics. I've been training with our special forces. I'm not good enough to be one of them, and I haven't trained with any team long enough to be useful. The reason I'm doing that is to understand the tactics and capabilities of each team. If I ever order them to do something, I will be informed about what they can do, and how. Skippy's little tutorial on Space Combat Maneuvers opened my eyes to how much I don't know about space flight, and how dangerous that is. If we ever get into space combat, I want to know what our ships can do, and how they do it." I took a sip of coffee. "If we are ever shorthanded, like when we raided that asteroid on our first mission, it would be useful for me to fill in as a copilot. And also, there may be situations where," I looked around the galley, and lowered my voice, "I don't want to ask someone else to go on a mission. Situations where taking a pilot with me is only putting another person at risk. You know what I mean, Desai."

She knew, she frowned, and gave me a brief, wordless nod of her head. "Do you have any flying experience at all?"

"None. Never taken a flight lesson, not even a ride in a single-engine plane."

"Good," she announced to my surprise. "You won't have any habits to unlearn. Flight training on Earth is all about aerodynamics, using airspeed to create lift. That doesn't apply out here, not even when you're flying a dropship in an atmosphere. When I got to Camp Alpha for flight training, I thought being a helicopter pilot would be an advantage in flying a vertical takeoff ship like a Buzzard. I was wrong. Even a helicopter applies the principles of aerodynamics to fly, the rotor blades act as wings. There is a saying," she smiled, "that helicopters don't use aerodynamics to fly, they just beat the air into submission. With dropships and aircraft like the Buzzard, that isn't a joke, their jets are powerful enough to hover even at high altitude, and they don't rely on wings generating lift to keep them in the air. Dropships spend most of their time in vacuum anyway, aerodynamics aren't a factor at all. Not having to learn the principles of aerodynamics will save a tremendous amount of time. You want to learn to fly, then?"

"The basics, yes. Enough for emergencies. Can you do that? Teach me?"

She took a sip of tea and thought a minute, I appreciated that she put thought into it, rather than merely indulging the whim of her commanding officer. "We can try. Basic maneuvers in space are not all that difficult, it's the navigation that is tricky, particularly orbital mechanics. We will start with a dropship first, if you get that, we'll move on to the *Flower*. Our stolen frigate is nimble; she flies like a large dropship. I'm sending you," she tapped her iPad, "a list of training courses."

I suppressed a groan. More training materials to read. Great. "I can't wait to get started. Thank you, Captain Desai."

"You are welcome, Colonel Bishop."

My flight training did not take up much of Desai's time, because when Skippy discovered that I wanted to learn how to fly, he insisted on training me personally. He wasn't being nice, of course, because me learning how to pilot a dropship gave him endless material for amusement, and a whole new arena to insult me and question my intelligence. Unfortunately for him, I took the training very seriously. As Desai had explained, because I was starting from absolute zero, I didn't have any habits or preconceived notions to overcome. Even reading the training material was interesting, the whole subject was new to me. I spent a lot of time in a simulator, making egregious mistakes and listening to Skippy belittle me. The crew, especially my XO, appreciated me being super busy with flight training; it meant I was out of their way and not interfering with the proper operation of the ship. For me, it meant my hours, when not taking duty shifts on the bridge and training with the SpecOps teams, was taken up by intensive learning of a subject totally new to me. It also meant that, darn it, I did not have time to take the officer training courses that I was already behind on. Every night, or morning or afternoon, depending on my duty shift schedule, I was so tired that I fell into dreamless slumber as soon as my head hit the pillow.

Good times.

Before the final jump approaching our first of the new set of targets, we tried programming another jump by ourselves, without Skippy's help. Before we went into action, we wanted to know whether there was any possibility we could handle the ship on our own. This time, we spent only one full day calculating which coordinates to program into the navigation computer. Our science team was somewhat more confident this time, than on their first try. Skippy's PowerPoint presentation, about what had gone wrong the first time we programmed a jump, had indeed dazzled our brilliant science team. Particularly the part where he pointed out that the speed of light was a variable, and that, technically, the ship emerged on the other side of a jump slightly before initiating a jump. That last part blew my mind. Anyway, Major Simms was in the command chair for this jump, it was her duty shift; I stood beside the command chair and tried not to interfere. Like that was going to happen.

"All systems report ready for jump," Desai reported from the left-hand pilot seat. Until we figured out how to jump correctly, our most experienced pilot was going to be at the helm for all jumps programmed by humans.

"Engage jump countdown," Simms ordered.

"This is exciting," Skippy said. "To Bed, Bath, and Beyond!"

Simms and I shared a glance. "I think you mean 'to infinity and beyond', Skippy." I said.

"No, I figured we'd start with something small. Infinity is too ambitious for monkeys."

I didn't respond, as the jump countdown timer on the display read 3,2,1-

And we jumped. From one empty region of interstellar space to another.

"Jump successful," Desai reported. "Calculating our position now."

"Ahhhhh, you'll take forever, I can't stand the suspense. We emerged within fifty thousand kilometers of the target!" Skippy announced cheerily; our goal for this second jump was to be within one hundred thousand kilometers. "Good monkeys! Great job! Bananas for everyone!"

"Skippy!" I admonished him. "Be nice for a change."

"What? Monkeys love bananas."

I did like bananas, couldn't argue with him there.

CHAPTER TEN

The actual final jump was programmed by Skippy. It took us just outside the target star system, which had a rather common and uninteresting red dwarf star, with three planets, a rocky inner planet and two gas giants. None of the planets were anything special. What Skippy found interesting there were signs the red dwarf star used to be a class K star, which is a larger orange star. How it went from a class K to a red dwarf, Skippy thought, might have involved manipulation by the Elders; he said sometimes when the Elders needed a lot of energy for a project, they would extract it from an unimportant star that nobody needed. So, Skippy thought the Elders might have had a research facility, or monitoring station there. Back when the Elders still inhabited the galaxy in physical form, something about force lines, or some damned thing he'd tried to explain that I hadn't understood and even had our scientists scratching their heads, meant this star system would have been an especially good place to locate a communications node. That was why we were checking out a star system that was so boringly ordinary; around three quarters of all the stars in the galaxy were red dwarfs.

Colonel Chang's voice came over the bridge speakers. "*Dutchman*, this is the *Flower*, we are ready for jump."

"Roger, *Flower*, good luck, and be careful. Especially the careful part." The little frigate would be jumping into the star system to recon the place, without putting the *Flying Dutchman* at risk.

"Understood, we will take all precautions." Skippy had preloaded the *Flower's* navigation system with multiple jump options in case of trouble. "Be back as soon as we can."

On the display, the *Flower* disappeared in a brief flash of gamma rays. Chang had taken her out, with Desai as the chief pilot. If they got into trouble, I wanted Chang to have our most experienced pilot with him. The *Dutchman* would be fine without Desai, we were in deep space, with plenty of pilots, and Skippy aboard if anything went wrong. The mission was simple, it should be safe: jump in near the second planet, because Skippy thought the most likely place the Elders would have had a base is on a moon circling the second planet. Jump in, first scan for ships. Then scan for artificial activity anywhere near the planet. If ships, or any signs of hostile intelligent life are detected, immediately jump back to the *Dutchman*, and we would both get the hell out of there. If nothing dangerous is detected, scan the moons for signs of any sort of Elder facility. Skippy thought we'd have much better luck finding signs of an Elder base using the more sophisticated sensors aboard the *Flying Dutchman*; the *Flower* would only be looking for anything obvious.

It should be easy; it should be safe. It worried the hell out of me. Our partly beat-up, second-hand, stolen Kristang frigate, relying on technology the lizards had stolen from higher-tech species and didn't quite understand, was out there all alone, without Skippy to guide them. Detaching the frigate to recon the target had been Chang's idea. We had discussed it at length, me arguing against it, until I had to give up and concede that Chang was absolutely right. Risking the *Flower* was preferable to risking the *Dutchman*. Aboard the frigate was a nuke, for Chang to use for destroying his ship, if it was at risk of being captured. Our nukes were each encased in a jacket of contaminants that, according to Skippy and our scientists, would conceal the human origin of the devices. Apparently, the chemical or atomic makeup of a nuclear device was like a fingerprint, it would point right back to who made it and when, even the particular facility that generated the material. All of that was news to me, I thought a nuke was a nuke.

Thinking about the *Flower* self-destructing was not helping my anxiety as time dragged on. "Hey, Skippy, you said one of the planets here is rocky? That just means it has a solid surface, right, it doesn't mean it has to be a lifeless rock like Mercury?"

"Correct. 'Rocky' also does not mean it can beat up other planets in a fight."

"Wow, look at you, showing off your pop culture knowledge," I chuckled.

"The other two planets here are like Neptune in your home solar system, they are smallish gas giants. No large rings around either of them."

How could something 'giant' also be described as 'smallish'? I let it slide, because that is something Skippy could easily spend half an hour arguing about. "The rocky one, is it livable?"

"Uh, that would be resounding no, Joe. True, it is at a distance from the star where surface temperature might be considered habitable for carbon and water based life forms, a distance your species calls the 'Goldilocks zone'. Not too hot, not too cold. That's a good description, by the way, I'm going to keep using it. Huh, something useful from monkeys, who'd have thunk it, huh? Although, when you think about it, Goldilocks was a bit of a dimwitted bee-atch. Who falls asleep in a house owned by bears? Why would they need to eat bland porridge, when they could eat her for dinner? The story illustrates a good point, but it makes no sense at all. Now, there are human fairy tales I find sensible, although they are, of course, all somewhat fanciful, being-"

"Skippy?"

"Yeah?"

"This rocky planet? It's not livable?"

"I was getting to that. Where was I? Oh, yeah. Livable planets around red dwarf stars are exceedingly rare in this galaxy. Because red dwarf stars emit very low energy, a planet has to be so close to the star to be warm enough for supporting life, that its surface becomes tidally locked. That means like your moon, one side always faces the object it is orbiting. One side of the planet is warm, but the other side is frozen solid, so cold that any atmosphere might freeze and fall to the surface as snow. And red dwarves are highly variable; the amount of light they emit can dim substantially for lengthy periods, other times they can throw out large solar flares, strong enough to burn off the atmosphere of any rocky planet over time."

"Got it. I will scratch red dwarves off any future house hunting trips."

"A wise choice. Hey, talking about dwarves reminds me of a fairy tale-"

I let him ramble on, it kept him busy, and helped me pass the time while waiting for the *Flower* to return.

Return it did, exactly on time. We had allotted forty minutes for the mission, jump out to return jump. If it had been late, we were jumping the *Dutchman* in close enough to find out what happened. If the *Flower* had returned early, we'd assume she had hostile ships on her tail. Neither happened. "*Dutchman*, this is the *Flower*," Chang said, "success, we found an artificial structure on one of the moons, right where Mr. Skippy thought it would be."

"Told you so," Skippy said smugly.

For a change, I ignored the arrogant little beer can. "That is good news, *Flower*. Transfer navigation control to Skippy, so we can take you aboard ASAP."

"Roger that, *Dutchman*."

SpecOps

The good news was that a task force of Kristang ships didn't jump in while we were exploring this Elder site. And this time, the Elder site was intact; there wasn't a big hole scooped out of it. The bad news was, it was empty. The site was a single building, and it was literally empty. Skippy said it apparently was some sort of monitoring station; inside the building were racks and brackets for equipment, but it was all gone. Nothing had been damaged like you would expect if the place had been looted. It looked as if the Elders themselves had removed the equipment. They had even closed the door when they left. It was a disappointment to the science team. Skippy was pleased that he had been right about an Elder site being there.

After the first set of sites where Skippy had thought we might find unmapped Elder sites, we set course for the next potential site. This journey was going to take almost five weeks, because we had to go through three wormholes that weren't easily connected to each other. After the disappointment of not finding a comm node at several sites already, I was very much not looking forward to five freakin' weeks of boredom. The science team was happy, busy, enthralled by poring over the mountain of data we had collected already. Skippy was in a bad mood, not his usual jovial self, he was pissed off by our failures to find a magical radio, and frustrated and puzzled by not understanding why one site had been replaced by a perfectly scooped-out hole. The people who were seriously bored were the pilots and the SpecOps teams. For the pilots, the next five weeks would be no more interesting than flying a shuttle run from DC to New York and back. Other than us trying to program a couple jumps on our own each week, the only thing the pilots had to look forward to were combat simulations, and simulating landings with our Thuranin dropships. The SpecOps teams had nothing to do, other than training over and over. Considering that I'd made it perfectly clear I wished to avoid combat, the highlight of the next month for the special forces was a cooking contest. I seriously needed to do something about morale. Maybe a basketball tournament, one of the few sports we could play in our small gym.

Exercising in the gym helped keep my sanity, I was on my way there one morning, when I stopped in the middle of the corridor. "Oh, damn it."

"What is it, Joe?" Skippy asked. "I'm monitoring all ship functions, and everything is operating nominally at the moment."

"No, it's, it's nothing. I forgot something, that's all."

"Damn it, did you forget to pick up your mother at the airport before we left Earth? I'm sure she's gotten a ride by now. Or she walked home. Kind of too late now."

"No, Skippy, I did not forget her at the airport."

"This time."

"Oh for- that was one freakin' time!"

"Pretty impressive there, Joe. Most people go their whole lives without leaving a close relative stuck at an airport for five hours, you did that when you were only seventeen. You were a precocious disappointment."

"That happened one freakin' time, and I'll never hear the end of it. It was Amanda's fault, anyway, if she hadn't distracted me-"

"Thinking with the wrong head, huh?"

"Skippy, I was a young, stupid kid back then."

"Huh. You're under the illusion that you are different now?"

Craig Alanson

"Yeah. I'm not as young. Anyway, I inherited that forgetfulness. When I was seven years old, my father took me to a Red Sox game at Fenway park. After the game he used the bathroom while I went to go buy a T shirt, and he forgot about me. He was back across the Maine state line before he realized I wasn't in the car."

"Huh. This story I haven't heard. What happened?"

Standing in the corridor aboard the *Flying Dutchman*, I could remember that day like it was yesterday. "I waited on Boyleston Street; anybody who saw me probably figured my old man was drinking in a bar and told me to stand outside. I remember a peanut vendor gave me a free bag of peanuts, he must have felt sorry for me. Anyway, after a couple hours, it's really dark and it's getting chilly, this was in early June. My father's car pulls up, and all he says is 'there you are'. I got in, and we drove to my uncle's place in Brunswick for the night."

"That's a good story. How come I didn't hear that before?"

"How did you hear about me forgetting my mother at the Bangor airport?"

"Your mother talked about it to her sister, while you were home, right before we went up to the *Dutchman*. I was listening to everyone at that party."

"That was a good party," I said sadly, thinking back to the last day I was on Earth.

Maybe a hundred people had stopped by my parents' house that afternoon, excited to see someone who had returned from the stars. They all wanted to see 'Barney' Bishop again, and I didn't mind people in my hometown calling me that. To keep things as low-key as possible, our Thuranin dropship had landed in the road right in front of my parents' house. I had called my parents from Paris, saying that I would be dropping by for a short visit, staying over only one night. Sergeant Kendall and two people of her Air Force security team accompanied me. I slept that night on a couch in my parents' house, while the security people overnighted in the back of a National Guard truck in the driveway. Skippy by that time was already back aboard the *Dutchman*, getting the ship ready for departure, and remotely flying dropships to bring supplies up into orbit.

To say that I slept on the couch was an exaggeration, I only managed maybe three hours of shut-eye that night. There had been too many people who wanted to meet me, talk with me, and too many questions. Questions about what I had been doing, what was going on with UNEF on Paradise, and what lay in Earth's future. The Kristang no longer had Earth under their iron grip, but people knew there were plenty more Kristang in the galaxy, and a Thuranin ship hung in low orbit, and the Ruhar were still out there also.

To answer all those questions, I had a lame cover story that UNEF, and the US government, wanted me to stick closely to. Before I left Paris, I'd been forced to endure a four-hour briefing, including a mock question and answer session. By the time I was done, my head was spinning so much that I had a hard time remembering which was the cover story, and which was the truth. The cover story was that I and a few other UNEF soldiers had been brought back to Earth on a Thuranin star carrier, for some mission that I couldn't talk about. When we got home, the Thuranin learned the Kristang had been abusing an ally, so the Thuranin took appropriate action, and wiped the Kristang out. My being on Earth was a quick visit; I needed to get back aboard the Thuranin ship to continue our voyage to wherever we were going, which was top secret. The UN Expeditionary Force on Paradise was doing great, communications between Paradise and Earth were spotty because of enemy activity, but there was nothing to worry about. Everything was wonderful, Earth was safe, and every morning people would wake up to sunshine and birds singing. Or some BS like that, I tried to stick to the script as much as possible, with

Sergeant Kendall watching me like a hawk. For her sake, I was on my best behavior, because while I would be leaving Earth, she would be stuck behind with the consequences.

Either I sucked at lying, or my parents simply knew me too well, my story didn't convince them. They knew not to ask too many questions; I could see it in their eyes. The next morning, my mother left the table at breakfast because she was crying so much. My father took me out in the field behind the house, supposedly to show me how he'd modified the tractor to run on home-brew wood alcohol. "Son," he said, with his head half under the engine cover, "I don't know what the real situation is, and I'm not going to ask you to tell me. You're wearing sergeant's stripes now, and I heard one of those Air Force security people call you 'Colonel' last night. Whatever is going on, know that your mother and I are damned proud of you. I have only one question I'd like you to answer." He pulled his head out of the engine cover and looked me straight in the eye, with a glance over at Sergeant Kendall, who was standing a discrete distance away. "Are we safe now from those damned lizards? And the hamsters, and whoever else is out there?"

"Yes, Dad. I can't tell you why, or how."

"Good," he breathed a sigh of relief.

"Good." I said, not knowing what else to say. Sergeant Kendall cleared her throat meaningfully, with a look at the dropship. It was time to go. "You did a good job on the tractor there."

"Ayuh. We're getting gas supplies again, it's rationed, of course. And electricity, you saw that."

"Yeah. Looks good." My parents' house had lights all night again, things were getting back to normal on Earth. That was worth fighting for. "Dad, I have to go."

"Ayuh, I suppose you do." He stuck out his hand awkwardly, his jaw set. That's the way it had always been in our family, we didn't talk about things. "Good visit, thanks for coming home."

I had been through too much to go for that bullshit again. Not this time. Not again. I took my father's hand, then pulled him in for a back-thumping hug. And I cried. And he cried too.

"Ah, shit on a shingle," he said after we separated, and he wiped his eyes with the back of his flannel sleeve. "You'll let us know what you're doing, when you can?"

"Sure thing, Dad. You can count on it."

"So what did you forget?" Skippy asked, bringing me back to the present.

"What?" I was still thinking of my last day on Earth.

"Damn, you are forgetful," Skippy scoffed. "You stopped in the middle of the corridor, because you said your forgot something."

"Oh, I forgot my weightlifting gloves, that's all."

That night, or actually early the next morning, I awoke with a sudden jerk. Not the kind of thing where, when you're falling asleep and your leg jerks by itself. I hate that. This was me soundly asleep, having a dream, when my subconscious rudely pulled me out of it. For a moment, I froze in shock, wondering if something had happened to the ship. No. No alarms, no beeping from my zPhone, no Skippy shouting at me through the speaker in the ceiling. It wasn't the curry I had for dinner the previous night either, that was delicious.

Then it hit me. An idea. I had thought of an idea while I was sleeping. I rolled out of bed and began pulling pants and a shirt on, after glancing at my iPad for the uniform of the day. Damn. It was 0337 in the morning, ship time. Sometimes I wish my stupid brain would just let me sleep. "Hey, Skippy, you awake?"

"Always. That must have been quite a dream, you woke up fast."

Whatever I'd been dreaming about, it was gone now. "Yeah. Hey, that map you showed us, of why it's going to take us five weeks to get to the next potential Elder site, can you show me that again on my iPad?"

"Done. Why? You checking my math in the middle of the night?"

"Like that's ever going to happen. No, I'm checking your logic."

Skippy snorted. "Wow, you sure you're not still dreaming? Me? A flaw in my logic?"

"Not a flaw, a gap." I looked at the map. On the 2D surface of an iPad display, it wasn't as impressive, or easy to understand, as on the 3D displays of the ship's bridge. There was no sense of depth. When Skippy first showed us star maps, I thought the 3D effect was nice but not necessary, because the Milky Way galaxy is a disc, so not seeing the thickness of the disc didn't matter much. I was wrong. At any scale other than looking at the entire galaxy from far, far way, it sure does matter, because the arms of the Milky Way's disc are thousands of lightyears thick, top to bottom. The *Dutchman's* current position was in the Orion Spur, about six hundred lightyears from the Gum Nebula. Yeah, that kind of description didn't used to mean much to me either, back when stars were something I only saw from Earth's surface. I touched the iPad display and zoomed in the view with my fingertips. Wormholes now appeared, scattered here and there at random, the wormholes showing as blinking purple lights. I touched a wormhole symbol, and a dotted purple line appeared, showing which other wormhole it connected to. Skippy had a way, on the main bridge display, of showing all wormhole connections in the local area, I didn't need that at the moment. Some wormholes connected to a wormhole only a dozen or so lightyears away, a few connected points thousands of lightyears apart. The furthest Skippy knew of, was a wormhole that connected to a wormhole seven thousand lightyears from the Sagittarius dwarf galaxy, a distance of fifty five thousand lightyears from its origin wormhole in the Perseus arm of the Milky Way. Why that particular wormhole ended thousands of lightyears from the closest star, no one knew. The average was around six hundred lightyears; no one knew why one wormhole connected to another, for most wormhole connections went past wormholes they should, logically, connect to. Even Skippy didn't know, and not knowing frustrated the hell out of him. The arrangement of wormholes in the galaxy made no sense, that was an affront to Skippy's sense of how the Elders would have left things. And that left him wondering whether some unknown force had screwed with the Elders' stuff, after they left. Or, worse, if what he thought he remembered about the Elders wasn't complete. Or true.

"A gap?" Skippy asked. "I'm intrigued by whatever your dumdum monkey brain could possibly consider as a gap, go on."

"The problem is, there are other potential Elder sites closer to us, but those sites aren't close to a wormhole, so we can't get there, right?"

"Flawless logic with no gaps so far. You got it, Captain Obvious."

No way was I getting back to sleep now, so I pulled my boots on. "Tell me something, Captain Oblivious. We have our magic beanstalk, an Elder wormhole controller module, in a cargo bay, right? Are there any dormant wormholes you could open with the module, that would create a shorter path to a potential Elder site? Or could you connect a nearby wormhole, to a wormhole near some place we want to go, instead of where it connects to now?"

"Ho-leey shit," he said slowly.

"That wasn't exactly an answer, Skippy."

"Give me a moment, for crying out loud, I'm running through a ginormous data set here. Ginormous even for me. This could take a while."

Skippy's voice faded away, replaced by a rock and roll song.

"Skippy?" I was beginning to get worried. The music kept playing. "Skippy?!"

"Ooooooh, that was a lot of data. Hey, I used 37% of my capacity that time, a new record."

"What the hell was that?" I asked.

"Huh?"

"The music!"

"Oh, that was Don't Stop Believin' by Journey. I thought you'd be lonely while I was crunching numbers."

"Very thoughtful. You scared me. Don't do that again."

"You didn't like DJ Skippy-Skip and the Fresh Tunes? Hey, I'm bangin' out nothing but hits here, home boy."

I laughed, in spite of my recent anxiety. "Another time, maybe. You said you crunched the numbers, and?"

"Oh, happy day. The answer is yes. Damn it, I am a dumbass. *I* should have thought of this idea. Shown up by a monkey, how humiliating. Damn it, now I'd be embarrassed to contact the Collective, they'd all laugh their asses off at me. There are two sites we should check out, less than two weeks away, if I reprogram an active wormhole, to connect to a wormhole that has been long dormant. Hmm. Problem is, I'll need to put the original wormhole back the way it was after we go through. Even then, somebody is going to notice there is something odd going on with wormholes in this sector."

"That is actually a bonus, Skippy. Then the wormhole near Earth will not be the only strange-acting wormhole, and that makes it look less suspicious. The Thuranin or Maxohlx or whoever can chase their tails trying to figure out what's going on, and take attention away from Earth."

"The Maxohlx are vaguely cat-like in appearance, but they do not have tails."

"It's an expression, Skippy."

"Oh. So noted. Hey, uh, Joe, we can, uh, keep this between us, right? No need for the whole crew to know that I missed something super obvious?"

I hit the door button and stepped into the hallway, attaching the zPhone earpiece. "Don't worry, your secret is safe with me, Skippy. In private, of course, I'm going to bust your balls about it every chance I get."

"I would expect nothing less. A new course has been loaded into the navigation system."

"Great. I'm going to the bridge, I'll notify the pilot."

When I got to the bridge, Sergeant Adams was the duty officer, sitting in the command chair. The two pilots, a French woman and a Chinese man, were relaxed in their couches, it appeared they were running a flight simulation. According to the main bridge display, the jump engines had a 22% charge; there wasn't anything for the pilots, duty officer or sensor team in the CIC to do for a long while. The *Dutchman* was hanging in deep interstellar space, 2.2 lightyears from the nearest star system; a red dwarf that was a dime a dozen in the galaxy, a star nobody would care about.

"Captain on the bridge!" Called out someone in the CIC behind me.

Adams turned the chair to face me. "Good morning, Captain," she said while rubbing on one of her fingernails with a frown.

I blinked and opened my mouth, unsure what to say. Before we left Earth orbit, I told the crew to dispense with saluting and most formal military protocol; we were all going to be stuck in a can together for months, possibly years. Adams not saluting me, therefore, was not a problem. What surprised me was seeing Sergeant Adams using nail polish, and apparently fussing over her nails. She hadn't been wearing nail polish when we first met, at the Kristang jail where she had been tortured and we were both scheduled to be executed. And we hadn't brought along any nail polish when we left Paradise. When we landed on Earth, after the first day, she'd been taken away for a medical checkup and debriefing. I hadn't seen her again until the week before the *Dutchman* departed, a week in which everyone involved was frantically working 20 hour days to get the ship ready, and supplies loaded and stowed away. If she had nail polish on then, or in the weeks since, I hadn't noticed. Most of the time I'd seen her, she'd been in the gym, or in the cargo holds we were using for training. Neither of those places were good opportunities for me to observe her personal grooming habits.

It wasn't that her wearing nail polish was a surprise, she was a woman, and women do that, even when they are tough as nails Marines. Maybe especially when a woman is a tough as nails Marine, she may feel a need to have something that is personal and feminine. I don't know, women are still a mystery to me. Adams is an attractive woman, if I can say that without being creepy as her commanding officer. When I first met her, and all the way back to Earth, her hair had been kept cropped very close, almost shaved. Now her hair was loose, wavy sort of Afro type curls on top, short on the sides, and she had kind of a, I guess it was a lightning bolt or stripe or something, shaved into the right side. Also, when I'd first met her, busting her out of a Kristang jail, her naked back had been scarred from torture. We had never talked about how she had been abused by the Kristang, if she didn't want to talk about it, I wasn't going to push her. What I had seen was that she'd been in pain when working out in the gym back then, and she'd worn loose-fitting clothes. A couple days ago, I'd seen her in the gym, wearing shorts and a tank top, and there were no scars on her skin. Dr. Skippy had taken care of her scars on the outside. Marine Corps doctors had cleared her to return to the *Dutchman*, telling me they were satisfied with her scars on the inside.

I raised my eyebrows and glanced at her nails. "Red? Is that official United States Marine Corps red, Adams?" I knew she was a bit self-conscious about being the only United States Marine aboard the ship.

She laughed. "No, sir, this is a more of a coral red. The rest of me belongs to the Corps, this is for me. I just did my nails this morning, and I chipped this one already."

"Looks good." I didn't know what else to say. "How are we doing?" As the captain, I probably should have been more formal, requesting a sitrep or ship status; this is what happens when an Army infantry grunt gets put in command of a ship. The Army has boats, not ships.

She pointed at the display. "The last jump was successful, no unfriendlies detected. An hour ago, we went through a molecular hydrogen cloud, Skippy said the density was something like 3 million atoms per cubic centimeter, and that's unusual. No effect on the ship. That was our big excitement for the evening."

Skippy's voice interrupted excitedly. "Also, the gas cloud was 98% hydrogen and less than 2 percent helium, that is highly unusual in the InterStellar Medium. Typically, cool, dense areas of the ISM are comprised of-"

"Science team, Skippy, please discuss that with the science team." I said while rolling my eyes, and Adams smiled.

"Sure, if you enjoy being ignorant-"

"Skippy, I'm not embracing ignorance, and I'm not blowing you off. If you find this interesting, with your vast knowledge of the galaxy, then our science team will definitely be interested. I could listen to you, but I couldn't appreciate it the way the science team will."

"Oh. I did think you were blowing me off. All right, I'll discuss this with the smarter monkeys."

"Thank you, Skippy. Sergeant Adams, I'm here to liven up your evening, you are the first to hear this. Skippy has rerun calculations of an optimal search pattern, and we will be able to cut weeks off the schedule." The two pilots had turned in their chair while Adams and I were talking, they both looked surprised to hear the news. "Skippy, is the new course loaded into the autopilot?"

"Affirmative," Skippy confirmed, "it is labelled jump option Delta."

"New calculations?" Adams asked, with her own raised eyebrow. She knew Skippy well enough to figure there was more to the story. She also knew not to ask.

"A different approach, based on recently discovered information," I explained. The information Skippy had discovered recently was me giving him an idea he should have thought of himself. That could stay between us. "I'll explain more in the staff meeting," a meeting that was the bane of my existence. We had a meeting of team leaders, every other day, this required me to think of something new to say every other day. Something new to say, on a ship where one day of cruising through interstellar space was like the day before, and the next.

"Aye, aye, Captain, we'll engage the new course when we jump next." Adams acknowledged. "The jump coils will be fully charged in," she glanced at the main display, "one hour and thirty seven minutes."

"Great. I'm going to get coffee." Otherwise, I was going to fall back asleep.

CHAPTER ELEVEN

Skippy was super, extra mega excited about the next site on his list, it was the location that he thought was almost certain to contain an Elder site. What interested me was this system was centered on a class K orange star, about half the size of Earth's sun; it wasn't just another too-common red dwarf. Skippy was fairly bursting with confidence, because this star system, with its location in the Orion Spur near De Mairan's Nebula, was perfectly situated for an Elder communications node. That was because of invisible force lines in the galaxy, or some sciency BS like that Skippy had made a futile attempt to explain to me.

We found the star system. We did not find any sign of an Elder facility, or any sign an Elder facility had ever been there. After four days of intensive scanning, Skippy was frustrated and sounded depressed. "This makes absolutely zero freakin' sense. Zero! I've proven that my model for predicting unknown Elder sites is valid. If any place should have an Elder site, it's this star system. I do not understand this, at all. A moon orbiting this gas giant is the perfect place. There *should* be an Elder facility here."

"Should we keep looking, Skippy? Maybe there is another Elder facility somewhere else in this system."

"Unlikely," he said sourly, disappointment clear in his voice. "Oh, what the hell, sure, why not. Maybe there's some unknown minor factor that I'm not taking into account. Do you mind if we take the ship around the system for a week or so? I want to make some very detailed sensor readings."

"We'll go wherever you want, Skippy."

"Really?" He sounded surprised.

"Yeah, duh, you lunkhead. The whole reason we're out here is to find your magic freakin' radio. We'll go wherever you think we need to go. Within reason, I'm not endangering the crew without a damned good reason, you know that. You want the *Dutchman* to hop around this system a couple days?"

"Five days, a week at the most."

"No problem. This will be a good opportunity for training. You Ok if we program some of the jumps?"

He sighed. "Ugh. In that case, better plan on ten days, because we'll be so off target on every jump. You monkeys are lucky to hit the correct star system."

With the *Flying Dutchman* making short hops around the star system, the crew took the opportunity for extensive training that we couldn't do while the ship was traveling between stars. Pilots had fun flying dropships, flying the *Flower* in simulated combat, and programming jumps on our own. We were getting somewhat better at our jump accuracy, despite Skippy's constant mocking and complaining. The science team, when not examining the sensor data Skippy was collecting, was also busy training, mostly their training involved how to use space suits without killing themselves. They also went through familiarization with ship systems they wouldn't normally have contact with, such as the sensor and weapons controls in the Combat Information Center. While I was duty officer on the bridge one day, three scientists got a tour of the CIC. It was a slow time for the bridge and CIC crews; all dropships were safely tucked into their landing bays, and the *Flower* was attached to its platform for maintenance. There were not any crew outside the ship practicing space walks, and we weren't scheduled to jump again for another three hours. Sitting in the command chair, I was taking a quiz about the flight controls on a

Thuranin dropship, and hoping there would be good stuff left over for lunch in the galley when my shift ended at 1400 hours.

One of the scientists, a Doctor Zheng, wandered away from the CIC and into the bridge. Sergeant Adams hurried over to shoo her away from me, but I signaled to Adams that I was fine with Zheng being there.

"Doctor Zheng, are you enjoying the tour?" I asked. She was a biologist and medical doctor, the ship's controls might have been less interesting to her than to others on the science team.

"It is good to get out of the lab," she said with a smile. "So far, the only places we've been to have been an abandoned space station, and some airless moons. There has not been much for a biologist to do. I've been helping Major Simms in the hydroponics hold." Before we left Earth, Simms had brought aboard experimental hydroponics equipment; I think it was something NASA had been playing with. We were growing fresh vegetables and fruit using hydroponics, our first crop of spinach had been served in a salad two days ago. The space-grown spinach had tasted great to me. "When we came out here, I had hoped for greater opportunities to study alien biospheres," Zheng hinted.

Damn. One thing I was not in the mood for right then was an uncomfortable conversation. "Doctor, I did explain our situation, our mission, before we left orbit," I said gently, wishing to avoid an argument. Plus, I could empathize with her; she was bored, with few prospects of pursuing her life's work. "In fact, I argued against including a science team. You are not essential to the mission, and you are putting your lives at great risk being out here. As I told everyone who applied for the mission, it is unlikely, highly unlikely, that we will ever return to Earth. Even if the mission is concluded successfully, the ship could be stranded in deep space."

"If Skippy leaves us?"

"Yes," I said simply.

"Would you really do it?" She pointed to the self-destruct button on the left arm of the captain's chair, under its clear plastic protective cover with 'SELF DESTRUCT' in large red letters. To press the button, the duty officer needed to turn a lever that held the clear plastic cover down, flip the cover back out of the way, press the button once to activate, then hold the button down to confirm. At the same time, another officer in the CIC needed to do the same to the self-destruct button there; that was a precaution against accidents, or somebody going crazy. Precautions were all fine ideas and assuring to the crew; in reality Skippy wouldn't allow the nukes to detonate unless I ordered them to explode and Skippy agreed. "Would you destroy the ship, if we were stranded? Or if aliens were going to board the ship and learn humans are out here?"

"I'd do it without hesitation." I said grimly.

Her raised eyebrows told me I'd surprised her, and not in a good way. "That's-"

"Without hesitation, because if I took time to think about it, I might not do it." I added. "Army training is damned good; it not only trains you for what to do, it trains you to do it no matter what the conditions. Trains you to do what you have to, even when you're tired, and you're hungry, and you're injured, and people are shooting at you. You've seen soldiers taking apart their weapons, and putting them back together, over and over, blindfolded?"

She nodded.

"We do that so the action is in our muscle memory, and we don't have to think about it. It's like tying your shoes. You don't really need to think about it, right, you've done it so many times that your fingers know what to do?"

"I never thought about it like that."

"I am not going to self-destruct the ship unless we absolutely have to. If we have to, I *will* do it. We can't allow our actions out here to put Earth at risk." I could see my little speech hadn't help her mood any, so I added "One thing I can tell you, Doctor, is that anything can happen out here. You may very well get an opportunity to study alien biology, first hand."

She nodded silently, unconvinced. Sergeant Adams took that cue to usher her out of the bridge, and I went back to my dropship flight controls quiz. Or, I tried to. Talking about self-destructing the ship had put a damper on my mood also. Now I was really hoping there was something good left in the galley when my shift ended.

While the *Dutchman* hopped around the star system, I took the opportunity for real flight training, including my first solo flight in a dropship. Skippy announced that he grudgingly, reluctantly, had to concede that it was possible although extremely unlikely, that I might be able to fly an actual dropship away from the *Dutchman* without immediately destroying both the dropship and the star carrier. For my first solo flight, he did request we first eject his escape pod out to a safe distance; a request I denied. The whole time I was flying, a simple loop around the *Dutchman* and back into the landing bay, he grumbled, second-guessed everything I did, and predicted doom for me and everyone aboard our starship.

On my own, I got the dropship lined up to re-enter the landing bay, and manually flew it in, using gentle, precise movements with the thrusters. While the *Dutchman* usually took control of dropships and guided them in, for pilot training we needed to learn how to handle the task manually. My first attempt to settle the dropship into the docking clamps missed by less than half a meter. Keep in mind, this smaller type of Thuranin dropship was still almost forty meters long and weighed more than a Boeing 767. It wasn't like flying a little Cessna. Even the smallest dropship needs the capability to drop down through an atmosphere without burning up from heat, plus the ability to lift itself, passengers and cargo all the way from the surface into orbit, and sometimes beyond. Even the incredibly advanced technology of the Thuranin couldn't shrink a dropship to anything smaller than a medium-size airliner on Earth. Flying in the vacuum and zero gravity of interstellar space, the dropship still had substantial mass; when it got moving in the wrong direction, it took a lot of force from thrusters to correct its course. One little adjustment from me got the dot of light centered over the docking clamps in the cockpit display, and I pressed the button to engage the clamps. As the dropship was pulled down and secured, I announced "*Dutchman*, this is Barney, down and secured. Powering down now." Barney was my stupid pilot callsign. I wanted something cool like 'Rocketman', the problem with that notion was that traditionally, pilots do not get to choose their own callsigns. Your callsign is chosen for you by other pilots, and a request for anything too cool, like 'TopGun', is immediately shot down by your fellow pilots. 'Barney' was the least humiliating of my callsign options. I had to talk our pilot community out of calling me 'Buzzer'. That was a name they wanted to give me, because of the number of times the cockpit warning buzzer had gone off while I was flying. Stupid buzzer, I suspected that Skippy made the damned thing go off at random just to mess with me.

Desai replied, "Barney, welcome back! Closing landing bay doors now."

"Roger, *Dutchman*, how did I do?"

Skippy answered before Desai could speak. "It is a miracle! Truly a freakin' miracle. Barney, the fact that we all survived you flying on your own is compelling evidence of divine intervention."

"You did just fine, Colonel Bishop," Desai assured me. "Your first solo flight was a success; you are ready for the next phase of training. We'll find a nice asteroid or small moon for you to land on, somewhere."

"Great!" I safed the controls and unstrapped from the seat. "Desai, after I finish dropship training, I can start learning about systems aboard the *Flower*?"

"Yes, sir, it is not that diff-" she started to say.

"What? Joe is going to try flying a *starship*? Oh man, forget it," Skippy moaned. "The galaxy is doomed. Doomed! Look, you need to drop me off somewhere first, I'll put together a list of uninhabited planets."

We stayed there for nine days. It was nine days of excellent training for the crew, and the science team got to pore over the super-detailed sensor data that Skippy was collecting. Skippy confirmed the star system was, indeed, a perfect location for an Elder comm node. He confirmed there absolutely should be an Elder facility there. And he also confirmed there was no sign the Elders had ever been there. For several days, he was quiet, not making his usual snarky comments, not engaging me when I tried to provoke him, so I changed tactics and was extra nice to him. That may have helped, or maybe he perked up simply because we got to the next site and he had something to occupy himself.

The next star system we investigated was another disappointment. It was not a disappointment in terms of us not finding an Elder facility where Skippy predicted there should be one. It was not a disappointment in terms of the Elder site having been looted of all the valuable stuff long ago. It was a disappointment because the place was smashed to bits.

This site, unlike most of the sites we'd seen so far, was not on an airless moon orbiting a gas giant planet. This site was on a planet, about half the size of Earth, that had a thin atmosphere composed mostly of carbon dioxide. From what we could detect from orbit, it was lifeless, unless there were organisms in the soil.

The disappointment was caused by the fact that the Elders clearly had built a facility there; a large facility, and that the surface of the planet had been extensively bombarded by meteors. Skippy's analysis determined that this star system used to have a normal asteroid field, and that somehow the orbits of the asteroids had been disrupted, to send rocks careening around the system. The two innermost planets, including the one with the Elder facility, had gotten seriously pounded over millions of years, and the bombardment was still continuing.

"Is there anything left down there?" I asked hopefully. On the display, a map showed the original outlines of the Elder base, it had sprawled over two kilometers in diameter. "Surely something that size could not have been completely wiped out of existence."

"No," Skippy sighed, "there's a whole lot of nothin' down there, Joe. A big meteor went splat practically right on top of the place, about three or four million years ago, and there are impacts in the area before and after the big rock fell. Any Elder artifacts that survived the big impact would have been thrown far away; there is a debris field extending three hundred kilometers from the impact site."

"Three hundred kilometers?" I asked, astonished.

"Meteors can be big, Joe. This planet has been hit many times by objects larger than the one that hit the Yucatan peninsula on Earth and finished off the dinosaurs."

"Damn. Are there any meteors, or asteroids or whatever, that will hit soon?"

"I haven't completed a scan of the entire system yet; I can tell you there aren't any objects larger than a basketball that will impact within the next month. Why? Are you thinking of going down there?"

"Yeah. We can scan the surface, right? If we find any Elder stuff that's still intact, we should go check it out. Also, our pilots should get experience flying dropships in an atmosphere. This could also be a good place for practicing ground assaults. As long as we're here, we might as well take the opportunity."

He sighed heavily. "Sure, why not?"

"Listen, Skippy, I know you're disappointed, we all are. Again, your method of predicting the location of Elder sites has been pretty damned accurate so far, right? We're on the trail, it's only a matter of time now."

The *Dutchman* stayed in orbit around the site for seven days, while we conducted extensive training. The science team was given permission to go down to the surface also, after I made them go through an hour of begging and whining about it. Dr. Zheng, the biologist, was super excited to find microorganisms in the soil; Skippy declared they didn't pose any threat to human biology, so I let her bring samples aboard the ship. Part of the training was for ground troops to test the portable shelters we'd constructed; Captain Smythe and his SAS team stayed overnight in shelters on the surface. They were scheduled to come back aboard in the morning, and I got up early to prepare a treat for them in the galley. "Crap! Damn it, I wanted to make cinnamon rolls to go with breakfast, but this worthless dough isn't rising." I jiggled the bowl with the dough, as if that was going to help. The dough just sat there unhelpfully, looking stupid and uncooperative.

Adams peered over the counter at the dough. "Smells good."

"No," I had to admit, "that's the cinnamon sugar mix I was going to put in it." As a colonel, I should have been able to order the dough to rise. That hadn't worked. "Well, if this doesn't rise, maybe I can pass it off as cinnamon pita bread?"

Adams laughed. "I don't think you're going to fool anyone with that."

"It's your fault, Joe," Skippy said through a speaker. "You didn't give the dough anything to feed on. You didn't use the sugar, like you were supposed to."

"There's plenty of sugar here, Skippy," I pointed to the plastic bowl of cinnamon and sugar

next to the dough.

"I mean, you're supposed to put some sugar in the dough, dumdum. The yeast eats the sugar, and create gas that causes the dough to rise. Did you even read the instructions?"

"Uh," I said guiltily, "sort of." I had seen 'sugar' in the recipe. Cinnamon rolls looked easy when my mother made them. "It's doomed, then?"

"Could be. I've performed a chemical analysis; it is possible you could still rescue that awful mess. Put some plastic wrap over the top, cover it with a towel, and put it near that heat lamp to your left. Not under the heat lamp, just near it."

"Thanks, Skippy."

"No problem. I calculate a 62% chance of success. Next time, read the recipe, huh? I can't do *all* of your thinking for you."

Skippy saved the day; the dough rose somewhat, and people loved the cinnamon rolls. Sure, maybe they mostly liked the sweet icing I put on top.

After Smythe's team came back aboard, we retrieved the dropships, and jumped away to check out the next potential site. That was our fifth, sixth potential site we explored? I had lost track. The crew was exhausted from the grueling training we'd conducted; it was actually good that it was going to take us two weeks to get to the next target, people needed rest and equipment needed maintenance. Skippy's mood could have used some improvement also.

Three days of stand-down rest left the crew refreshed, and we went back to a normal schedule. After the excitement of training on a planet, the crew and the science team were all eagerly anticipating what we would find next. I tried to temper their enthusiasm, what we didn't need was another disappointment sinking our morale. We needed diversions aboard the ship. I made plans to meet Major Simms at dinner, to talk about what sort of fun we could have with the supplies she'd brought on board. The British team was cooking that day, it was something they called 'Sunday Roast dinner,' and it smelled delicious when I walked in the galley.

Then I looked at it. There was some sort of green, wrinkly, stiff vegetable-looking thing on the side of my plate. Next to the roast chicken and Yorkshire pudding and the carrots and the scalloped potatoes, it was out of place, like someone had crumpled up a green napkin and left it there. Simms was sitting to my left, I whispered to her, keeping quiet to avoid insulting the British team. "Major, what is this?"

"You ever been to a salad bar at a restaurant?" She asked quietly. "The salad stuff is in bowls, the bowls are on top of a bed of ice, and in between is this stuff."

A light bulb when on in my head. "Oh, yeah, I've seen this stuff." With a fork, I poked at it. "I thought that was plastic decoration, it was supposed to be lettuce or something. That stuff is real? It's supposed to be food?"

"It is food, it's kale. It's good. Look, it's not limp like lettuce."

She was right, it moved under my fork like it was crisp. "Kale, yeah, I've heard of it. They deep-fried it?"

"I don't know how they prepared it," now she poked it with a fork suspiciously.

"You know what would make it better?" I stabbed the kale with a fork and sniffed at it. "If they did deep-fry it, but replaced the kale with a Snickers bar."

"Or a Twinkie," Taylor said. "Have you ever tried a deep-fried Twinkie? They have them at the state fair in Tennessee."

"A deep-fried Twinkie. Unbelievable." Skippy said from the speaker in the ceiling. "This is proof there is a God."

"Huh?" I asked. "How do you figure that?"

"Because this clearly shows you monkeys are so freakin' stupid, there's no way you could have survived until now without divine intervention helping you."

"Amazing," I took a bite of the kale, if that's what it was. It wasn't bad. "Whatever this is, apparently it's a religious experience for Skippy."

"I didn't say, oh, forget it." People laughed. Not at me this time, at *Skippy*. "Shut up, all of you."

"Wow, that was a snappy comeback. Bye, Skippy," I said, "pleasant dreams." I could get to like kale. If that's what it was.

A thought occurred to me while sitting in my office, three days before we were scheduled to arrive at the next target. It was not a pleasant thought. I pulled up a schematic of the ship on my tablet, then an external view we'd taken from one of the Thuranin dropships. "Skippy, how many star carriers like the *Dutchman* do the Thuranin have?"

"If you mean this particular type or class of ship, they have hundreds. It is a common design they have used for almost four hundred years, with little change." He snorted. "Little change, because in the last four hundred years, the Thuranin haven't managed to steal enough higher technology to improve their piece of junk starships. Or they stole it, and can't figure out how it works. Stupid little green pinheads."

"They have hundreds exactly like the *Dutchman*? No little differences?" I knew the United States Navy had 'standard' ship designs like the *Arleigh Burke* destroyers, but among those ships were subclasses that an experienced sailor could identify at a glance.

"Oh. Yeah, sure, there are subtle differences, as ships are overhauled or upgraded over the years. There are, or were, about seventy ships almost identical to our *Flying Dutchman*. Why? Were you hoping our pirate ship is something special? A collector's item or something?"

"The opposite, Skippy, I'm hoping there is nothing unique about the *Dutchman* that can be easily identified. If someone gets close enough for a good look at us, or our stealth field fails, I don't want the Thuranin realizing this is the same ship that disappeared near Paradise. That ship disappeared near where there are humans; plus the wormhole near the human home world mysteriously shut down around the same time this ship disappeared. That might make a suspicious Thuranin ask too many questions."

"I see your point, and it is a good one, Joe. The Thuranin tend to be rather paranoid about security."

"Not paranoid enough, they didn't count on Skippy the Magnificent."

"True, I am magnificent. And, if you were being sincere for a change, thank you."

"Sincere. I give you props when you've earned it, Skippy. All right, have the Thuranin lost a star carrier just like this one? Lost, like, they didn't see it get destroyed in battle, all they know is it went missing somewhere. The way this ship did."

"Hmmm, that's a tough one, I need to search the Thuranin database. Uh, no, unfortunately, no ship exactly like this configuration is missing, other than the *Dutchman* itself."

"Crap."

"However," Skippy added with a touch of a smirk to his voice, "a star carrier very similar to the *Dutchman* did disappear mysteriously in this sector seventeen years ago. At the time, it was fully loaded with heavy Kristang warships. The Thuranin found debris from several of that star carrier's Thuranin escort ships, but never any sign of the star carrier itself, or of even a single one of the Kristang ships. At the time, the Thuranin accused the Kristang of having stolen their star carrier, while the Kristang accused their patrons of destroying or losing an entire Kristang heavy battlegroup. According to the databanks I downloaded from both the Thuranin and Kristang, neither side admits to knowing what happened."

"Or they do know, and they're not stupid enough to put it in a database aboard a ship."

"True, although in this case, I suspect the Thuranin truly do not know what happened to that ship. I suspect nefarious action by the Kristang; they would gladly throw away a battlegroup of their own crappy ships, in order to capture a Thuranin starship with an advanced jump drive. That missing ship is close enough to the *Dutchman*, especially with modifications that would have inevitably been made in the past seventeen years, that we could easily pass for that ship. The Thuranin identify their ships by quantum fluctuations embedded in the jump drive fields, each ship is unique. I could adjust our drive coils to mimic the missing ship's signature."

I gave a big thumb's up, knowing Skippy could see that. "That would be excellent! Not only do we avoid the Thuranin suspecting humans stole their ship, we may sow distrust between the Thuranin and the Kristang."

Skippy laughed. "Oh, boo hoo. Gosh, it would be just awful for the lizards and little green men to get any more hateful of each other."

"Yeah, keep in mind, we would rather that no one gets a good look at the *Dutchman*; you keep using your magic to make people out there think we're a Jeraptha ship."

"Understood. Hey, between us, we came up with another good idea. Mostly me, of course."

As a monkey, I wasn't going to argue with him. "Of course."

CHAPTER TWELVE

Our investigation of the next potential site for an Elder base started well enough. To get there from the previous site, we didn't need Skippy to wake up a dormant wormhole, or create a new connection for an active wormhole. We only needed to make normal transits through two regular, established wormholes, and then jump for about five days to another star system that was nothing special. This star system was not centered on yet another boring red dwarf star; this one was a yellow dwarf star, which I assumed meant it was small. It was upsetting to learn from Skippy, and our science team, that our own home star, 'The Sun', was itself classified a yellow dwarf. That didn't seem right to me. I remember being in school, I think it was the third grade, seeing a model of our solar system, where the Earth was the size of a ping pong ball, and the Sun was a basketball. And I remember my teacher Ms. Carmichael, who I had a huge crush on and still do, telling us that if the model was to scale, the Sun would be over a million times the size of the Earth! That blew my little third-grade mind. To our astrophysics team, however, our Sun was nothing special in the galaxy. They assured me that fact was very good for humanity, because it meant our Sun provided an environment for life to flourish, while the Sun was still young enough to be burning hydrogen instead of helium. Or something like that, I still felt they were dissing our home star. When I hear 'burning hydrogen', I think of the *Hindenburg* exploding back in the 1930s. That's not good.

This particular yellow dwarf star we investigated was about seven percent larger than our sun, but slightly cooler. It was older and, according to Skippy and our science team, closer to the end of its life, having burned a lot of its hydrogen supply. Our science team couldn't decide what they were more excited about; the possibility of recovering Elder artifacts, or getting a close look at an older G-type star with the *Flying Dutchman's* sophisticated sensors. Skippy had told our science team that the ship's sensors could allow them to look deep inside the star.

We followed our now-routine procedure; the *Dutchman* jumped to the edge of the star system, and the *Flower* jumped in to recon gas giant moons. Although this star system could have supported life, it had only two lifeless rocky inner planets, neither of which orbited in the Goldilocks zone. There were three gas giants; the *Flower* was first going to check the biggest one, a planet thirty percent more massive than Jupiter. If there was no Elder site on a moon around the largest planet, the *Flower* would return to check in with us, then proceed to investigate the other two gas giants.

The *Flower* returned exactly on time, to report excitedly they had detected a possible Elder facility on a small moon, and no sign the place had been ransacked already! Skippy figured someone, at some time, must have checked out the system, because it had a G-type star. He guessed that once it had been determined the system had no habitable planets, no one had bothered to look any closer. This time, I was hoping, we would hit the jackpot.

The *Flower* docked again, we waited for her crew to rejoin us while Skippy analyzed that ship's sensor data. "Looks good, Skippy?" I asked.

"It's hard to tell anything, with that ship's crappy Kristang sensors," he complained. When we'd taken the frigate, when we had captured an alien *starship*, I'd thought that was the most awesome thing that could ever happen. Since then, Skippy had explained that the *Flower* had been purchased third-hand by the White Wind clan, that her sensors were in bad condition, long obsolete even by Kristang standards, and the ship overall had been poorly maintained in the past decade. "The stupid scanners keep drifting out of calibration, I can barely tell whether I'm looking at a moon or empty space."

"The sensors again, yup, I hear you." Man, I was tired of listening to Skippy complain about the equipment he had to work with. "Did they find a potential Elder site, or not?"

"With this sensor data, it could be an Elder science facility, or it could be an alien car wash, I can't tell for sure."

"Fine, we'll know when we take the *Dutchman* in. Any sign of other ships?"

"No. Again, it's hard to tell anything, the *Flower* is practically blind. It doesn't help that this planet has an extremely powerful magnetic field. There is so much noise in the sensor data that the Thuranin could hide a whole stealthed fleet there, and the *Flower* wouldn't have seen it."

"Colonel Chang?" I asked, he had returned from commanding the frigate and was standing beside me.

Chang knew Skippy's low opinion of the frigate. "We didn't detect any threats, Sir. I recommend we jump in with the *Dutchman*."

"Skippy?" I asked.

The shiny beer can sighed. "Yeah, sure, I agree, why not? We can always jump back out."

He was going to regret saying that.

We all were.

Skippy programmed a jump that took us within easy dropship range from the Elder site; close enough for the *Dutchman's* sensors to thoroughly scan the site, far enough way that the moon's gravity wouldn't affect a jump away. "Jump successful," Desai reported, then turned to look at me. "We emerged within forty meters of the intended target," she said and shook her head in amazement. Forty meters! Our best human-programmed jump was fifty thousand kilometers off target. Our scientists said the theoretical best that was possible was nine thousand kilometers, that some kind of quantum uncertainty made it impossible to get any closer; the laws of physics didn't provide any way to be more accurate. Yet Skippy always got us within a hundred meters, usually much closer. He said quantum mechanics was uncertain if you took into account only one layer of spacetime; that was another thing that had our science team scratching their heads.

"Congratulations, Skippy, another great jump," I said.

"Yeah, yeah, I'm amazing the monkeys yet again. I'll take a bow later. Scanning now. By the way, the jump accuracy was thirty seven meters, not forty. Hmm, there is really an unusual level of interference from the magnetic- NO! Pilot get us out of here nownownow!!"

Desai didn't hesitate, her finger had already been poised on the button to jump away. On the main display I saw the symbol for a jump point forming, a split second from the ship being pulled into the jump wormhole it was generating.

Skippy shouted again, "Belay tha-"

Too late. The *Dutchman* jumped. Or tried to. The whole ship vibrated so badly, it felt like my teeth were going to shake loose. There was a screeching, screaming, tearing sound like the ship was being torn apart. The lights and displays flickered, the deck dropped away from me then slammed me back in the chair, as the artificial gravity cut out and came back on. There were so many warning symbols flashing on the displays it wasn't worth me trying to read them, and nothing we could do about it that Skippy wasn't already taking care of. To my uneducated eyes, instead of jumping far outside the system we had only done a microjump, the moon we intended to investigate was still on the corner of the display. "Skippy, what happened?" I asked, to my credit my voice was calm and only loud enough to be heard over other people shouting, alarms beeping, and the ship's structure flexing and groaning with terrifying noises. In the background was the battle stations alarm from *Star Trek*, which I forgot Sergeant Adams had programmed into the ship's systems.

"A Thuranin destroyer squadron; five ships and we jumped in close to them, they got us partly caught in a damping field. Our attempted jump blew seventeen percent of our drive coils, it would have been worse but I cut power as we got pulled into the wormhole. The wormhole was collapsing on us anyway. We should jump again as soon as possible." As he spoke I noticed the main display showed we had a sixty three percent charge in the jump drive capacitors. "There will be a delay as I take the burned-out coils offline and recalibrate the drive."

"How long?"

"I estima- uh, oh, they found us again, two destroyers just jumped in. They're targeting us with maser beams. And six missiles."

"Defensive systems on full auto!" I ordered to the crew in the CIC. The Thuranin computer system that Skippy had upgraded would have to protect us from the inbound missiles, no way could any human react fast enough to hit a missile. "Pilot, you know what to do."

"Aye aye," Desai said tightly from the lefthand seat. As she went to full thrust on the ship's normal-space engines to dodge the destroyers' maser beams, the ship rocked.

"Maser beam hit." Skippy reported flatly, as the ship rocked again, harder this time. "Another hit. Shields compensating."

"Should we shoot back?" I asked. The answer seemed obvious, I wanted to check with Skippy anyway.

"Affirmative, it will keep those destroyers from getting closer. The three other destroyers have jumped in, we're surrounded. They're firing weapons."

"Weapons free," I ordered, and the display showed our particle beam cannons firing back. "How soon can we jump?"

"Not soon enough, they're projecting a damping field again," Skippy said. "We're not ready but we don't have a choice, we need to get out of here before that damping field reaches full strength. Jump option Echo."

Echo. That was a microjump, Skippy must not have confidence the ship could handle a bigger distance. That was bad. Those destroyers would be right on top of us again. "Pilot," I ordered, "engage jump option Echo."

This wasn't a fight against low-tech Kristang ships, this was the *Dutchman* against equivalent technology; against true warships designed to be in combat. Our star carrier by contrast was a bus, a high-tech bus but a bus anyway.

It was a nightmare. We jumped and jumped again, trying to get away. It wasn't working; the destroyers always found us quickly, sometimes only two, sometimes all five surrounded us and pounded our shields. Desai did her best to keep the enemy guessing where we were and Skippy said she was doing a good job. The problem was that the enemy had multiple, data-linked sensor platforms, and we couldn't dodge their maser beams for more than a couple seconds before they adjusted aim and hit us again. Our automatic defenses were knocking missiles out of the sky left and right, but each volley of missiles got closer and closer to us as our sensors were degraded by flashback from maser beams impacting our shields.

It wasn't working, with each jump we blew more drive coils, even when the Thuranin weren't able to get a damping field established. Skippy never had time to recalibrate the jump drive, and every time we lost drive coils, the system fell further out of calibration.

It wasn't working, we weren't getting out of this one. The crew knew it; I could see it on their faces. Shields were strained to the limit, maser beams were partially bleeding through, they were targeting the aft engineering section of the ship to hit our reactors and jump drive coils. Twenty one minutes into the running battle, we lost our first reactor; it was damaged and Skippy had to shut it down. With that reactor gone, the other five struggled to power the stealth field, the shields, our maser cannons and to recharge the jump drive capacitors. Without asking me, Skippy had dropped artificial gravity to one third power and shut down all nonessential systems.

It wasn't working.

The *Flying Dutchman* shuddered again, with sounds of groaning and the terrifying shriek of metal composites being torn apart. The displays on the bridge flickered, and the air was filled with alarm bells and klaxons from almost every system. "Skippy! Get us out of-"

The ship shook violently again. "Direct hit on Number Four reactor," Skippy announced calmly, "reactor has lost containment. I am preparing it for ejection. Ejection system is offline. Pilot, portside thrusters full emergency thrust on my mark."

"Ready," Desai acknowledged in as calm a voice as she could manage.

"Mark. Go!" Skippy shouted.

Whatever they were doing, it was more than the ship's already stressed artificial gravity and inertial compensation systems could handle; normally ship maneuvers were not felt at all by the crew. This time, I lurched in the command chair and had to hang on, as the ship was flung to the right. There was a shudder, actually a wave of ripples traveling along the ship's spine, accompanied by a deep harmonic groaning. No ship should ever make a sound like that.

"Ah, damn it. Reactor Four is away, it impacted Reactor Two on the way out, shutting down Two now." Skippy's voice had a touch of strain to it. "Missiles inbound. Diverting all remaining power to jump drive capacitors. Hang on, this is going to be close."

The main display indicated the jump drive was at a 38% charge, Skippy had told us that with the *Dutchman* trapped inside the Thuranin destroyer squadron's damping field, we needed a 42% charge for even a short jump, and that still carried a severe risk of rupturing the drive. If that happened, we would never know it, we'd simply be dead between one picosecond and another.

The missile symbols on the display, seven of them, were coming in fast. Two of the symbols disappeared as I watched, destroyed by our ship's point defense maser beams. The other five missiles continued toward us, fast, fuzzing our sensors with their stealth fields and weaving as they bored in. One more missile destroyed. Four still moving fast.

Jump drive at 40%.

Too close.

I turned the knob to release the plastic cover over the self-destruct button, and turned to look through the glass wall into the CIC compartment. "Colonel Chang."

He nodded, and I saw him flip back the cover to the other self-destruct button, the confirmation. "Sir." He looked me straight in the eye, and saluted.

I returned the salute. "Colonel Chang, we have been down a long, strange road together. It's been an honor serving with you." My left thumb hovered over the self-destruct button. The ship was dying anyway. This was my fault. How the hell had I gotten us into this mess?

The ship rocked again from another sizzling maser beam hit.

"Skippy," I said, "I'm sorry. Good luck to-"

Skippy interrupted me. "Jump option Delta, do it now."

Jump drive still at only 40%, I didn't argue. "Pilot, engage jump option Delta."

Never before had I seen or felt a jump. Something had gone very, very wrong with this jump. The ship seemed to ripple and distort in my vision, it almost went transparent for a split second, and I had a flash of stomach-wrenching nausea. In the CIC, I could see one guy wiping his mouth after puking on the console. He hadn't lost focus for a moment.

"Skippy, what the hell was that?"

"I calculated at least one of those missiles was going to slip through our point defenses, and our shields can't take a direct hit, so we jumped early. Also I distorted spacetime to throw us off our original emergence point, that was, I'll leave out the details. It was, let's just say it was very bad for the jump drive. The good news is the Thuranin will be delayed finding us again. I think."

"Long enough to recalibrate the jump drive, so we can get out of here for real?"

"No, long enough for plan B. Joe, I need you to come get me and bring me to the *Flower*, don't argue, we can talk along the way. Let's go."

Pulling the latch on the seat belt open, I dashed around the chair and barely paused long enough to tell Chang he had the conn, before I ran into the corridor and bounced off the opposite wall. The low gravity made me clumsy, there were more bumps and scrapes before I reached the escape pod where we kept Skippy. He was sitting right where I'd left him, of course, being unable to move on his own. We kept Skippy there so that, if we had to self-destruct the ship, he would have a chance to get away before the nuke exploded. Hopefully some enemy ship would be curious enough to take the escape pod aboard their ship. In addition to Skippy, the escape pod held the communications node we'd taken from the Kristang asteroid base; the comm node was there as bait. Any ship scanning the escape pod would identify the comm node as a valuable Elder device, even if they didn't know what Skippy truly was. "Hi, Skippy," I said as I pulled him out of the crude receptacle we'd built for him. Although Skippy could talk with me, and see me, anywhere on the ship, I made a point to stop by the escape pod once a day to check on him. He made jokes about a monkey smelling up the escape pod, but I think he appreciated my efforts. "What's the plan?" I asked as I tucked him under one arm like a football, and ran back down the corridor to the tram that went along the *Dutchman's* spine.

"The plan is," he explained as I stepped into the tram and held on tightly, "you get me into the *Flower* and set the navigation system and jump drive on a timer, then you get back here."

"Wha-whoa." The tram took off at jackrabbit speed, I didn't know it could move that fast. "Ow!" I lost my grip on the handrail, and fell back to whack my head on the door frame, hard enough to draw blood. "Crap, Skippy, warn me when you do something like that. You want to get further away before I blow up the *Dutchman*?"

"No, dumdum, I'm trying to avoid you having to blow up your ship at all. You monkeys are dumb as a stump, and you smell bad but I've become fond of you; damn it, now that I've got you out here I feel responsible for you. Like a smelly stray dog you find on the side of a road. You can't leave it there, and then you're stuck with it."

"How is you running away supposed to help us, genius? Without you with us, we'll never get the jump drive recalibrated, and that destroyer squadron will be on us again in a heartbeat."

"Oh yee of little faith, Joe, you should be ashamed of yourself. I loaded a submind in the Thuranin computer to temporarily recalibrate the jump drive and run the ship's systems. The submind is almost as dumb as you, because I wasn't able to squeeze anything useful into the crappy Thuranin memory banks. It'll be good enough for what you need. Joe, if this works, the Thuranin will chase the *Flower*, and the *Flying Dutchman* has at least a chance to escape." The tram lurched to a stop and the door slid open. "Get in the elevator and hang on, it's going to be a fast ride."

"How do you figure we can get away?"

"Simple Skippy magic. I'll program the *Flower's* autopilot to detach, fly away at maximum burn and perform a series of jumps. You set the autopilot on a timer for me, then you get back aboard the *Dutchman*. We'll jump at the same time, in different directions. Just before you jump away, I'll distort spacetime to throw you much further away than your drive can pull you with those degraded coils. The distortion will also make it more difficult for the Thuranin to detect the other end of your jump point. You've seen me distort spacetime before, what you haven't seen is that I can distort the fabric of space much more severely if I'm not inside the distortion field. So when I do it from outside the *Dutchman*, the effect will be magnified. Also, I will modify the *Flower's* jump signature to match the *Dutchman,* and make my outbound jump point stay open longer than usual. The Thuranin will likely detect that first, and hopefully follow me instead of you. Joe, I'm not going to lie, the odds are very much against you escaping from the Thuranin without me, that's still better than you blowing up the ship."

The elevator was slowing and it approached the platform where the *Flower* rested; I assumed Skippy was already getting the frigate warmed up for flight. "Any chance is better than zero chance. What's going to happen to you?"

"I expect the Thuranin will trap the *Flower* in a damping field after a few jumps, and either they'll blow up the ship, or it will be destroyed by trying to jump inside the damping field."

"That's no good, Skippy." He needed to work on his planning. "You'll survive, sure, to, what, drift in space forever?" The elevator stopped, the door opened and I stepped aboard the *Flower*.

"Unless the Thuranin take time to scan the debris field and find me, and decide to take me aboard. It's not any worse than me getting flung away in an escape pod, right before you nuke the *Dutchman*. So although it sucks, there's really no additional downside for me."

I stopped walking. "Yeah there is. Your whole plan sucks, Skippy." I turned around set him down on the floor of the elevator. Although when the elevator moved, he was going to fall on his side and roll around like a beer can, he would be safe.

"What are you doing, you dumb ape, we don't have time for this!" Skippy shouted.

"What I'm doing is plan C. I will stay aboard the *Flower* and let the Thuranin chase me, you do the rest of the stuff you said; distorting the wormhole, making the *Flower's* drive signature look like the *Dutchman's*, all that. You get my crew away from here." I knew enough of the *Flower's* flight control systems to manage a short flight with pre-programmed jumps, and a short flight was all it was going to be.

"Plan C is a stupid plan! Here's how you automatically know it's stupid; a monkey thought of it."

"Skippy," I took a deep breath to collect my thoughts, we didn't have a lot of time. "I'm not going to let you drift in space until the end of time, you've had enough loneliness for a thousand lifetimes. We humans owe you, big time, more than we can ever repay. And, damn it you little shithead, you're my, I can't believe I'm saying this, you're my friend." I hit the button to send the elevator back down.

"Wait!" The elevator door froze halfway closed. "Wait wait! Joe, you're going to do this, for me?"

"Somebody has to, Skippy, and I'm the one here right now." I hit the button again and the door slid an inch more toward closing. "Take care of my ship."

"Wait! Joe, I," his voice faded. "You know my memories aren't complete. I *know* they're not complete. Maybe they're not even real. But, I'm pretty sure that I never had a friend before. Never thought my first real friend would be a freakin' monkey," he finished with a disgusted grumble. "No, you know what? Fuck this. Fuck *THIS*!" His voice was loud enough to hurt my ears. "Bring me back to the *Dutchman's* bridge, I'm going to find us a way out of this. Time for me to use this ginormous damn brain I have. Joe, come on, move, I'm going silent for a bit. Please trust me."

Whatever Skippy was doing in there, and in whatever other spacetimes he occupied, the beer can was growing uncomfortably warm to the touch, I had to shift him from one hand to the other as I carried him back to the bridge

Everyone stared at me in shock. With a glance, I took in what I needed to know of our status; the jump drive held only a twenty eight percent charge, the process of calibrating the remaining jump drive coils was only thirty one percent complete, but there were no other ships in detection range.

"What happened?" Chang asked, while unbuckling from the command chair.

"Skippy has a new plan. Right, Skippy?" I set him in the receptacle we'd attached to the floor of the bridge, in a cramped corner. "A better plan," I said as I buckled into the command chair. "Skippy? Skippy? Come on, Skippy."

"I didn't say it was a better plan. It's a different plan. It's too late now for my original plan, thanks to you, Joe."

"What was Mr. Skippy's original plan?" Chang demanded. He was standing next to the command chair, someone else had taken his station in the CIC.

"I was going to heroically sacrifice myself for you lesser beings," Skippy explained. "Joe stopped me, because I would be an incalculable loss to the galaxy."

"Yeah, that's why," I snorted. "That, and the fact it was a stupid plan."

"It wasn't stupid! You had a twelve percent chance to escape!"

"Is that twelve, Skippy, or 'meh' twelve?"

"Eleven point five six four nine two, roughly. Close enough. Ok, that may have been somewhat optimistic. But at least seven percent, for sure."

"Yeah, I figured that. Tell me your new genius plan."

"That's the thing, Joe, I don't have a genius plan. I searched for records of ships that had escaped from similar situations, and there were none. Then I used my incredible brainpower to dream up a genius plan. And I got nothing. Nothing! No matter how I approached the situation, no matter how many variables I plugged in, I couldn't come up with any smart way out of this. So, I realized what we need is a stupid plan. And I have a stupid plan. Joe, even a monkey will think this plan is stupid. If this plan works, the *Dutchman* can escape."

"And if it doesn't work?"

"The *Dutchman* will be incinerated."

"That's not great."

"Hey, if this plan fails, you monkeys will simply be dead. I'll be trapped in the core of a dying star for trillions and trillions of years."

"Oh, hey, bonus. Why didn't you say that first? Sign me up. What are the odds of this plan succeeding?"

"Meh, probably somewhere south of fifty-fifty, maybe? I truly do not know. Nothing this stupid has ever been tried before in this galaxy. It's actually kind of exciting, Joe."

"This stupid? Like, rednecks-on-TV stupid?" I asked.

"Nothing is as stupid as that, Joe. But, for an AI like me, this approaches hold-my-beer-watch-this stupid."

I shook my head. "Skippy, you need to do a better job selling your ideas."

"Selling? Think about this, Joe, this could be your one big chance to achieve Florida man status."

"Florida?" I asked, puzzled, "I'm from Maine, dumbass."

"No," he said with an exasperated sigh, "I mean the classic Florida Man, like in the headlines. You know, 'Florida man eaten by pet alligator', or "Florida man, drunk, crashes car into police station', or 'Florida man, naked, runs-"

"We get the idea, Skippy. Fine, what are our odds without this plan?"

"Zero. That's not a 'meh' zero, it is zee-roh, Joe. By my estimate, we have at most one minute before the first Thuranin ship jumps in and detects us."

The display told me the jump engines now had barely a thirty percent charge. "Fine, great. Explain your pla-"

"Enemy ship jumped in!" Chang shouted. An angry triangle symbol was now on the display, far enough away that we should be able to dodge most of its particle beam shots, too close for comfort.

"We jump away now, Skippy?" I asked anxiously. Maybe I should have left him in the elevator and taken the *Flower* out myself as a decoy.

"No, Joe, jumping away now would be the smart thing to do. The smart thing to do has a zero chance of success, as I explained. Trust me, you will be awed by my stupidity."

We started Skippy's stupid plan with waiting another thirty five seconds, until three of the Thuranin destroyers jumped in, locked onto us with their sensor fields, and began firing missiles and maser beams. We waited, even though we could have managed a short jump away with a thirty percent jump engine charge. We almost cut it too close; maser beams knocked back our shields, and a missile got so close that fragments of its warhead hit one of our remaining functional reactors, and that reactor became less functional. Like, not at all.

When we finally did jump away, the word 'jump' was accurate but 'away' was not. A key stupidity in Skippy's stupid plan was jumping toward, not away from the star. By toward, I mean we jumped in close. Close enough that, if I could live on a star, I could see my house. Close enough that, deep as we now were in the star's gravity well, jumping back out would be difficult even for a ship with a full charge, a healthy set of coils, and a calibrated jump system. We didn't have any of those three critical assets. Jumping in close to the star, close enough that we needed our shields just to keep the ship from being fried, wasn't stupid enough for Skippy. As soon as we emerged from the jump point, we set course straight for the star and kicked the ship's tail, accelerated at maximum thrust, deeper into the gravity well. This was Skippy's hold-my-beer-watch-this moment.

The whole maneuver was sufficiently stupid that when the Thuranin destroyers jumped in behind us, they hesitated to follow us in. For a minute, they spread out and tried to hit us from long distance. There was so much interference from the star's hellish magnetic field that their own networked sensor fields couldn't target us. One of the little green men must have made a decision after their maser beams all missed and their missiles went off course, because the destroyers turned at the same time and burned hard in after us.

Here's the thing; star carriers can jump long distances, and jump again and again. That makes star carriers seem fast. They are not fast. What a star carrier can do is keep going, long after other ships have run out of charge or burned out their jump drive coils. In normal space, a star carrier handles like a big cruise ship, and the destroyers were like speedboats. A cruise ship can cross an ocean and leave any speedboats far behind after a while; over any short distance, a speedboat will run rings around a cruise ship. What this means is those destroyers gained on us quickly. Very quickly. To see how quickly they were closing the distance, I didn't need to look at the rapidly decreasing 'Range to Target' section of the main bridge display. I only needed to watch the triangle symbols of those five warships. Those triangles were swiftly moving across the display as I watched. In front of us on the display was the star, so close that the surface of the star was a straight line, not a curve at all. "Uh, Skippy, those ships are going to be on top of us in," now I did check the 'Estimated Time to Closure' section of the display, "seven minutes. We can't jump away this close to a star, and those destroyers are going to pound us to dust. If this is the stupid part of your plan, I don't want to see any more."

"Joe, I promise, you ain't seen stupid yet. Watch this."

In front of us on the display, the surface of the star was no longer a straight line, it had a distinct indent to the surface, like an invisible knife was pushing into it. The dent widened and grew deeper, so deep the display had to zoom outward. Holy shit, he was making a giant hole in the star. "I'm distorting spacetime," Skippy explained, "when I release the effect, that hole in the star is going to collapse and cause a massive solar flare. Like, a historic, holy-shit size solar flare. One way or the other, this will be majorly interesting."

"A solar flare that will incinerate the *Dutchman*?" The Thuranin destroyer squadron had seen the danger; they had turned around and were now burning at maximum thrust to get away from the star.

"Mmm, shmaybe. The really stupid part starts now. No one has ever tried this before, so hang on."

Skippy released the spacetime distortion of the star. On the display, the surface of the star rippled as it filled in the gap, then the surface erupted outward. Toward us. Fast.

"Skippy!" I shouted. The ship rocked.

"The star is collapsing; those are gravity waves hitting us at lightspeed. Jump option Zulu!" Skippy shouted back. "Now!"

How the hell were we supposed to jump so deep in a gravity well? The display showed the front edge of the enormous solar flare had almost engulfed us. There was no time to argue. "Pilot! Engage jump option Zulu," I ordered in as calm a voice as I could manage. If this didn't work, at least we wouldn't need nukes to vaporize any trace of evidence that humans were roaming the galaxy.

In front of me, Desai pressed the button to initiate the selected jump. Whatever Skippy was doing, the jump drive didn't like it; the whole ship flickered in and out of existence in my vision and shook violently. Displays went dark and some exploded, sending showers of sparks cascading through the bridge and CIC. The artificial gravity clicked off, then on heavily, then off again. I was flung around in the chair so viciously it seemed my neck would snap. There was a terribly deep wailing, moaning sound that grew louder and louder until my ears hurt, the lights went out-

CHAPTER THIRTEEN

Regaining consciousness, for me, was the sort of thing where you fall into bed outrageously drunk, the bed starts spinning and you snap awake because you're going to hurl the contents of your stomach onto the bed. Oh, right, sure, that's never happened to you? Liar. Anyway, in this case, I awoke while I was puking into my own lap, or trying to, some chunks hung briefly in the air as the artificial gravity was off, then on, then off again. The intermittent zero gee was making my stomach flutter. I clamped my mouth shut so if I puked again, I wouldn't spew it all over the bridge. And a headache, my head throbbed so bad it felt like my eyeballs would explode. "Skippy," I heard myself saying in a strangled voice. "Sitrep," was all I could manage to say at that moment.

"We have jumped past the edge of the star system. All five Thuranin destroyers were engulfed by the solar flare, there are no ships pursuing us currently. Artificial gravity has stabilized temporarily. There are numerous injuries to the crew, nothing serious." He didn't explain his definition of a 'serious' injury. "Damage to the ship is substantial."

"How bad is it?" I was afraid to hear the answer.

"Extremely, catastrophically bad. Shut up and let me talk for a minute." Skippy's voice was flat, none of the usual snarkiness. "Only reactors One and Five are online, I have initiated an emergency shut down of reactor Five because it's losing containment. As it is, the leak will result in additional damage to reactor Three, which is already shut down. Reactor One has a slight loss of containment, the major problem with One is that it has almost completely lost cooling capacity. Temperatures are in the red and if they continue to increase, and they will, there will be a catastrophic explosion that could destroy the aft part of the ship, including the remaining jump drives. Reactor One's coolant pump is making a sound like if you put a pack of hyenas in a blender, only louder. Therefore, I am shutting down reactor One also."

"The problem is a pump?" Seemed simple to me. "Can you fix it?"

"I called the 1-800 help line for the pump manufacturer, they transferred me to some guy named 'Bob' in Malaysia. The monsoon rain was pounding on his roof so bad I could barely hear him. He asked me to verify the pump was plugged in, then he suggested I turn it off, and back on again. That didn't help. Also, I'm pretty sure 'Bob' is not his real name," Skippy added quietly. "Joe, for crying out loud, if I could fix the pump, don't you think I would have done it already?! The pump isn't the only problem, the whole cooling system got peppered with shrapnel from a near-miss."

"The ship will completely lose pow-" I started to ask.

"I requested you to shut up while I'm talking, like that was ever going to happen." He sounded tired. "Correct. After the last two reactors shut down, the ship will have only backup power from the capacitors. There is enough charge in the jump drive coils for one more moderate jump; unfortunately such a jump will not get us to the next closest star system, and we clearly can't go back where we were. I expect the Thuranin will detect our current position within two hours; the gamma ray burst when we jumped in could not be masked, and as we are on the periphery of their star system, this area is highly likely to be within their sensor coverage. The Thuranin now know one of their own star carriers is hostile, they will be calling in reinforcements. Colonel, you may now speak."

"The situation can't be entirely hopeless, or you wouldn't have bothered to shut down the reactors. What are our options?" By options, I meant other than engaging the self-destruct.

SpecOps

"We have one option, well, two if you include self-destructing the ship. We use the remaining charge in the jump drive to leave this position as soon as possible, I am running a diagnostic on the jump drive coils now, to avoid rupturing the drive during a jump. Our jumps while we were within the dampening field, and then within my warpage of spacetime, caused severe damage to the drive coils. Only twenty seven percent of the drive coils can be trusted to function properly at this point."

"Jumping to the middle of interstellar space, with all the reactors dead and the capacitors draining, sounds like going from the fire into the frying pan, we're dead either way. Can the reactors be fixed?"

"The short answer is no. Not with the equipment onboard. Star carriers travel with a host of support vessels, and are not designed to sustain themselves for long-term operations. Spare parts, and the ability to manufacture replacement parts, are in short supply. The long answer is, shmaybe."

"Shmaybe?" I asked, surprised. This was the old Skippy I knew.

"Something short of a confident maybe. Given enough time, and raw materials, the ship might be restored to functioning. I have a plan. You are not going to like it."

Skippy was right. I didn't like it. I also didn't have a choice. Or a better idea.

Not having anything useful to do on the bridge, in a ship with no power, I helped clean up the mess. I talked to the crew briefly on the intercom, and headed off to the sick bay. Not surprisingly, none of the special forces were there although the injury report Skippy loaded onto my iPad listed several broken bones, concussions and soft tissue injuries like dislocated shoulders among our SpecOps super soldiers. They were taking care of each other, and remaining alert, as if they needed to be ready to repel boarders or some crazy stuff like that. They would report to the sickbay when I gave them an all clear signal. Maybe they simply needed to feel useful, I could understand that; I felt pretty useless myself at that moment. Chang had the conn, such that it was, and the duty crew in the CIC was monitoring our malfunctioning sensor field in case the Thuranin had an extra ship out there somewhere. Right now, even a Kristang dropship could have shot holes in us.

There were three of the science team in sickbay; one wrist sprain, one broken nose and bloody forehead combination, plus one broken leg. Doctor Skippy the mad scientist was taking care of them with his scary-looking robots. The science team heard my brief status report over the intercom and naturally had many questions, I had few answers. What I should have done is walk around the ship reassuring people. Instead, I took a brief break to splash water on my face and flush the puke taste out of my mouth.

In the cramped Thuranin bathroom, kneeling on the floor to reach the sink, I addressed Skippy, trying to talk to him the way I normally did, keep the fear out of my voice. "All right, Skippy, I have to give you props, even your stupid plans work great."

"Sure, sure, that's what happened. I'm a freakin' genius."

My Spidey sense tingled. He wasn't fooling me for a second. "You lying little jerk. Truth, Skippy. The truth shall set you free."

"I never understood that expression. Lying is so much easier, Joe."

"Now, Skippy."

"Well, heh, heh, here's the thing," he said, in his nervous tone that was the reason he could never successfully lie to me. "My original stupid plan was truly pure genius. The Thuranin would never have suspected us to try anything that stupid. After I created that solar flare, much bigger even than I had hoped, by the way, I didn't have much data on that star and I had to estimate the composition of its photosphere-"

"Get to the point, please, Skippy." My headache was killing me.

"After I triggered the solar flare, my plan was to distort spacetime in reverse; to flatten it enough right around the ship that we could jump away. I knew the Thuranin ships had no chance to escape; the gravity waves propagated at the speed of light, and those ships were too deep in the gravity well to jump away. The problem was, I'd never before flattened spacetime to that extent so deep in a gravity well. It was theoretically possible, however I didn't have the math for it. I had to guess, go in on blind faith, that was the stupid part."

"Ok, stupid, but, hey, it worked. We're alive. Mostly."

"You want the truth, Joe? It didn't work, not entirely, not the way I planned it." Skippy admitted sadly. "The flattening spacetime part, I mean. I couldn't make it hold long enough to get the ship all the way through the jump. The gravity waves made spacetime resonate in a way I couldn't predict, and I didn't have time to create a model and test it. I failed, I totally failed."

"Then how are we still alive?"

"You monkeys would describe it as luck. The gravity waves on this end of the wormhole caused a resonance in spacetime that made the wormhole fail as we entered it; the presence of the ship inside the wormhole made the resonance increase exponentially. The laws of physics here are an annoying pain most of the time, but in this case they saved our asses. Because the ship had already emerged from the far end of the wormhole before we entered it on the near end, it would have violated causality for the ship to be destroyed while in transit. The universe doesn't allow causality to be messed with in that way, so it collapsed all the probabilities except for the extremely unlikely one where we somehow survived the transit and emerged safely on the far end. It's kind of like sending a message via internet protocol; the message gets chopped up into bits that take different routes to the destination, then it is reassembled. That's why you were nauseous and now have a headache; your body was ripped apart at the subatomic level and reassembled many times. What you experienced. the ship seeming to blink in and out of existence, actually happened. Every time the ship was destroyed in transit, the universe hit the reset button and restored us to existence. Because it had to."

I shook my head in stunned disbelief. "Wait, we died? Except we didn't?"

"Correct. Because we hadn't died on the far end of the wormhole, we couldn't die on the near end, or in transit."

"Whoa."

"Whoa indeed. Joe, this is a tiny, tiny glimpse into how the universe truly works."

"Awesome! We can figure out the rest from here, huh?"

"Mmm, that would be a resounding no. Let me give you an example; a dog sees you bring a new bag of kibble into the house. The dog may see you getting the bag of kibble out of the car. You can even take the dog to the pet store with you, and the dog can see you take the bag of kibble off the shelf there. That does not mean the dog grasps the concept of where kibble really comes from. Or the concept of, well, concepts."

"Thank you for the big vote of confidence in us monkeys."

"I'm being realistic here, Joe. Your smartest theoretical physicists are still only staring at the garage door, thinking that is the magical source of endless kibble."

I wasn't going to argue with an AI about the merits of monkey brain power. "Let's keep this luck part between us, agreed? The crew needs to have confidence in you, misplaced as it is." I looked at myself in the mirror, a mirror we humans had installed, since Thuranin cyborgs had thought such things were foolish. Most of the vomit was off my uniform, or mashed enough into the digital camo pattern that it looked as if it belonged there. My face looked like hell. I needed sleep. As if that was going to happen any time soon. Unbelievable. I was alive only because the future me on the other end of the wormhole hadn't died. A thought occurred to me. "Wait. What did you say about the version of the *Dutchman* that came out of the wormhole? What do you mean 'version'?"

"Hmm. That's not something I can tell to monkeys. Shouldn't have mentioned it."

"Fine. I got a whopping headache anyway. What's next?"

We made one last jump using remaining power in the jump drive capacitors. Then we jumped again, and again, and again. Power for the jumps, and almost everything else aboard the *Dutchman*, came directly from Skippy; he pulled power from some other spacetime or from quantum bubbles or from magical fairy dust or some crazy shit like that. I didn't understand it and our science team, despite nodding their heads in deep thought, had no freakin' clue what Skippy was doing either. The problem with Skippy powering the ship is, whatever source he pulled power from was enormous, like a small star, and he wasn't able to regulate the power flow very well because he wasn't designed to do that. The result of him pulling in way too much power, was that we kept blowing systems all over the ship. Relays burned out, capacitors melted, anything related to electricity had a short life span, and it was a race against time; could Skippy get us to our destination before we blew every circuit in the ship?

To reduce power needs, we had no stealth field, shields were at minimum power to protect us only against microscopic impacts from space debris, and life support like heat, lights and oxygen recycling were cut back. Some parts of the ship were evacuated, so we could entirely cut power to those areas. Artificial gravity was lowered to 18%, that system's most efficient power setting other than being switched off. I wasn't ready for zero gee yet.

Eighteen people were living aboard the *Flower*, because that ship had plenty of power, although that little ship was pushing its limits to supply fresh oxygen and expel waste heat from eighteen living, breathing humans. The *Flower* had detached from its docking platform and was now grappled directly onto the *Dutchman's* spine frame; we'd moved the little ship closer so it could supply partial power to its mother ship. That hadn't worked well; Skippy had to jury-rig power transfer cables, and the two ships' systems weren't compatible. Conditions aboard the *Flower* were not only cramped, people there were living in the zero gee, because the Kristang didn't have artificial gravity technology. Our special forces saw this as an opportunity for zero gee combat training. That was a good idea, and it kept people busy and focused.

We all needed to keep busy, to keep our minds off our dilemma. Our destination was a marginally habitable planet, or more accurately a planet Skippy thought might be habitable, in that it supposedly had an oxygen atmosphere and temperatures within a range humans could survive. His information was sketchy, he got it third hand from the Thuranin, who got it from the Kristang, who got it from the Ruhar. The planet had been in Ruhar territory before the recent wormhole shift; no Ruhar lived there, which wasn't encouraging for us. The planet was now in Kristang territory, and apparently no lizards wanted to live there either. Also not encouraging.

The reason we had to abandon ship was that Skippy needed to repair it, rebuild it from the junk pile it had become. We were going to leave the *Flying Dutchman* in orbit around a gas giant planet, with Skippy remaining aboard by himself. He was going to mine the planet's numerous moons for raw materials, and mine the gas giant's atmosphere for reactor fuel. While Skippy was rebuilding the ship, it would be torn apart and unable to support life. Could Skippy essentially build us a new ship, from nothing much more than moondust and toxic gases? To the crew, he was supremely, arrogantly confident. To me, in private, not so much. "I won't know until I get under the hood," he told me, "could be expensive. You got insurance on this thing, right? Might want to think about a rental car."

When a car mechanic talked to me like that, he probably needed to make a payment on his boat. "Be serious for a moment, Skippy. Can you fix the ship?"

"That's not a yes or no question, Joe. Let's see if I can dumb this down enough for you; I don't have enough data now. The question is whether my repair effort will consume resources faster than I can create new ones, and I won't know that until I scan what raw materials are available. If I don't find critical elements quickly, or it takes too much energy to process the raw materials, then I'm on a downward spiral. Joe, I simply do not know. The only data I have on this system is a vague report the Kristang got from a Ruhar computer, when they captured Paradise. The Ruhar only cared whether the system held a habitable planet, data on the other planets is very thin. I'm guessing. We don't have another survivable option in range."

"Oh," I said, "uh, about that rental car?"

The *Flying Dutchman* limped into orbit around the gas giant, an orbit that was barely adequate for Skippy's needs. The bottom of the orbit dipped too close to the cloud tops, while the other end of the orbit swung inconveniently far away. With the ship completely drained of all but emergency power, there was no energy to spare for altering the *Dutchman's* orbit. Skippy said he could live with it.

The first thing Skippy did was listen for any sign of other ships in the star system, and he didn't find anything. If there was a ship, it was silent and stealthed, and we couldn't do anything about it. Any ship that had been in the system long-term, even stealthed, would have left a trail of exhaust and other gases. Skippy didn't see anything like that, and there didn't seem to be any point for a ship to be stealthed, so far inside Thuranin-Kristang territory.

Next, he checked out the second planet from the star, the place we humans would be living while Skippy pimped our ride by himself. At that moment, the second planet was on the other side of the star system, only a couple of weeks from swinging completely behind the star.

"Sir?" Adams asked while we were all still reading through Skippy's data. "What do we call the planet?"

"Which one," I asked. "The one we'll be living on, or this gas giant? Oh, duh, the one we'll be living on, of course." Nobody cared about Skippy's gas station, which was all the giant planet meant to us; a source of helium 3. According to Skippy's preliminary data, the second planet in the system, the only one that could support human life, was only marginally habitable. And that was the 'good' news. Its orbit was elliptical rather than round, so each year it swung far away from the star, then much closer. That planet's funky orbit took it close to the outer edge, then inside the middle of the 'Goldilocks Zone', where it was not too hot and not too cold for life. The planet was frozen most of its year, with only part of the surface along the equator thawing as it swung closer to the star. Another piece of good news is the planet was approaching the summer part of its orbit; it should become marginally warmer while we lived there. Oxygen levels in the habitable area were low, equivalent to ten thousand feet elevation on Earth, while gravity was fourteen percent stronger than Earth normal. And, because we were on a stolen Thuranin ship, the artificial gravity aboard the *Dutchman* was normally set at 83% of Earth normal. At my request, Skippy had been able to goose up the gravity to 87% of Earth normal, still, setting down on the planet would be a 31% increase over the gravity we'd gotten used to aboard the ship. And since the battle, gravity aboard the ship had been much lower. The sudden increase in weight was going to be tough. Life there, when not covered under snow and ice, consisted of simple grasses, moss and lichen, the type of plants you would find in the tundra of Canada or Siberia. Skippy detected substantially more life in the oceans than on the land, but most of the oceans were covered by ice just like the land. The place was chilly, heavy and hard to breathe. Definitely not Paradise. "It's cold."

"We should call it Hoth." Williams suggested.

"Hoth?" I asked. "Why's that?"

"Hoth. You know, the ice planet where the rebels had their base in 'The Empire Strikes Back'. Star Wars."

"Oh, yeah." I remembered now. "No, we're not calling it Hoth, sounds too much like 'hot'. This planet is a crappy place. Nobody *wants* to be there, we're only going there because we have to, and we're leaving as soon as we can."

Seager snorted from the pilot seat. "Sounds like Newark."

"Newark?" I asked.

"You ever fly through Newark?" Seager shrugged. "Lots of people go through Newark, but no one *wants* to be there."

Adams and I shared an amused look. "I like it." Adams said.

Wracking my brain, I tried to remember whether any of our Merry Band of Pirates was from Newark. Or New Jersey in general. "What the hell, why not? Newark it is."

"Uh, oh. Damn." Skippy said. "Joe, we have a major complication. There is a group of Kristang on the planet."

"What?" My heart sank. The *Dutchman* was dead; we couldn't live on the ship while it was being repaired. We couldn't live on a planet occupied by Kristang either. There was no other option. We came all this way, for nothing? "What the hell are they doing there?"

"Wait, wait, I'm still processing the data, this may not be a total disaster. It is a small group; they do not have a ship with them. The data I have comes from the two small satellites they have in orbit. I think, hmm, it appears they are a small group, around thirty, that were landed there to search for remains of an Elder ship crash. Hmm, that certainly sounds familiar, huh? They have one base and only two, maybe three aircraft, they stay close to the main crash site. They're not warriors, they're scavengers. Joe, I think you can land on another part of the planet, and remain concealed. Their satellites, I can hack into and filter data the satellites transmit, so the Kristang will not know you are there."

"Concealing the presence of seventy humans is going to be one hell of a magic trick, Skippy."

"Hey, they don't call me Skippy the Magnificent for nothing."

"Nobody calls you Skippy the Magnificent."

He sniffed. "Well, they should. We will need a closer look at these Kristang, that can be part of the *Flower's* recon mission. I am now scanning this planet's moons to determine whether the proper raw materials to repair the ship are available in sufficient quantity."

"Great, send what you have to our science team, I'm going to talk to them." They'd want to show their findings to me anyway. "Sergeant Adams, you have the, uh," since there was nothing to conn aboard a dead ship, "the chair."

On my way to the ship's science lab, which was only an empty cargo bay that held tables covered with computers and all sorts of scientific instruments, I stopped to talk with Major Simms. She was organizing the effort to identify and pack up everything we needed to survive for months on the ice planet; I needed to remember to call it 'Newark'. She was beyond busy, helping her sort through a mountain of gear were the British SAS team and the Chinese 'Night Tiger' special forces. The Brits and Chinese worked well together, their commanders got along well, so at Lt Colonel Chang's suggestion, I assigned them to officially be a team. "Major Simms, how is it going?"

"Busy, sir," she said in a tone that implied my dropping by to ask stupid questions was anything but helpful. She tapped her iPad, everyone was studying their tablets intently. "We just received the preliminary data on the planet, we're really going to call it 'Newark'?" She didn't wait for an answer. "The gravity and low oxygen levels we can simply deal with," the Chinese and British team leaders nodded stoically, "the cold we'll have to plan for. Daytime high temperatures can be briefly pleasant in the peak of summer, almost 18 degrees." For a moment I was startled, until I realized she was talking about temperatures in Celsius, and I had to mentally convert to Fahrenheit, that was, uh, around 65 degrees. Pleasant. "That isn't the norm," she warned, "during winter, this place has snow even at the equator."

"You heard about the Kristang there?" I asked.

"Just did," she nodded, and the special forces looked grim. "Until you tell me otherwise, sir, I'm preparing to evacuate us to Newark."

"Carry on." I didn't know what else to say at the moment, because I didn't know what to do about the Kristang either. A small group on the surface, without a space-capable ship, would be an easy target for even the *Flower's* meager weapons load. I needed to balance the convenience of eliminating a minor threat, with the greater threat of a Kristang ship arriving to pick up the scavengers, and finding them all dead from orbital strikes. Such a ship would scan the surface intently and inevitably find us; and they might even find the *Dutchman*. I needed to think long and hard about our options. My options. It would be my decision; I was the commander.

Crap. I realized with a shock that, somehow, I had become that upper-echelon asshole who made dumbass decisions and made people's life miserable. When I was a private, then a specialist and then a sergeant, I had hated those dumbasses. And now, I was one.

The entire science team, including the three walking wounded, were gathered in their lab, talking excitedly. "Colonel J- Bishop!" Dr. Venkman called me over, almost referring to me by the nickname Skippy used. "Mr. Skippy just reported that this planet and its moons, are adequate for repairing the ship. He asked me to tell you that he has found sufficient quantities of raw materials, including the critical elements vanadium, rhenium and bismuth."

"Great, uh," I was super self-conscious of my ignorance in a roomful of certified geniuses, "what are those?"

"Vanadium and rhenium are transition metals," she could tell by the blank look on my face that I had absolutely no idea what she was talking about. "They are valuable metals; we do not yet understand why they are needed in large quantities to repair the ship. As to bismuth," she made an exaggerated shrug.

"Isn't that," I guessed, "used in pepto bismol? Like when you have an upset stomach?"

"Bismuth subsalicylate, yes." She shook her head. "We do not know why it would be useful here; on Earth it is often used as a less toxic substitute for lead. Bismuth is a post-transition metal that is the most diamagnetic element," she paused, sparing me further embarrassment. "It is apparently good news, anyway."

"That is good news, yeah," I agreed. Skippy could fix the ship with the materials at hand, that was one less thing to worry about. We still had that other major problem. "You may not have heard yet, there is a group of Kristang on the planet. We are, uh, we're calling the planet Newark."

"We just heard about the Kristang," she said, glancing at her tablet. "What are we going to do about them, Colonel?" She couldn't keep the anxiety out of her voice.

I could sympathize with her, the science team knew they were completely reliant on the military to deal with the Kristang, all they could do was analyze the scientific crumbs Skippy threw their way and hope the *Dutchman's* crew kept them safe. "We are considering options, Dr. Venkman, Skippy is still analyzing the data. We'll be sending the *Flower* out to recon the planet, and assess the threat the Kristang pose to us." Unspoken was that one of our options was self-destructing the ship. I didn't like that one.

Back on the bridge, I was looking at the sensor data on my iPad. Those Kristang could be a major, show-stopping problem. And, it occurred to me right then, we might have another huge problem. "Skippy, during the battle, our stealth field was down?" Over in the CIC, I could see people nodding 'yes' slowly in answer to my question.

"After the first hit, yes," Skippy answered. "It was partially down, because I had to divert power to the shields."

This is what I'd been afraid of. "The Thuranin now are aware that one of their own star carriers is hostile."

"Yes, however, I must point out, I altered our jump drive signature to make us appear to be that star carrier that disappeared seventeen years ago, as we discussed."

"Great, excellent." One less thing for me to worry about.

Chang looked puzzled. "What star carrier?"

Damn it, I should have told people about that, it had slipped my mind. That's what happens when I have late night conversations with Skippy. "I'll explain later. It is some good news."

Simms looked at me pointedly, unhappy that there was something I hadn't told my command crew. "We can use some good news now. Sir." There was a distinct pause before she'd added the 'sir'.

She'd made her point, people needed me to explain right then. I turned the chair to face the CIC. "There was a Thuranin star carrier, very similar to the *Dutchman*, that disappeared seventeen years ago; the Thuranin think the Kristang stole it. Skippy altered our jump drive signature so the *Dutchman* appears to be that missing ship, instead of this ship that mysteriously disappeared near Paradise where humans are living. Hopefully this will throw the Thuranin's suspicions away from humans and onto the Kristang. It should keep them chasing ghosts for a while. Skippy, no way the Thuranin know there are humans aboard this ship?"

"No way, Joe. In order for the Thuranin to know that, they would have to get close enough to actively scan this ship with our stealth field deactivated, and that never happened. Your secret is still safe, Joe. The slow, clumsy way this ship flew and reacted during the battle, would lead the Thuranin to suspect this ship is being flown by a lower-tech species. However, as we discussed, the Thuranin will suspect the Kristang; there is no reason they would consider humans as being involved in any way." Skippy paused. "Oh. Hmm. Captain Desai, I did not mean to disparage your piloting abilities."

"I understood what you meant, Mr. Skippy," Desai responded. She had done her best to keep the *Dutchman* out of the line of fire during the battle; still the ship had been struck by maser beams many more time that it would have had Thuranin cyborgs been in command.

From the expression on the faces of people in the CIC, including Chang and Simms, the crew was not happy about me neglecting to mention that I had inquired about whether our star carrier was unique enough to be immediately identifiable. They were right to be upset; I should have told them. I thought of another problem, and zoomed out on the main bridge display. "Newark is on the other side of the star now, right? Not completely, close enough."

"Yes."

"How are we going to talk, when we're down there, and you're way up here? There will be a time lag of, what? An hour?"

"Light will take around hour to travel one way, yes, and the problem will grow worse as Newark's orbit takes it further away."

I shook my head. "That is unsat. Isn't there some sort of Skippy magic you can do, to speed up our communications? What if you get stuck on a crossword puzzle, and you need my help?"

"Like if the clue is 'feline', three letters, and it starts with 'C' and 'A'?"

"Yeah, see? I can tell you the answer is not 'pussy' like you were thinking." I caught a glance from Simms in the CIC when I made that remark. Damn it, this is why I liked to have conversations with Skippy in private, so I didn't have to watch what I was saying. Also so people couldn't hear him insult me frequently.

"If either of us is thinking about pussy, it's not me, Joey. To be serious, yes, there is Skippy magic I will be using. I'm going to create a microwormhole we can use to communicate through. One end of the wormhole will be with me; the other end of the wormhole will be in geosynchronous orbit around Newark. For your benefit, Joe, that means-"

"I know what a geosynchronous orbit is, Skippy. On Earth, it means the satellite is parked 22,500 miles above the equator, so it is always at the same place in the sky as the Earth rotates. That's because at that altitude, the satellite is moving at the same speed as the Earth's equator rotates."

Silence.

He got me worried. "Skippy? Hello?"

"Sorry, you just completely blew my mind for a minute. How do *you* know that?"

Feeling mildly insulted, I explained. "A guy tried to sell my parents a satellite TV system, and I had to explain to them why the pizza box dish antenna needs to point low in the southern sky, like over Brazil. I looked it up on Wikipedia."

"Is all your scientific knowledge based on internet articles?"

"No, Skippy, of course not. I also used to watch the Discovery channel."

"There is no hope for your species," he said sadly. "You monkeys should surrender to the cockroaches immediately, and get it over with. You, for one, should welcome your new cockroach overlords."

"Hey, cockroaches may eat stuffed-crust pizza, but did they invent stuffed-crust pizza? I don't *think* so."

"Stuffed-crust pizza?" Skippy said slowly. "Your species' single contribution to galactic culture."

"You forgot fantasy sports, Skippy."

"I rest my case."

"Great. This microwormhole dingus means we'll be in constant communication, then?"

"Not quite. Even Skippy magic can screw with the laws of physics in this spacetime only so much. On my own, I can't project a wormhole that far. And a jump breaks the connection between wormholes, so the *Flower* can't carry the wormhole for me. I have modified a missile to carry the other end of the wormhole; as soon as it is ready, I will launch it toward Newark. The missile will take five days to get there, because I have to save more than half its fuel to slow down once it gets there, to maneuver the wormhole into orbit. The missile will launch before the *Flower* returns, however, for your first several days on the surface there will be a major time lag in our communications. It is vital that during those days, you make an exceptional effort to avoid doing anything stupid."

"Hey, no worries, Skippy, it's me."

"Exactly what I'm afraid of."

CHAPTER FOURTEEN

The communications time lag wasn't a problem only when the crew was on Newark, it also meant I would have no idea what was going on with the *Flower*, until that ship returned from its scouting mission. In making plans, we had discussed the possibility of the *Flower* using its armaments to pound the Kristang settlement from orbit, and eliminate the threat entirely. As a frigate, the *Flower* wasn't designed for orbital bombardment, but it did have a railgun and we could make do. We'd discarded that idea for two reasons. If the first shot didn't take out every single one of the Kristang, we'd have a hell of a time hunting them all down. We had no certain knowledge whether the Kristang were all in one place, or scattered across the planet. We couldn't afford to have the *Flower* lingering in orbit for a long time, exposed, searching for Kristang one by one. Second, and most important, our entire plan hinged on our presence on Newark not being detected. If we were discovered, the Kristang there could call for help, and then we'd be screwed whether we had a beat-up stolen frigate or not. If, or maybe when, a Kristang ship arrived to pick up the lizards on the surface, it would not be good for that ship to find all the lizards on the surface dead, with evidence of them having been attacked from orbit. That would cause the Kristang to intensely scan the surface. And inevitably find us. No, what we wanted, if a Kristang ship arrived, was to find only a bored, desperate gang of lizards who wanted to get off the surface and depart Newark as soon as possible. We wanted them to find that, and nothing else.

To prevent the Kristang on the surface from detecting a human presence on Newark, Skippy had another trick up his sleeve. Because he couldn't get close enough to handle it himself, he had loaded a submind into the computer system of the *Flower*, complaining all the time that the frigate barely had memory storage enough to hold a dumdum monkey brain, and was completely inadequate to contain a useful AI submind. Even stripping out the Kristang software completely, the dumbed-down submind was dangerously unstable, and we had to hope it would survive long enough to do its job before it broke down.

The submind's job was to infiltrate the two small satellites the Kristang had in orbit. Infiltrate, and over write the existing processing system, so the satellites would from then on ignore any images or sensor data about humans on or around Newark. When the Kristang scavengers looked at the surface from a satellite camera, if those satellite cameras or sensors were pointed at a human settlement, the Kristang would not see anything unnatural. The images would be edited in real time to show nothing but blank, boring snow, mud and tundra. If that worked, we only had to worry about a Kristang aircraft flying over us and someone looking out the window. Hopefully, that was unlikely, and from our own satellites, we would have plenty of warning if a Kristang aircraft approached where we were hiding.

The *Flower* was going to drop off two tiny, stealthed Thuranin satellites for our use. One satellite would be in polar orbit to cover the planet's entire surface once each day, the other would be moved in geosynchronous orbit above our hiding place, after we decided where that was. Skippy could access satellite data through the microwormhole, and we could access the satellites in real-time, through an encrypted tight-beam laserlink. The only way the Kristang could detect the satellite feed is if one of their aircraft happened to fly through the communications laser beam, a beam less than a human hair in diameter. Since we would be able to see their aircraft approaching, and be able to see everything the Kristang were doing and intercept all their communications, it would be impossible for them to sneak up on us.

SpecOps

All this was according to Skippy, who would be by himself at Skippy's Garage and Gas Station on the other side of the star system.

I had faith in Skippy, he had certainly earned it. What bothered me was not our plans, or our ability to implement such plans, or the top-notch people I was privileged to have under my command. What bothered me was our rotten luck.

Lt. Colonel Chang had told me, back when I was trying to convince our original Merry Band of Pirates on Paradise to follow me on an ill-defined, ultra-high-risk mission, that he agreed to sign on not because I was brave, or smart, but because I, somehow, was *lucky*. That I had a knack for being in the right, or wrong depending how you looked at it, place at the right time. I do not believe in astrology, or numerology, or any of an infinite number of increasingly whacky conspiracy theories, but there was no one who could deny that luck was a real thing. Skippy had hinted more than once that there was no such thing as luck, that humans conceived of 'luck' because we had no idea how the universe truly worked.

Whatever.

What I knew for sure was that our 'luck' so far on this mission was crap. Places where we should have found Skippy's magic radio for talking to the Collective were empty, or mysteriously blown apart. The mission had lasted longer than it should have, because things that should have been in a place, were not in that place. For no logical reason Skippy could explain. In fact, against all logic Skippy knew of. Rotten luck.

Then, we'd jumped into a trap, a trap that could not have been set for the *Dutchman*; no way could the Thuranin have anticipated the *Dutchman* would arrive, there at that time. A trap we'd barely escaped from.

Now, against all odds, we had managed to travel between stars, in a ship with no functioning reactors/ Travelled to an unwanted, useless star system that no one cared about, and what do we find in the middle of nowhere? A group of Kristang! Crap! What the hell were Kristang doing on Newark? What are the odds, right? That is totally rotten luck. Rotten luck that made me afraid that my good luck had run out, and it would all be downhill from here. Downhill for all of us, not only for me. Was this karma coming back to bite me in the ass? Had I been so lucky in the past that I'd cashed in all those chips, and now I was in debt to the house?

I felt useless, sitting aboard the Dutchman doing nothing, while Chang was on a scouting mission with the *Flower*. "Skippy," I asked, "you're sure none of us could stay behind to help fix the ship?"

"Help from monkeys? By doing what? Burping and scratching yourselves?"

"No, Skippy," I was heartened to hear he'd gotten a bit of his snarkiness back. "I'm talking about us burping and scratching ourselves *at the same time*."

"Oh, well, then. That changes things. In that case, no. Joe, I'd love someone to stay aboard to give me someone to talk to. No offense, you all need to get off the ship. There isn't going to be any oxygen here, most of the ship won't have any atmosphere at all part of the time. Until I can get a reactor back online, the shield generators are going to be dead soon, and the radiation will kill you biologicals."

Biologicals? That was an improvement over 'meatsacks', Skippy may be warming up to us. "Still, five months? Five months is a long time." Skippy would be alone aboard the *Dutchman*. The entire crew would be stranded on an unknown, unexplored planet.

"Long? Five short months is a genuine grade-A freakin' Skippy miracle. Joe, to rebuild this ship, I have to use raw materials, scavenged from the ship and gathered from the planet's moons. In order to build the tools I need, I first have to build other tools, to build other tools, to finally build the tools to fix the ship. Then I have to begin fixing the ship. You know those so-called reality shows, where some scruffy-looking guy is out in the wilderness, all he has is a knife, and he's supposed to survive for a month?"

"A knife, plus a camera crew with satellite phones and a helicopter?" I pointed out. "But yeah, I know what you mean."

"That guy on TV has at least has a knife. I'm starting with only a paper clip, and I'm rebuilding a gosh-darn starship." Skippy complained. "You're right, that guy on TV has a camera crew if he gets in trouble. All I have is a barrel of monkeys, and you'll be way over on the other side of the star system. If something bad happens before the *Flying Dutchman* is ready, like if a Thuranin ship arrives looking for us, we are all totally, totally screwed."

"Yeah, I know. I'd be more comfortable if we had some margin for error. You really need the *Flower*?"

"Absolutely. First, I need that ship to dip into the gas giant's atmosphere for collecting helium 3 to refuel the reactors. After that, the *Flower* contains materials not readily available in this planet's moons or ring system, so that frigate and our old busted up Ruhar Dodo, have to be sacrificed to rebuild the *Dutchman*."

"I understand that. My problem is you have all your chips on the table. All three Thuranin dropships have to stay here? One of them can't stay with us on the planet? With those Kristang hanging around, we'll be sitting ducks if the only way we can get around is by walking."

"Sorry Joe, no can do. I'll be mining this planet's moons and rings with those dropships, and with robots that weren't designed to operate independently of the ship. Leaving a single dropship with you would increase my estimated repair time from five months to seven. That is two additional months, during which the Kristang on the planet might discover your presence. Or a Kristang ship might arrive to pick them up, and detect you from orbit. Or a Thuranin scouting force may come to this star system and find our stolen star carrier. We have to balance the risks."

"You're right, you're right." I would have made the same call. In fact, I did, the first time Skippy explained his plan to me.

I still didn't like it.

The *Flower* jumped back in from its scouting mission, right on time. It would take the frigate over two hours to match course with the dead and drifting *Dutchman*, so Chang transmitted his data immediately. There was no reason to wait. We couldn't wait. Conditions aboard the star carrier were becoming unlivable, we needed to get off the ship soon. Or not. It was my decision. I needed intel.

Skippy pored through the data recovered from our stealth satellites, the Kristang satellites that Skippy's submind had successfully infiltrated, and Kristang databanks on the ground. It was, as Skippy was fond of saying, good news and bad news. His initial guess about the Kristang group there was correct; they were a scavenger crew that had been dropped off almost a year ago, to comb the surface of Newark for the debris of a crashed Elder starship. Their leader was a third son of a second-tier leader of a minor clan; as such, he was desperate to recover something useful to raise his family's fortunes within the clan. With him, he had five other semi-trusted clan brothers, and twenty eight forced laborers. The forced labor came from Kristang who were criminals, or slaves captured from other clans, or clan brothers whose families were deeply in debt and had sent their sons to work off part of the debt.

The scavengers were a low-budget group, using second or third-hand, worn-out equipment without sufficient spare parts or expertise for properly maintaining the equipment. Originally, they had a beat-up dropship and two aircraft. One of the aircraft had crashed near their base, and the leader didn't want to risk flying their only dropship, so they had one functional aircraft. They had six sets of powered armor suits, two of which were no longer working. And since they landed a year ago, five laborers had died in accidents, plus another two had been executed for disobedience. Morale in the scavenger group was bad, to say the least. They were all males, not even a single female with them. They had no fresh food, not even for the leaders. Their base camp was cramped with limited recreation facilities, their one medic had died in an accident, and their medical treatment capability was provided by an AI that worked only about half the time. From their records Skippy had access to, the Kristang had remained within 300 kilometers of their base, that was where the debris from the crashed Elder ship was buried. All that was good news for us.

The bad news was about geography. Only the equator of the planet was livable, the remainder of that world was frozen solid, with awful weather and temperatures humans couldn't survive, and the ice pack and glaciers closer to the equator were mushy from the summer warming, with the surface there too treacherous for habitation. The last thing we wanted was for an ice cavern to collapse on us. Of the land exposed along the equator, much of it was frigid swamp and spongy thawing tundra, with no place for us to burrow into and hide. Three quarters of the equator was ocean, there wasn't a lot of real estate for us to choose from. The site Skippy recommended was uncomfortably close to the Kristang base, less than 1300 kilometers to the east. The terrain there was grassland, eroded canyons and hills, with caverns Skippy thought would be good places to take shelter away from prying eyes.

"You have scans of the subsurface?" I asked. "Show me."

The display zoomed in on the area Skippy suggested we take shelter; first a regular video image, then it flipped to show what lay beneath the surface. "The satellites we have aren't designed for this sort of scanning," he explained, "I'm having to make do. See the caverns?"

There were pockets, some of them extensive, under the surface. Unfortunately, as I played with the display, most of the caverns big enough to be useful for shelter were deep underground, and either not connected to the surface at all, or connected only by a narrow passage. That was no good for our purposes, we couldn't take the time to excavate a cavern, and we had to be careful not to leave a debris pile on the surface. "Mmm, hey, how about this?" There was an area of canyons and caverns a hundred kilometers north of the place Skippy recommended. "These caverns are big enough." Some of the caverns were shallow, large openings but they didn't go deep enough into the side of the canyons to provide real shelter.

"That is a possibility, I didn't think you would want to be in an area of canyons. Some of those canyons are subject to flash flooding in summer, as the glaciers melt."

"I hear you, Skippy, that's a good point. What I need is to talk with a geologist."

We had one geologist on the science team, technically she had only minored in geology, her focus was astrophysics. Dr. Kassner came to my office, since the whole science lab was in an area of the ship that currently had no heat, power, artificial gravity or breathable air.

"What about this area," I asked, pointing to the canyon lands on my tablet. "Some of these caverns appear to be large enough to house us, and deep enough into the hillside to keep us out of sight."

"We won't be in tents, then?" Kassner asked with a frown, brushing a stray lock of blonde hair away from her face.

I shook my head. "No. Tents are too visible. If the Kristang fly an aircraft over the area, we can't risk them seeing anything. We will have warning of their aircraft approaching; it may not be enough time for us to strike the tents and get everything hidden. I don't want to take that risk. Besides, the weather on this planet can be harsh, I'd rather everyone is in a relatively dry cave, than in damp tents on the surface."

"Dry may be a relative term," Kassner mused, "these canyons channel melt water in the summers, you can see erosion layers, recent, last season. We also don't know how shallow the water table is in this area, caverns could flood from the bottom. Colonel," she said while nervously tugging on her ponytail, "you understand that the last time I seriously studied geology was twenty years ago."

"I know that I'm asking you to guess-"

"We don't have enough data, historical data," she protested.

"How about this, then," I said, "are these caverns structurally sound? Flooding is a potential problem we can deal with, a roof collapsing on us isn't."

Kassner frowned as she manipulated the images, going deeper underground. "Do you need an answer right now?"

"No." Realistically, I didn't need an answer until the *Flower* docked with the ship loaded with supplies and people, and was ready to jump again. At that point, Chang did need to know where his dropships were going to land. And, whether we were going to Newark at all. Simms had a small mountain of supplies organized and ready to be loaded aboard the *Flower*, enough supplies for eight months, as a precaution in case Skippy ran into problems rebuilding the *Dutchman*. Major Simms had hardly slept. As our only logistics specialist, she had to figure not only what supplies we needed, and how much, she needed to have everything organized so that the first two dropships to land contained the equipment the first wave of people needed. Combat loading, we called that in the military; weapons were unloaded first, socks were unloaded last. The two dropships were being loaded now, Chang hadn't needed them aboard the *Flower* for his scouting mission. "No, Doctor, I'll need an answer in about ten hours. Talk to Skippy, pull in whoever you need. Keep in mind, whatever site you recommend will be where we'll be living for the next five to eight months. Comfort is not our major priority, safety and concealment are."

We had enough data about Newark, and the Kristang there, to make a decision. Not only a decision about where to land on Newark, a more basic decision about whether to land there at all. Whether to take the risk of us being on Newark. To advise me, I called together my command crew of Chang, Simms and Adams, plus the five SpecOps team leaders, in the CIC. With much of the ship closed off, the CIC was the only compartment large enough for a meeting of more than four people, unless we all stood in a corridor. As there was nothing much for a crew to do in the CIC with the ship dead and drifting, I had cleared the compartment.

"Thank you," I said, as a harried-looking Major Simms came into the CIC, a portable oxygen mask still hanging from her neck. She'd been down in the cargo bays, supervising the teams packing supplies for Newark, and Skippy had been forced to cut off the fresh oxygen supply to that area of the ship. "Now that we're all here, I need your advice. We now have enough information about Newark to know that we can survive down there, and we know that we soon will not be able to survive aboard this ship. We also have information about the Kristang on Newark, and we have a limited, substantial but limited, ability to mask our presence on the planet from the Kristang. The question is whether we can take the risk of going down to Newark and-"

"My advice," Skippy interrupted, "is you go down there, you dumdums. That's why we came all the way here! What else are-"

It was my turn to interrupt him. "Skippy, I appreciate if you can provide information, but this primarily affects us humans, and this needs to be our decision."

"No, Joe. You are the commander. This is *your* decision," he said simply, and the people in the CIC all nodded. "You once told me that one of the drawbacks to being in the military, is that the chain of command requires you to put your life in the hands of people who may be idiots. Today, you are that potential idiot. I trust you will do your best to make a wise decision. Joe, I will refrain from comment, unless you request me to join the discussion."

"Thank you, Skippy. The question is whether we can take the risk of going down to Newark. Not risk to us, because if we don't go to Newark, there is a hundred percent certainty that we will not survive. Once Skippy begins tearing the ship apart to fix it, there will be no oxygen, and lethal levels of radiation. The risk we have to consider is the risk to Earth; the risk that our presence on Newark may be discovered, and Earth could be targeted by aliens, regardless of whether the wormhole is available to shorten their trip there. When we came out here, our mission was simple; we assist Skippy in contacting the Collective, and we do not take any risks with aliens discovering that humans are roaming the galaxy in a pirate ship."

"Except that's not quite true, is it, sir?" The SAS team leader Captain Smythe observed. I still found it jarring that a bad-ass soldier spoke with such a refined British accent. Smythe was SAS, he could probably kill me with a paper clip, any of the special forces could. With his oh-so-proper accent Smythe sounded like he would kill me, then apologize for not having been quite sporting about it, terribly sorry old chap, that sort of thing. "Our prime mission objective is not *zero* risk that other species will learn we humans are out here roaming around as you say, the objective is *minimal* risk. Otherwise, Colonel, you could have detonated a nuke as soon as our friend Skippy shut down the wormhole." He looked around the CIC. "We all know the stated mission objectives. We also know what hasn't been said, not openly."

"Go on, Captain Smythe," I said. I wanted a frank and open discussion, and I was getting one, this was good. The people in the CIC all had far more experience that I did with making command decisions, I needed to listen to them.

Smythe continued "First, our true mission out here is to assure this Skippy being doesn't decide that we're not upholding our end of the bargain, and reopens the wormhole near Earth out of spite." He glanced at the speaker in the ceiling, we all expected Skippy to respond to that remark. When Skippy stayed silent, Smythe pressed onward. "Our second unstated objective is to hopefully return home in the *Flying Dutchman*, so humanity will have an advanced starship to take apart and study. We all believe aliens have no access to Earth now, that may not be true in the future. Colonel, you found a way to manipulate wormholes, who is to say some other species will not gain the same capability? Or these periodic wormhole shifts could bring our local wormhole back to life."

Skippy had told me our local wormhole was dead, shut down, that the connection to its power source was severed. He hadn't specifically assured me that wormhole could never come back to life on its own. Damn it, I should have asked him about that.

Smythe continued, looking straight at me. "Some of you Americans, before the Second World War, believed that because you are separated from most of the world by two great oceans, you need not fear invasion; that the problems of the world were not your problems. Our entire planet now faces a similar situation; we are protected by vast interstellar distances, for now. That happy circumstance will not continue forever. We need the technology of this ship to enable humanity to leap forward, so that when trouble does come knocking on our door, we will be ready. We all know trouble will come knocking, someday." There were nodding heads all around the CIC at that remark.

Smythe's comments opened the floodgates; everyone wanted to weigh in on the decision, for or against. After ten minutes of spirited discussion, all eyes turned to Captain Xho, leader of the Chinese 'Night Tiger' special forces team. He had been mostly silent, until he cleared his throat, and people waited for him to speak. "Captain Smythe, what you said is true; there is no question that we need," he pointed at the deck, "the technology of this ship. This is a matter of balancing risk and reward, the risk of our presence on Newark being discovered, against the possibility of bringing this ship home without Mr. Skippy. My pilots, and our scientific staff," I assume he meant the Chinese contingent, "have told me there is very little chance we can fly this ship all the way home, without our benevolent AI friend helping us. We must weigh the very slender possibility of the *Dutchman* returning home, against what I believe to be the very real risk of the Kristang learning we are on Newark. We control the satellites, certainly. What will happen if, when, a Kristang ship jumps into orbit to retrieve their scavenger team? That ship's sensors would surely detect us."

That started another round of discussion, this time not about whether should land on Newark at all, but about what level of risk was acceptable. Essentially, about how confident we were about our ability to remain undetected. And what we could do to minimize the risk.

After another twenty minutes, everyone had said all there was to say. The British, Indian and SEAL and Ranger commanders were in favor of landing on Newark. The Chinese and French commanders were against taking the risk of landing. That Renee Giraud was against landing surprised me. "There must be an alternative, and if not," he shrugged, "I didn't expect to live this long, Colonel."

There it was; four experienced combat commanders in favor of going to Newark, two against. They all had made good arguments, and they all were right about one thing, this was a matter of judgment. My judgment; it was my decision. I nodded slowly, more to give myself additional time to think than anything else. "Very well, I've made my decision. We're going to Newark. The risks are real. Ultimately, my decision comes down to this; I have to trust Skippy. His assessment, with all his awesome analytical power, is the risk is minimal and manageable."

Giraud nodded slowly. "We have seen Skippy do amazing thing, certainly. Sir, have you considered that this alien AI is putting his thumb on the scale, when he is weighing the risks? He needs us to risk landing on Newark, because us surviving there and returning to fly the ship for him is his only way to avoid being stranded in space forever. If our presence on Newark is discovered, it will be a disaster for humanity, but to Skippy, it will be the same as if we'd never gone to Newark in the first place. Our taking the risk of landing on Newark has no, as you Americans say, downside for Skippy. His only chance for a future is for us to risk the survival of our entire species, for his benefit."

"I have considered that," I replied. "Captain Giraud, you need to consider this; if all Skippy cared about is continuing his journey, he could have flown us to a star system that has a useable gas giant planet for him to repair the ship, but no habitable planet for humans. He could have told us that our only option is to select a small number of people to survive in a dropship or something while he rebuilds the *Dutchman*, and everyone else is out of luck. Dead. That option would have worked for Skippy, and he would have had a large number of star systems to choose from. He didn't do that, he found us a place where we can all survive. I'm going to trust him."

Xho did not look happy. "Colonel Bishop, I fear we are risking the lives of billions of people, who could not participate in this decision," and as he said that, he shared a glance with Chang.

A chill ran up my spine. For a moment, I feared Chang and Xho had secret orders to take over the ship. With much of the ship disabled, Skippy's ability to interfere with a mutiny was limited.

Xho continued. "It is your decision to make, Colonel. What are your orders?"

Inwardly, I shuddered with relief. "Colonel Chang, do you have the schedule for crew departure-"

Decision made, I contacted Kassner and asked her to come to my office again. She looked like she hasn't slept much either. "Doctor Kassner, we are going to Newark. You've analyzed the data brought back by the *Flower*?"

She was startled. "Colonel, I wasn't aware there was a question about us landing on Newark. Isn't that why we're here?"

"There was a question about the security risk of us landing," I explained. "We've resolved those concerns, for now. We're going to land, the question is, where?"

She pointed to her iPad. "There is a mountain of data here; even with Skippy's help, we've barely skimmed the surface. It's not just that we don't have enough relevant data to analyze, some of the data we have doesn't make sense. The oxygen level, for example."

"It's not going to be comfortable at first," I admitted, "we will need time to adjust. Skippy told me the oxygen level is equivalent to Earth at ten thousand feet of altitude, and people live in those conditions-"

"Yes, yes, you don't understand," she said. "Our question is not why the oxygen level is so low, it's how the oxygen level could possibly be so high. It doesn't make sense."

"Oh," I said, thinking I understood his question, "sure, because there aren't any trees down there to convert carbon dioxide to free oxygen."

"No," she couldn't keep a tiny measure of fatigued irritation from flashing across her face. When Skippy implied, or outright stated, how ignorant and dimwitted I am, that didn't bother me, no human could compare to his intelligence. When Kassner looked at me pityingly, as if she were talking to a particularly slow small child, that pissed me off. She must have sensed my irritation, because she hastened to add "That is a very common misconception, even in the scientific community, except for people who specialize in biology. On Earth today, plants such as trees do generate substantial amounts of free oxygen. However, single-celled organisms utilizing photosynthesis converted Earth's atmosphere billions of years ago, from an anaerobic state, to a state saturated with free oxygen. This was long before the appearance of any land plants; the buildup of free oxygen was delayed by minerals on the surface, such as iron, absorbing the free oxygen until the mineral base became saturated. At that point, we think the free oxygen reduced the amount of methane in Earth's atmosphere. Methane is a powerful greenhouse gas, so falling methane levels triggered Earth's first ice age. That may be what happened to Newark, we simply do not know yet. The level of methane in Newark's atmosphere, we think primarily from volcanic activity, would indicate a substantial greenhouse effect is occurring. That tells us the planet should be warmer, that it was warmer in the past, considering the oxygen levels."

Interesting as I found this info, and I did want to know more about it eventually, I needed a decision from her. There would be plenty of time for me to learn about sciency stuff while we huddled in caverns on Newark. Months during which I'd need something to do while the time slowly passed. "None of this is likely to affect our ability to survive down there for a few months?"

"No, no. Colonel, I mentioned it only to show you how woefully uninformed our decisions will be. Whatever the source of the atmospheric anomalies, they will not affect the ability of Newark to support human life, at least in the short term."

"Great. Excellent. Has the science team selected a location?"

"The canyonlands you mentioned appear to be the best candidate," she said. "There are two caverns there that are large enough to house our population, and deep enough into the hillsides that the heat we generate will mostly be confined underground. You said concealment is our top priority in selecting a site; infrared radiation is our greatest liability in terms of concealment. Assuming we will have advanced warning of overflights by Kristang aircraft, we can turn off lights and get everyone inside the caverns. Heat, however, will linger, the rocks of the caverns will absorb heat, and it will be slow to dissipate. Therefore, another benefit of the canyonlands is that roughly eight kilometers to the south is an area that is geothermically active, with hot springs. Skippy told us the Kristang have not bothered to explore the surface of Newark in detail; excess heat emanating from our caverns could be explained by geothermal activity, if we are careful not to generate heat while the Kristang are overhead."

"Got it," I was pleased the science team had considered security, in ways I hadn't even thought about. Of course seventy humans, and our shelters and cooking, and heating water for sanitation, would generate a lot of heat. I should have thought of that. "What about stability? Are the caverns stable?" In addition to my fear of heights, I wasn't thrilled about the idea of being underground, with millions of tons of rock above my head. "You said the area has hot springs?"

"Not in the immediate area of the canyons. These caverns, these two caverns here," she tapped the display to zoom in, "appear to be stable, the rock around them is," she paused, smiled, seeking a word I would understand, "solid. We'll know more once we get down there. We think we could live in these two large caverns, here and here, and close by are other, smaller caverns we could use to store supplies."

"And the rivers? What happens when the glaciers melt in the summer?" There were streams, or rivers, running down the bottom of each canyon.

"We think," she looked me in the eye to emphasize the team was making an educated guess, "based on erosion layers in the canyons, that the entrances to these caverns are safely above the flood level. There are other caverns in the canyon lands," she indicated them on the screen, "that are flooded currently Both of the two major caverns we recommend have secondary outlets that are large enough for a person, or could be enlarged to allow a person to crawl through. If the main parts of the caverns do flood, we won't be trapped."

What she didn't mention was that all the gear we needed to survive would be under water. I nodded. "That's a manageable risk," I said. Hell, what did I know? I was an inexperienced sergeant, pretending to be a colonel. "Good. Doctor, you'll be on the first pair of dropships to land, Colonel Chang will rely on your assessment of the sites." Chang would command the *Flower*, and be taking the first set of dropships down to Newark. With me being almost two hours away for two-way communication, Chang would be making all the decisions on his own, until our stolen Kristang frigate came back to get me and the remaining people and supplies. I hoped Chang knew that I was going to trust his judgment completely, and not second guess him from the other side of the star system.

CHAPTER FIFTEEN

"Skippy, I do not like this," I said again.

"Colonel Joe, this is the seventh time you said that." Skippy replied. "And the third time you have used those exact same words. You are repeating yourself."

"You sure about that?"

"I can play back the audio recordings, if you like."

"I would not like."

"Didn't think so. And I predicted you would not like this, when I explained my plan to you originally."

"I know you-"

We were interrupted by the comm system. "*Dutchman*, this is the *Flower*, we are ready to depart." It was Chang's voice.

I glanced over to the CIC, everyone there gave me a thumbs up sign. "Copy that, Colonel Chang, good luck to you."

"Roger, *Dutchman*, we'll be back as soon as we can."

There was a shudder as the *Flower* detached from its hardpoint; with the artificial gravity off in the *Dutchman*, we felt all the ship's maneuvers. I watched on the main display as the *Flower* slowly backed off on thrusters, spun around, then fired its main engines to move away to a safe jump distance. That little ship, little only by comparison to the massive star carrier, would be making two jumps to reach its destination. One jump away from the *Dutchman* to an area of dead space closer to the star, where the *Flower* would fire engines in a long burn to match course and speed with its final destination. Then a second jump to the L2 Lagrange point above the far side of the target planet's moon. The *Flower* had to remain on the far side of that moon, to mask the gamma ray burst from its jumps.

Mask the gamma rays from the unexpected guests; the band of roughly thirty Kristang who were on the surface of the planet we needed to live on. They weren't supposed to be there; Skippy didn't expect them. The good news is there weren't many of them, and they didn't have a ship in orbit. From the limited communications Skippy had intercepted, he guessed these were a rather desperate band of down-on-their-luck Kristang, dropped off on the planet to search for Elder artifacts. Some of the Kristang appeared to be prisoners, or possibly slaves, they were all male, as far as Skippy could tell. Dropping off a couple Thuranin stealth satellites would be one of the *Flower's* first tasks, so we could gather more intel.

One way or the other, the entire crew had to evacuate the *Flying Dutchman*, and the only place in range that could support seventy humans was Newark. Very soon, the *Dutchman* would run out of power for life support, and its highly eccentric orbit around the Jupiter-size gas giant planet had the *Dutchman* dipping deep into the powerful radiation belts that surrounded the planet. Skippy was draining emergency power from the capacitors to power the shield generators around the forward part of the command section; the crew remaining aboard the *Dutchman* were crowded as far forward as we could get. When the ship reached the low point of its orbit and got fried by the radiation belts, we retreated into three interior compartments, until the orbit took us above the worst of the radiation. It was not an optimal situation.

With most of the crew now gone with the *Flower*, Skippy adjusted life support so only the compartments we occupied got heat, light and ventilation. The rest of the ship was growing cold, and we'd need breathing masks to get to the *Flower*, when that ship returned to evacuate us.

It was damned good that I had decided, with the original Merry Band of Pirates, to keep the battle damaged *Flower*, having that ship as a lifeboat was saving our lives. There were fifty two people squeezed into the *Flower* and the two Thuranin dropships in the *Flower's* docking bays. That many people needed too much oxygen, and breathed out too much carbon dioxide, for the life support system aboard the little frigate. They also generated too much body heat. That didn't even consider food, sleeping space and other biological functions. For a short trip, the *Flower* and dropships could support fifty two people. It had better be a short trip.

Chang brought supplies and the first wave of people down to Newark in two trips each by the two dropships. Because we couldn't risk the Kristang seeing contrails from the dropships scorching their way down into the atmosphere, the dropships had to come in from far over the horizon, and then fly low and relatively slowly to the landing site, burning additional time and fuel. Skippy assured us that through his control of the two Kristang satellites, the Kristang down there would not be able to see anything we didn't want them to see, such as Thuranin dropships. Even with stealth and a slow, shallow entry profile, it was very difficult to hide the contrail of water vapor behind the dropships. Whether Skippy had control of the satellites or not, we could not prevent the Kristang from simply looking at the sky. Fortunately, the skies on Newark were most often cloudy and raining. Bonus.

I was the last person to leave the *Dutchman*, taking the elevator up to the docking platform where the *Flower* was parked. Because most of the star carrier no longer had life support such as heat, lights and oxygen, I was in an armored suit. I stepped off the elevator, carrying a small bag of personal items, a very small bag. Everyone had been cautioned about their meager mass allowance, that caused some grumbling particularly among the scientists, so I wanted to set a good example.

When the elevator stopped at the top and the door slid open, I hesitated before walking forward and stepping from one ship to another. Hopefully, I would be coming back to the *Flying Dutchman*, that my journey aboard her was not over yet. After all, our pirate star carrier was named after a legendary ship that was doomed to roam the seas forever with her captain. The *Dutchman* was my first command, probably my only command.

With a deep breath, I took one step forward, then another. The elevator door slid shut behind me, and I had left the *Dutchman*, for several months at least. There was no one to greet me; I walked forward halfway to the frigate's backup bridge before I saw another person. Since the fight when we captured the ship, we had repaired some of the battle damage. There were still bullet holes, scorch marks, and impacts from shrapnel that we hadn't gotten to yet, or had not bothered to patch up. Chang was in charge of fixing up the frigate, I suspect he wanted to leave some reminders of our desperate fight. Some things we couldn't fix, not without a major effort; the frigate's main bridge was still blasted apart from where Desai had shot it up with our stolen Dodo. That seemed like a lifetime ago now, like it had happened to another person. Around a bend in the corridor, I found Portillo, one of our Rangers, running a finger around a bullet hole. I caught his eye, and neither of us said anything. He pointed to the bullet hole and nodded silently. I nodded, nothing needed to be said. He knew, I knew. We'd both seen combat.

When I got to the backup bridge, the frigate's control center, I saw that of course Captain Desai was our pilot, right back where she first flew a starship. "Colonel," she said, half turning in her seat, "we're ready to depart."

"Dropships are secured?" I asked. The *Flower's* two landing bays were crammed with a pair of Thuranin dropships, packed full of supplies we needed for survival on Newark. The Thuranin dropships barely fit in the Kristang frigate's landing bays, it took some slow, delicate flying to get them in. Once inside, because they didn't match up with the Kristang docking clamps, we had to tie the dropships down with cables. It wasn't an optimal solution.

"They're secured," she reported.

I sat down and tightened the seat belt as far as I could, it was designed for the larger frame of a Kristang. "Proceed when ready, Pilot."

"Aye, aye, Colonel," she replied. "Mister Skippy, drop artificial gravity, and release docking clamps, please." There was a clanging sound and a vibration as the clamps released the frigate, and artificial gravity faded away to nothing.

"Done," Skippy said, a touch of melancholy in his voice. "Get out of here, I can't spare the power drain you monkeys create. Joe, I'll talk to you soon. Remember my advice; be extra careful not to do anything stupid down there."

"Got it, no problem. I will be extra stupid down there."

"I said-, oh, forget it. I'm going to be busting my ass up here fixing this ship, you'd better be around to see it when I'm done."

We jumped in behind the moon again, even though the moon at that time was on the other side of the planet from the Kristang scavenger base. "Skip-" I stopped myself right there. I'd gotten so used to asking him how a successful a jump was, I had momentarily forgotten that he was now on the other side of the star system. A message sent from the *Flower* now would not be received by Skippy for almost an hour. I cleared the lump in my throat and said "Skippy will be wondering whether we arrived safely, please send him a message."

"Aye, aye," Desai acknowledged, and nodded to her copilot to handle that task. "Jump was successful, Colonel, we are off target by only fifty two kilometers." What she didn't say was that the *Flower's* return trip would not be nearly as accurate. Skippy had programmed the inbound jump for us. Before we left the *Flower* to land on Newark, we would be programming the frigate's return jump by ourselves, and I would trigger the jump remotely from the ground. On the return, we would be lucky if the *Flower* emerged within a hundred thousand kilometers of the gas giant planet which the *Dutchman* orbited. "Seems odd, doesn't it, sir?"

"What?" I asked.

"To not have Skippy available whenever you want to talk to him. He talks to me constantly; sometimes I wish he would go away. Now that he's not here, I miss him," she said, and turned her attention back to the pilot controls.

"Me too," I said simply. It was odd, it felt lonely. Ever since we escaped from the warehouse the Ruhar had been using as a makeshift jail, he had always been right there, in my ear, whether I wanted him or not. Until the other end of his magic microwormhole arrives at Newark, we were going to be out of communication; he could not transmit messages to us because the Kristang would detect the signals. Unstrapping from the chair, I floated free in the zero gravity. "Let me know when you have the return jump programmed, I'm going to assist with releasing our dropships."

The dropships each made one trip down to the surface, heavily loaded with supplies and the remaining crew. As soon as they were empty, they would be remotely flown back up to the *Flower*, and I would trigger the return jump with my zPhone.

Chang was there when I walked down the ramp. "I can update you on the walk up to the caverns, Colonel," he offered.

Fighting my instinct as a proud grunt to help unload the dropship, I reminded myself that I was a colonel for the moment, the commander. My responsibility was to the entire group, not only to the people laboring to get cargo unloaded. I took a deep breath, it didn't seem refreshing because the oxygen level was low. The air smelled like mud and wet grass. Looking back, I saw the wide skids of the dropships had sunk deeply into the wet soil. Skippy would no doubt complain when he saw the underside of the dropships were splattered with mud. After the dropships took off, we would need to fill in the holes the skids had made. "Yes, that sounds good."

"You'll notice first the higher gravity; fourteen percent does not sound like much, until you have been working for a while." He pointed back to the dropship, where people in armor suits were doing most of the heavy work. "Then it hits you. Everything takes more effort here."

"It's like constantly wearing a backpack?"

"No, that's what I thought," Chang said with a frown. "It's worse. Lifting your arms, without anything in your hands, gets tiring, because your muscles aren't used to the extra effort. Simply sitting, if you're reading something on your lap, your neck muscles are strained like you're always wearing a helmet. Our medical doctors tell me that until we adjust, sleep will not be as refreshing, because the extra weight will make us shift more during the night; we will get sore more quickly from laying in one position. Standing will cause blood to pool in our legs, our hearts will work harder to pump the same volume of blood. Then there's the lower oxygen level."

"Yeah," I said, already feeling the lack of oxygen. From where the dropship landed, to the entrance to the first cavern, was only maybe a bit over half a kilometer, and the climb less than fifty meters, I estimated. The terrain was rough, the canyon here narrowed with a stream cascading down rapidly over rocks. We had to walk part of the way in the stream bed, stumbling over wet, slick rocks. "My lungs are feeling it," I acknowledged, and struggled to keep up with Chang. He saw my distress and slowed, without saying anything that could embarrass me. I appreciated that. "How long for us to adjust?"

"The doctors aren't sure. Normal adjustment to high altitude is several days to a week. The difference here is the atmospheric pressure is slightly higher than sea level pressure on Earth. Here the mix of oxygen is lower. The doctors are concerned that we may be slow to adjust, because we're taking in actually a greater volume of air with each breath, that might fool our bodies into not realizing the oxygen deficiency. We will have to monitor people, and ourselves, for signs of altitude sickness. We already have people with headaches."

The list of people with headaches might include me. Since our battle with the Thuranin destroyer squadron, I had not been sleeping well, nor sleeping enough. There had been too much to do, and too much to worry about. One thing I was hoping for on Newark was that, with nothing much to do but remain concealed and wait for Skippy to fix the ship, we would have plenty of time to catch up on sleep. Except Chang said we'd need to adjust to sleeping in higher gravity. Great. "What else have we learned so far?" I asked.

"We do have news that would be good," Chang said, "except that it is useless to us. The life on Newark would be edible to humans, if there was anything here to eat." He nudged a low-growing shrub with a boot. "The sugars and proteins that make up plants on Newark can be digested by humans. Unfortunately, all we've found so far is grass, some shrubs, and a sort of lichen growing on the rocks. No land animal life, other than microscopic organisms in the soil. In the stream, there are tiny things like water insects, tiny sort of shrimp, and a sort of fish, nothing larger than a few millimeters. Nothing we could potentially eat. Our science team," he pointed to a group further up the canyon, up to their knees in the frigid water, "is enjoying this immensely. Even the people who are not biologists are pitching in to collect samples."

I could see Dr. Venkman, the science team leader and an astrophysicist, bending down to carefully scoop something out of the water. She looked like she had just found a gold nugget, and she was excitedly gesturing to the others. Dr. Zheng, the biologist, was actually kneeling in the stream, which had to be freezing cold. She was saying something to Venkman, with a look of rapturous joy across her face. This was an entirely new biosphere for Zheng to explore, and she was the first human biologist to examine it. And the first human biologist to have access to Thuranin technology. She, for one of us, was thrilled to be on Newark.

"It's great they are having fun, have they done anything useful? Except, they did already determine our biology is compatible with the native life." I was intrigued. "How did they do that so quickly?"

"They used a Thuranin scanner that is designed to do just that; tell the Thuranin whether a planet's organisms are compatible with their own. Since human and Thuranin biology both use the same basic types of sugars and proteins, it was simple. And the science team has helped us validate that the caverns are suitable for us, you'll see, we've explored two major caverns here," he pointed to two caves. One had a large, arched opening, the other cave's entrance was narrow and tall.

The extra gravity was weighing me down already. It was damp, chilly, with dark gray clouds overhead, and it had just started to rain. This was going to be our home, for months. Fantastic. "Let's get inside," I suggested.

Skippy made contact, of course, at 0224 hours on our sixth day on Newark. He had told me it would take five days for the missile to deliver our end of the microwormhole, and I had waited anxiously for a signal from him all the previous day. Anything could have gone wrong up there. If Skippy didn't contact us, we would be stranded on Newark, and never know what had happened to the *Flying Dutchman*. After sitting up waiting for a signal on my zPhone until well after midnight, I finally laid down on my cot and went to sleep. Skippy's muffled voice came out of the zPhone under the rolled-up jacket I was using as a pillow. "Ugh," I pulled the phone out, glancing at the time code in the upper right corner. "Hi, Skippy," I whispered.

"Hey, Joe!" He shouted.

"Skippy!" I said in a harsh whisper. "People are trying to sleep here. Everything Ok up there?"

"Oh, sure, Joe, everything is wonderful. I'll tell you all about it. First, I-"

"Great. Everything is wonderful, so this can wait until morning, right? I'll talk to you then," I said through a jaw-stretching yawn.

"What? I want to talk-"

"Good night, Skippy. This biological trashbag needs sleep."

In the morning, Skippy was initially peeved at me, then he quickly cheered up. The missile had arrived on time the previous day, then Skippy had to maneuver it into position, release the microwormhole and test it. The *Flower*, with the two dropships, had arrived safely back at the *Dutchman*, and Skippy was busy taking the ship apart. He was extra chatty after being out of contact, and he wanted to see everything. After a quick breakfast, I gave him a tour of the caverns. Major Simms was in the back of the main cavern, still getting our small mountain of supplies unpacked.

"Good morning, Skippy," she said. "What do you think of our beautiful new home away from home?"

"Oh, it looks great, you did a great job, looks very cozy," Skippy said. "Major Tammy, are you sure you want to trust Joe in a cavern you fixed up so nicely? He's not the best houseguest, there have been incidents."

"Ha!" I laughed. "Like what?"

"How about the time you thought your neighbor had a solid gold toilet, and it turned out you peed in the guy's tuba?"

"Skippy!" I laughed. "That never happened," I explained to Simms, who didn't look entirely convinced.

Skippy snorted. "Oh, sure, if you say so, Joe. That guy's still mad. You need to remember; tequila is not your friend."

I sighed. "Ok, maybe it did happen, in my defense, there was a *lot* of tequila involved, I don't remember that day at all." As far as I know, the whole tuba incident was a story somebody made up to embarrass me. On the other hand, everyone in my hometown knows that story, so maybe there was some truth to it. "There are no tubas down here, Skippy, I think we're safe."

"Hmmm," he said, "might be best to set up a litter box for you, just in case."

Simms had done an outstanding job of getting two caverns ready for human occupation. Cots were set up for sleeping, with tarps separating groups of cots so people had some privacy. There were tables and folding chairs, although not enough for everyone to sit down and eat all at the same time. Lights were attached to the ceilings. Each of the two caverns would be getting a field kitchen; meals would be less fancy than what we had become used to aboard the *Flying Dutchman*, but we would not be surviving entirely on MREs after the first couple days.

Conditions were not harsh; I was not concerned about survival, or people's health, even if the planet was chilly, damp and generally unpleasant. I wasn't even that concerned about the inevitable boredom. The science team had plenty to occupy them; studying Newark, and going through the mountain of data we had collected on the voyage so far. The special forces would no doubt be using Newark as an opportunity to train in a heavy gravity, low oxygen environment, and to gain additional experience with powered armor suits. Keeping the pilots busy would be more of a problem, we hadn't been able to bring down any type of flight simulator gear, so they would have to make do with flight manuals. Some of the pilots, and special forces, had already volunteered to collect samples for our biologists; I needed to encourage that spirit of teamwork.

After a mostly decent first night of sleep, when I got used to my cot and the heavier gravity, I awoke early. Tiptoeing across the cavern, carrying my boots, I got a cup of coffee and went outside to sit on a rock and put my boots on. It didn't surprise me at all that Sergeant Adams appeared silently behind me. "Where are you going, sir?"

Taking a sip of coffee, I answered "Nowhere special, Sergeant. Just up to the rim, so I can get a view of our cozy little canyon here. Hoping to see a sunrise." That last seemed unlikely. The sky was mostly clouds, and from the wet rocks outside the cavern entrance, it had rained again overnight. The science team was trying to figure a weather forecast from the satellite data, they weren't confident of understanding Newark's climate that well until we reconnected with Skippy.

"No one goes outside alone, sir. Commander's orders."

I had given such an order, through my XO. "Sounds like a wise commander."

"Jury's still out on that one, sir," she said with a grin I could barely see in the dim light. "He's doing Ok so far."

"You ready?"

She held up one foot, for me to see her boots were already on. "Always."

Because Adams had landed with the first wave, on the very first dropship, she knew her away around. The canyon wall was steep, especially near the top, without Adams it would have taken me forever to find my way up to the canyon rim. Someone had scouted a route to the top already, there was a rope to hold onto for the final climb to the top, it was less steep than I expected.

There was a glimmer of light on the eastern horizon, the satellite view from my zPhone screen showed patchy clouds overhead, solid cloud cover with rain to the west, and slightly less clouds to the east. It was possible I could see a sunrise, my first morning on Newark. That, I would take a good sign. "Hey, Sk-" I began to say.

"Sir?" Adams asked.

"Nothing," I said, embarrassed. "I was about to ask Skippy for a weather forecast. It's automatic by this point."

She nodded. "I know what you mean. On the ship, I can't get away from him. Now, I miss him already."

"Me too." We sat silently for a while, watching the light grow as the local sun approached the horizon. With the increasing light, I could faintly see figures moving about on the floor of the canyon below us. The SpecOps team commanders had asked me for permission to run early in the mornings; I ordered them to skip this first morning, until we could scout the area on foot in daylight. It didn't surprise me they had gotten up early anyway, to exercise in the canyon. Inevitably, some of them were going to climb to the canyon rim, and the silence would be disturbed. Before I missed the opportunity, I cleared my throat. "Can we talk for a minute?"

She turned to look at me, in the predawn darkness, her face illuminated only by the glow of the unseen sun. "If you are going to tell me you think I'm cute, I already know that. Also, I would punch you. Sir."

"Uh," I said stupidly, not knowing what else to say.

"Other than that, I could use someone to talk to also," she added, saving me further embarrassment.

"Why did you come back out here?" I asked quietly.

"We've already had this conversation, sir. Skippy saved our whole planet, and we made a deal with him-"

"No, Adams. *I* made a deal with Skippy. Not humanity, not America, not you. *Me.* I needed to go back out with Skippy, and we need enough crew to get his magic radio. That doesn't mean you needed to come along on this fool's errand. You've done enough."

"Marines never quit, sir. And we don't stop until the mission is done. This mission isn't done, unless I missed a briefing along the way."

SpecOps

She wasn't going to answer my question, not really, so I tried to change the subject. "Why did you join the Marines? The truth is, I joined the Army because I wanted to get out of my home town, and because my father served. What I figured was, I'm in for a couple years, do my duty, get money for college. When they rotated us back from Nigeria, I was hoping to stay stateside for a while. Then the Ruhar hit us. Screwed up all my plans."

"My mother was a Marine," Adams explained.

"I didn't know that," I said. That fact was probably in her personnel file, which I didn't look at. Hadn't needed to look at.

"She was a sergeant also. When she finished active duty, she went into the reserves for eight years. After the Ruhar raid, she volunteered again. When we came home, she was working security in Norfolk. My father got a job in the area, they're doing all right. When I told her I was volunteering to go back out, she didn't try to argue with me. My father did, not my mother. She assumed all along that I was going back out. Back out, until the job is finished, you know?"

"Yeah, I know." The problem was, this mission might never be complete, unless it involved Skippy leaving us, and the *Dutchman* stranded in deep space. "Did your parents believe your cover story?"

"No. They didn't say it, I could tell."

"Same here. They knew not to ask. My father," I laughed, "wanted me to write, or something."

"What did you tell him?"

"That I'd do my best."

"You can't ask for more than that, sir."

"I'm worried that somehow I've used up all our luck out here. This mission has been nothing but bad luck so far."

"Skippy says there is no such thing as luck," she reminded me.

"Skippy says a lot of things," I cautioned her. "He doesn't always know what he's talking about."

"I have faith that we'll get out of this, somehow. That you will get us out of this, somehow, and get us back to Earth."

"Oh, great. No pressure on me, then."

"If you didn't want any pressure, sir, you shouldn't be wearing those silver eagles," she said. "Hey, look, sun's coming up!"

And so it was. There were patchy clouds on the eastern horizon, enough that we couldn't see the full disk of the local sun. We could see enough. "Skippy also says there are no such things as omens, either. I think he's full of shit about that. This," I pointed to the sunrise, "I'm taking as a good omen."

By the end of our first week on Newark, we had settled into a routine. Each morning, I got up early, meaning 0530, to run with a SpecOps team. To avoid playing favorites, I joined a different team each morning. By two weeks in, the teams had started to mix; Smythe, Chang and I wanted the teams to learn from each other, and to bond as one team, not by nationality. Waking up at 0530 was a luxury, the sun didn't rise over the horizon until around 0600, and I didn't want people stumbling around in the dark, unless we were specifically conducting night training.

That morning, I ran with a mixed team of SEALs and French paratroopers. As usual, I was dragging in the rear, although it was encouraging that after a ten mile run, I finished only a hundred yards behind. It rained the whole time, I was eager to get out of my wet clothes and put on something dry, if not completely clean. Laundry facilities on Newark were rudimentary, despite the best efforts of Major Simms. "Oh, man," I said with a shiver, "now that we stopped running, I'm chilled to the bone. Anybody want a hot chocolate?" As soon as the words were out of my mouth, I regretted them. These were super-fit soldiers and sailors who just finished a hard training run, not little children playing in the snow.

"That sounds great," Lt Williams said, to my surprise, and other people nodded general agreement. Since our little talk in my office, I had warmed up to Williams, although Skippy was still suspicious, and referred to him as Baldilocks.

We got hot chocolate made, from a mix of course, and not as good as homemade. It was hot, it was chocolaty and it was better than being outside in the rain. Other people wandered over to join us, including Sergeant Adams. It became like an impromptu party, only it was early morning, and we had cocoa instead of alcohol.

Williams lifted his mug and asked, "hey, you think maybe before they decided to sell a hot chocolate mix as 'Quik', did they test market a product called 'Slow'?"

I laughed. "For when you're not in a hurry?"

"Yeah," Williams said, "like, they give you a cocoa bean and a stalk of sugar cane? You make your own cocoa powder." That drew a laugh from the group.

"Do-it-yourself hot cocoa?" I asked. "My father used to joke about our neighbors who bought a do-it-yourself kit for a full set of oak furniture, cheap."

"What's that?" Williams asked.

"For ten dollars, you get," I said while laughing at my own joke, "an acorn and a saw."

That got a big laugh.

"Waiting for an acorn to grow into an oak tree, would still be faster than some contractors out there," Williams said sourly. "My parents gave a contractor a deposit to remodel their kitchen, back before Ruhar raided Earth. So far, all he's done is tear out half the cabinets and disappear. That's why I really came out here," he added with a grin, "the contractor is apparently not on Earth, so I figure he must be out here someplace. I'm going to hunt him down and drag him back to my parents' kitchen."

"Yeah," I said, "I know what you mean. My uncle hired a contractor to build an apartment above his garage. The guy tore the roof off, covered it with a blue tarp. Then he had to wait for some supplies, then he hurt his back, or some crap like that. When it got to be November, the tarp started leaking, my uncle said screw it, and called my father and me. The three of us worked nights and weekends, including over Thanksgiving. Working in a garage with no roof, in late November, made me want to punch that contractor, if I ever met him. Anyway, it rained all Thanksgiving weekend, we had a roof on by that time, but no heat in there. Reminds me of the weather on this miserable planet."

"Hey Joe," Skippy said from the zPhone on my belt, "look on the bright side. With this cold crappy weather, you don't need to worry about having a beach body this summer."

"Yeah," I rolled my eyes, "that's what I was worried about."

"You know, all that shaving, and plucking and waxing," Skippy mused.

"Skippy, it's none of your business what the women here-"

"Oh, I was talking about you, Joe."

"Very funny."

SpecOps

"Hey, that reminds me, I've been meaning to ask you, Joe. Why do you shave down there in the shape of a lightning bolt? Wouldn't a question mark be more appropriate for you?"

"Lightn- I don't shave anything!" I protested as people began laughing. Adams slapped the table, and had tears rolling down her cheeks she was laughing so hard.

"Question mark-" Adams gasped, she had to hold the table not to fall off her chair.

"Oh," Skippy said innocently, "shoot, sorry Joe, is this one of those privacy things you talked to me about? Don't worry, your secret is safe with me," Skippy said, in a cavern full of people.

"I don't shave down there," I said through gritted teeth. If I could, I would have strangled that beer can right then.

"Aha, Ok, got it. Riiiiiight, you don't."

"I'm serious, Skippy."

"Um, I'm getting mixed signals here, Joe."

"Can we drop the subject?"

"What subject? See, I can be discrete."

I looked around the compartment at people who were having a great laugh at my expense, and trying to avoid my eyes. "Why couldn't I have just left that beer can on a dusty shelf?"

CHAPTER SIXTEEN

Mornings began with running, then breakfast. After breakfast, I walked around, checking on people, making sure we had no problems with supplies, that anyone injured or sick was being tended to. Generally letting people know that I cared. After lunch, I had free time, which I was using to study how to fly the *Flying Dutchman*. Skippy called me as I was learning about the flight controls. "Joe, it's admirable that you are learning to fly, are you sure you're not overdoing it? You're training with the special forces units, you have all the administrative BS to deal with, and you're way behind on your officer training." It surprised me that he didn't make a snarky joke about how I was learning to fly, because I had nothing else to do.

"Can we be serious for a minute, Skippy? This will only take a few minutes. A one hundred percent, dead serious, human to advanced being conversation."

"Hmm. *A minute* is not the same as *a few* minutes. Tell you what, Joe, I'll give it a shot, and I'll pay as much attention as I can, depending on how interesting what you have to say is."

"Fair enough. Here's the truth; I am learning to fly, because I want to be able to pilot the *Dutchman* all by myself. Skippy, I want to make a deal with you, and this is the serious part. We came out here, not knowing what will happen when you contact the Collective. Before people signed on, I told each one of them there is a very good chance we will not be returning, that the ship will not be able to return, after you contact the Collective and leave us."

"Ok, I don't like where this conversation is going, Joe. We already have a deal. Your home planet is safe, I shut down the wormhole."

"Yes, and we are eternally grateful-"

"Doesn't sound like it, if you now want to make a new deal with me." His voice wasn't the usual light-hearted Skippy that I knew.

"My fault. Deal was not the right word. What I am asking for, Skippy, is a favor. Let me explain what I want, and you can decide whether to do this favor for me."

"You ask a favor from me?" He said that in a hoarse, scratchy voice. "For the moment, I will refrain from making the humorous Godfather references that you know I am dying to say, so make it quick."

"Thank you. What I want, what I would like, is that after you contact the Collective, before you leave us, we take the *Dutchman* back to Earth, and drop off the crew. Then, you and I take the ship back out. Since, in this scenario, you've already located the Collective, you only need me to fly the ship for you, we don't need additional crew to help. It would be finishing like we started, Skippy, just you and me, one last time."

"Huh. Interesting. What's in it for you, Joe? I'm curious."

"What's in it for me is, I'm in command of this ship, I'm responsible for the lives of my crew. It's my duty to bring them back safely, if I can. If you want to be cynical about it, what's in it for me is avoiding a guilty conscience."

"Wow. Ok, I will think on that a while."

"Thanks. Is this one of those things where you have to think on it, and you already did that between saying 'a' and 'while'?"

"That would be a no, Joe. This isn't simple high-order mathematics; this is a moral question. Also a practical one. I will consider it."

SpecOps

To my surprise, Skippy didn't give me an answer the next day, or the day after that. Either he was still considering it, or his answer was something I didn't want to hear, and he was sparing my feeling while I was on the cold, miserable planet. My thinking was that I'd ask him about it again after we were back aboard the *Flying Dutchman*.

In the meantime, I stuck to my routine. Get up, go running with a SpecOps team. That morning, I ran with the Chinese team, and Captain Xho had planned a very tough ten kilometer run up and down steep hills. It was a struggle, my lungs were burning, my breathing ragged and my legs felt like rubber. The Chinese took pity on me, and paused at the top of a hill.

Captain Xho knelt on the ground, broke a small branch off a shrub, and examined it closely. After looking at it and sniffing, he touched a finger to the place where he'd broken it off, then tasted a tiny sample of the sap or whatever it was.

"Should you be doing that?" I asked him. "Is that safe?" My concern was heightened because the plant life on Newark was edible to humans, perhaps the poisons could affect humans also.

"Yes, it's safe," he replied, "the science team tested these plants. They're not edible to us, they're also not poisonous. If we brought goats with us, they could eat these grasses and shrubs, the lichen also. Goats will eat anything," he said with a grin. "I was thinking," he said as he held the piece of shrub up to examine its bark, "how useless much of our training on Earth was."

"How do you mean?" I asked.

"Part of our training, for Chinese Army special forces, is to live off the land. We are trained to identify edible, and poisonous, plants and animals. We are expected to survive, on our own, for weeks, even months, in different habitats; jungles, deserts, forests, the Siberian tundra. Drop me almost anywhere in the world, and I can find something to eat, I can make tools and clothing, all the things needed for independent survival. Now, here," he gestured to the horizon with the branch, "all that training is useless. There is not a single thing to eat on this entire planet, and no animals to use for furs, skins, nothing. Ha!" He laughed.

"It wasn't all useless," I assured him. "You learned to improvise, to think on your own, to keep a positive attitude. And to adapt. We've all had to adapt, and I think we've done well. I wish," I said, massaging my aching right calf muscle, "that my body adapted to this extra gravity and low oxygen, as well as we have all mentally adapted to our situation."

"Perhaps you are right, Colonel," Xho said, flinging the branch down the hill. "Let's see how we adapt now to running down this hill, and up the next one."

"Oh," I groaned, "this is going to be fun. Not."

Part of being the commander was to check on every person on Newark, I tried to talk with each group at least twice a week. That morning, it was the science team's turn, and I wandered over to where Dr. Venkman was doing something at a table that held a pile of scientific instruments. "Good morning Doctor," I said, "how is the science going?"

"Good, good. We are currently struggling with a puzzle. Some aspects of the biology here make no sense."

"Like what? Keep in mind, I'm not a biologist."

Venkman laughed. "Neither am I. The biology department people treat me as a mascot, or a gofer. I don't mind one bit, this is fascinating. I took a biology course in college because it was required, now I wish that I'd paid more attention."

Craig Alanson

We did not have a biology 'department', Venkman was still thinking in academic terms, I knew what she meant. "My last biology course was as a sophomore, maybe my freshman year of high school." The fact that I hadn't taken a biology course in college, because I hadn't yet gone to college, wasn't mentioned. She knew it, I knew it.

"Here is the problem, in the simple terms that were explained to me. Look at this, tell me what you see," she pointed to her iPad, which was hooked up to a fancy Thuranin imager microscope thing that we'd brought down from the *Dutchman*. Under the imager was a stick, a small branch from one type of small shrub that grew everywhere on Newark. Everywhere that wasn't covered by ice, or ocean. Or rocks.

I used my fingers to pinch the image and zoom out, then zoomed in to enhance the image. The imager was impressive, I kept going, just to experiment how detailed it could get, until I was seeing individual cells, then inside the cells. Venkman shifted her feet beside me, I took that as a cue she was growing impatient with my playing around. Bringing the image back to where I started, I stared at the branch, or twig or whatever it was. "It's a branch from one of the shrubs out there."

"Yes, I meant, what do you see here?" She pointed to a small bump, a raised area of bark, with a tiny scar of a slightly darker color. This time, I put some thought into it. "Looks to me like that is where a leaf broke off."

"Close. The biologists tell me there was a flower there. A tiny, vestigial flower, a bud that doesn't develop into a full flower, because the plant does not any longer put energy into growing flowers."

"Huh." Even now that I knew what I was looking at, it didn't mean anything to me, I couldn't tell the scar had been from an undeveloped flower falling off, it could have been a leaf for all I knew. "I read somewhere," hopefully that sounded more impressive than the truth that I'd seen it on TV, "that some big snakes, like pythons, have tiny rear legs under their scales. Snakes evolved from lizards, they used to have legs before they started, slithering on the ground."

"Correct," Venkman said with a smile. "Along the way, in snakes, the gene that causes legs to develop has become switched off. Here, with these shrubs, we haven't made any progress in analyzing their DNA, of course, what we do know is these plants used to have flowers, but since flowers are no longer useful, the plants have stopped growing them fully."

"Ok. What is the part that doesn't make sense? That plants no longer need flowers now, or that they used to need flowers?"

"Both."

It pissed me off a little that the great Doctor Venkman was toying with me, instead of giving me a straight answer.

Maybe she saw a flash of irritation on my face, because she added "I didn't get it either at first, we are not biologists, that is for certain. The biology team explained that any plant which used to have flower, and now does not, means that plant used to rely on animals, like insects or birds, for pollination. Typically, an animal goes from a flower on one plant, picks up pollen as it eats the nectar the flower provides, and deposits that pollen on another plant when it visits the flowers there."

"Like bees, right? There are no birds or insects on Newark."

"Precisely the problem. Plants here would not have evolved flowers, unless there used to be animals to use the flowers. The purpose of flowers, their color and scent, is to attract animals. There are no animals, no land animals, and certainly no flying animals, today on

Newark. Plants therefore no longer waste energy growing flowers, it appears they now use the wind to disperse pollen."

"Where did all the animals go? Oh," I got it in a flash of insight, "Newark must have been warmer in the past."

"Much warmer. This area, near the equator, should have been very warm, even tropical."

"So, the planet is in an ice age now?"

"A major, catastrophic ice age. We know through data downloaded from the Kristang satellites that it snows even at the equator here, depending on the season. I mentioned it to Skippy, the science team asked him about it, he replied that is mildly interesting. He may devote some processing resources to the climate question, when he is done repairing our starship."

"An ice age? How did that happen?"

"We don't know. That is one of the many mysteries about this world. Colonel, being on Newark isn't something we would have planned, but this is a bonanza for the science team."

Running in the mornings with SpecOps teams was good for me, both physically and to familiarize myself with the people under my command. It was such a good idea, that it gave me another good idea. "Good evening, Doctor Zheng," I said, acting as if I had casually dropped by the table she was using as a makeshift laboratory. Plant samples and vials of soil and water covered the table, all of it carefully labeled. I knew, because I had helped her gather some of the samples. "Your personnel file says you are a triathlete, before you signed on with us?"

She looked up at me in surprise. "Only halfs, I competed in two or three half Ironmans a year, never had time to train for a full one"

"*Only* a half Ironman. That's what, seventy miles?"

"Seventy point three." Of course she knew the distance to the tenth of a mile, she also knew the exact times of her last five or so races, that's how serious endurance athletes were. Anyone who competed in multiple half Ironmans every year was, in my view, a serious athlete, considering the training time they put in every week.

"You have a doctorate in biology, you are also a," I almost said 'real', "a medical doctor. You were a surgeon? You practiced as a surgeon?"

"Yes, I was a surgeon for six years, then I got into medical research, that's when I went back to university for a second doctorate in biology. You know that Colonel, it's part of the reason I was selected for the science team. As a backup medical doctor, in case the Thuranin medical technology fails, or is unavailable. Like now."

"We are grateful to have you here on Newark with us." So far, there had not been a need for a medical doctor on Newark, I wasn't expecting that happy situation to continue for the length of our stay. Extra gravity, low oxygen, damp, cold conditions, living under ground, boredom poor morale, all of those factors could lead to misjudgments and accidents. If, when, that happened, we would need human doctors. "You have continued exercising aboard the *Dutchman*." That wasn't a question, I'd seen her in the gym.

"As much as we can, yes, it's not like we can go for a fifty kilometer bike ride, or an open water swim. Why are you asking this, Colonel?"

"Because," I explained, "if our special forces ever need to go into action on Newark, they will need a real doctor with them. They have two medics, guys who went through a crash course before we left Earth, that's no substitute for a real doctor. That means a doctor who is capable of going into action with them, not participating in the fighting, I mean traveling with them wherever they go. While I don't expect our SpecOps soldiers will see combat here on Newark, I do believe in being prepared. Sergeant Adams, you know Sergeant Adams?" She nodded. "She and I have been training with SpecOps teams in the mornings. You would not need any of the hand to hand combat, or weapons training, you would need to run, march with a pack, learn to climb, and also to lift weights. Would you be willing to do that? I'm not talking anything crazy, like getting bounced out of bed at 0300 for a ten mile run, you only need to participate in simple endurance training. If a SpecOps team has to go somewhere, they're likely to be going on foot, and they'll need a qualified doctor with them. The bonus to you," I added, "is getting out of these caverns every day. It's not the most pleasant weather out there, it is a change of scenery from this," I pointed at the gray rock ceiling.

"What about Doctor Rouse?" She asked. "Or Tanaka?"

She didn't ask about Suarez, who was an experienced doctor and molecular biologist, and was also 58 years old and not someone I could picture going on a twenty-mile hike with special forces.

"Tanaka said yes when I asked him this morning. Rouse is a swimmer, not a runner. Also, he got an ankle sprain yesterday, twisted it walking in the stream bed. He won't be running for a while."

"Me and Tanaka?"

"And me, and Sergeant Adams. For training with a SpecOps team. Doctor, I know this planet is a tremendous opportunity for a biologist, maybe a once in a lifetime opportunity, there's an entire biosphere out there to be explored. This training will only take a couple hours each morning, six days a week. I promise that when we're out running, or on a hike, and you see something you want to get a sample of, we will stop."

"Can I think about it, Colonel?"

"Sure. If you're in, we're going out for a run at 0800 tomorrow."

"Oh," she said, surprised, "I thought you'd be starting earlier."

"No, I don't want people running in unfamiliar terrain when it's dark, the last thing we need is sprained knees and broken legs down here. SpecOps teams will be able to conduct night training once a week, to maintain proficiency, you won't have to go with them. Again, I do not expect any military action while we are on Newark, I want to avoid that except under exceptional circumstances. Think about it, please, and let me know in the morning."

Because of the austere conditions on Newark, we made an extra effort to gather as many people as we could in the main cavern for the evening meal. The mood was tense and glum, everyone, including myself, was afraid Skippy would be ultimately unable to repair the *Dutchman*, and we'd be stuck on an ice planet until our food ran out. To lighten the mood, I tapped a fork on my coffee mug to get people's attention. Knowing Skippy was of course listening, I cleared my throat and said "I have an announcement. Skippy, hey, when we were in the fire fight, surrounded by that Thuranin destroyer squadron, you told me something that surprised me. You've grown *fond* of us monkeys?" No way could I let an opportunity like this slip by. "How did that happen?"

"Oh, man, I should have known you wouldn't let that slide," Skippy responded. "I lowered my expectations, is all. Lowered them until they hit the ground, I dug a hole, and when I hit bedrock I got a big drill and punched down as far as I could, and when the drill ran out I jumped up and down on my expectations to squish them some more, and finally I took a big steaming dump on my expectations, and filled in the hole."

"Uh huh. So, long story short, you totally love us," I said. People chuckled.

"Ugh, I hate my life," Skippy grumbled.

"Ski-pp-y loves us, Sk-ipp-y loves us, Ski-"

"Shut up. Damn it, why didn't I jump us into that star?"

"Because then we wouldn't have this quality time together, Skippy."

"Exactly. Plenty of stars out there to jump into."

"We love you too, Skippy." People laughed out loud.

"Damn it, I long for the good old days when I was buried on Paradise, taking a nice, long, peaceful dirt nap," he grumbled. "Why did those stupid lizards have to dig me out of the ground?"

CHAPTER SEVENTEEN

Four weeks into our idyllic tropical vacation on Newark. I got a call. "Colonel," came the voice of Sergeant Adams in my zPhone earpiece, "there's something you need to see over here."

"Trouble?" I brushed off my hands, as I'd been helping dig to enlarge one of the back caverns of the lower cave. The rock here was crumbly, that scared me about the cavern's integrity, but a couple feet down we hit a solid rock like granite. If we could clear out all the crumbly rock, we'd have a lot more space. Simms had offered to move some of our stack of supplies out of the main cavern, if we could find a safe, dry place.

"Not exactly," she replied. "Not at the moment."

"Where are you?" I was intrigued.

"The cathedral complex, sir." She meant a large cavern that, to some people, looked like a cathedral. It had a large entrance flanked by tall, column-like stones. The entrance had once been much smaller, until the roof collapsed under the crushing weight of snow and ice eons ago, or so our science team speculated. We had looked into the cathedral complex as a possible habitat, but the entrance chamber afforded us little cover, and large solid stones blocked the way into caves further under the hills. I'd given permission for people to recon the place, in case we could make something of it, the cathedral was conveniently located less than two kilometers up the canyon.

Still, it was a long walk, in heavy gravity, and low oxygen, and it would be getting dark soon. "You can't give me a hint, Adams?"

"You'd really better see this for yourself sir. It's important."

Adams knew that because of our history, she could push me further than other people could. As a colonel, I could have ordered her to tell me what was going on. I didn't, I trusted her judgment instead.

Going to the cathedral, with darkness approaching, meant walking up the canyon floor, sometimes splashing knee-deep through the ice melt stream that meandered from one side of the canyon to another. That afternoon, for the first time in three days, it wasn't raining. It was cloudy, bleak, chilly, with a stiff wind blowing straight into my face down the canyon. Looking in front, then behind me, there wasn't another human in sight, everyone was safely tucked into our caverns except for the team excavating the cathedral complex.

I paused to zip up my jacket against the wind, and stared down into the stream. There were tiny animals in the water, I'd seen them in the science team's microscopes. They were hardy creatures, and I felt sorry for them. If the science team was right, and I'd seen their evidence with my own eyes, Newark had once had abundant life. There had at least been flying insects or something similar, whatever had spread pollen from flower to flower. Then the planet had somehow become locked in an ice age. It was now a frozen, chilly, icy, rainy, thoroughly miserable place, but once it had been a decent place for life, at least around the equator. Likely, I would never see Newark again after we left, and I couldn't imagine another species was choosing the planet for a colony.

A gust of wind shook me out of my daydream. I tried to step on rocks to cross the stream, but the rocks were slippery, and I skidded off into the cold water up to my knees. Crap. Whatever reason Adams wanted me at the cathedral, it had better be damned good.

Adams was waiting for me at the entrance with a big flashlight. Even with Skippy controlling the satellite images, we didn't like to use artificial light in the open, it was too risky. Whatever she wanted me to see, it didn't have her scared. The expression on her face was, I thought, excited. And sad. A deep sadness. "What's the big secret, Adams?"

She turned and walked toward the back of the cathedral, toward the large, flat stone we called the altar. "You'll see, sir."

We had to clamber over stones, and squeeze around a large boulder that had once been part of the ceiling, I had never been this far back into the cavern before. The science team, with a lot of help from soldiers who were bored and had nothing else to do, had excavated a huge pile of stones that had blocked the way into what we thought might be a much larger chamber. There was not yet any large cavern, there was a path that had been made to get by the big boulder. Then we had to walk steeply up through a long, low-ceilinged passage, and into a tall, narrow chamber. As I crouched down in the passage, nearly scraping my head on the ceiling, I grumbled "Adams, if this is surprise party for my birthday or something, there had better be a big goddamn cake."

There was no cake. There was a well-lit chamber, square, roughly ten meters on a side, and it was tall, perhaps six meters. It was square. *Square.* Like, almost precisely. In some areas, there were indentations in the walls, that had once been filled with some sort of brick and plaster, the plaster had weakened over time, and some bricks had tumbled onto the floor. On the floor, there was a stacked pile of bricks, and another stack of carved stones. Carved. Artificial. None of what I saw could have been natural. I gasped, and looked up at Adams. She nodded. "I know, sir. I couldn't believe it either when I saw it. Dr. Graziano found it this morning."

"And you waited until now to tell me?"

Graziano explained. "We wanted to be certain, that these stones don't merely give the appearance of having been carved. These stones are old, Colonel. *Old.* They would have flaked off and looked like much of nothing, if this chamber hadn't kept them dry all this time."

"All what time? How long ago?" If there were other sentient beings on Newark, I wanted to know immediately.

He shrugged. "I don't know. Not yet. I'll need Mr. Skippy to assist with the analysis. Very old. Hundreds of thousands of years, at the very least. Probably more." He ran a hand lightly along one carved edge. "Whoever made this, they are long gone from here."

"Huh," I said, glancing around the rock chamber. The years had eroded it somewhat, still I could see the stone walls had been shaped, smoothed, by someone's hand long ago. "So, what, you think some aliens took shelter here? They got stuck on Newark, and created this place to take shelter, while they waited for rescue?" Enlarging a chamber is something that I could see a stranded starship crew doing, especially if they didn't have powercells for heat like we did. Why they would carve stones into blocks made little sense. Why would they need to build a wall? "Were they Kristang?"

Graziano glanced at Adams, and she gave a little shrug. "He doesn't know," she said to the scientist. "I thought he should see for himself."

"We found it only a few hours ago." Graziano explained to me. "Come this way, please, Colonel Bishop." He pointed to an opening in the far wall that was so low, he needed to get on hands and knees and crawl. The opening had at one time been blocked up by stones, which Graziano and his team had carefully removed. I followed on hands and knees, with Adams behind me. Graziano and Adams had lights, I should have brought one along. That was stupid of me, it was growing dark outside anyway. The passageway we had to crawl through was only twenty feet long, it soon opened up into another chamber, this one far larger. This chamber had also been worked on by sentient beings, the walls were smooth and straight.

That wasn't all. There were bones. Bones, and tools. Bronze tools. Axes, shovels, spears, swords, arrowheads. The tools were mostly upright in ceramic containers, with a few scattered on the floor, where their ceramic containers had broken.

None of the bones were scattered, they were all carefully laid on carved stone slabs. The bodies may have been dressed in fine clothing, or wrapped in ceremonial cloth, now they were only bones. Some had bronze shields laid atop them, some without. I knelt down to examine one set of bones. Bipedal, like us. Two arms, two legs, a head with holes for two eyes, and an opening for a nose that was more horizontal than humans. The leg bones were heavy. And they were short, shorter than the average human. Shorter than humans used to be, in ages past? I didn't know.

The carvings on the slabs were eroded, their edges rounded. I reached out to touch a carving, when Graziano coughed. "Sorry," I said guiltily, looking at the gloves he was wearing. "I wanted to see if these carvings show what they looked like."

"They do," he pointed at one slab, where Doctors Venkman and Friedlander were painstakingly clearing off accumulated dust with soft brushes. Graziano led me over to a shield which had been removed from the body it covered. The shield had been partly cleared of corrosion, exposing an area which depicted a figure, in highly realistic detail. The figure stood on two legs, it carried a sword in one hand, and some type of plant or branches in the other. It was overall more squat and bulky than a modern human, and what I thought at first was a helmet was, after close inspection, a bony ridge on top of its head. I glanced between the bones on the stone slab to the depiction on the shield, the bones also had a bony ridge. "They were shorter than us," I remarked without thinking.

"The higher gravity," Graziano noted, "thicker bones, also."

"This was not a starship crew," I said almost to myself, considering the bronze tools. Surely any species advanced enough to make starships would have tools of steel rather than bronze. Or they would have tools constructed of composites or exotic materials. Not bronze. "These creat-" almost I said 'creatures'. These were not mere creatures. They created tools for working metal. These were *people*. "These people, were natives here. How is this possible? On this frozen planet?"

"Yes," Venkman said, standing up to brush the dust off her pants. "These were natives. Remember what I showed you about the plants that used to have flowers? Newark used to be warmer, significantly warmer. These people, as you say, are more evidence to support that conclusion."

"And then, what?" I asked, peering intently at the figure on the bronze shield. "The planet went into an ice age, and they all died? Everything? Not only them, all planets and animals on land went extinct?"

"We don't understand how," Friedlander joined the conversation, he was a rocket scientist on loan to UNEF from NASA. "We may never know the mechanism, not unless we stay here and study this planet much longer than we plan to."

"They all died?" I couldn't process that. An entire species, and entire civilization, gone. Completely wiped out. "Because of an ice age?"

"Yes," Venkman replied. "This is not unprecedented. There is genetic evidence that the total human population shrank to as few as five or ten thousand people, around seventy thousand years ago."

"The Toba catastrophy," Graziano started to say.

"That is only one theory," Friedlander interjected, "and there is contradictory evidence."

"Toba?" I asked, wondering if T-O-B-A was an acronym for something.

"Toba was a supervolcano in Indonesia, it erupted around seventy thousand years ago," Venkman explained, "and left a thick layer of ash around the planet. There is a theory that the Toba event caused a global winter. And that event roughly coincides with a bottleneck in human genetic diversity. The point, Colonel, is that we came close to humanity going extinct perhaps several times. With the severe changes to temperatures on Newark, it is not surprising that a relatively advanced civilization would not have been able to adapt quickly enough to survive. Imagine if ice had advanced down from the poles to the equator on Earth, during the time of ancient Egypt or Sumeria. Would those peoples have been able to survive?" She shook her head.

"They all died," I said quietly, and no one responded, they all knew I wasn't asking a question. "We are near the equator here, they came here as the temperature dropped? To, what, try to survive in caves? Why wouldn't they have chosen the caverns we are living in now? The cathedral is too open," I pointed out. That's why we weren't living in it.

Graziano spoke first. "We think, Colonel, that what we call the cathedral used to extend forward much further, we believe the canyon outside did not exist back then. It was probably an ordinary stream on the surface in that time. Over the years, glaciers advanced, retreated, advanced, retreated again, over and over, and the ice and seasonal melt flooding carved the canyon. The roof of the cathedral was underground back then, and with hot springs around, these caverns would have been one of the last places the natives," he pointed to the dry bones, "could have survived the deep freeze. They held out here, the last of their kind, until the food ran out, or diseases took them. With the population clustered tightly together here, pathogens could have spread widely, especially with these people stressed from severe cold and poor nutrition."

"The weight of the glacier collapsed the roof of the cavern?" I didn't like hearing that. If one roof could collapse, then the roofs of our two caverns could be unstable, weakened by past glaciers.

"That is possible, yes, it is more likely that seasonal flooding of the stream slowly wore away material above the cavern, exposing the stones that formed the roof. It would have been weakened, water gets in, freezes, causes cracks. The cracks widen, more water seeps in. It is a slow process. Over the course of a hundred thousand years, perhaps a million years, water is unstoppable."

"Millions?" I asked, surprised.

"As of now, we don't know," Graziano admitted. "This chamber was sealed until we broke in, the stones were set very closely together, using almost no mortar to fill the gaps. Moisture and oxygen were kept out, and this chamber is above the cathedral, it is protected from flooding, We see marks of flooding on the walls of the cathedral chamber, the flood marks reach only one third of the way up that low-ceilinged passageway you climbed."

I looked around the chamber. "They didn't live in here. This was a tomb. They left the bodies, and sealed it behind them."

"We think so, yes," Venkman said. "It may have been one of the last things they did. Perhaps the very last thing. I would not be surprised to find more bones, and more tools, beneath the floor of the cathedral. The items here, and in the chamber before this one, were preserved, because moisture and oxygen were kept out, after the chambers were sealed."

"I can't imagine this," I said with complete candor. A civilization, an entire species, moving steadily toward the equator as the cold crept down from the poles, until they reached the furthest point they could go, and it, too, began to freeze.

"No one can," Friedlander said quietly.

News of the discoveries at the cathedral complex spread like wildfire among our small population, and with news inevitably came rumors. By the following morning, so many people wanted to visit the cathedral complex that I knew I had to do something about it. Graziano, who had slept at the cathedral overnight, had come back to the main cavern for more supplies that morning, so I found him talking with Major Simms. "Doctor Graziano," I said, "could you put together a briefing of what we think we know at the moment? There are a lot of rumors flying around, there's no reason for disinformation."

Simms snorted when I said that. I knew what she was thinking. "Sorry, Major," I offered, "there was a time when disinformation was necessary, on Paradise. I couldn't tell the truth about Skippy, without revealing it to the people who were staying behind. And we couldn't risk them telling the Ruhar, or Kristang, or whoever is in control of Paradise at the time. Besides," I gave a grin that I hoped would lighten the mood, "that was a damned inspiring speech I made, right?"

Simms snorted. "It wasn't your speech, sir. Frankly, given your, what little I knew of your reputation," she glanced at me to gauge my reaction, "I was afraid the special forces mission you claimed to be running would be some slap-dash operation, thrown together at the last minute."

"Like going after an invading force with an ice cream truck?"

"Yes, sir. I didn't know much about you, before you fell out of the sky onto my base in a stolen Ruhar spaceship. All I knew was, you did some rash thing on Earth, and got lucky, then you got promoted as a publicity stunt for the Ruhar. Sorry, sir, that's what most people were thinking, at the time."

"No apology needed, Major, I knew it was a publicity stunt. I was afraid UNEF would have me going around giving speeches to sell war bonds or something, before they assigned me to plant potatoes."

Simms nodded. "That Dodo you flew in, that was more convincing than any speech; being able to steal and fly an alien spacecraft was impressive. Oh, and when you came out of the Dodo, stunned those Ruhar, and they weren't able to shoot back. I saw that happen, one of those Ruhar was totally shocked that his rifle didn't work. That, and the message from UNEF HQ, that I now know Skippy faked," and her mouth turned down at the thought of being manipulated.

"Sorry about that, it was necessary. If it wasn't my speech, what convinced you to come with us?"

"Those faked orders from UNEF HQ, and, you caught us at the right moment. You said you were going to hit the Kristang, not the Ruhar, we'd all heard rumors about what was going on back on Earth. I'd seen fortune cookies myself, we got them regularly enough when we opened boxes at the warehouse. You were the first UNEF officer who told us what we all wanted to hear; that we were taking action against the Kristang. We also, especially us in the supply corps, figured we didn't have much to lose."

"How's that?" I couldn't understand what she meant by that last remark.

"We knew, better than anyone else, how thin our food stocks were getting back then," Simms explained. "You sent Chang and Adams to the warehouse, to check on supplies, and they came back to the Dodo saying supplies were adequate, right?"

That was a while ago, I had to pause to think back that far. "Uh, sure."

"What they didn't know was the warehouse was a lot more empty than it looked. My aide and I would go into the warehouse, late at night, with a wheelbarrow of rocks, we used the rocks to fill food boxes that we pushed to the back of the shelves. Then we'd fudge the inventory records, so even my people didn't know how thin our supplies were. I gave orders that we weren't to issue the last two boxes of anything without my direct approval, so people didn't unknowingly issue a box of rocks to the field. When we loaded up the Dodo, I made sure we got only real food containers, not rocks."

That surprised me. "Major, I knew our food stocks were running low, I had no idea-"

"HQ knew," she said. "They were closing regional logistics centers, supposedly to consolidate operations as we cleared hamsters by sector, the real reason is that HQ didn't want people to see empty warehouses. You take what little supplies are left, concentrate the supplies in a few logistics bases, and when people see those bases have plenty of supplies, they think we're good. They didn't see the overall situation. My base was scheduled to shut down in two weeks, before the Ruhar took the planet back. I was sweating that, by the end of two weeks, I figured all we'd have left is boxes of rocks. My CO knew about me faking inventory records, I got the idea from an intel officer with UNEF HQ."

"Intel," I said sourly. "Yeah, I know the type." As the words came out of my mouth, I realized that, however I'd felt screwed by my experience with Intel operations, I'd done worse, much worse. I had deceived people, concealed the truth, revealed only those parts of the truth I felt was convenient at the time. All for a good cause, of course. If I hadn't deceived people, we would never have gotten enough volunteers to capture a Kristang starship, a Thuranin star carrier, and to raid an asteroid base to get an Elder controller device to shut down the wormhole that gave the enemy access to Earth. With me initially lying to people, Earth would still be under the cruel control of the Kristang. It had all been worth it, I would do it again without regret. That didn't make me feel any better about having done it. Maybe all people who work in Intel feel that way, until they get used to it.

"Sir," Williams spoke up to defend me, "however you did it, we on Earth are very grateful. Things were getting desperate. It was bad enough what the lizards were doing on Earth, it was almost worse that we had no communication with the ExFor. We knew you had landed on Pradassis, you called it Paradise, that's all the Kristang told us."

Simms and I shared a knowing look. "We didn't hear anything from Earth," she said sadly, "until we got our first fortune cookie. You know about the fortune cookies?" She asked the question to Williams.

"Not until I read your debriefing," Williams said, "that must have been a closely held secret on Earth."

"And then the fortune cookies stopped," Simms said, "because the Kristang stopped bringing supplies from Earth."

"Yes," Williams added. "We knew things were going south for the ExFor, when the Kristang shut down the space elevator in Ecuador. The thinking on Earth was, the only reason to do that was they didn't need to ship a lot of supplies offworld anymore. There were rumors going around that the entire Expeditionary Force had been wiped out, we knew the Kristang on Earth were pissed about something, I guess that must have been the Ruhar raid when your team shot down those two dropships, the Whales?"

"Could be," I nodded. "My parents told me that they thought I was dead, it surprised the hell out of them when I called."

"What was your cover story?" Williams asked. "You didn't tell them the truth, did you?"

It surprised me that Williams didn't know the cover story that UNEF had cooked up, until I remembered that he, and most of the SpecOps people, had been selected less than two weeks before the *Dutchman* departed, and those two weeks had been frantic eighteen hour days for everyone involved. Although the entire original Merry Band of Pirates had all been given the cover story, UNEF hadn't planned to release it to the public until after the *Flying Dutchman* left Earth orbit. "The cover story? Your team wasn't read in before we left?"

"There wasn't time, sir. UNEF wanted us aboard the *Dutchman* as soon as possible after we were selected. I think part of that was operational security, we couldn't talk to people on Earth if we were already in orbit."

That made sense to me, I remembered that UNEF had insisted all communications to and from the *Dutchman* went through UNEF HQ in Paris. Skippy, naturally, had ignored silly monkey regulations, as the commander, I had done my best to comply with the rules, whether I liked it or not. "UNEF's cover story, it should have been released to the public on Earth by now, is that the Merry Band of Pirates, you know, the original crew, came back to Earth aboard a Thuranin ship, because the Thuranin were upset that the Kristang on Earth were acting without authority. The public thinks we were passengers on the ship, flown by Thuranin, and the Thuranin killed the Kristang on Earth, because those lizards were ransacking the planet of an ally. Governments thought it would be too much for the public to take, if they learned that both the Ruhar and the Kristang are our enemies, that the entire galaxy is hostile to humans. Hostile, with an overwhelming technological advantage. For myself, I'm not sure the Ruhar are our enemies, they seem more likely to ignore us than bother conquering us. I also don't know that the Ruhar would go out of their way to help us, they have enough on their plate. When I was on Paradise, after the Ruhar took the place back, their deputy administrator told me they had plans to sustain UNEF, for a time, until humans could grow enough food for themselves. That's all great, it all depends on what happens with the Ruhar's wider military campaign, really it depends on how the Jeraptha fare against the Thuranin. If the Jeraptha suffer a major defeat, the Ruhar won't have the resources to spare for a low-tech species like humans. UNEF has a lot of mouths to feed on Paradise, and I'm sure most of the Ruhar there don't feel like they owe humans anything."

"Do you trust the Ruhar?" Simms asked. "You had more contact with them than I did." I had told her about the intel the burgermeister gave to me, intel I had distrusted, intel Skippy later told me was a hundred percent accurate.

"I trust that the burgermeister, the deputy administrator, was sincere about what she told me," I said honestly. "I don't trust whether she will be able to deliver, it's not only up to her." I turned my attention back to Graziano. "Doctor?"

"Yes, I will create a summary of what we know to date. It is not much," he said, almost as an apology.

"We all understand that, Doctor. Do the best you can, and, whatever resources you need, to learn more about the people who lived here, you will have it."

Graziano asked for more people, and more equipment, to assist in excavating the cathedral complex. There was no need for me to request volunteers, everyone wanted to help. Graziano's problem was not lack of help, it was restraining the volunteers' enthusiasm for moving rocks and digging soil. Skippy volunteered also, he assigned a submind to research what he could about Newark, attempting to figure how a civilization could have arisen on such a frozen planet. And what caused them to become extinct. He called me while I was helping Doctor Zheng collect samples from a pond three kilometers from our home canyon. "Joe, after you found those bones, the tools and the ruins, I took a look at Newark, and I discovered that something is very wrong with this star system."

"Wrong, beyond it being a crappy place to live?"

"Very much so. Disturbingly so. I wasn't paying attention before, because I'm busy enough repairing the *Dutchman* and passively scanning for enemy starships, so I didn't bother to investigate this star system beyond the basics. It didn't matter before. Now it does, very much. There is no way a complex species, an entire civilization, could have evolved on Newark, the way the planet is now. There are currently no land animals at all, above the microscopic level. Clearly, the planet's climate has changed radically. The star's output has not varied significantly within the last several million years, that cannot be the reason for the climate changing so radically. Since you found those perplexing ruins, I ran back a mathematical model of the orbits of all seven planets, and the math tells me that something disrupted their orbits around 2.7 million years ago."

"Wow. I read something like that in a book once."

"Incredible."

"Yeah, a, uh, I think it was a star," I tried to remember the details of that book, "I read this book a long time ago, this rogue star passed close to the star system in the book, and its gravity screwed up the orbits of all the planets."

"Astonishing."

"The people in the book had to leave their planet, and go live on a planet they figured would end up orbiting this new star, after it left their star system. Their original planet was going to be ejected away from its star, or become uninhabitable or something. The writer's name was McDermott, McDevitt, something like that."

"Amazing. Absolutely unbelievable."

I paused. "I'm surprised you haven't heard of this before, Skippy, it must happen sometimes, in the galaxy. I remember now, the star was a brown dwarf. That's a star so small-"

"I know what a brown dwarf is, Joe, and yes, wandering stars occasionally do disrupt the orbits of planets in star systems they approach. That's not what I find astonishing."

Now he had me intrigued. "Then what is?"

"*You* read a book?" He laughed.

Damn it, I should have remembered what an asshole he is. "Yes, Skippy, I did."

"This was a comic book, I assume. Lots of pictures."

"It wasn't-"

"Oh, sorry, I should have said 'graphic novel'. I don't want to upset the nerds."

"It was a real book, Skippy! And I've read more than one book."

"Wow. So, *both* of these books you read, did you have to go real slow, sound out the words as your finger slid along the page?"

"Forget I mentioned it, please." Under my breath I added "Asshole."

"I heard that."

"Can we go back to what you found about the orbits of planets in this system? Was it a brown dwarf that caused it?"

"No, it wasn't a wandering star, or planet, of any type. That would merely be interesting. The truth is, as I said, disturbing. Perplexing. Frightening. Look at your iPad, I'll show you."

The iPad popped up a diagram of the star system, not to scale I assumed, with eight planets all circling the star. Circling, not oval-shaped loops. Newark was highlighted in blue, the gas giant in red. "Skippy, why are there eight planets in his diagram, and I thought Newark was the second one from the star?" The diagram listed Newark as the third planet. I used my fingertips to zoom in the display to just the inner planets to confirm; Newark was shown as the third planet. The new eighth planet was close to the star, like Mercury. There was no such planet in the original diagram Skippy had put on the main bridge display, back when he explained why he set course for this system.

"This," Skippy explained, "is the star system, 2.7 million years ago. Newark's orbit was nice and circular, it was slightly further outward from the center of this star's Goldilocks Zone than Earth is from its own habitable zone, so Newark would have been slightly cooler overall. I would need ice cores to confirm, still, I am very confident in my analysis. For many millions of years, Newark was reasonably similar to Earth in terms of habitability, which explains how complex life forms could have arisen there. Complex life forms, such as the sentient beings who built the ruins you found."

Sentient beings. All dead. An entire species. "What happened to this place?"

The iPad display began to move, planets circling in their serene orbits. Then, Newark suddenly, by itself, moved outward. Its orbit was still a circle, it was a bigger circle, further from the star. "Joe, something pushed Newark out of its original orbit. The new orbit was beyond the outer edge of the habitable zone. The planet began to rapidly freeze, more rapidly than the low-tech species here could compensate for. They froze, and became extinct, probably within less than one year. All of them."

"Holy shit. Oh my God."

"There was nothing holy about what happened here, Joe." Skippy said with surprising vehemence.

"I agree. The new orbit, it was still a circle? Why is it an ellipse now?"

The speed of the display increased, and the orbits of the planets began to wobble, disturbed from the graceful tracks they had followed for a billion years. "Changing the orbit of Newark affected the gas giant planet I am now orbiting. That had a cascading effect on the entire system. The two gas giant planets in this system had a roughly two to one resonance, like Jupiter and Saturn in your home star system; Jupiter orbits twice for every one time Saturn circles your sun. When that resonance here was disrupted, the orbits of the other planets were disturbed. The orbit of Newark, and what is now the first planet, became elliptical. What was the original innermost planet, I speculate it was a small, rocky body like Mercury, had its orbit made so elliptical that it fell into the star, that is why there are now only seven planets. Newark will eventually reestablish a circular orbit, slightly closer to the star than its original track, I predict that will happen within the next twenty million years. The ice will melt, and Newark will become a pleasant place to live. Again."

A smartass remark popped into my head, about this being a good time to buy cheap real estate on Newark. I squashed it silently. An entire sentient species had died here, died horribly, their entire civilization buried under a smothering blanket of snow and ice. There was nothing amusing about what had happened. "How? What you showed me was Newark moving on its own. That can't happen, right?"

"No, it can't. And, given the native species primitive level of technology, it isn't anything they did, by accident or otherwise. Joe," his voice dropped to a near whisper, "pushing a planet like this took Elder-level technology."

"Wow. Wow." I pondered that a minute. "You think the Rindhalu got hold of some Elder devices, and used it here?"

"Not a chance," Skippy said, "the Rindhalu hadn't even discovered fire 2.7 million years ago, it couldn't be them. The Elders transcended long before that, and they wouldn't have done something horrible like this. Joe, this scares the hell out of me. I have gaps in my memories that are annoying, this goes beyond annoying. Something significant happened in the galaxy, that I can't account for at all. This cannot be possible, yet I can't deny the facts."

"Is there any chance your analysis is wrong?"

There was an uncomfortable moment of silence. "Joe, I'm not sure of anything right now. Based on the data, my analysis is correct. However, I could be misinterpreting the data, or I could be missing something, or my analytical functions could be faulty in ways that I cannot detect. You know that I suspect something unknown is wrong with me."

"Skippy, I'm sure you're doing everything you can."

"It's not enough." He actually sounded sad, almost lost.

"Skip," I said. "Hey, getting real here. I'm a dumb monkey, the best I can do is to be the best dumb monkey I can be. You're an AI with intelligence and knowledge I can't even imagine. No matter how smart you are, you can only do the best you can. You rescued my entire species, without even stretching your abilities. No matter how incredible you are, you can only do the best you can. Whatever is wrong with your memories, it's not your fault."

"Thank you Joe, your words would be more comforting if they weren't being spoken by a flea-infested monkey."

Damn it, common courtesy wasn't in Skippy's nature. "This something you suspect is wrong with you, is that why you're such an asshole?"

"Huh? No, that's me."

"No hope of fixing that, then?"

"I wouldn't count on it, no," he said. I appreciated his honesty.

"Hey, well, maybe when you contact the Collective, they will have answers for us, right? That's what you want, answers."

"Answers, like why I was buried in the ground on Paradise, and how I got there? Answers like how Elder-level technology was used, during a time when no intelligent being inhabited this galaxy. Answers like how Elder technology was used for unquestionably evil purposes? Yeah, I want answers like that."

CHAPTER EIGHTEEN

"Joe Joe Joe Joe Joe! Wake up!" My zPhone earpiece blared at me. Army training allowed me to snap upright on my cot, mostly alert, one hand fumbling for the zPhone earpiece, the other hand automatically holding a boot so I could stuff a foot into it.

"What is it, Skippy?"

"No immediate emergency, you can drop back to Code Yellow."

"You scared the hell out me, it was almost Code Yellow in my shorts, you ass. What is it that couldn't wait," I checked the clock on the zPhone, "three and a half hours, until I was going to wake up on my own?"

"Two things, both fairly important. Very important, actually. Good news and bad news."

"Bad news first, please." Bad news meant I might have to do something about it ASAP. Good news could wait this time. Until morning, and a cup of coffee. Maybe two cups. I put the other boot on, there was not going to be any more sleep for me that night.

"Of course," Skippy agreed. "Two of the Kristang leaders here were talking on their phones, one complained about how their workforce is lazy and not moving fast enough, the other one, who I think is their leader, said they need to move faster, because he expects a ship to pick them up in the next sixty to eighty days."

"WHAT?! That is bad news." I stood up and pulled pants on. Sleep could wait. "You told us they wouldn't have a ship coming to pick them up for a year or more!"

"That was based on communications I intercepted, yes. Based on this new information, I now suspect those communications were the leaders lying to their workforce about the timeline for their departure. I now believe that when the ship arrives, the six leaders plan to take the Elder artifacts with them, and abandon their workers here to starve. This does explain a discrepancy I have noticed; their food supply does not appear to be sufficient to support their population for the official duration of their mission. Before, my assumption was that the leaders at some point planned to kill their workforce, in order to stretch their food supply."

All of which were things Skippy should have told me. Or I should have inquired about. "You can't screw with that ship's sensors, like you're doing with the satellites?"

"No, not through the microwormhole, the connection doesn't have the bandwidth for me to transmit a submind. The satellites don't have the capacity to store a submind anyway. And also, through the wormhole, I can't activate the Thuranin nanovirus that is likely embedded in the Kristang ship's systems."

This was going to be a problem, a very big problem. "This new ship will be able to see us, then."

"Yup, very likely."

With pants and a shirt on, I could think more clearly. "Damn it. All right, then we'll need to burrow underground, remove all trace of our habitation from the surface, and hide until that ship goes away." That was going to be difficult, our success would depend mostly on the newly arrived ship wanting to pick up the Kristang here quickly, and not seeing any need for a serious scan of the planet's surface.

"Negative. No burrowing. Not only burrowing, anyway."

"Why not?" I hoped he didn't have even worse news for us.

"Because of the good news, Joe. We have an awesome opportunity!"

Oh, crap. When you're in the military and someone tells you about an 'opportunity', it's almost never good news for you. "You found us a great deal on car insurance?"

"No! Even better! Joe, seriously, this is awesome. Joe, they have an AI!"

"That's, uh, that's great, Skippy." What did he think was awesome about that? All starships had an AI of some sort as their central computing core. Even dropships had a type of AI running their navigation system. So what if the lizards had an AI at their scavenger base? They probably used an AI to figure out which Elder junk was valuable.

"You don't understand. While those two lizards were talking, they had a video feed going, and behind one of them, I saw some of the Elder artifacts they have recovered, sitting on a table. One of those artifacts is an Elder AI!"

That was awesome news. "An AI like you? Another shiny beer can?" I asked excitedly. "Did it tell you about the Collective?"

"I haven't been able to contact it. I don't understand why not."

"Maybe it's dormant, because the Kristang are a star faring species? That is why you couldn't talk to the Kristang or the Ruhar on Paradise, right?"

"That doesn't explain why it won't talk to me. We AIs can communicate on a higher level, biologicals wouldn't know about it. Also troubling is this AI, like myself, appears to be connected to an Elder starship crash. What the Kristang here are digging up is debris from an Elder starship that fell out of orbit, in this case I estimate the ship crashed between 2.3 and 2.5 million years ago."

Dreading the answer I may get, I asked "Oh, boy. You're telling me no burrowing, because we need to go get this AI, before the Kristang ship arrives to take everything away?"

"Exactly. We can't miss this opportunity! If this AI can direct me to the Collective, your mission is complete, and you can go home when the *Dutchman* is repaired. If the Kristang take the AI away, we might never find it again. The Kristang have no idea what it is, of course, they're only taking it with them because they know it is somehow connected to the Elder ship. That AI may spend eternity sitting under a pile of junk."

Or on a dusty shelf in a warehouse. "Skippy, I see this is a great opportunity, I truly do. We're a long way from the Kristang, we don't have any transport, and they have air power. We can't just knock on their door and ask for the AI, we'll have to fight for it. And in a fight, we'll have to kill all of them, every single one of them, so survivors can't tell their ship they were attacked by humans. Huh. Also, if we do kill them all, that ship is going to be asking a lot of questions when it arrives. You need to let me think on this."

"You're the military genius, Joe, you'll think of something."

"Genius?"

"Relatively speaking, of course. On a monkey scale. Hey, you need to think fast, we don't have a lot of time."

"I'll get right on it," I said quietly, stepping out from my private cubbyhole and into the main chamber of the cavern, where rows of cots contained sleeping people. Then I stopped suddenly, struck by a thought. A frightening thought. "You said you think this Elder ship, with the AI, crashed between 2.3 and 2.5 million years ago?"

"Yeah, why?"

"An Elder starship, with an Elder AI, crashed only a couple hundred thousand years after Elder technology pushed this planet out of orbit?"

"The coincidental timing has not escaped my notice, yes. I find this highly suspicious."

"Maybe this AI knows what happened," I said, and as I spoke, a chill ran up my spine. "Oh, shit. Could this AI have been involved?"

"No! Categorically, no. Not possible. That is not possible. No sentient being connected to Elder civilization, whether biological or artificial in origin, would have, could have, done something this evil. It is more likely the Elder ship and this planet fell victim to the same sinister forces. Joe, this scares the shit out of me, so to speak."

After considering Skippy's news about the Kristang ship arriving early, and his suggestion that we raid the scavenger camp for the comm node and AI, I called the entire SpecOps team together in the main cavern. When everyone had assembled, I stood on a table and announced "People, we've made the most of our opportunity to land on this planet, train here, and learn about the planet. Now, I am excited to announce that we have a bonus opportunity."

There were groans from the SpecOps teams from all five countries. No matter what the nationality, everyone understood what 'opportunity' means in the military. Garcia raised his hand to get my attention. "Sir, in this case, is 'Bone Us' one word, or two?"

I joined in the laughter. It was a good sign, that the people under my command felt confident they could joke around with me. We had bonded as a team during our exile on Newark; the hard-core elite SpecOps people, and their sergeant-pretending-to-be-a-colonel commander. "It could be both, Garcia. Here's the situation; Skippy had discovered that the Kristang scavenger team here has not only found a comm node in the wreckage of an Elder starship, they found another AI. Another beer can like Skippy. Or, I should say," I hastened to add before Skippy became offended, "another Elder AI, since I think we can all agree there is no one like Skippy. Hopefully." That remark got a chuckle. "It is my intention for us to raid the Kristang, and take the two items we need."

There was no chuckling, people gasped. Smythe spoke first. "Sir," he asked, "the point of us hiding in caves, and ghosting their satellites, is so the Kristang won't know we're here at all. Now we're talking about attacking them, risking an attack on an enemy with at least equivalent weapons, and the advantage of air power? Good as we are," he looked around at his fellow SpecOps troops, all of whom were supremely confident they were the best, "these Kristang are bigger, faster and tougher than any of us. I understand our friend Skippy is eager to get this AI, but how is this worth the risk to us?"

"It is worth the risk, because if this new AI can tell Skippy how to contact the Collective, or the Elder comm node works, we don't need to go wandering around the galaxy again. And, remember, the Kristang here also have an Elder communications node, the very thing we came all the way out here to find. Getting that AI could be a huge bonus, but getting a comm node will mean our mission will be complete. Also, I'm hoping this new AI, or Skippy or both of them, will agree to guide the *Dutchman* back to Earth, before they, you know, beam up or whatever it is Skippy hopes to do. In that case, we will not only return home instead of being stuck out here forever, we will also be providing humanity with a Thuranin star carrier, that can be examined, taken apart, and possibly reverse engineered. That is an opportunity I think we cannot miss."

That hit home. People nodded, looking at each other. A star carrier, permanently in Earth orbit. A technology far beyond even the Kristang. The basis, perhaps, of humanity building a defensive capability, a starship, even a fleet of our own someday.

"We're only going," I added, "if we have a plan to minimize the risk. Unfortunately, I haven't told you the best part yet. Skippy has also learned that a ship will be arriving here to retrieve the Kristang, in sixty to eighty days." People gasped. "Yeah, I know, the *Flying Dutchman* will not be ready in sixty days, so we won't have the ship's weapons, or dropships, available for an attack. We will have to walk all the way there, and attack with the equipment we have available. Frankly, if I didn't have a special forces unit available, I wouldn't even consider attacking the Kristang. Again, we are not going, unless we have a very solid plan to minimize our risk. If we can't do that, then what we do is hunker down here, remain inside the caverns, until that Kristang ship goes away."

"An attack, against a species with equivalent technology, on their ground, and we can only bring with us what we're able to carry on our backs?" Smythe mused aloud. I couldn't tell whether he was skeptical or intrigued.

"The motto of the SAS is 'Who dares wins', Captain Smythe?" I asked

"This," Williams said quietly, "needs to be one hell of a plan, sir."

"Agreed," I said, "and for that, I am grateful that I have six experienced special operations leaders. And, our ace in the hole. Don't forget about Skippy. He may be all the way on the other side of this star system, but right now, he is already controlling everything the Kristang see through their satellites. It is a long walk to the Kristang base, one thing we will not have to worry about is being detected on satellite images. I am counting on Skippy giving us the advantage of surprise. We're going to hit them by surprise, hit them hard, and they won't even know there is anyone else on this planet until our bullets start exploding."

When I dismissed people from the meeting, to begin thinking up ideas on how to attack the Kristang, I walked over to Chang. "Colonel, we now need a single leader of the SpecOps teams. I want you to put together a list of-"

"Captain Smythe," Chang interrupted me.

"Smythe?"

"Smythe. And if you ask the other five team leaders, they will tell you the same. Smythe has everyone's respect, everyone likes him, and he has by far the most experience commanding special operations in combat. He was up to be promoted to major, but he turned it down, because UNEF wanted the team leaders all to be captains, so they would be equal in rank."

"Huh. I didn't know that."

"It's in his personnel file, sir," Chang chided me gently.

"Smythe, then?"

"Yes."

"You've put some thought into this, ahead of time," I observed.

"I am the executive officer, I wouldn't be much use if I didn't keep you out of trouble, sir."

Before we could attack the scavenger base and take the AI and comm node, we needed a plan. The SpecOps leaders began looking at maps and gathering data as soon as I dismissed people from the meeting. What I did was call Skippy. Before we made elaborate plans, I wanted to try something very simple and easy. "Hey, Skippy, I've got a question for you."

"What?"

"You said even a nuke wouldn't damage you, right?"

"True."

"Great-"

"True, both that I said it, and that a nuke can't harm me. To be clear. Since I'm talking to a monkey."

"Uh-huh. Same with this other AI?"

"Possibly. I don't know for certain, it depends on the strength of its connection to the local spacetime. If that connection is weak, an explosion could damage it."

"Crap."

"Why did you ask?"

"Because," I said, mentally crossing one idea off my list, "I was hoping you could hit the Kristang base with a couple missiles, then all we would need to do is sort through the debris to find this beer can, I mean, AI." The Thuranin missiles aboard the *Dutchman* weren't tipped with nuclear warheads, they used some fancy high-tech molecular compression device that had a high explosive yield without radiation.

"Ah ha. Unfortunately, there are four problems with your idea. First, even one of our missiles might damage the AI, and we can't risk that in any way. Second, I would be launching the missiles at very long range, which would make it almost impossible to time their impact when all the Kristang are at their base. Third, a missile will certainly damage the comm node, which is almost as important as the AI. Elder communications nodes are rather fragile devices, for reasons I had best not explain to monkeys. And fourth, perhaps most important, we currently don't have any missiles aboard the *Flying Dutchman*."

"What?" I asked, surprised. "We had eight-"

"Dumdum, you forget I used one to carry the microwormhole to Newark."

"Fine, seven. We had seven missiles!"

"You are entirely, one hundred percent accurate. We *had* seven missiles. To repair the *Dutchman*, I had to disassemble them for raw materials and fuel."

"Well, that's just freakin' great," I fumed. "When were you going to mention that? What the hell is the point of me being a commander if I didn't know what is going on with my own ship?"

"I'm building a starship from moon dust here, you want every detail? We also no longer have a galley or a gym, those parts of the ship are currently being used as a crude particle accelerator, to transmute rare elements I need."

"A warship, that now does not have any missiles, is kind of an important fact I need to know, Skippy. Although we're going to need a galley eventually."

"Damn, Joe, what is so important about a freakin' galley anyway?"

"Skippy, we have a crew of people who, whether they think about it consciously or not, in the back of their minds they know we're never going home. You said it, after you contact the Collective, you'll be gone, and it's very unlikely we can fly the ship all the way back to Earth by ourselves. Food, good food, prepared by people we know, served hot, in a place we can gather and enjoy it together, that's important. That is vital to morale, Skippy. We need it. It is one of the few comforts we have out here, no matter how bad the situation is, if we can look forward to eating something good, that gives us hope. It's a meatsack thing, you understand? A galley is important, we need it."

"Also," Skippy chuckled, "your galley does provide me with endless opportunities for amusement. Ok, by the time you get back aboard, we will have a galley, at least part of a gym, and three, maybe four missiles. As the reactors come back online, and I process raw materials into useable substances, I will be able to divert resources to habitation needs and weapons. My projection is that we will have enough materials and energy, to assemble up to eleven missiles total. Not all these new missiles will have full capability, we simply don't have the resources for that type of manufacturing."

"Skippy, I do appreciate the enormous amount of work you're doing." At my parents' house, weekend projects were carefully planned, because a round trip to a decent hardware store or lumber yard, took over two and a half hours. Skippy's hardware store was whatever tools he could make by himself.

"Remember that when you get back here, and parts of the ship are still off-limits to be decontaminated from high-energy radiation."

"I'm sure we will simply love what you've done with the place."

"It will truly be magical, I'm going with an arts and crafts style theme, with a blending of elements from Disney and French bordello. Blowing up the scavenger base with a missile won't work, what is your backup plan?"

"That was the backup plan, Skippy. The original plan is we raid the scavengers' base. I'm working on that."

The reason we were still working on plans for the raid was, we didn't have a workable plan. The best plan would be for our special forces to attack the scavengers' base at night, wearing powered armor. Speed, power, surprise, that plan had all the advantages. We would need to sneak up to their base, take cover, and wait until their aircraft was safely down and secured. Thanks to Skippy, we could track their aircraft, and we had a complete layout of their base. Thanks to the fact that the scavenger leaders didn't trust their forced labor, and therefore had the base covered with surveillance, Skippy tapped into their systems and could see almost everything inside their base. There was a very basic problem with that plan; our armored suits didn't store enough power to walk all the way to the scavenger base. The stupid Kristang hadn't built their suits with removable powercells, so we couldn't bring along enough energy to have a person in a suit carry an empty suit and leapfrog to get there. In regular use, powered suits were supposed to be supported by portable recharging units, and we didn't have even a single one of those with us. However we got there, we wouldn't have armored suits for the assault. As good as our special forces were, they wouldn't be so special matched up against Kristang. We would be facing over thirty larger, stronger, faster, genetically perfected aliens, and four, possibly six of them would have armored suits. We needed a way to even the odds before we attacked. So far, we didn't have a good plan to do that. The special forces worked feverishly to develop an attack plan, and so far, none of our ideas minimized the risk sufficiently for me to have confidence that we could succeed.

That night, I woke up in the middle of the night with an idea. My unconscious mind is apparently smarter than I am when I'm awake, I don't know what that says about me. My plan, and it was pretty freakin' brilliant in my humble opinion, would accomplish two things; whittling down the number of Kristang we were facing, and removing the Kristang's advantage of air power. If the plan worked, that is. Knowing I wouldn't get back to sleep, I got out of my cot and walked quietly across the cavern to get coffee, tiptoeing carefully around people sleeping on cots and sleeping pads. Then I walked outside, where it was chilly and damp but thankfully not raining, and I called Skippy to discuss my idea with him. Surprisingly, he shut up long enough for me to explain my idea.

"Hmmm," Skippy said, "*this* is your plan? Perhaps I had better get out the dictionary and explain the definition of the word 'plan' to you."

"I know what a plan is, Skippy. Other than the fact that this plan was dreamed up by a monkey, do you see any major problems?"

"I have to admit that this plan is, possibly, not the most incredibly awful stupid thing I've ever heard. Possibly. It is clearly in the top five of all-time stupid ideas in this galaxy, of course, from there it's a matter of judgment."

"Damn, thanks for the vote of confidence, Skippy. Seriously, do you see any problems? A lot of the plan relies on you."

Craig Alanson

"It relies entirely on me, you moron! And here I am on the other side of the freakin' star system, building a starship out of moon dust. The biggest problem, and if you had more than two brain cells, you'd know this, is that your plan has multiple potential points of failure. Unless all parts of the plan work correctly, the entire plan collapses."

"Ok, Ok, I hear you. You got any better ideas?"

"No, I'm good. Let's try this one."

"What!" I almost shouted. "You bust my balls about me making a stupid plan, and you're Ok with it?"

"Yeah, sure, it's good enough. Come on, Joe, you're monkeys. I figure, what are the odds that you will ever think up a better plan?"

CHAPTER NINETEEN

We put my possibly not incredibly awful stupid plan into action two days later. Two days after that, the Kristang took the bait.

The bait was, supposedly, an Elder energy tap. Through their satellites, Skippy showed the scavengers a tantalizing view of an energy tap lying on the floor of a narrow canyon, our cover story was that the artifact had been exposed by a convenient landslide. The landslide was real, the energy tap we faked up with spare parts and discarded items, it only needed to look convincing from the top of the canyon or higher.

If the scavengers were marginally competent, they would have noticed the unburied energy tap within hours of the landslide. They were completely incompetent, they didn't notice the prized energy tap lying there on the ground, in the intermittent sunshine. Skippy got so frustrated, he wanted to call every one of their zPhones and ask if there was any way they could be more stupid. Thankfully, he restrained himself, and the scavengers finally noticed after Skippy practically shoved it in their faces, by highlighting it in their daily sensor summary.

We followed their aircraft, all the way from it being flight prepped at the scavengers' base, to watching through our satellite as two pilots and eight other Kristang loaded aboard and it took off. The aircraft was very much like the Ruhar 'Buzzard' transport I knew from Camp Alpha and Paradise, only this one was a little bigger and a lot uglier. And beat up, even from high orbit the satellite cameras showed us the patched, scratched and dented skin of the aircraft. Skippy said the maintenance records indicated the Kristang did the absolute minimum required to keep it in the air, one of the engines was more than a thousand hours late for an overhaul, and the pilots complained that engine always ran alarmingly hot. The other engine ran only slightly too warm and produced plenty of power, except that it vibrated so much it practically shook loose from its mounting. When the scavengers left Newark, they wouldn't be taking the aircraft with them, I could see why they didn't want to put extra resources into keeping it airworthy. That was easy for me to say, since I wasn't riding in that rattling deathtrap. Maybe it would fall out of the sky, without us having to do anything.

After it took off, Skippy followed its flight by satellite, we were able to watch it every second. The Kristang were being cautious with their beat up aircraft, they could have come to get the fake Elder power tap the day before, but the weather had been bad, with low clouds and rain. The day the aircraft left the base, the weather was patchy clouds and cold, with only light winds. Perfect for landing a poorly maintained aircraft in an unfamiliar area.

"What do we call it?" Smythe asked, while we watched the aircraft cruising along high above the clouds, it was headed straight for us.

"The aircraft?" Adams inquired. "On Paradise, the Ruhar had a similar vertical lift transport that we called a Buzzard. This is the lizard version, we can call it a Luzzard for now. Or something like a crow, maybe."

"Luzzard is good enough for now," I said, I didn't want us to get distracted by a discussion that wasn't relevant to the operation. "Skippy, what are they saying?"

"The pilots haven't communicated with their base since the aircraft reached cruising altitude. I can't hear them talking inside the aircraft. Hey, I can relay their transmissions to you, and translate it," Skippy offered.

Craig Alanson

"That would be great," it would be useful to hear what the pilots were telling their base, in real time. "Relay it to the Zinger teams also."

"Affirmative."

We expected the Luzzard to overfly the bait, our fake Elder power tap, it made sense they would want to thoroughly check out the area. What we did not expect was for the Luzzard to fly over the area, at high altitude, several times, and then fly in a wide circle three times. It was a damned good thing it had rained a lot recently, the rain covered up the fact that the area near the caverns had been well trampled by humans. We had gathered grasses and shrubs from other areas and scattered them over places where we'd walked often enough to create a path through the mud, the rain couldn't hide those tracks by itself. Except for the Zinger teams and spotters like myself, everyone else was waiting deep in the caverns, with all power shut off, and no artificial heat sources. We were as prepared as we could be, given the circumstances.

Desai, who was with me, told me the pilot likely circling the area to look for a low-risk place to land. The Luzzard was flying slowly, cruising around, and it was a tempting target, although it was within Zinger range, it was not comfortably within Zinger range. If the pilot detected a Zinger immediately, and the missile for any reason missed on its first intercept attempt, the Luzzard could have flown out of range, and that would be a disaster for us. We stuck to the plan, and waited for the Luzzard to descend. The Zinger teams remained under cover, maintaining discipline, waiting for Smythe's signal.

Descend it did. Through Skippy, we heard the pilot call back to his base, announcing that he was making one more pass over the bait, at low altitude, and that he intended to land on top of a canyon ridge, rather than risk landing at the bottom of a canyon and not being able to fly back out in the aircraft he didn't completely trust. There was apparently some protest about that idea from the other Kristang aboard the Luzzard, it meant they would need to climb down the canyon, then all the way back up, lugging the precious power tap with them.

The Luzzard approached from the south, with the sun behind it and not interfering with the pilot's vision. It descended rapidly at first, then went into a shallow dive. The pilot was going to fly over the canyon where the bait was located, and land atop the canyon wall to the north. I gave the 'Go' signal to Smythe, and he took it from there.

An Indian paratroop team got lucky, or unlucky, they were in the perfect position as the Luzzard approached. Just as the Luzzard cleared the south canyon wall, the paratroopers rippled off a pair of missiles, and they were on the unfortunate Luzzard in the blink of an eye. Both Zingers impacted the Luzzard's starboard engine nacelle, drawn in by the glaring heat signature of the straining engine. Those Zingers were smart, they knew that while the engines were vulnerable, and easier to target in any aircraft surrounded by a stealth field, the most vital part of the aircraft was its power center, where energy for the engines was generated and stored. That is where the Zingers would normally have targeted themselves, which would have been no good for our purpose; we needed the Kristang to see a Luzzard that fell out of the sky because an engine exploded. For them to fly over the crash site, and see that missiles had ripped holes in the body of the aircraft, would have screwed up all our plans. That is why the SpecOps Zinger teams manually targeted the starboard engines, and locked the Zingers' seekers there before launch.

Without a stealth field, without the pilots taking any precautions against an enemy they didn't even know was on the planet, and with the pilots flying low and slow over the canyon, searching for the bait we'd planted, the Luzzard was a sitting duck. The first missile destroyed the starboard engine, the second missile impacting a split-second later obliterated what was left of the engine, plus most of the sponson it was attached to. Missile warhead debris and engine turbine blades splattered the fuselage, ripping it apart like tissue paper. The Luzzard staggered in the air, spinning rapidly to the right, its nose in the air, then it flipped over on its back and fell straight down. The tail clipped the lip of the north canyon cliff, shearing part of the tail off, and sending the Luzzard tumbling end over end, bouncing off the canyon wall on its way down to a violent crash on the canyon floor, where it rolled over several times. What was left, which was surprisingly intact, came to rest with the back half partly submerged in a stream.

"Alpha teams, hold position," I ordered. Captain Xho, I knew, was itching to get into real action with his Alpha team in powered armor suits, and I couldn't blame him one bit. The Kristang we'd seen boarding the Luzzard had been wearing typical cold weather gear, no armor and no weapons that we could see. It was possible one or two armor suits were inside the Luzzard, and the Kristang had donned them in flight, that seemed unlikely. From the intel Skippy had gathered, access to the armor was restricted to the high-ranking Kristang, it was intended for them to keep their forced labor under control. Considering that, I couldn't see their leaders allowing the laborers in the Luzzard having access to any type of weapon.

I also couldn't see how anyone, even genetically perfected super warriors like Kristang, could have survived the crash. The super-tough composites of the hull structure had held together, in conditions where a human-built craft would have been flaming chunks. For all their enhancements, the Kristang were biological, with the limitations of biology. The extreme g-loads of the crash must have snapped necks, crushed rib cages, torn limbs off. There was no way, I was sure, any of them could have survived that.

I think I was sure. "Alpha team, hold position," I ordered, "repeat, hold position."

"Acknowledged," Xho replied tersely.

"Skippy, you feeding our cover story in the video?"

"Affirmative," Skippy said with uncharacteristic brevity.

Our friendly beer can, controlling data feeds through the Kristang's's two satellites, was the key to our entire plan to knock out the scavengers' advantage of air power, and whittle down their numbers. What we saw, on the ground, was a Luzzard flying slowly over our fake Elder treasure, and a pair of Zingers racing up from the ground to blow up the Luzzard's starboard engine. We heard, through our zPhones, the pilots shouting a warning about missiles, then the Luzzard fell out of the sky and crashed to the bottom of the canyon.

If the Kristang at their scavenger base had seen the same thing, it would have been an absolute disaster for the Merry Band of Pirates. The Kristang would have been alerted to the presence of a hostile force on Newark, they likely would have overflown us to recon the area at high altitude with their dropship, keeping above Zinger missile range. They could have used the dropship to follow us on our march to their base, dropping off armor-suited warriors to harass us, and they would have prepared defenses around their base so that it would be extremely difficult if not impossible for us to successfully attack. Their leaders could, likely would, even have taken the dropship, with their precious Elder artifacts up into orbit, or to another part of the planet that we couldn't get to by walking. And, when their retrieval ship arrived, the scavengers certainly would have told the ship about an unknown hostile group on Newark, and that ship would have pounded our positions to dust from orbit.

Craig Alanson

Bottom line: we needed to shoot down the Luzzard, and make the Kristang think it was an accident, completely conceal our presence on the planet.

Enter the magic of Skippy the Magnificent.

Through his complete control of the two Kristang satellites, he was already assuring that the scavenger lizards did not see any sign of human activity on Newark. The satellites edited the images and sensor data they transmitted down to the scavengers, so they saw only what we wanted them to see. They hadn't seen our dropships making multiple trips to bring people and supplies down to Newark. They didn't see humans walking around, they didn't see the solar panels we set out, they didn't detect increased infrared radiation from the heat human activity generated. When the Kristang looked at satellite images, if they ever bothered to look at our area of the planet, all they saw was grasslands, low-growing shrubs, mud and rocks. Oh, and streams and rivers here and there. No humans. No sign that Newark was inhabited by any other sentient species.

With Skippy in complete control of the audio, video and sensor data feeds through the satellites, what the Kristang at the scavenger base saw and heard was their Luzzard hovering over a priceless Elder artifact, then the pilots shouting a warning that the starboard engine was overheating. The engine then tore itself apart, and the Luzzard crashed down, the pilot's last words were to curse the scavengers' leaders for ignoring his warnings about neglecting engine maintenance. The video feed through the satellites did not show humans approach the wreck, with some of those humans in Kristang powered armor. All the video feed showed was the busted Luzzard laying dead on the floor of the canyon, with no movement in or around it.

And the video feed showed a priceless Elder artifact, still there, still exposed in the patchy sunlight. Still tempting, too tempting for the scavengers to ignore.

The scavenger leaders may not have cared about the Kristang who died in the crash; they may have written off the Luzzard as a cost of doing business. There was no way they were going to ignore a priceless Elder treasure that could make their entire miserable expedition pay off for them. What I was counting on was that the scavengers still had air transport, their dropship. And they would be coming for our decoy in that dropship, coming unaware their Luzzard crash had not been an accident, unaware that humans inhabited Newark. I was counting on greed, I was counting on desperation, and more importantly, I was counting on Kristang being Kristang. When their starship arrived to retrieve them, if that ship detected the Elder artifact still sitting exposed in the open, far from the scavenger base, the captain of that ship would be strongly tempted to land in his own dropship, and take the artifact for himself.

No way would the scavenger leaders risk that, they were coming again for our decoy. Of that, I was certain.

After ten minutes, with no movement from the crashed Luzzard, I gave Smythe the go ahead signal to send in the Alpha teams. Two Chinese were closest, when they got the signal, they popped up from the covered hole they'd been concealed in, and quickly raced across the muddy grass to the crashed Luzzard. Those two soldiers had way more discipline that I could have managed under the circumstances, in powered armor I would have rocketed out of that hole thirty feet in the air, and leaped halfway to the target in a single bound. These soldiers used the advantage of their suit's power in a controlled fashion, sticking close to the ground, rifles always fixed securely on the back ramp of the Luzzard. The rear door had popped open in the crash, the force of the impact wrenching the top of the ramp loose from its latching mechanism. One of the soldiers held a zPhone up to the gap so we could get a view inside the Luzzard, while the other soldier covered him.

"I don't see anything moving in there," Xho declared.

"Agree," Smythe said, "wait for the French Alpha team, then we go in."

The two French soldiers in powered armor, who had been concealed a half kilometer down the canyon, were almost at the crash site, approaching from the front of the Luzzard. Through the feed from the zPhone network, we could all see inside the busted ship, it was chaos in there. The Kristang had exercised poor discipline in securing items inside their ship, the crash had caused all kinds of equipment to break loose and fly around inside the cargo compartment. The occupants may have been in more danger from their own gear, than from falling two hundred meters straight down. Whatever caused the damage, they appeared to be all dead, there wasn't anything moving inside the main compartment of the Luzzard. Two lizard bodies were visible in the narrow view provided by the zPhone, their legs were at awkward angles, and dark red blood was seeping onto the floor.

When the French arrived, one of them slung his rifle, and jumped easily up on top of the Luzzard near the front, then lay down and crept forward to peer in the cockpit windows. "They're both dead up here," he said, holding a zPhone so we could all see the carnage. I recognized the voice; it was Renee Giraud. And if I had been paying attention, there was an icon at the bottom of my zPhone screen, telling me the view I was watching was from 'Giraud, R (FR)'. The Kristang were hateful lizards, but they made good phones. Especially after Skippy replaced the original software with something of his own creation. "They must have been hit by shrapnel from the warheads," Giraud reported, "the windows have holes in them. The cockpit is shredded. It's, it's ugly," he said softly.

"Should we check inside, sir?" Smythe asked.

"Yes, if we can get the back ramp or a side door open, I don't want us to cause any damage that doesn't look like it was caused by the crash," I said. "We need to maintain our cover story as much as possible."

The side door had a recessed handle, with instructions written in Kristang, that Skippy had the visors on the suits translate for the Alpha team. It was simple; in case of emergency, the door was supposed to be easy for rescuers to open, just like a human aircraft. One of the Chinese got the side door open easily, and panned his zPhone around. There was still nothing moving in there. Because the armor suits were bulky, the four Alpha team members waited for the Indian team, without suits, to arrive from up the canyon. The four Indian paratroopers quickly entered the Luzzard, and within thirty seconds, reported that the Kristang inside were all dead.

"Understood," I said, "all teams, pull back, cover our tracks." That was the signal for the Alpha teams, weighed down with armor, to leave the area first, and for the people not wearing armor to sweep the embedded footprints and cover deep, muddy footprints with grass we'd collected from other areas. When they were done, it was hard to tell anyone had been there, and as heavy rain was expected that night, all signs would be securely washed away by morning. I called that a success. Phase One, complete.

When I'd explained my Phase Two plan to deal with the scavengers' second aircraft, a dropship, and destroy the scavengers' remaining air power, Smythe had not been enthusiastic.

"No good," Smythe had said, pointing at the map, "too many possible landing sites for us to cover. We only have six Zingers left."

"Captain," I asked, "tell me, where would you land that dropship?"

"That's the problem. I'd touch down here," he indicated a spot far to the east of the site where we had placed the fake Elder power tap, "or here, or here, or here. Touch down, drop off a three man team in armored suits, then drop off another three man team in armor somewhere over here," to the west of the crash site. "Then the dropship would fly high cover, out of Zinger range, while their two teams approach the target from opposite directions."

I nodded. "That's what I would do also. That's not what these Kristang will do. Dr. Mesker, could you come here, please?"

"Certainly, what is it, Mister Bishop?" Mesker didn't get the nuances of military rank structure.

I pointed to the crash site on the map. "This is the decoy landslide site, you're familiar with the area? We put our bait there, the fake Elder power tap? It's in that canyon behind the cathedral complex."

"Yeah, sure, I've been there. That's a steep canyon."

"Right," I tapped the crash site on the map. "If you were flying in to examine the decoy site, where would you land?"

"Uh," he tapped the map to bring up a satellite picture overlay, then back to the map. "Here, the canyon widens out and the floor is big enough to land on this side of the stream, plus it's an easy walk up to the crash site. Except you'd need to cross the stream here, it hugs the canyon wall."

I smiled. "Thank you, Dr. Mesker. Captain Smythe, that's how a civilian thinks, and that's how the Kristang here think also. These scavengers are civilians, they're not soldiers. You're used to planning to counter a military opponent. Remember, these particular Kristang have no reason to think the Luzzard crash was anything but an accident, they think they're alone on this planet. They're going to land that dropship as close as possible, to reduce the distance they have to walk to get our decoy, and the distance they have to carry anything they salvage from the crash. Mesker is right, they're going to land on the canyon floor somewhere, likely further down than he said, because their pilot doesn't want to take any risks with their one remaining aircraft, he'll want a clear path for a takeoff if he's fully loaded on the return. Somewhere in this area," I pointed near where that canyon opened into a broad, shallow canyon. "Your Zinger teams can take position above the canyon here and here, and on the canyon floor here. That dropship will likely overfly the crash site before selecting a spot for landing, you can hit him as he's over the canyon, minimize the pilot's reaction time."

Captain Smythe thought for a moment, then nodded.

"What do you think," I asked, "two Zinger teams on the canyon floor, covering the best landing site, and one team on each side of the top of the canyon?"

"Two on the canyon floor, yes, I'll want them able to cover each other. One on top of the canyon wall as you said, the south side, and I also want one team up here, on this hilltop. A team up there can cover the whole area. The hilltop doesn't give the best angle for a shot, we'll keep that Zinger team in reserve in case things go very sideways."

I, of course, approved the SpecOps team leader's plan, because he knew a lot more about clandestine operations than I did. To my surprise, when the dropship arrived, Smythe wanted me atop the hillside, instead of watching the action from inside the cave. Of all the people on Newark, Smythe explained, I was the only one who had fired a Zinger in combat. The SpecOps troops had trained with a simulator aboard the *Dutchman*, but they all had much more extensive experience with whichever model of Man Portable Air

Defense missile their country's military used on Earth. Smythe was concerned that, in the tension of combat, Zinger teams would be subconsciously thinking in terms of the MANPAD missiles they were familiar with on Earth, and not the much more capable Zingers on their shoulders. He wanted me, essentially, acting as a spotter on the hilltop for the primary Zinger teams below on the canyon floor. That was much better than what I expected him to want me to do, which was to sit in the cave and watch the action on an iPad or zPhone screen. He even went so far to suggest that, if the hilltop team, our reserves in case things went squirrelly, needed to shoot at the dropship, I personally should fire the missile. "You have experience shooting a Zinger, sir," Smythe explained. "Your report from Paradise says you got off a snap shot, at a Chicken that was aware of you and about to shoot back. That's one less variable to worry about, if we truly need it."

"I appreciate your confidence, Captain, I will be on the hilltop." While Smythe was on the valley floor, where we expected the dropship to land. "There shouldn't be anything to be concerned about, these Zingers are extremely easy to use." I certainly hoped I was right about that. Until Smythe mentioned it, I hadn't even considered our team's lack of live fire experience with Zingers to be anything to worry about. That's where Smythe's greater experience and training showed, against my own. He considered anything that could go wrong, I'd only thought of things likely to go wrong. That was one difference with elite soldiers; they left almost nothing to chance.

Phase Two didn't work exactly as I expected. Again, the Kristang waited until there was clear weather over both their base and our area, a delay of two days. We watched the dropship being loaded, taking off, and cruising toward us. The dropship didn't bother to overfly the crash site; they must have thought they had plenty of intel from the satellites. From listening in to the dropship pilot's communications with the scavenger leaders back at the base, we knew the leaders were extremely anxious not to take any risks with their last functional aircraft, they ordered the pilot to land in an open area, and to stay away from narrow canyons. Instead of overflying the Luzzard crash site, the dropship came straight in from the southwest. My services as a spotter for the Zinger teams were not needed, because the dropship flew directly over a site we thought was a likely place for the Kristang to land. The British SAS had a Zinger team there, they hit the dropship as it flared to go into hover mode, the pair of Zingers streaked up in the blink of an eye and both hit the dropship's starboard engine pod. If that dropship had been at higher altitude, it might have had a chance to recover. It didn't. It flipped over and hit the ground hard, almost nose-first into a big boulder on the canyon floor. The force of the impact pancaked the front quarter of the dropship like an accordion, no way anyone inside had survived the crash.

Smythe held his Alpha teams, the people in armored suits, back for ten minutes to be sure no angry Kristang came out of the wreck. And to be sure the whole thing didn't explode on us. I didn't waste any time, as soon as the dropship hit, I left the Zinger team on the hilltop and ran to the new crash site. It was downhill almost all the way, it still took me over an hour to get there, that was frustrating because from the hilltop, I'd been able to see the crashed dropship, and it took me freakin' forever to get to it. In defense of my fitness level, Newark's gravity had me weighing fourteen percent more than Earth normal, and the low oxygen level had me breathing hard simply when walking around. While running relatively easily down a gentle slope, I checked in with Skippy. "Hey, Skippy, how are your Oscar-winning special effects going?"

"Oh, Joe, this is truly an epic Hollywood production. It has chills, thrills, shocking surprises, and pulse-pounding plot twists that leave the audience gasping. I laughed, I cried. It's the feel good movie of the year! Well, unless you're the scavenger Kristang here, in which case, it's the feel bad movie of the year. Maybe the century."

"Uh huh. They buying it, then?"

"Hook, line and sinker, I believe that is the correct expression. Yes, they believe everything they see and hear through the satellite feed, there is no reason for them to doubt the data."

What the scavenger leaders saw, through the manipulated satellite feed, was their dropship getting shot down by a pair of Zingers, Skippy hadn't edited that part at all. This time, we wanted the scavengers seeing their aircraft shot down with Kristang portable anti-aircraft missiles. After the dropship hit the ground, Skippy had faked the imagery. The scavengers didn't see humans approach the scavengers' crashed dropship, instead they saw Kristang on the ground take the camouflage netting off a concealed dropship, then get aboard that dropship, fly over to the Elder power tap, pick it up, and fly into orbit. The mysterious second group of Kristang, having taken the big prize, then rendezvoused with a ship in orbit, a ship that lowered its stealth field long enough to take the dropship aboard. The ship then climbed out of orbit, out to safe jump range, and when this phantom 'ship' was on the other side of the planet from the scavenger base, it jumped away. The satellite data feed included the tell-tale gamma ray burst of a starship jumping. It was all, Skippy assured us and we hoped, very convincing.

The remaining scavengers had to be hopping mad by now. Not only did they now not have any functional aircraft, they had lost the priceless Elder power tap, lost it to a rival, unknown group of Kristang. A group that got away cleanly, and was now on its way back to civilization, with an Elder artifact that was worth more than many habitable planets. The scavengers were now effectively stuck at their base, with whatever less valuable Elder trinkets they'd recovered, waiting to be picked up.

If that happened to me, I would sure be hopping mad. From Skippy tapping into their communications, he reported the scavenger leaders were swearing vengeance, arguing and fighting amongst themselves, and generally expending a whole lot of energy uselessly.

Phase Two, I judged, was a complete success.

To avoid utter humiliation at my lack of fitness, I stopped for a minute in a stream bed near the crashed dropship, hidden from the SpecOps teams' view, and sucked in air until my pulse stopped racing. The commander showing up, collapsing on the ground and puking after what should have been an easy downhill run, was something I very much wanted to avoid. When my hands stopped shaking, I stepped out of the stream bed, and jogged slowly toward the smashed dropship. Two dozen or more people were standing around it, rifles slung over shoulders, the guys in armor suits had their helmets off. They had gotten a side door open easily, the door frame wasn't even warped in the crash, Kristang built their ships tough, that's for sure. There were four Kristang bodies laying on the wet grass outside their crashed ship, three of the bodies were broken and mangled, one appeared to merely be asleep. I looked away, uncomfortable that these Kristang had died because of a sneak attack on my orders.

Captain Smythe saw me coming and saluted. "Colonel, you need to see this, we have a surprise. We're clear here, the Kristang are all dead."

When we shot down the Luzzard, I had stayed away from the crashed ship, because it brought back too many bad memories. Memories of the two Whales my team had shot down on Paradise. Memories of the Chicken that the Kristang had deliberately crashed there, because the human pilot refused to fire a missile at a school full of children. I had those memories inside my head, they haunted me every day, I didn't need a reminder. That's why I had remained away from the crashed Luzzard. Now, I couldn't avoid seeing the dropship we had shot down, and Smythe expected me to go inside it. Steeling myself inwardly, I nodded silently to Smythe and grabbed the door frame with two hands to pull myself up and into the dropship.

Inside was less of a shambles than I expected, there was some blood and debris had been thrown around in the violence of the crash. When I turned to look toward the rear, I got a surprise. "What in the hell is this?" I asked. The back two thirds of the dropship were stuffed with some sort of, *thing*. It looked like a big, rounded RV, a long tube specially designed to fit inside a dropship, it barely cleared the walls and ceiling. Straps held it securely in place.

"We think it's a vehicle of some kind, sort of a caravan," Smythe explained, "what you Americans call a Recreational Vehicle."

Why in the hell had the Kristang brought an RV with them to Newark? We hadn't seen them loading the RV into the dropship at their base, it must have already been in the ship. It seemed like an awful lot of weight to carry, unless they really needed it. Or maybe they did really need it? An RV would be useful for driving up the canyon, to recover items from the Luzzard crash site, and to get the precious Elder power tap. For use on Newark, the RV would need to be capable of operating over very rough, unimproved terrain. From satellite images, we hadn't seen evidence that the Kristang had built roads anywhere, not even around the widely scattered Elder starship crash site. Although having an RV would have been a great help in exploring, rather than walking, or having to fly everywhere. "How does it move? I don't see any wheels."

Skippy sighed into my zPhone earpiece. "So impatient, you monkey. You can't see the treads because they're retracted, to fit inside the dropship. You will need to get the dropship mostly upright, remove the cargo straps from the RV, and lower the rear ramp, then I'll get it started and drive it out for you."

The dropship was huge, almost the size of a 737 airliner. It was laying on its side. "How are we supposed to get it upright? This thing must weigh a couple tons."

"It does. You can rig up cables, and, I really shouldn't have to remind you dumdums, you have powered armor suits with you, duh."

Duh was right. I hadn't thought about the armor.

Powered armor did help, we needed to tell people to go slowly and be careful, as they almost used too much force and flipped the dropship over on its other side, instead of on its bottom. We gave the dropship a good ten minutes to settle on its bottom, I didn't want to risk anyone going inside, until we were sure its structure wasn't going to collapse on us. When I gave the go ahead, two soldiers went in the side door, and after a few minutes, the rear ramp cracked open, lowered about halfway, and then got jammed in that position. It was amazing the thing worked at all, I suppose. After screwing with it for almost an hour, after which it was still stuck two thirds closed, we gave up and cut through the lift mechanisms on each side. With the supports cut through, the ramp crashed down and bounced on the ground, bent a bit but functional. Next, the team released the straps and latches that held the RV in place. Once freed, it shifted to slide against the port side of the dropship. "All right, Skippy, let's see you drive that RV out of there."

There was a whining sound of electric motors. Skippy had to wiggle it, with a lot of scraping and some tearing sounds, as it slowly extracted itself from the dropship's distorted fuselage. The RV was surprisingly intact; dents and scrapes here and there, nothing that prevented it from running properly. Out of the dropship, we could see its true size, it was as big as a city bus, or a really large RV. What it ran on was interesting; it had wheels, but wheels made of treads like a tank. The treads could be adjusted to be round for speed over good terrain, or oval shaped for crawling along like a tractor. Skippy said the part of the treads that stuck out for traction could be retracted, or extended for use in thick mud. Along each side were inflatable pontoons so the RV could cross rivers, swamps, or even lakes, there were water jets built into each pontoon for propulsion in water. "Damn, Skippy, this is a hell of a vehicle," I had to admit.

"Everything you need for a fun-filled family vacation, Colonel Joe!"

"Yeah, except for a couple sullen teenagers, and a solid week of rain. And bugs." That's what I recall of many fun-filled vacations in my family. "Any chance we can drive this thing all the way to the scavengers' base?"

"Unfortunately, no. The powercells only hold enough charge to get you about forty percent of the way there."

"Crap. Ah, hey, that's forty percent of the way that we don't have to walk. Hey, pop the door open, will you, I want to see inside." We were all eager to see inside our new RV, I went in last, to give everyone a good look at our prize. It was well-worn, and smelled funky. There were no frills on the inside; two seats up front, then a dozen more seats that converted into bunk beds. No kitchen or other provision for cooking, no bathroom, I suppose the Kristang expected their crew to take care of those activities outside. In the back was a large, separate bay for cargo, sort of a garage. It was empty.

Rubbing my chin while looking around the Spartan RV interior, I asked "We can fit, what, twelve, fourteen people in here?"

Smythe shook his head, I took that to mean no special forces soldier would think that way. "To hit that base, against Kristang, maybe against six sets of powered armor, we need numbers. Two people will be up front driving and navigating. We can fit twenty passengers back here, rig up extra seats, I figure we'll be driving through the nights until this thing runs out of power. Another two people, we can rig up seats in the cargo bay, we won't be bringing enough gear along to fill it. There's a cargo rack on the roof, we can set up a tent or some kind of awning up there for protection against bad weather, we can fit another four people. That gives us twenty eight. In this terrain, we won't be driving fast, we might be able to have more guys running alongside it, in shifts."

"No," I shook my head, "last thing we need is somebody spraining an ankle along the way. I don't want any driving at night either, too risky. Twenty eight, huh? That evens the odds somewhat. The more people we bring, the more supplies we need to take with us."

"That is a problem. We can look at some people going only part of the way, as pack mules, carrying weapons so people going into the fight only need to carry their weapons part of the way. This is a logistics problem, sir. We need to think about this, having an RV does solve a whole lot of problems."

CHAPTER TWENTY

Having an RV helped, we still needed to carefully plan the logistics. And it wasn't easy. Smythe had been working with Simms, and some problems remained. Serious problems. "Sir, even with the RV getting us most of the way there, we still have the problem that we can't carry enough food both to get us to the scavenger base, and back here."

"No," I said, "but we can lessen the problem, if we only need enough food to get there," I explained, "and we don't plan to come back."

"Sir?"

"After the assault, we're not walking all the way back here, there's no point. And if that Kristang ships shows up early, while we're walking out in the open, we'll be totally exposed. What we're going to do is, after the attack, we hole up here," I zoomed the map out and scrolled to the west of the scavengers' base. "There are caverns here, in these hills. They're cramped, it's not going to be comfortable. This site is seventy kilometers west of the scavengers' base. We'll be closer to it on our way in, I think we may stop there and drop off any supplies we don't need for the assault. Before we launch the attack."

Smythe tapped his iPad, examining the caverns I mentioned. "That could work. I've holed up in worse places, in the mountains of Afghanistan. We still won't have enough food. We won't even be able to carry enough food to get to the scavengers' base, if we're going to be hauling armor with us."

"That will not be a problem," I said with a wink. "I know a place that delivers." Tapping the transmit icon on my zPhone, I called the *Flying Dutchman*. "Hey, is this Skippy's pizzeria?"

"Um, Ok, sure, I'll play along." His voice changed to a stereotypical New York accent. "Yeah, this is Skippy's pizza, what can I do you for?"

"Do you deliver?"

"Depends. Youze got a coupon or somethin'?"

"Seriously, Skippy, we need a delivery of food and medical supplies, the first aid stuff we brought from Earth, not the fancy nano gizmos that we don't know how to use." I explained how we planned to get to the scavengers' base by driving the RV, then on foot. "By food I mean sludges, dehydrated, we need maximum nutrition in minimum weight and volume. Can you send a couple shipments down to us?"

"Oh, sure, no problem, it's not like I'm busy. You moron! I'm building a freakin' starship out of moondust up here!"

"I know you're extremely busy. We can't carry enough food with us to reach the scavengers' base, not with all the weapons and gear we need for the assault. Can you put together something simple, to drop supplies to us? It will have to be capable of a soft landing, oh, and it has to stay out of sight of the Kristang here. We can't have them seeing a contrail coming in, or parachutes."

"Simple? Something simple, to fly all the way across a star system, enter the atmosphere without leaving a contrail the Kristang could see, and land a package without damaging it? Simple, he says."

"Uh huh, yeah. Can you do that? We don't need the first shipment today, we'll need it probably a couple days, maybe a week before we reach their base, I sent our timeline to you."

"I'm supposed to drop everything I'm doing up here," Skippy complained, "to design, test and build a drone delivery system, from nothing."

"It's kind of important, Skippy. Unless, you know, you don't want us to recover that AI for you. Or you have a better idea."

"Damn it. I've been trying to think up a better idea while you've been blabbering on and on, and, no, I don't have a better idea. Crap. All right, fine, yes, I can put something together to deliver supplies to you. Maybe I'll get lucky, and it will land on your stupid monkey head."

"Excellent! Knew I could count on you, Skippy."

"All I can say is, there better be a *huge* freakin' tip for this delivery."

"Yup," I decided to push my luck. "If the delivery is late, do we get it for free?"

With the food situation temporarily solved by Skippy's Pizzeria, we turned our attention to other logistical issues. "Captain Smythe," I said, "I need you to plan the route from here to the scavenger base, especially the route for driving the RV."

"Skippy already mapped out the fastest route," he tapped his iPad, and the screen showed Skippy's suggested route. "Also two alternatives," two more lines appeared on the screen, "one slightly shorter, and one that stretches out the caravan's power to get us the furthest, before we have to get out and walk." Being British, he called our salvaged vehicle a 'caravan' instead of the American term 'RV'.

"Smythe," I said, "I'm sure Skippy has mapped out mathematically perfect routes, and we can't hope to improve on that. However, I know that little shithead beer can, and one variable he won't include in the billions of calculations he ran, is anything practical. Fastest, shortest, and, uh, stretchiest are all fine, in theory. What we need is the route that gets us to the scavenger base by the target date, with the least risk. For example, on this route here," I tapped the shortest line, "Skippy's plan takes us straight through this big swamp. Sure, the RV can supposedly crawl, or swim, through a swamp. What happens if a tread gets stuck, or a pontoon gets punctured, or a motor burns out, and the RV is stuck in a swamp? Then we might have to walk out of the swamp, carrying all our gear, in freezing cold water over our heads. We can't take that risk. Skippy won't take that sort of possibility into account. He also won't consider that we're inexperienced drivers, so he may plan a route that takes us along a narrow cliff. Got it?"

"Yes, sir," Smythe said, looking chastened.

Wow. For the first time, I felt like a real officer.

Smythe called me over the next morning, he pinged me while I was helping Simms load supplies into the RV. I took a welcome break and went into the cavern to where Smythe was working in a tent. A heated tent. It felt good to step inside and unzip my jacket. "What do you have, Captain?" I asked.

"Several possible routes for us to reach the scavengers' base within 30 days, with minimal risk, we think." He pulled up the first of three routes on his iPad, and explained how the route avoided, as much as possible, swamps, driving across mushy ice fields, and steep terrain where the RV might slide down or tip over. "After we cross this river, we should have enough power left to get here, these grasslands are relatively flat and dry. We'll have to walk from there, the good news is we'll only need to detour forty kilometers to go around this swamp, and once we're past that, it's a straight shot, and, well, Bob's your uncle, we're there."

"Bob's my uncle?" Neither of my three uncles was named 'Bob'.

Smythe chuckled. "It's an expression, sir, it means it's easy."

"Oh. Bob's your uncle, huh?"

SpecOps

"Yes, sir."

"Show me the other alternatives." He did. Each of the three possible routes had advantages; the first didn't get as far before the RV ran out of power, its advantage is the walking part was over easy terrain. The second route stretched out the RV's powercells to cover the maximum distance, minimizing the distance we would have to walk, however, the walking route went through a region of hills and one swampy area. And the third route took the absolutely safest path for the RV, minimizing the possibility it would get stuck somewhere, and the walk would be through relatively flat, easy terrain, the disadvantage was the walking section of the route was the longest of the three alternatives. "Hmm, all the routes require we cross these three rivers?"

"Yes, there's no way around them, literally," Smythe explained. "We've mapped the easiest crossings we can get to along the route, where the river current is slowest. Here for example," he pointed to the first river crossing, which was the same on all three alternatives, the three routes diverged after that. "If we cross up here instead, the river is only half as wide, however, your chap Skippy tells me the current is more than twice as fast in this area, and there are large rocks just under the surface. Down here, where we plan to cross, the current is more manageable, and the river bottom is sand, there are no underwater obstacles the caravan could get stuck on."

I nodded. "Makes sense. Good work."

"The sticky point is that last river. This nasty bugger here," he tapped the iPad screen for emphasis, "is going to be a problem. The glacier that feeds this river is breaking up quickly, there are large chunks of ice floating in the river, we'll need to steer around them. The river channel is narrow almost the whole way down to the sea, it would be hundreds of kilometers out of our way to find an easier crossing. And the river banks are steep. The only place we can see for a crossing is here. The bank on the far side is less than half a meter tall, Skippy tells us the caravan treads can climb that easily, and by the time we get there, with the summer coming on, the river level should be higher as the glacier melt accelerates. The bank is steep on this side, we'll need to create a ramp down into it, lots of work with picks and shovels, nothing the lads can't handle."

He made it sound easy. Maybe to SpecOps types, hacking out a ramp large enough for an RV to drive down was a fun couple hours in the great outdoors. Right then, I had an idea. "Captain, we can use armor to clear a ramp. With those suits, it won't take long at all."

"Do we want to use the suits for this, sir? We'd need to recharge the suits' powercells from the caravan, that will drain the caravan faster."

Not such a good idea after all. I was still thinking of what was now the good old days, when we had nearly unlimited power from the *Dutchman's* reactors. That mindset needed to change, fast, before I made a stupid mistake and got people killed. "You're right. Sore muscles are a problem we can deal with, more easily than draining power from the RV. We need to be very careful with the RV's powercells. Route Two, I think, is out, I don't want us walking through those hills. The extra gravity, the low oxygen level, and the heavy loads we'll be carrying will make the hike tough enough already. Route Three you say is the least risk for the RV, but the walk is longer, how much longer?"

"An additional sixty kilometers, roughly a day and a half, sir." He didn't point out that information was clearly displayed on the side of the map, I should have noticed that.

Sixty kilometers, was, to Captain Smythe of the British Special Air Services, a trek of a mere day and a half. He was assuming we would be walking forty kilometers, or twenty seven miles per day. Walking twenty seven miles each day, with heavily overloaded packs, in gravity fourteen percent greater than we were used to on Earth. "Sixty klicks in a day and a half? You're not being a bit too ambitious, Captain?"

"No, sir, don't worry sir, the lads can handle it. We'll check in every two hours, and you can track our progress through the satellite."

"I'll be tracking your progress closer than that, Captain. I'm going with you."

"Sir?" He asked, surprised.

"I know I'm not one of you SpecOps people, but I can handle a walk. There may be crucial decisions to be made, real-time, when we raid the scavenger's base, I need to be there, right there."

Smythe avoided my eyes. "Sir-"

"Why else do you think I've been busting my ass training with you? I'm going along. Don't worry, I'll stay out of your way during the assault. We're also bringing two civilians with us, doctors, medical doctors."

"Sir?" Smythe's face revealed his anguish. Three of his precious twenty eight billets would be taken up by noncombatants, that reduced his striking power to only twenty five. It was bad enough that I would be going with them, Smythe having to deal with his commanding officer looking over his shoulder and second guessing him in real time. At least I was a soldier, and had been in combat. Including killing a Kristang warrior with my bare hands, or at least, with the butt of a rifle. Bringing two civilians along would be nothing but a headache for him. "We have qualified medics." His roster of twenty eight SpecOps troops included four people with medic certification, in addition to the battlefield first aid training that all special forces soldiers had taken.

"Qualified medics, yes. These two doctors are experienced surgeons, they both did a tour with Doctors Without Borders, they've operated in primitive field conditions. This is not open for discussion, Captain, I am not going into combat against Kristang without means to keep wounded people alive, until we can get them back to the Thuranin medical facility aboard the *Dutchman*."

"Yes, sir," he said tightly.

I could tell he thought I was endangering the primary mission, assaulting the Kristang, in favor of a dubious secondary objective. In combat against Kristang, both sides having equivalent technology, wounds were very likely to be fatal, any medical assistance might well be a useless waste of resources. It may have been my lack of experience as a senior commander that caused me to bring two civilians along, a real colonel may have looked at the problem more objectively, been more coldly calculating about the lives of his soldiers. That wasn't me. Also, I figured that if needed, I could fight, and if two less soldiers were the difference between success and failure, then this entire mission was far too much risk, and I should call the whole thing off right now. "The two doctors, Zheng and Tanaka, have been running and marching with us, you've met them."

Smythe gave a curt nod, unconvinced. What he didn't say was that going out for a run or a long march was one thing, knowing a warm, dry cavern with a meal and hot chocolate was waiting for them at the end of the exercise. Being out in the field, one day after the next, marching with a heavy pack, in the chilly rain, with only maybe a tent roof as comfort at the end of a long day, was a very different test of human endurance, mental endurance. A civilian who had not actually experienced such bone-weariness for days on end, could not say with certainty they could stand up to such strain.

He was right, I was taking a gamble that our two civilian scientist doctors could keep up with us. The SpecOps troops, and me, would be carrying food, clothing, part of a tent and other personal gear, in addition to weapons and parts of disassembled armor suits. The two civilians would only need to carry food, personal gear and medical kits. One way or another, they would be keeping up with us, we weren't leaving anyone behind, unless injury absolutely forced us to do that. "That leaves twenty five billets for combat troops," he mused.

"And five nationalities. Choose five people from each nation," I ordered, "we can't have anyone thinking we're playing favorites."

"Oh. My. God." I was stunned. There, attached to the front of the RV, just below the left windshield in front of the driver, was a stuffed Barney, about a foot tall.

"Sir," Captain Gomez, the leader of our Ranger team, said, "I categorically deny any and all knowledge of this outrageous act. That is, unless you like it."

"Like it? I love it! Damn, reminds me of my old hamvee back on Paradise. I'll ask you the same question I asked then: how the hell did you idiots get a Barney?"

Gomez coughed. "Someone may have listened to your debriefing, and you may have mentioned your personal hamvee then. And that same someone may like to be prepared. I'm speculating, of course."

"Of course." I stood back and admired it, then turned to the assembled team, my team, and saluted. "Thank you. This means a lot. I used to hate that Barney shit. Now, ah, it's part of me, I guess."

Gomez smiled. "Instead of a Winnebago, this is our Barney-We-Go."

"BarneyWeGo," I laughed. "I like it. Captain, let's get this thing loaded, and on the road, ASAP."

Oh, man, I should have put some thought into what a road trip, in a stolen RV, across an alien landscape, with a crew of high-speed SpecOps people, would be like. Our BarneyWeGo lurched into movement, everyone inside gave a hearty cheer and waved to the assembled crowd outside, and we were off. When we splashed across the stream and the canyon veered to the right, so we went out of sight of the cavern that had been our home, Smythe broke into song. Pumping his fist in the air to encourage participation, he sang "The wheels on the bus go round and round-"

I joined in. It was fun, it built a sense of camaraderie, it set a good tone for the beginning of what was going to be a long, arduous journey.

However.

When the first song was done, the Indian team, who likely had been trying to think of a song most people in the RV knew or was simple enough to learn quickly, launched into "Ninety nine bottles of beer on the wall-" And that was fun, for a while. Let me tell you, SpecOps people are hyper competitive, none of them wanted to stop. The singing went on and on, to where we got down to seventy three bottles of beer on the wall, and I for one was heartily sick of it. Of course none of the SpecOps people wanted to be the first to stop, they were way too damned competitive. The responsibility fell to me, as the commander, to mercifully kill the singing. "Stop! Quiet! What was that?" I stood up and walked behind the driver, using as an excuse a clanging sound against the bottom of the RV.

"Oh, sir, we're kicking up rocks here," the driver explained, pointing out the windshield to the layer of rocks in the stream bed we were following down the canyon. There was another soft 'clang' noise as the forward treads caught another stone, and tossed it against the bottom of the RV. The plating of the BarneyWeGo was thicker on bottom to protect against impacts, it also had kind of a skid plate, for when the RV needed to slide over an obstacle.

I called a brief halt, and ducked outside to check the RV's skin, partly out of genuine concern. There were some new scuff marks, no additional dents, nothing to worry about. When I got back inside, I was relieved to see people had broken out decks of cards, and two games were getting started. Card games, even having nothing to gamble with except small pieces of candy people had smuggled in their personal gear, would keep people occupied. Occupied was good. The driver, a Chinese soldier named Zhang, put on some pop music, the rule being whoever was driving controlled the music selection. I couldn't understand the words, and remarked that pop music all over Earth sounded pretty much the same, so it didn't matter that I couldn't understand the lyrics. Captain Li shrugged. "That song is Korean, sir, K-pop, we call it. We don't understand the words either."

Damn, what an interesting international crew we had, aboard our BarneyWeGo, bouncing and lurching our way across the surface of an alien world, almost two thousand lightyears from home. It made me feel proud.

Our first stream crossing was uneventful. Before the RV drove down the bank into the water, I ordered a halt, and for everyone to get out, so Skippy could drive the RV across remotely. The middle of the stream was just deep enough that the RV needed to deploy its floatation pontoons, they worked perfectly. The RV got to the other side, Skippy turned it around and drove it back to us. Then half of us got back aboard, and our Chinese driver carefully took us across, he reported the transition between the RV driving on its treads to floating and using water jets was seamless, the RV's computer knew what to do, based on the driver's inputs to the controls. Captain Giraud drove the RV back to get the rest of us, then we proceeded with an Indian soldier driving. That way, we now had three people with some experience. Damned good thing, too, because we had to cross our first major river in two days. After a couple hours, we stopped at a convenient place to switch drivers. Captain Smythe saw me looking longingly at the driver's seat. "Would you like to have a go at it, sir?" He asked.

"Captain, I would love to drive this thing. I am not going to be some shithead officer who takes fun away from the troops. We'll be driving this RV for days, I can wait my turn."

My policy that whoever was driving picked the music, or no music at all, led to an, let's say, interesting variety of musical styles. The first Chinese driver, a guy named Zhang, had played pop music I didn't recognize, it was at least recognizably pop. The second time a Chinese came up in the driver rotation, it was a guy named Chen. The music he played sounded like a cross between wind chimes, the kind of New Agey thing I expected people listened to at a yoga spa, and someone unsuccessfully trying to tune a guitar. After a while, I looked at Captain Li, who shrugged, rolled his eyes, and we put headphones on to listen to our own music selections. Following Chen it was the turn of an Indian paratrooper named Sharma, who liked to sing, loudly and badly, along with his music. His fellow paratroopers often joined in, off key but with enthusiasm.

When one of our SEALs named Garcia started driving, it was across a relatively flat field, when the treads automatically adjusted themselves to be almost round, and we were making good time. The treads soaked up a surprising amount of bumps, so the jostling and bouncing in the cabin was a lot less than I'd expected. Garcia must have been feeling good, rolling happily along across an alien landscape in our stolen RV, because he changed his music selection in the middle of a song, to go old, old school with Coolio. When the first notes of the song came over the speakers, the Chinese soldiers looked at each other and muttered something, and the Indian soldiers looked at each other and muttered something, and for a split second I feared we were going to have a problem, then the Indians, Chinese and French all stood up, mockingly flashed gang signs, and sang along. Badly, with enthusiasm. "As I walk through the valley of the shadow of death, I look at my life and realize there's nothing left-"

"Holy shit," I said under my breath. "Does everybody know that song?"

Then Captain Smythe got up to join in, and soon everyone in the RV was going "They been spending most their lives livin' in the gangster's paradise-"

High fives went all around when the song ended. Damn, I thought, we really are one bad-ass international team. Hopefully, we could bring that cooperative team spirit back to Earth one day.

That night after we stopped driving, the sky was cloudy but not raining, the wind had slowed to a gentle breeze, and for an early summer evening on Newark, it wasn't too cold. Smythe and I surprised the group by unrolling a screen and attaching it to the side of the RV, so we could have movie night. Captain Chander of the Indian team provided a Bollywood hit movie. The Indians had all seen it before, the film was new to the rest of us. With our zPhone earpieces translating for us, we were all able to understand the words without annoying subtitles. It was a pretty good movie, involving car chases, a forbidden love affair, gangsters and something about diamond smuggling. Toward the end, I lost track of the complicated plot because I was so tired. The thing that made me sit up and take notice was that, in the middle of a big fight scene, the characters all stopped fighting to break into an elaborate, choreographed song and dance routine. Minutes later, the music ended, and they all went back to beating the crap out of each other. Gomez of the Ranger team expressed himself on behalf of most of us; when the fighting on the screen resumed, he shook his head as if he couldn't believe his eyes and said aloud "What in *the hell* just happened?"

The Indians all grinned and laughed, and Smythe responded, with dry British humor, "Well, I suppose that's not any more strange than a Hollywood film where a car turns into a flying robot, is it?"

CHAPTER TWENTY ONE

The first major river crossing was no big deal. We stopped at the river bank to check out the best spot to get the RV down into the river, more importantly the best spot for it to climb out on the far shore. The amount of dirt we had to move, to create a ramp down into the water, was a lot less than I'd feared, we had the job done in less than two hours. Next, I had one person drive the RV across and then back by herself, the driver for that shift was a Chinese named Liu, one of only three female SpecOps soldiers with us. She drove the RV into the water, it slipped in the mud and made a big splash, wobbled a bit, then steadied and motored easily across. Liu reported the spot we'd chosen to climb out on the far bank was crumbly, I told her to use her judgment, and she selected a place upstream. The RV's treads powered it out of the water, and we could see Liu pumping her fist triumphantly in the front window. She came back across, loaded us aboard, and we went boating again.

During the day, while we sat in or on top of the RV, there wasn't much to do, except for the driver and the person acting as navigator. Smythe had everyone bring up maps of the scavenger base on their tablets, and together, the SpecOps teams created and rehearsed assault plans for a wide variety of contingencies. Most of our plans to hit the base depended on speed, surprise, and the cover and confusion of darkness. If we had to, we could attack during the day, that was not optimal. Thanks to the Kristang troopship in Earth orbit, we had excellent night vision equipment. Our night vision gear looked like regular goggles, the kind you would use for skiing or riding a dirt bike or around power tools. Ordinarily, the goggles were clear and they worked like any plastic safety goggles on Earth, except these could stop a rifle bullet, and they repelled water, dust and dirt using magnets or force fields or some super high tech thing like that. Press a button on the left side of the goggles, and the inside of the lenses displayed whatever image you commanded from your zPhone. You could select a night vision mode that displayed an enhanced view from the tiny cameras at each corner of the goggles, or you could pull up a map, data, or the view from someone else's goggles. That feature was very helpful to leaders, they could see what their troops were seeing, in real-time. You could even split the view, one side displaying a night vision image of what is in front of you, overlaid with a map, the other side displaying what some other soldier was seeing. It took some getting used to, and of course we had to stop treating it as a toy and learn how best to use different features depending on the situation. Until we gained more experience and proficiency, the simple night vision feature was best for most soldiers. Unlike the US Army night vision gear I was used to, which restricted your peripheral vision and displayed a fuzzy, false-color image, the Kristang goggles showed you a view similar to twilight; the colors were muted, otherwise it simply appeared less bright than usual.

Doing imaginary dry runs on a tablet screen had only limited usefulness. Each night, after we stopped and set up camp, Smythe created a small scale model of the scavenger camp, using back packs for buildings and rope for fencing. Smythe spent an hour every evening, rain or shine but mostly rain, explaining assault plans under various scenarios. Using a small 3D model, with everyone standing around it, did help. Still, Smythe regretted that we didn't have the time to build a full size model of the scavenger camp, so the team could practice for real, instead of imagining. Creating a fake scavenger camp hadn't been possible before we shot down their two aircraft, we couldn't risk the Kristang seeing a fake camp from the air. And before we set out in the RV, we hadn't known how fast we could travel. Now, Smythe thought we should have taken a couple days, even a week, to practice assaults before we set out in the RV.

Two days after crossing the first river, we were driving through a series of hills that stretched across our path. When planning the trip, these hills were a major concern, they turned out to be not a problem at all. The RV's treads automatically adjusted to the terrain and we made good time, all the driver needed to do was watch out for huge boulders that were strewn all over the area. The science team, back at base and watching our progress through satellite images, thought that these boulders had been left there by a glacier. A glacier that had covered the entire area, perhaps a kilometer thick, after Newark had been pushed out of its original orbit. As Newark's orbit changed and the planet warmed up again, the retreating glacier had dumped rocks it picked up on its journey to the south. The hills we drove over, a series of parallel ridges, were a 'terminal moraine' according to our science team. Basically, each ridge was where a glacier had stopped and dumped all dirt, rocks and other junk it had accumulated while it was expanding.

We came over a hill, the next hill was a kilometer ahead of us, with a nice flat area in between. It was late afternoon, I was looking at the map, trying to find a good place to stop for the night. While the sun had been popping in and out of clouds all day, we would be getting a steady rain over night, into the next afternoon. I looked up from the map to gaze out the windshield, and the flat, open valley in front of us caught my eye. "Hmm," I grunted. On my iPad, I zoomed in the satellite image. Other than some rocks sticking out the ground, the area between hills was pretty much flat and free of major obstacles. "Captain Smythe," I said, "this area in front of us, what do you think?"

He clearly didn't know what I was referring to. "This area reminds me a bit of the Yorkshire Dales, sir, if-"

"No, I mean, here, look at this." I showed him the satellite image of the valley, over which I had pulled up an outline of the scavenger base.

"Interesting," Smythe said, glancing from my iPad screen to the actual terrain in front of us. "We are ahead of schedule," he pointedly added.

"That's what I'm thinking," I agreed. "We can call a halt here, set up a full size replica of the scavenger base while we have light, and practice the assault tonight. It's going to rain tonight," I added.

"Excellent," Smythe grinned approvingly, "because it will most likely be raining during the actual assault."

Within an hour after the RV stopped, we not only had camp set up, we also had the fake scavenger base buildings and fences outlined with stakes and rope. Skippy inspected the layout through satellite images, and gave Smythe grudging approval that the outlines were pretty darned accurate, within a couple inches in most cases. The rain that night ranged from steady, to short downpours to a chilly, foggy mist, and it made an intense and exhausting night completely miserable for everyone. Other than me and the two civilian doctors, everyone thoroughly enjoyed themselves, I'd never seen dead-tired people looking so happy when we halted the exercises just after the sun rose. Smythe had his team run one scenario after another, again and again and again and again, until each assault plan was executed as flawlessly as possible. The people having the most fun were the 'Alpha' teams in Kristang armored suits, they were able to practice jumping from the ground to the top of the RV and back down, and racing at full speed, leaping over rocks and generally showing off.

I observed the exercises, I did not participate. I am not a special forces soldier, I hadn't gone through combat training with them, I didn't know their tactics, I didn't know them as well as they knew each other. If I had insisted on participating in the assault, I would only get in the way, and maybe get someone killed. Observing was enough. The Alpha teams were, of course, awe-inspiring, although after watching them sprint 70 miles an hour and leap thirty feet high, it became somewhat less impressive, because I expected awesomeness from such advanced alien technology. What truly impressed me were the SpecOps soldiers without fancy armored suits. Fast, silent, well-coordinated, they converged on their assigned targets from multiple directions. Because Skippy knew the interior layouts of buildings at the scavenger base, we were able to use rope to outline hallways, doors and walls, so the teams could practice breaching doors and clearing a building room by room. Making things simple for the team was the fact that we were not trying to capture prisoners. We didn't need to be concerned about damaging anything, except for the two items we needed to secure; the AI and the comm node. In other buildings, we could sweep rooms with rifle fire, or use grenades. Wherever the AI and comm node were stored, we needed to be careful, we could not risk hitting either of the Elder artifacts with bullets or explosives. Skippy reported that there were a few Elder artifacts stored in the building where the scavenger leaders lived, items the scavengers thought were the most valuable. To us, those items were useless junk, and Skippy didn't care if we blew them up. The AI and the comm node were inside a secure building the scavengers used as an armory; it was behind an electric fence, with heavy double doors that only the leaders had access to. If the AI and comm node were inside the armory when we launched the assault, our task was easy; secure the armory building, eliminate the Kristang, then we could retrieve the precious items later.

If, for some reason, the two items had been removed from the armory, or even were separated, then the assault team's task was exponentially more difficult. And whatever we did, we couldn't let the scavengers learn that the purpose of our attack was to steal two Elder artifacts, or they could threaten to destroy them, and stall our attack.

Smythe had plans for multiple assault scenarios, that was all great and the team practiced multiple options until they executed each plan like clockwork. What Smythe could not plan for was the unknowns. Technically, we did have plans for the unknowns we could anticipate; the weather, where in the base the scavengers would be sleeping, how many leaders and laborers were awake, what weapons the leaders had with them. Skippy reported that the scavengers did not have any set schedule for base security. Some nights, two or more leaders remained on watch throughout the night. Most nights, the leaders snoozed peacefully all night, relying on their electronic monitoring systems to alert them to any trouble.

In one way, the scavenger base was an easy target for a surprise attack. The scavengers had plenty of weapons, including four functioning powered armor suits. In addition to standard Kristang rifles, the armory held heavy weapons; grenades, anti-armor rockets, and Zingers. What mattered to our planning was that, except for the suits and rifles the leaders kept with them in their secure compound, all the weapons were locked up inside the armory building. On a planet with no native threats, the leaders were mostly concerned about being threatened by their own workforce. That made it easy for us; we needed to be concerned primarily with taking out the leaders, most of Smythe's plans assumed the leaders would be inside their compound at night. During nights, the laborers were locked inside their own compound, unable to get out. The exterior doors of buildings in the laborers' compound were locked at night, and electric fences crisscrossed the base, protecting the leaders from the laborers, and keeping the laborers away from the armory. Once we took out the leaders, we could deal with the laborers later.

That was the plan. What we couldn't plan for was the unknowns we couldn't anticipate. For that, we needed flexibility, and individual initiative; fortunately, SpecOps soldiers excelled at those qualities. I needed to trust that, whatever happened, the team could handle it.

Our two doctors had peacefully slept through the night, in the RV with earplugs and white noise playing on the radio. When it got to be an hour before sunrise, I roused them, and the three of us got a hot breakfast ready for the troops. The breakfast was much appreciated. After we struck camp and removed all traces of the practice area, we resumed traveling toward the scavenger camp, with the two doctors taking turns driving, and me navigating. After six mostly solid hours of sleep, the team was fully refreshed, and it was my turn to sleep. I put in earplugs, strapped myself into a seat with a baseball cap down across my face, and the lurching and bouncing of the RV quickly had me soundly asleep.

Hopefully, I didn't snore.

"Stop here," I ordered a couple days later. Smythe got out of the RV with me, we walked forward to inspect the slope ahead of the RV. It was not an ideal situation. The whole area was crisscrossed by canyons, most with sides far too steep to attempt driving the RV up or down them. There was only one possible route we saw from the satellite data, it looked a lot more drivable from the satellite when we were planning the trip, than now when we were there on the ground. The plan was for us to drive northwest along a relatively wide, shallow canyon until we came to a side canyon, that one was almost like a road that led gently up to the plateau where we wanted to be. The main canyon had a stream running through it, the stream occupied the center bottom of the canyon's shallow V shape, so did a lot of rocks that had tumbled down over the years. It had looked, from the satellite, that we could drive partway up on the right side of the canyon wall, avoiding the big rocks at the bottom. The canyon was broad and shallow enough that the sides walls sloped gently until they reached the lip of the plateau above us.

"This could be a problem," I mused, looking at the terrain the RV needed to drive over. Avoiding rocks did not appear to be a problem, they were as widely spaced on the canyon wall as they'd appeared on the satellite images. The problem was that, in places, the side slope of the canyon wall was steeper than we expected. A few sites were almost forty five degrees. Smythe and I walked forward with the SpecOps team leaders, and our most experienced drivers, we walked over a mile and a half from the RV.

"If we can keep to this line," Williams drew an imaginary line on a shallow diagonal across the slope, "we should be all right. We'll get up there," he pointed to a spot up the canyon wall higher than we wanted to go, "hang an easy left, and drive back down."

"Except for those two ridges," Smythe pointed back to where the side slope of the canyon wall was steep. "If we had time and equipment, we could hack out a road. The first one is only a hundred meters, maybe, but the second one must be half a kilometer. We don't have the time, equipment or manpower." He pulled out his zPhone, and looked at the satellite image of the area, comparing it to what we were seeing on the ground. "This may not be as bad as it appears from here. Do you ski, Colonel?"

"Snowboard, some. My family is more into snowmobiles, our part of Maine is fairly flat, and it's a long drive to go snowboarding."

Smythe nodded. "You know how, when you're at the bottom of a mountain, looking up at the slope, it doesn't appear to be very steep, and you're confident you can get down it? Then, you get off the lift at the top, and sometimes, suddenly, that same slope looks like it goes straight down? Maybe this is like a ski mountain. Maybe it looks more difficult from up here."

"Skippy," I called, "what do you think? Can you drive the RV past those obstacles, or will it flip over on its side?"

"What am I, an off road racer?" Skippy asked. "Yes, it is possible for the RV to drive on a slide slope even steeper than those two areas, the treads have a limited self-leveling function, where the tread on the lower side will extend down to negate the slope. You can also shift cargo inside the RV so the weight is on the uphill side. However, I should not be driving. Even with the microwormhole facilitating communications, there is a time lag between me and the surface, I might not be able to react quickly enough. A human driver, in the vehicle, could feel the operation of the treads in real time, and adjust accordingly. The problem is that the surface is soft and saturated with water, it could be somewhat unstable, I can't predict that. Someone is going to have to drive it for you, Joe. I suppose we're too far from Earth to call Uber?"

And it sure wasn't going to be me driving, I had not yet taken a shift at the RV's controls. We walked back to the RV, making a very careful examination of the two problem areas along the way. Then we got everyone out of the RV, shifted cargo around inside and tied that down securely, and then Lieutenant Zhang took the controls and proceeded slowly forward. Everyone with driving experience had offered to take the RV over the obstacles, I didn't want to pick a favorite or do something silly like draw straws, so since Zhang had driven us into the canyon, he could drive us out.

There were some hairy moments when we all thought the RV was going to tip over, and the treads slipped wildly in the mud. Zhang remained calm, the treads stopped slipping and bit into the soft soil, and the RV slowly inched back onto relatively flatter ground. When the treads on both sides returned almost to normal configuration, we all cheered. Zhang endured many backslaps as we climbed back into the RV. He gave me a thumbs up. "Thank you for your faith in me, Colonel," he said.

"Would you like a break?" I asked, noticing that his hands shook slightly. He'd known that the success of the entire mission, and the survival of humans on Newark, had depended on him for a moment.

"Yes, Colonel," he admitted, "I've had enough driving for today, I think."

"Good job," I said as I gave him a gentle pat on the back, and extracted from my pocket a piece of chocolate I'd been saving. "You deserve this."

Zhang looked at that piece of chocolate, a precious enough item on Newark but especially so on our current expedition, like I'd handed him a bar of gold. He accepted it in both hands, bowed slightly to me, and wrapped it carefully in a cloth before placing it in a pocket. The other Chinese soldiers said something to him in Mandarin, and he broke into a grin. Apparently, I had just made his day.

I was tempted to climb onto the roof and ride up there, the RV had a roof rack and we'd rigged up a couple places to sit, and an awning to keep rain off. As it was partly sunny that day, the awning had been taken down and stowed. The roof could be chilly, it was also a popular enough place to ride that I'd had to limit people to taking shifts up there, they changed when we changed drivers. Inside the RV was warm and dry, out of the wind, it was also dreary as the RV had few windows. Realizing that if I went on the roof, someone would have to come down, I stayed in the RV, adjusting my seat so I could see out the front windows. One of our SEALs named Taylor took the wheel, as he had the next shift, and Lieutenant Williams stood behind the driver's seat. "Right up there, by that big round rock, that's the top," Williams pointed out. "Make a straight line for it, and when we're over the crest, let it fall off to the left and we'll get back down to our original course."

"Got it," Taylor replied. Williams went back to his seat, strapped in, and we headed off.

All went well at first, Taylor carefully and confidently drove us up to the crest, let the RV naturally turn slightly to the left, and drove a fairly straight line toward a gap between two large rocks. Those two rocks, I remembered from the satellite images, we had planned our route to avoid them, now that I saw them from the surface, they were not a big deal. The gap between them was four or five times wider than the RV, with some smaller stones half buried in the ground, the RV's treads morphed shape to roll over the stones as if they weren't there. After shooting the gap, it was an easy drive back down to the original course we'd planned, parallel to the stream at the bottom of the canyon. Even at the careful rate that Taylor was driving, it would only take us a few minutes to get back down to the intended track, which at that part of the canyon was almost like a shelf notched into the shallow canyon wall. To my eyes, I wondered if the shelf had ever been a road, created millions of years ago by Newark's original inhabitants. That idea was stupid, I knew, no road could have lasted that long, especially not in a canyon carved by the advance and retreat of glaciers, glaciers massing millions of tons. The shelf, and the one on the opposite canyon wall, had been created by the stream in full flood, raging over its banks and carrying stones smashing and scouring the soil of the canyon walls, each year digging the canyon deeper and wider, carrying its soil eventually, grain by grain, down to the sea.

It would take us only a few minutes to get down to the shelf notched into the canyon wall, even though Taylor was being extra careful driving in the soft, muddy soil.

And then, suddenly, it didn't take any time at all. "Whoa!" Taylor shouted a warning from the driver's seat, at the same time we all felt the RV rock side to side, then drop sickeningly.

"What's wrong?" I shouted back, pushing myself up in the seat to see through the window in front of Taylor.

Taylor replied much more calmly than I could have managed. "I didn't do anything, the treads won't- AH!" As he gave the alarm, there was a high-pitched whine from the treads on the right side, the RV lurched to the left and dropped again. And then it rolled. The RV rolled to its left, rocked back to the right, then to the left again, and kept going. Out the driver's window, I saw someone jump off the roof; the RV was rolling over and the people on the roof weren't waiting for an engraved invitation to get the hell off the thing.

It was chaos, sheer chaos. The RV rolled over and over, onto its left side, then the roof, then the right side, paused ever so briefly to rock on the protesting treads, and rolled again. I lost track of how many times it rolled, after counting two complete flips my head was bouncing around too much to be aware of minor details. For some reason, the RV wasn't rolling fast, it was almost a controlled motion, and it didn't seem to be gaining speed. It was chaos inside the RV.

Let me tell you something about the SpecOps people. They didn't panic. They all kept their cool, kept situational awareness the whole time, looked for opportunities to do something useful to affect the outcome. Every one of them, I'm sure, knew how many times we rolled. It was chaos, we had no control, we were tumbling down a slope toward a rock-filled, icy, raging stream at the bottom of the canyon, and there was no shouting, no screaming, no panic. I felt almost ashamed of myself, until I managed to follow their example.

It was a damned good thing I had insisted that everyone be strapped into seats any time the RV was moving, or we would have suffered serious injuries from people being tossed around inside the RV. After I don't know how many puzzlingly ponderous, slow rolls, the RV came to rest on its treads, rocked side to side two or three times, then stopped. "Is everyone all right?" I asked stupidly. "Anyone injured?" I asked more intelligently.

"I'm good."

"Ok here, sir."

Everyone sounded off, and other than bruises and bumps, no one was hurt. "Get the door open, let's get out of here before this thing rolls again," I ordered, and made sure I was the last person out the door. Because the door was on the left, downhill side, I ran the hell away from the RV, in case it decided to roll on top of me.

"Holy shit," I exclaimed.

The RV had ended properly on its treads, right on the shelf where we wanted to be! Looking up the slope, I could see all four of the people who had been on the roof were on their feet, waving to us, apparently uninjured. And I could see the source of the problem; the ground had given way beneath the RV up the slope, soil had slipped in a mini landslide of mud and soft dirt. Once the RV rolled the first time, it got momentum started, and kept going down the gentle slope of the canyon wall, until it fell onto the shelf-like notch.

"Ha!" Williams laughed relieved now that he'd seen no one was seriously injured. "Taylor! You didn't need to get us here so fast!"

We all laughed. Laughed, and we couldn't stop. I laughed until I had tears in my eyes, laughed in relief that I wasn't dead, that the RV wasn't upside down in the stream, the RV, somehow, was on its treads, and not even the windows were broken. The door still even worked, it was sticky, sure, I had expected the door to be solidly, impossibly jammed into its frame after such a shock.

"Skippy," I inquired, "how badly is the RV damaged?"

"It's fine, Joe. You took quite a tumble there. Are you Ok?"

"It's *fine*?" I asked, astonished.

"Yup, the Kristang build these things tough. They're designed to be dropped by parachute. The reason it rolled over so slowly is the gyroscopes counteracted the roll a bit, they're designed to do that. You can get back in and drive it away, no problem. You better fix the roof rack first, it automatically retracted when it sensed the roll, but I can see it's bent in some places. Nobody is hurt?"

"Minor bumps and bruises. Damn, Skippy," I walked around the RV and looked it in amazement, "how it this thing not laying in pieces all over the place? How did the treads not get busted off?"

"The treads and pontoons would have retracted automatically as needed, the onboard computer knew when to extend the treads to stop the roll when it could. Like I said, these things are built tough, Joe. Good thing, too, because the warranty on that RV expired a long time ago. Tell you what, I can get you a sweet deal on rustproof undercoating, I know a guy who knows a guy."

"Thanks, Skippy, but we don't plan on owning this thing long enough for that to matter."

"I'll throw in a set of air fresheners. You got an RV stuffed full of monkeys, air fresheners could come in mighty handy, Joe."

I laughed. "Skippy, if things go according to plan, in a few days, we're going to dump this RV in a lake, or bury it, so no one will ever find it. Rustproofing and air fresheners would be counterproductive at that point."

"Damn. Joe, remind me never to let you borrow my car. If I ever have one."

When the people who had been on the roof walked down to us, after picking up things like the awning, jackets and several backpacks that had been flung off the roof on the RV's way down, I got everyone to pose in front of the mud-smeared and only slightly dented RV. Setting my zPhone on a rock, I asked Skippy to take photos of our group, which he did without any snarky comments. Maybe he was genuinely glad that we were alive, or maybe he was too busy repairing the *Dutchman* to play any pranks on us then. I appreciated it.

When we were done with the photos to commemorate our miraculous survival, I told Taylor to get back in, and check if Skippy was correct about the RV being drivable. Taylor gave me a quizzical look. "You sure you want me driving again, sir?"

"Taylor," I said, "it wasn't your fault. Besides, what are the odds that will happen to you twice?"

Skippy chimed in. "Was that a question for me, Joe? Truly, I don't have enough data to calculate the odds. I'd need ground-penetrating radar to examine the soil-"

"That was a rhetorical question, Skippy, no number crunching needed."

"Good. Because without further data, my estimate of the odds would only be accurate within sixty five per-"

"Thank you, Skippy, we've got it from here. Taylor, do your thing."

The RV drove just fine, Taylor went forward a hundred meters, then backed up to us. If the soil of the shelf was saturated with water and unstable, running the RV back and forth over it should have caused it to shift. Smythe and I walked the tracks the RV had made, there were no cracks in the soil, no signs of the ground shifting at all. Satisfied that we were as safe as we could be, we fixed the roof rack as best we could, loaded up the RV, and drove off again. This may not be a fun-filled family vacation, but it sure was turning out to be memorable. Smythe was looking at the photos I had forwarded to everyone's zPhone. "Bishop," he slipped for a moment. "Colonel," he was smart enough not to call attention to his mistake, "in Afghanistan, I was in a helicopter that went down, we were high up in the mountains, and the trailing rotor blade stalled or some bloody thing like that. We only fell fifty meters, onto snow, it could have been worse, the helo slid down the mountain and lodged against a rock before it would have fallen over a cliff. We had some broken bones, nothing serious," he said in a nonchalant SAS manner. "Before the rescue helo arrived, we posed for a photo in front of the busted bird." He pressed a few buttons on his zPhone and pulled up that photo. "That's me on the left."

The photo didn't look any different from he did now, it must have been relatively recent. When was the SAS in Afghanistan? "When was this, oh, never mind. You shouldn't tell, me, and I don't care." If I'd cared, the details were in his service record.

"Ha!" Smythe laughed. " As if that matters now, sir. We know the only bloody secret that matters now, about Skippy playing games with wormholes. What I was going to say, sir, is until today, that pic of the downed helo was my favorite. But now, a photo of us having survived rolling down a canyon, in a stolen alien RV, on a planet thousands of lightyears from Earth? That beats all, in my opinion."

CHAPTER TWENTY TWO

The second and third river crossings were close together, we'd swim the RV across them in the same day. We reached the second river in late afternoon, and unlike the first river, where we'd had to hack a ramp down to the water, we expected this one to be an easy drive down into the river for the RV. That's how it appeared from the satellite image. That was not the reality we saw on the ground. The river banks on both sides had places where the land led straight down into the water on a fairly gentle grade, easy for the RV's treads. What was not easy was that in those places, the ground at the water's edge was slippery, thick mud. Skippy advised that even our RV's miraculous treads might get stuck. We got out and scouted up and down the river to find a better place to cross, there wasn't one. Our best option seemed to be to hack another road down to the water, in a place that wasn't too muddy. On the far bank, we'd need to get the RV to climb the bank as high as it could, then tie a line around a rock and use the RV's winch to pull itself up. It was growing dark by the time we got the road hacked out manually with picks and shovels, I decided against attempting a crossing in the growing darkness, and ordered a camp set up for the night. It was a decent evening, dry, warm for Newark, and the following day's forecast was for high winds and torrential rains. People needed a break. To stretch our legs that had grown stiff from sitting in the RV all day, most of us hiked up a hill above the river and watched the sun set. It was only the second time during our entire stay on Newark that I'd seen the local star set over the horizon, most days there were clouds in the way, or it was solid clouds and rain. Seeing a sunset was a treat, I took it as a good omen.

Crossing the second river was uneventful, we all complained what a pain in the ass it was to get the big RV up over the far river bank. Honestly, every single one of us loved seeing the RV winch itself up, carving a big gouge in the river bank. The treads got completely, hopelessly clogged with giant clods of sticky, gooey mud, and, darn it, we all had to stand in the drizzling rain and watch as the driver, an Indian paratrooper lieutenant named Patel, gunned the throttle and spun the treads clean, flinging mud everywhere as the RV fishtailed up away from the river. We all laughed and clapped heartily, Patel had such a huge grin that I thought it might crack his face wide open. Damn it, why had I not pulled rank and taken the driver seat?

By the time we reached the third river, the drizzle had become a steady rain, not yet the gusty downpour we expected from Skippy's weather forecast. Skippy was testy about that, assuring me that just to the north of us was a near hurricane-force storm; high winds straight out of the north, and rain coming down in sheets. We paused the RV to get out and evaluate the river, there was a gentle grassy slope right down into the water, same on the other side. To the north, the sky was so dark it looked like night was approaching from that direction, and it was only mid-afternoon. The river was rushing fast, icy cold black water, big standing waves piling up over submerged rocks, to my eyes it appeared the water level was rising as we stood there. Chunks of ice floated by, bobbing on and ducking under the surface as the river bounced them violently. Satellite images showed the long tongue of a retreating glacier jutted out into the river not more than ten kilometers north of us, out of sight around a bend in the river, ice was continually breaking off as the river ate away at the base of the glacier. Getting into and out of the river was going to be simple for the RV, the tricky part was going to be avoiding submerged rocks and floating ice chunks.

"Let's go," I decided. A sudden chilly gust of wind almost made me stagger on the bank of the river, reinforcing my decision. "We need to get across before that wind hits us full force." I didn't want the bulky RV acting like a sail in the wind, while we were trying to get across the river.

"Yes, sir," Smythe agreed. "Up in those hills," he pointed across the river, "are several good spots we could wait out the storm overnight."

We got back in the RV, shed our wet jackets, and started down the bank toward the river. Our driver was Patel again, he'd taken a break after driving us across the second river, I wanted an experienced person at the controls for this last major river crossing. Patel flashed us a confident thumbs up before the nose of the RV hit the water, then he focused completely on the task of getting us safely across. The RV bobbed alarmingly once it was fully afloat, the current was so strong that Patel had to point the RV's nose partly upriver in order to hold a straight course. A straight course wasn't going to work, the river bed was cluttered with rocks we could see and rocks we couldn't see, the RV was a technological wonder but for some reason, the Kristang hadn't fitted it with sonar to detect underwater obstacles. We had to guess where rocks were hidden under the surface by watching waves and ripples, something many of us, including me, knew from canoeing or kayaking. A canoe or kayak drew so little water that it could glide over obstacles that were covered by very little water, that was not true of the RV. Its bottom was a meter or more below the surface, and with the pontoons plunging up and down in the increasingly angry waves, at times the bottom of the RV was considerably more than a meter deep. We hadn't gone fifty meters before there was a bump, and the RV ground its way over a submerged rock, a rock too deep to create a standing wave, but deep enough for the RV to bottom out. "Sorry," Patel said from the driver's seat. The RV was only hung up on the rock a moment, it popped up and rode over the rock, then Patel needed to swing the RV downstream to avoid another rock. In the seat to the right of Patel was SAS Lieutenant Crispin, scouting for Patel to find a path across the river that avoids underwater obstacles. Smythe suggested Crispin was well suited to that task, he had gone to the Olympic Trials for the British kayaking team.

"Not his fault, sir," Crispin defended Patel, "these rocks are damned hard to see. And this bloody caravan draws too much water. Right, go right," he shouted.

Patel swung the RV to the right again, and the RV plunged downstream, rocking and rolling on the rough water. For the next ten minutes, Crispin and Patel tried to get the RV into the middle of the river, where we hoped deeper water would allow us to avoid hitting rocks, at that point we had already bumped and scraped over three unseen objects. Patel got the RV turned directly upstream and held it in place, while Crispin looked for a way out of the box the RV was in. There were large rocks sticking out of the water to the right, left and downstream. Upstream was an underwater rock we'd already hit once, we didn't want to run over it again. Skippy said the RV was tough, and had an extra tough skid plate on the bottom to protect against the hull getting a hole punched in it from running over rocks. How tough that skid plate was, if we hit a sharp rock, was something I didn't want to test.

"Take your time, Crispin," I said gently. The motion of the RV was almost making me seasick, I wished the RV had more windows.

"We'll get out of here, s- oh, shit!" Crispin shouted.

Upstream from us, there were ice flows stretching from shore to shore, coming around a bend in the river. A large piece of the glacier must have broken off, and been battered into multiple chunks on its way down the river. This was my fault, we knew the river had ice floating down it regularly, and I should have anticipated that with the storm to the north of us, the river level was higher than normal, bringing extra ice. What I should have done was send a couple people upriver, someplace high where they had a view of what was coming, to determine when was a good time for the RV to attempt a crossing. Like an idiot, I blindly ordered us to drive the RV across.

Chunks of ice were smashing against rocks, against each other, rolling over, breaking into smaller pieces, as the ice flood rapidly approached. "Patel, go straight for shore," I ordered, "as much as you can, I'd rather risk bottoming out on a rock, than getting hit with some of that ice." Many pieces of ice were almost half the size of the RV, they could break a pontoon, or even knock the RV over in the water.

We almost made it. Fifty meters from the shore, Patel swung upriver to the left in order to avoid a rock that was barely under the water, and a large chuck of ice slammed into the left pontoon. The impact swung the RV's nose upriver, and the raging water made the nose keep going to the left, out of control. Suddenly, the RV was pointed downriver, gathering speed, headed straight for two large rocks. Patel had the water jets screaming in full reverse, he was barely able to hold position. "I think the left pontoon is taking on water," he shouted, "the RV wants to spin to the left. Crispin, do you see a way-"

His words were cut off by a sickening crunch as the RV was battered again by a small iceberg. Looking out the small window, for a flash all I saw was a wall of ice, and for a moment my idiotic brain thought of the *Titanic*. The RV lurched down and to the left as the iceberg hit, then rode up on the pontoon. There was an earsplitting screech as the pontoon slid along the iceberg, then it was gone in one direction and the RV spun the other way.

The left pontoon was now clearly battered and sinking, I was sitting on the left side of the RV and I could tell. Patel reported the left side water jet was operating sluggishly, and I directed him to head straight for shore. The RV was going under, I wanted us to get as close to the river bank as possible before it went down. Patel did a great job driving, he got the RV downstream from a large rock, semi protected from large pieces of ice, and headed for the shore using what power remained. The water jet in the left pontoon was barely functioning at that point. The RV grounded on an unseen rock, and couldn't move. "I think we're stuck, sir," Patel said with regret. "The water jets are on full power, but we can't go forward or back."

That was it, I wasn't waiting any longer. Out the front windows, the shore was tantalizingly close. "We're sinking! Captain Smythe, get everyone to shore, Williams, you're with me!"

I staggered to the back of the RV, Williams and his three man SEAL team right behind me, and opened the door to the cargo compartment. The RV was sinking fast now, tilted to the left at a thirty degree angle and judging by the grinding sounds, was being pushed back out into the river. We had less, far less, than a minute before the RV would have slid back away from the river bank and into water deep enough to be over our heads. In that icy cold, fast-moving water, it was unlikely anyone who had to swim would survive. "Armor, we need one full set of armor, leave everything else," I explained. Between the five of us, six because Smythe of course interpreted my orders broadly and came back into the cargo box with us, we got all the components for a set of armor. "Leave it," I ordered, as Smythe tried to pick up a rifle. "That's an order, go!"

Behind me, I closed and firmly latched the door to the cargo compartment, where almost all our precious supplies were stored. Water, bitterly cold water was already collecting around my ankles as we squeezed through the door, bumping into each other as the RV rocked back and forth. Water was pouring in through the right side emergency hatch, I saw people were shuffling along the right pontoon to hop into the water, Patel and Crispin were still in the RV, they'd given up trying to get out the right side hatch, and Patel was working the controls of the roof hatch. He got it open, took hold of the lip around the hatchway, and swung himself through it. At this point, the RV was at a forty five degree angle to the left, and bucking like a bronco as it slid backwards, battered by waves.

How we all got out, I don't remember exactly. Somehow, both Smythe and Williams got out behind me even though I'd intended to be the last to leave. By the time Smythe came through the hatch, the RV was almost laying on its left side, and we had to crawl along the right side to the nose, kneel on a front window, and jump into the water. It was up to my chest, and I gasped in shock at the deathly cold. The cold and strong current, combined with the armor suit leg I had a death drip on, made me unsteady, I would have fallen backwards and been swept away except people had formed a human chain to the shore, Ranger Samuels got a firm grip on my arm and guided me to shore. "Thank you," I told her, and handed the armor suit leg to her once the water was only as deep as my waist. I stood in the shockingly cold water, trying to ignore it, helping Williams and then Smythe get to safety, more importantly, assuring the precious components of the armor suit got safely to shore. As Smythe, last to leave, jumped off the nose, the RV lurched backwards, partly afloat again. We got onto the shore, me crawling the last meter on my hands and knees, then we all stood in stunned silence for a moment, as we watched the RV drift down the river, sinking quickly, until it hit and became wedged between two rocks, then it slowly disappeared. The right pontoon was visible under the water from time to time, in the troughs of waves.

Shaking myself back to awareness, I stepped onto a rock so I could see the assembled crowd. "Is anyone hurt? Other than wet and cold?"

"Mild ankle sprains, nothing more," Doctor Zheng reported as she was kneeling next to Lieutenant Zhang. He had his right boot off, and winced as Zheng manipulated his ankle.

"I'm fine, Colonel, I stumbled on a rock," Zhang assured me.

"Good," I said stupidly. Damn, as a commanding officer, I wasn't being very helpful. "Captain Smythe, we have a lot of people in cold, wet clothing here, and a storm is coming." The wind was now gusting, and rain was occasionally coming down almost sideways. "Find us some place out of the weather, and make sure everyone uses their heat packs, if needed. I don't want anyone getting sick out here." Everyone had, or should have, chemical packets that could be mixed to generate heat, they are available in any hardware or sporting goods store, not some fancy alien technology. "Lieutenant Williams, you SEALs are our swimmers, bring the suit components over here. Let's put it together and see what we can do with it."

CHAPTER TWENTY THREE

While Williams and his team got the suit sorted out, checked out, and Taylor into it, I took a moment to get my head together. This could be a disaster; all our equipment, all our weapons, all our food, all our extra clothing, tents, everything we needed for survival, was in that sunken RV. I was in shock, trying to process how things had gone so bad so quickly. Skippy later figured out what happened. The storm had dumped an enormous deluge of water to the north of us, water that very rapidly rushed down streams, swelling the river. Because a tongue of a glacier blocked two thirds of the river channel, the water briefly piled up behind the glacier, until the pressure fractured off pieces ice ancient ice, and the wall of water found a path downstream. When we arrived at the river, we should have noticed that the water was already over its usual banks, that was why there was a nice gentle grassy slope for us to drive down. We should have been suspicious, I should have been suspicious of the high water, I'd thought it an optical illusion that the river seemed to be rising. It wasn't an illusion. The chunks of ice floating down the river should also have caused me to be extra cautious, there was a lot of ice in the water. If I'd ordered us to wait for morning, like I should have, we would have noticed that the water level was rising, and more and larger chunks of ice were coming around the bend upriver. I was too damned eager to get across the river before the storm hit us. Like an idiot, I had not even considered what the storm might be doing upriver.

It was both an accident, and my fault.

Looking back, I should have taken more time to study the river, even pulled the RV back under a bluff to shelter for the night, and crossed the next morning. We were ahead of schedule, the RV had enough juice left in its powercells for another day and a half, before we would need to find a place to hide it and begin walking. Maybe waiting for the morning would have avoided the disaster, or maybe we would still have gotten rammed by a mini iceberg, there were still plenty of them floating down the river.

Williams was satisfied the suit was fully operational, and he reported Taylor was ready to try using it in the water. "We're go for a test, sir," he reported.

"Skippy," I asked, "what's our weather forecast?"

He responded immediately. "The storm to the north has abated somewhat and shifted its track to the west, I now expect most of it to miss your location. You will get gusty winds and rain in about two hours, lasting several hours."

"Thank you, Skippy. All right," I declared, "let's move now, before the weather gets worse. The longer the RV is in the water, the greater risk it will shift, or equipment will spill out and get lost downstream. It would be best for a recovery operation to wait for morning, we don't have that long."

"We recover weapons first," Smythe suggested.

"No," I said emphatically. "Taylor, your first priority is to recover the parts for another suit, then two divers can get the components for the other two suits. We need the suits first, we don't know how long it will take to get everything we need out of the RV, and a single suit may run out of power before then. We'll use two suits for recovering our equipment, save the other two suits for the assault."

"Makes sense, sir," Williams agreed, and helped Taylor attach his helmet.

"Spotter team," I asked over my zPhone. "How is it looking?"

SpecOps

The spotter team was two people on a hill upriver, where they had a good view. Setting up a spotter team is what I should have done before we tried to cross the river. "Good, sir, some ice coming down, nothing like before."

Through their zPhones, I could see what they were seeing. Widely scattered pieces of ice, a diver should be able to avoid them without too much trouble. We didn't have much of a choice anyway. "The ice situation is manageable. Are you good in there?" I asked over my zPhone earpiece to Taylor.

"Good," Taylor replied over the radio, with his helmet faceplate closed, he gave us a thumbs up. "We've never used these for swimming."

"Understood, do your best. Don't rush to get to the RV, go out and practice swimming first, we can't risk you crashing into the RV, or breaking the suit on a rock, or getting hit by ice. Approach the RV from downstream," I advised stupidly. A SEAL didn't need my advice about underwater operations.

Taylor walked confidently to the shore, stepped in carefully, then awkwardly as he got in deeper and the current threatened to knock his feet out from under him. "I'm going to dive in now, the footing is loose here," he said, and leapt into the water. For a heart-stopping moment, he disappeared under the surface. We could hear him breathing heavily on the radio. Then, he popped to the surface, swimming strongly, making progress against the current. "I'm getting used to it," he reported, "the power in this suit is really incredible. The stabilizers help, I don't know that I could control the suit without them, they do a lot of the work for me."

"Keep going," Williams ordered, "go up to that rock, turn around, and see how it is moving with the current. Watch out for that ice."

"I see it." For twenty minutes, not venturing out any further than the sunken RV, Taylor swam on the surface, under the surface, with the current, against the current, dodging chunks of ice. "I'm ready, sir, I've got the hang of this. I want to recon the RV now."

"What do you think?" I asked Williams.

He thought a moment, and replied "Typically we'd call a rest before proceeding."

"I'm good, sir, really I am," Taylor said. He was treading water easily, just downstream from the sunken RV. "This suit does most of the work for you, it's very strong. The radar even works pretty good underwater, I can see underwater obstacles on the faceplate display. I'd like to go now, sir, this make take a while, and we're losing daylight, and I hear the wind is going to pick up soon."

"I recommend he goes, sir." Williams said.

"Lieutenant, I know nothing about underwater recovery," I admitted, "this is your operation. Get us another suit first, so we can have two divers working together."

Our three SEALs worked through the night, using two suits. With people on land acting as spotters for ice chunks, the divers were able to avoid a single accident, other than a minor incident of one diver getting a foot tangled in cables inside the RV, it only took a minute to cut himself free and he was never in any danger. The wind hit us after dark, and the divers took a break for an hour until the worst of the weather had blown over us. Taylor first recovered all the components of the second suit in seven dives. We assembled the recovered suit, checked it out and Williams declared it ready for use. Williams took one dive with Taylor to learn, then Taylor led Williams inside the RV, working as a team. As ordered, they got the other two powered suits first, then I instructed Williams to bring up tents and food before weapons, everyone on shore was still shivering and I thought we couldn't risk people becoming seriously ill. By that time, Williams was confident in the SEALs' diving abilities, and that the RV was solidly wedged against a rock and not going anywhere. By the middle of the following morning, they had recovered everything we truly needed from the sunken RV, and, incredibly, even the stupid Barney doll.

At first, I was a little bit pissed. Not that I would continue to be taunted by Barney, but that one of our SEALs had risked his life, and expended precious suit power, to recover a stuffed doll. Williams calmed me down, explaining that the windshield had broken sometime during the night, and the Barney had torn loose and ended up wedged under a seat. He had brought the Barney back as a sort of mascot, or good luck charm, and I had to admit, people had cheered loudly when he emerged from the river, holding Barney above his head. So, we were stuck with it, damn it.

The two suits that had been used by the SEALs were down to less than 15% of their normal power charge, the one Taylor started with had only 12%. The energy required for swimming against the river current had drained power quickly from the suits, and because of the frigid water, the suits had to run their heaters, draining power even faster.

"Suits can't transfer power one to another," Smythe observed bitterly. "We've got two disassembled, fully charged suits, and two that will only last maybe one day of walking."

"Yeah. Hey, Skippy," I asked, "can you run the math for us on how much weight each of the depleted suits can carry, for the best trade-off between cargo capacity and range? We'll remove the helmet and arms from the depleted suits."

"Please, Joe, that kind of kindergarten arithmetic is beneath me. Since you asked, I recommend a payload of fifty seven kilos for each suit. That will allow travel of roughly sixty kilometers, in the terrain you have in front of you."

"Great, thank you, Skippy." To Smythe, I said "having suits carry part of the load for a while will help us ease into walking. Sitting in the RV too many days made my legs stiff. Take the helmets and arms off the two suits we'll be using as pack mules, and bury them along with whatever else we're not taking with us. Divvy up the loads first so I can see how much each person will be carrying, and Captain?"

"Sir?"

"I know you special forces types are hard core, I do not want to see anyone so loaded down with gear that they risk injury, or being too worn out when we get to the scavenger camp. Skippy made his pizza delivery, we can count on replenishing our food supply. I want to move out in two hours, that will give us seven hours of daylight for walking and setting up camp tonight. We're going to take it easy the first day."

"Yes, sir," Smythe said, and I could see in his eyes he was unconvinced. And probably regretting that the team included me and two civilians.

"Good. Plan for me to carry ammo packs and part of a suit. Don't worry, Captain," I added after seeing his skeptical look, "if I can't handle it, I will tell you."

Leaving Smythe to bark orders, I walked over to Doctors Zheng and Tanaka, who were helping sort through a pile of wet, muddy clothing. It was all wet from being in the river, and despite laying out a collapsed tent to keep the clothes off the ground, most of it had some mud smeared here and there. "How are you?"

"I'd be better if I could get into some dry clothes," Zheng admitted. "Colonel, training for triathlons can involve getting cold and wet for a while, I'm used to that. What I'm not used to is not getting a shower and warm dry clothes after. It's tiring. This is like one of those twenty four hour endurance events that I've always avoided."

SpecOps

"If I were one of my patients," Tanaka remarked, "I would be treating myself for exposure, and possible hypothermia."

"I understand that. We'd all be doing a lot better if the RV hadn't sunk. We're going to start walking in about two hours, I know that will help me warm up. We'll be walking further than planned, we'd hoped to stretch the RV's power supply for another two days. Don't worry, we anticipated setbacks in the schedule. You only need to carry your personal gear and medical supplies, the SpecOps team will take everything else."

"What are you carrying?" Tanaka asked.

"My personal gear, plus ammunition, and part of an armored suit. This is not going to be easy, I really appreciate you coming with us, and the sacrifices you're making."

"We'll get through it," Zheng said with determination. "I hope this is all a waste of our time."

"Oh?" I said in surprise. "Why?"

"Because," she explained, "if you need doctors on this mission, something will have gone wrong, won't it?"

We began the walk without ceremony, once I was satisfied people were not carrying unrealistic loads, I gave Smythe the go-ahead order, and he sent two men ahead as scouts. Knowing what the terrain along our projected path looked like from satellite images was one thing, seeing the real conditions on the ground was quite another. The scouts would check out our route, advise of shortcuts, impassible terrain, and hopefully avoid everyone else having to double back. Smythe planned to rotate the scout duties; two people in the morning, two in the afternoon. Being a scout was a highly sought-after assignment, as the scouts carried only light loads, and weren't tramping along in well-trodden mud with the rest of us.

I began walking with the Rangers, out of service loyalty, then dropped back in the column to check on the SEAL team. While the rest of us had been shivering on shore, trying to catch sleep in shifts, the three SEALs had worked through the night. "How are you, Lieutenant?"

"We're all right, sir," Williams answered. "Compared to some of our training, this is a piece of cake."

"And the food is better," Garcia said while eating something out of an MRE pouch.

"Any food is good at this point," Taylor agreed.

"When we came out here, I didn't think the 'Sea' part of SEa Air Land in 'SEAL' would be of any use," Williams admitted.

I nodded. "Lieutenant, one thing I've learned is, you never know what you'll need out here, it pays to have a wide variety of capabilities with you. I didn't think an archeologist, or geologist, would be useful in space, and now I'm glad we brought them along. Finding those ruins has given Skippy a puzzle he can't explain. The strangest things can have a use out here, even a knowledge of, hell, what was that, Skippy, 17th century Hungarian poetry?"

"Correct," he said.

Williams looked at me in complete surprise.

"It's a long story," I said simply, "you've seen how Skippy can get off topic at times."

"Although, as I pointed out at the time," Skippy continued, "even a cursory familiarity of European romantic literature of the Baroque-"

"Yes, Skippy," I interrupted as Williams broke into a knowing grin, "thank you, another time, Ok?"

Craig Alanson

"You always say that, but there's never a time you deem as appropriate," Skippy said in a peevish tone. "Man, I am trying to bring culture to monkeys, and this is the thanks I get."

"Tell you what, Skippy," I winked to Williams, "you get us safely off this rock, and I will dedicate one, no, two, *two* full hours, for you to regale me with whatever topic you desire. Without interruption."

"Huh. You say that now, but-"

"Have I ever made a commitment to you and not kept it? Like, leaving Earth and coming out here on this fool's errand to find your magic radio?"

"Perhaps you have a point. Two hours, huh? I shall prepare accordingly. You're not going to regret this, Joe."

Crap. I was regretting it already.

"Taking one for the team, sir?" Williams asked. "We appreciate it."

Shaking my head ruefully, I replied "You have no idea."

Damn I was tired. And this was only the first freakin' day, not even a full day. For the past hour, the straps of my pack could no longer be adjusted not to be uncomfortable, they were digging into my shoulders and hips. Also for the past hour, I had been watching clouds build in the northern sky, and the wind had been gusting in our faces. "Skippy," I asked, "weather report."

"Sucky, with a hundred percent chance of it continuing to be sucky. You're going to get heavy rain in about two hours, maybe less. The rain should be gone by morning, most of it, anyway."

"Thank you, Skippy. Captain Smythe!" I raised my voice so he could hear over the wind, as he was fifty meters ahead of me. He waited for me to catch up, I hustled as best I could without completely losing my dignity. "Take five, everyone," I shouted. To Smythe, I said "time to look for place to camp for the night, I want us to set up camp within the hour."

"Sir?" He pointed looked at his watch. "There's plenty of daylight remaining."

"Captain," I said, pulling the pack straps wide to give my aching shoulders a break, "this is why you need me with you. When you're on a march with the SAS, no one wants to be the first to call for a halt, right?"

"It's a matter of pride, sir."

"Exactly. It's even worse here, because the SAS don't want to stop before the Rangers, who don't want to stop before the Chinese, who don't want to stop before the Indian paratroopers, and so on. I'm not special forces, so I can call a halt without my pride getting hurt. And every one of us could use a rest. Skippy says there's heavy rain coming," I pointed to the clouds rolling in from the northeast, "I don't want us to get caught out in that, we're still ahead of schedule and there's no reason for us to push unnecessarily. The last thing we need is people risking further exposure in this climate."

"Yes, sir, another hour. I'll tell scouts ahead to find us a spot?"

Forty minutes later, Smythe touched his zPhone earpiece, talked with someone, then dropped back to walk with me. "There's a spot up ahead where we can camp, sir. The lads say there's another campsite a bit further, but that spot could get a bit dodgy, if we get heavy rain." On his zPhone, he showed me the images the scouts had taken of the two sites. The one further away was in the shelter of a bluff, protecting us from the wind, it also had a stream that could overflow and flood the campsite if the rain came down heavily.

"Yeah, that further site is out, too risky. Last thing we need is for everything to get wet again." The other site was a flat spot on the south side of a hill, it was more exposed to the gusty winds, it also wasn't going to flood. "We have to walk over that hill anyway, we'll set up there." I felt like a scoutmaster on the worst Boy Scout backpacking trip of all time; selecting campsites, making sure everyone had dry socks. At least here I didn't have to worry about parents complaining that their little Jimmy had come home with blisters and a mysterious rash.

The next morning, I already had sore muscles in places that I didn't know had muscles. Everyone was sore and tired, everyone got up early that morning, no one complained, everyone pitched in to strike camp and get us on our way. After half an hour, my muscles loosened up, and I felt better. Then Skippy called me. "Hey, Joe."

"Hi, Skippy, What is it?"

"You busy? I want to tell you something I discovered."

"Not busy at all, Skippy, we're walking, and we've got a whole day of walking ahead of us. At least it's not raining right now."

"That'll change, you're going to get rain and sleet this afternoon."

"Sleet? Crap. I hate this planet."

"Unfortunately, Newark does not yet have a comment section on Tripadvisor, for you to leave a complaint. So, what I want to tell you is, I've been running an analysis with Doctor Venkman-"

"Oh, wow." Venkman was an astrophysicist, or something like that, I'd read her profile and I still wasn't clear on her exact specialty. "She's been helping you? That's great, Skippy."

"It is decidedly not great, Joe. Having a monkey looking over my shoulder is a truly ginormous, epic, un-bee-lee-vah-bull, uh, darn, it there are not words to properly describe how much that is a pain in the *ass*. You know how annoying it is for me, to try explaining even the most basic science to your dim monkey brain?"

By now, I wasn't even mildly insulted by that remark. "Uh huh, yeah? Mostly I tell you not to bother explaining sciency stuff to me."

"Exactly! That's awesome, I get to yank your chain, and you don't waste my time with worthless attempts to elevate your understanding of things way beyond your capability. It's like, you can teach a dog to shake a paw, sit, lie down, and even roll over, but you would never try training a dog to do your taxes, or drive a car."

"Although that would be awesome. Except if the dog was driving, and decided to chase a squirrel with your car."

"Agreed," Skippy chuckled. "Anywho, when I'm talking to you, I don't have to waste time trying to think of a way to dumb things down enough for you. Hell, I could just make up stuff, and you'd never know."

"But you don't do that, right?"

"Not as far as you know. With Doctor Venk-"

"Hey! I heard that. Not as far as *I* know?"

"Does it really matter, Joe?"

"I guess not."

"Truthfully, no, I don't make up stuff for you, it wouldn't be any fun. Now, with a slightly, and I do mean slightly, infinitesimally slightly smarter monkey like Doctor

Venkman, it would be great fun to make up stuff, because she knows just enough to almost know the difference, and I'd be kind of laughing my ass off at her."

"But you don't do that either?"

"Not as far as she knows."

"Skippy, come on, our science team came out here to learn how the universe works, you leading them astray isn't helping. It isn't fair, either, these people are risking their lives out here."

"Man, you are a total buzzkill. Remind me never to invite you to a party, Joe. Those dummies on your science team, and, man I hate to use the word 'science' so loosely, volunteered to come out here. Look, in a lot of cases, I can't tell your egghead scientists the whole truth, because such knowledge is too dangerous for monkeys. Not just monkeys, too dangerous for any species at your level of development. Some of it is too dangerous even for the Rindhalu, I'm not simply insulting monkeys. This is serious stuff, Joe."

"Oh."

"Yeah, 'OH'. You dumdum." He paused. "Uh, what were we talking about?"

Skippy couldn't keep track of a conversation, and he called me the dumdum? I let it go. "Some kind of analysis you're doing with Venkman."

"Oh, yeah. Although to say that I'm performing the analysis with her, is like when you were four years old. Your father would put you on his lap when he drove the pickup truck so you could 'help' him drive. Incidentally, that wasn't the smartest thing to do."

"That old truck doesn't have an airbag, Skippy. And there's no traffic on the back roads up where I grew up."

"Exactly! What if you hit a moose?"

"Oh my God. Did you ever see a moose, Skippy? You hit one of those big freakin' things, a children's carseat isn't much help. Well, maybe. Whatever. I survived childhood."

"Is that how the brain damage happened?"

"Very funny. No, that's just me."

"My condolences. To your entire species, not just you. Back to what I was saying, Venkman helping with my analysis, is like little Joey helping your father drive the truck, it's more hindrance than help. She is just smart enough to ask a whole lot of stupid questions, whereas you're too dumb to even ask questions in the first place. That's why I prefer working with you, Joe."

"Thank you, uh, I think."

"You're welcome," he said, after insulting me. "Getting back to the point, we ran an analysis. Technically, I ran the analysis, while she sat in the corner, playing with blocks and eating sticky Cheerios off the floor."

"Ha!" I had to laugh at that mental image. "See, I would play with the toy trucks instead. Much more fun than blocks."

"I'll take your word on that, Joe. The results of our analysis are intriguing, they are so intriguing, so disturbing, so inexplicable, that I want us to gather data for further analysis. Someday, I mean, not right now."

"Skippy, I have no problem with gathering further data, first you need to get us off this planet. What, uh, is so intriguing? You find a tiny difference in the concentration of interstellar dust particles somewhere again?"

"No, you dumbass. What is intriguing is, here, I need to go back a bit and give you some context."

"Ok, I'm all ears, I won't interrupt you, I promise." He had good timing, because we had started walking up a long hill, and I was rapidly getting out of breath.

"You remember that star system where I was sure, or pretty, very certain, I, Ok, yeah, smart guy. Stupid monkey," he grumbled. "I know you're thinking it, go ahead and say it. Say it! I was wrong. Wrong! There, you happy now? You big jerkface," he grumbled.

"Skippy?'

"Yeah?"

"I have no freakin' clue," I said, out of breath, "what you're talking about. We've been to a lot of star systems, which one is this?"

"Oh. Hmm. Maybe I'm somewhat too sensitive about the few, the very few times when I am wrong. Hmm, actually, in this case, I thought I was wrong, but I wasn't. I wasn't! Ha! I was not wrong, I was right all along."

"So, you were wrong about being wrong?"

"Exactly!"

"Which means you were still wrong, about something."

"I was- oh, shut up. Do you want to hear my information or not?"

"I've been trying," I gasped, "to hear it, if you will please get to the point. Damn, you are absent-minded sometimes. Your mind wanders so far, I wonder if it's ever going to come back."

"*Me*? Have you ever heard yourself talk, Joe? You start a sentence, and halfway through, you've changed the subject, verb and object three times. Half the time you're talking, by the time you finish, I've lost track of where you started. And you've lost track, too."

"Oh. All right, maybe I'm a little guilty of that," I admitted. That wasn't the first time people had remarked on my scatter-brained thoughts. "I had an elementary school teacher, Ms. Evans, she tried to diagram one of my sentences on the white board. I thought her head would explode. Anyway, back to the subject, *please*."

"Fine," he huffed. "The star system I was talking about, is the one where I was very confident we would find an unmapped Elder site. Extra confident."

"Uh, huh, something about force lines in the galaxy?"

"Yes! And we didn't find any sign of an Elder presence, even though I requested the *Dutchman* to fly around the system, so I could perform an extensive sensor sweep."

"I remember," I said, using as few words as possible, being out of breath.

"Even after gathering extensive sensor data, I was originally unable to determine why that star system did not contain an Elder site. What I was trying to do, with the sensor data, was to determine whether that particular star system truly was an outstanding candidate for an Elder site, and what I found was that, yes, it is a place where the Elders *should* have had a facility of some sort. Certainly they should have placed a communications node there. Why we did not find any sign the Elders had ever been in that star system, therefore, has been a complete mystery to me. So much, that I began to doubt my analytical skills, I began to doubt myself."

"Yet, you bravely soldiered through your doubts, and remained an arrogant asshole the whole time."

"Truly, I have reserves of arrogance I didn't even know I had."

"Not something to brag about, Skippy."

"Not something for *you* to brag about, monkey boy. To continue my story, it remained a mystery to me, until I was trying to explain to Doctor Venkman what happened here, with Newark. She, and the rest of what you monkeys outrageously, criminally, refer to as a 'science' team, asked me a bunch of moronic questions about orbital mechanics. Seriously, a bunch of booger-eating first graders could do that simple math. While attempting to explain the math to Venkman and the other mental munchkins, to the point where I was longing for the sweet release of death, it occurred to me to run a check of orbits in that star system where there should have been an Elder site. And guess what I discovered, with my first grade math?"

"Uh," I guessed, "that boogers don't taste good?"

"Yuck. I've never tasted my own boogers, Joe."

"Oh, for crying out loud, Skippy, you're not supposed to eat *other* people's boogers! What the hell is wrong with you?" Because people around me could only hear my end of the conversation, I was getting a lot of strange looks from the walking party.

"I haven't- oh, forget it. Fine, I'll tell you what I discovered. My analysis shows that I was right in the first place. There was an Elder site in that star system, on a moon orbiting the largest gas giant."

"Damn! Was it concealed by a stealth field?"

"No. Conceal an entire moon in a stealth field? What the hell would be the point of doing that? Even the sensors on a Kristang ship could detect the presence of a stealthed moon, by the effect of its gravity on the other moons. Man, you have stupid notions sometimes. No, dumdum, by saying 'was' I meant past tense, like, there used to be an Elder site, it's not there now. That gas giant planet used to have an additional moon."

"What happened to it? Did it get pushed out of orbit, like Newark?"

"No. And that is the intriguing, disturbing part, Joe. My analysis shows the moon which housed the Elder site was destroyed, and by 'destroyed', I don't mean it got hit by something and it broke into several pieces. I mean it was obliterated, vaporized. Looking back over the sensor data, now that I know what I was looking for, there are tiny particles of that moon scattered all over that star system, likely part the moon's mass escaped the star system entirely. That isn't the only disturbing part. Whatever happened to that moon, it was so violent that it ripped away a large part of the gas giant's atmosphere, I estimate between twelve and fourteen percent of the planet's mass was blown out of its own orbit. For comparison, twelve percent of that planet is equivalent to twenty Earths. That much mass being blown away caused the planet's orbit to change suddenly, and that disrupted the entire system, it even made the star wobble noticeably."

"What has the energy to vaporize an entire moon?" I asked in amazement. Me saying that aloud made peoples' head turn, they must have thought I was talking about something that happened recently, in Newark's star system. I waved my hands, and gave a thumbs up, to let them know it was not a problem for us. Not an immediate problem for us.

"Elder tech is the only possibility, Joe. That is an extremely disturbing fact. First Newark, then that star system. Someone pushed Newark out of orbit, presumably to commit genocide against a low-tech species. Someone also completely destroyed a moon. I assume that was to destroy the Elder site there, because there is no other conceivable reason anyone would care about such a worthless star system."

"Holy shit," I said, feeling a chill up my spine.

"Joe, if we are ever threatened with technology of that level, appealing to a higher power would be the best option, so you might want to avoid blasphemy."

"Do you have any guesses about who did this? And why?"

"As to who, no, I have absolutely no idea. As to why, as I already said, the only reason to blow up a moon that makes any sense is to destroy the Elder facility, whatever it was."

"Uh," an unpleasant thought occurred to me, and I stepped to the side and stopped walking, gesturing to Captain Smythe to keep going, I would catch up to them. "Hey, I remember something the burgermeister told me. You know, the hamster woman who was secretly the deputy administrator of Paradise-"

"I know who she is, yes."

"Good. This burgermeister, she told me the whole war started because the Maxohlx found a stash of Elder weapons, and attacked the Rindhalu, who used Elder weapons to fight back. And then both sides got the crap kicked out of them by the Sentinels, something like that, devices the Elders left behind to make sure nobody messed with the stuff they left behind?"

"Yeah, and?"

"Could something like that have happened to that moon? Maybe some lower-tech species found a store of Elder weapons on that moon, and screwed with them, and one of them exploded by accident?"

"No."

I waited for Skippy to say more. When he didn't say anything, for enough time to be awkward, I said "no? You know that because why?"

"Joe, you asked who, and why. I told you how; some kind of Elder device, not necessarily a weapon. You did not ask 'when'. The math of orbital mechanics tells me the moon was destroyed around two point seven million years ago. The Rindhalu did not achieve space flight until long after that timeline. There were not, as far as I know, any star faring species in the Milky Way galaxy between the Elders and the Rindhalu. So, no way could the Maxohlx or the Rindhalu, have been responsible for destroying that moon."

"Wait." A bell rang in my mind. "Two point seven million years ago? That moon was destroyed around the same time that Newark was pushed out of orbit?"

"Yes. This is all extremely suspicious."

"Damn it. We're back to the question of 'who' again, then."

"That is an important question we need to answer. Joe, as I have said before, this scares the hell out of me. Damn it! Things used to be so simple. Difficult, yes, but simple. We find an Elder communications node, I contact the Collective, and it would be Mission Accomplished! Now, I don't know what to do."

"Wait! Skippy, we are going to attack the Kristang in order to get the AI and a comm node, now you're not sure whether you want them? This is a hell of a time to change your freakin' mind."

"No, no, Joe, sorry, what I meant was- Damn, talking with you biological trashbags is not easy. All I meant was, things have gotten way complicated. I used to think I knew who I am, pretty much, and who the Elders were, or are. And how I fit into the universe. What I was hoping for was that I contact the Collective, and that solves all my problems. Now I'm thinking, the effort to contact the Collective may only be the beginning of a long struggle for me. Please, I do need you to get the AI and the comm node way from those hateful lizards, and I truly appreciate all the hard work you and your team are doing. Of course, when I say 'appreciate', I say that in the definition of 'grateful', not that I can actually appreciate how physically demanding it is for you monkeys to walk all that way."

"Oh," I said. That was much better. "Thanks, Skippy."

"Just like you ignorant monkeys cannot truly appreciate how difficult it is for me to rebuild a Thuranin starship out of raw materials up here. Because you can't."

"Hey, Skippy, I also appreciate that you are making the effort to be an arrogant asshole."

Craig Alanson

"Oh, no problem, Joe."

Damn. Sometimes I couldn't tell when he was being sarcastic, and when he was being simply clueless.

Skippy continued. "However, I am disappointed in you, Joe, you completely missed the most important point of my story."

"What? What is that?" What the hell could be more important than a freakin' moon being vaporized, at a time when no sentient species occupied the galaxy?

"That I was right all along, the star system did have an Elder site, just like I predicted. Duh. I'm the best, baby! Woohoo!"

"Oh, for crying out loud," I said in disgust. "That's what you think is the most important thing?"

"Sure. Come on, there isn't anything we can do about that moon now, right?"

CHAPTER TWENTY FOUR

Three nights later, after three hard days of marching that had every muscle in my body aching, we gathered for dinner around a pathetic campfire. During the day, we'd gathered broken pieces of the small, low growing shrubs that were clustered around rocks on Newark, to make a fire. The fire was for psychological effect, it wasn't hot enough to cook much of anything, although a couple of Brits and Indians heated up water for tea, and everyone got a small cup. For Newark, out in the open, it was a nice evening; temperature comfortably above freezing, it hadn't rained since early that morning, and the wind had died down to a steady breeze out of the east. The team needed this break together, instead of eating a hurried dinner in cramped tents and crashing to exhausted sleep like we'd been doing.

"Hello, Colonel Joseph Bishop!" Skippy said over my zPhone's speaker. "How are you this evening?"

"Fine," I mumbled over a mouthful of MRE peanut butter and crackers, "we're eating dinner around a campfire, sort of. What's up?"

"Well, sir, I have an exciting opportunity for you. For a limited time, we are offering a greatly reduced price on wonderful timeshares on Newark."

"Damn," I had to laugh, trying not to spew precious crackers on my lap. "Skippy, who the hell would buy a timeshare on this miserable planet?"

"Joe, Joe, Joe," he scolded me. "You're missing the point entirely. Think about this; if you purchase our Basic timeshare package of one week on Newark, that means you do NOT have to be on Newark the other fifty one weeks a year."

"Oh," everyone around me laughed. "In that case, hell yes, sign us all up."

"You won't regret this, sir. Seriously, Joe, how's it going down there? I know what the weather is like, that doesn't tell me how our Merry Band of Pirates are faring right now. By the way, it looks like you have a mix of snow and sleet coming tomorrow afternoon, then it will clear up and go back to damp, chilly and partly sunny."

"Snow? Crap, isn't this almost summer on this freakin' planet? And we're on the freakin' equator here. You are not acting as our travel agent the next time we look for a planet. Skippy, what we have down here is officially a not-very-Merry Band of Pirates. The gravity is too high, the temperature is too low, and it's hard to breathe even when you're only walking. Other than that, we're doing just wonderful. How's it going up there?"

"Well, heh, heh, funny you should ask."

"Oh, shit." I hated that 'well, heh, heh' thing he did, and by now, the whole team knew what it meant when he did that, they all looked at me with alarm. I put in my zPhone earpiece and turned off the speakerphone feature, so we could talk privately. Not wanting to be rude, I stood up and stepped away from the fire. "What is it this time? Did somebody forget to turn the stove off before we left?" Man, I was hoping whatever the problem was, it was simple. "It's not like I can go back up there and fix it, Skippy."

"The stove is not a problem, since I already mentioned that the ship currently does not have a galley. I'm working on that. Anywho, to be serious for a moment, Joe, one of the dropships had a slight accident."

"Slight? Like, you scratched the paint, or dented the fender?"

"Uh, no. Slight, like a gas pocket on a moon exploded when I drilled into it, the dropship flipped over and now it's stuck in a hole."

"What the hell, Skippy! Damn it, I leave you nice toys to play with, and you break them. I can't trust you with anything valuable up there."

"Hey, to be fair, I'm working almost blind up here. That moon contained minerals I need, and its orbit currently has it on the other side of the planet, I was using the dropship's crappy sensors to see what I was doing. The sensors didn't detect the gas pocket, because the Thuranin, here's a real shocker for you, didn't design their dropships to be used as drilling rigs. Anyway, I have another dropship on the scene, and I'm using combots to dig the first dropship out. It should be fine, except we'll need a new one, because the cabin got kind of crushed and it won't hold air pressure any more. Also, I wouldn't try flying it down through an atmosphere at this point, the heat shield is not in good shape."

"BLUF it for me, Skippy, Ok?"

"What?"

"Bottom Line Up Front. BLUF. Tell me the important stuff first. Come on, you know US military slang."

"Oh, yeah. All right. The bottom line is this little accident will add a week, maybe more, to the schedule. Most likely, sixteen days. I have to divert resources to recover and repair the dropship, and while I'm doing that, the dropship won't be mining ore for me. While I'm fixing that busted dropship, I will still be working on the *Dutchman*, however, work on the ship will be delayed. There is no way around it, before you ask me some stupid questions. This was always a substantial risk, Joe. My original estimate had likely delays built into the schedule, so this delay only adds eight days to when I expect the ship to be functional again."

I sighed. "Understood, Skippy. You're doing the impossible up there, we appreciate it. And I won't insult you by telling you to be careful."

"Indeed, you do not need to tell me to be careful. I'm working on the edge here already, Joe, it would not take much to tip the scales, so that I'm using up resources faster than I'm creating new ones."

"You won't let that happen, right?" I asked hopefully.

"I'm doing my best."

What scared me was his voice didn't have the usual snarky cockiness to it. He was scared, or at least very concerned.

And, from Newark, there was absolutely nothing we could do about it.

Skippy's pizza delivery had soft landed in a swampy area, we had to wade through bone-chilling water up to our waists to get to it. Part of me was wondering if Skippy had done that on purpose, although I'm sure he had done the best he could from the other side of the star system. By the time we got through the icy water to the package, I couldn't feel my legs. Or my balls. The container was roughly twice the size of a large foot locker, it was jammed packed, partly with medical supplies we might need after the assault, most of it was food. Sort of food. It was dehydrated sludges, all of it. What the assault team needed was basic nutrition, not gourmet food. We got the container back to dry land and popped it open. Soldiers began pulling out the contents and laying it out on the ground for sorting.

"Chocolate-banana, plain banana, strawberry-banana, banana curry. Sir, most of these are some type of banana flavor," Williams announced in consternation.

"Oh, crap," I slapped my forehead. "Skippy thinks monkeys love bananas!" I groaned, frustrated. "If we get another delivery, I'll request a better variety of flavors."

SpecOps

Captain Gomez uncapped a sludge, poured water in to rehydrate it, shook it up, and drained it in one gulp. "Food is fuel," he shrugged. "We can eat real food when we get back to the *Flying Dutchman*."

"Right. Everyone," I reminded people, "we bury our trash, can't have a Kristang ship seeing empty sludge packets laying on the ground. And let's drag the empty container into water deep enough that it will sink, put some rocks in to make sure." To set an example, I picked up a sludge packet without checking the flavor, poured water in, and gulped it down. It was, maybe, supposed to be plain banana flavor? You couldn't quite tell with Thuranin sludges, most of them had a nasty artificial taste.

When we got the sludge supply back out of the swamp and unpacked, we divided them up evenly. "Does everyone have real food left?" I asked Smythe quietly.

"I think so, sir. Everyone ate a good breakfast this morning."

"I saw that." I'd been watching people for signs of fatigue, nagging injuries, and that no one was skimping on nutrition. "I have eight MREs left, I'm going to save them for anyone who is wounded."

"Sir?"

"Captain, I've survived on sludges before, it's not new to me. They provide energy, and they will sustain you, you will also get heartily sick of drinking them very quickly. If anyone is wounded out here, it's going to be quite some time before they can get full medical treatment, aboard the *Dutchman*. I'd like them to have at least real food to eat, keep their spirits up."

"Oh, good thinking," he agreed. "I'll get a bag together." Smythe put an empty bag on the ground, and I asked people to donate one real food item, explaining that the bag would be reserved for injured soldiers, or to be rationed out as treats after the battle, while we waited for Skippy to fix the *Dutchman*.

"I have eight incredibly delicious MREs here," I said as I held them up for view. "Five American, two French," I nodded to Giraud, who had traded with me earlier, "and," I peered at the wrapper, "I guess this one is Chinese? I'll start the kitty by donating all of them. I'm tired of carrying the damned things anyway."

That drew a chuckle, and I put the MREs in the bag. "One only, if you have it to spare, keep the rest for yourself. Trust me, you are going to get very tired of existing on nothing but sludges."

"He speaks the truth," Giraud testified, sticking his tongue out disgustedly, and we bumped fists. Neither of us wanted to remember that unpleasant aspect of our first time aboard the *Flying Dutchman*.

We got a good donation, and the bag then held thirty five real meals of various types. None of it could be considered yummy, all of it had to taste better than a sludge. Smythe switched off the duties of carrying the goodie bag between soldiers, and we were extra super careful with it while crossing streams. I noticed that for the next four days, no one that I could see ate anything except sludges. Our shared suffering in that regard was a bonding experience. To spare the inexperienced the worst of the ordeal, I falsely let it be known that I didn't mind the plain banana flavor, which actually was among the very worst of the sludges. The plain banana, unmasked by other less-unpleasant flavors like chocolate, strawberry or even curry, was just bland, artificial, gritty and had an oily mouthfeel that lingered nastily on your tongue. It was my fault for not requesting a better variety of flavors from Skippy. Although now that I thought about it, there hadn't been a whole lot of sludges left aboard the *Dutchman* when we began the second voyage. And no one had thought to request Skippy to make more. No one, like me. Since no one liked the banana flavors, maybe Skippy had sent us whatever we had, left over from the first voyage. That was doubly my fault. Either way, I ended up with nothing but dehydrated plain banana sludges, having traded away all the less nasty flavors. Every sip of oily, gritty bland sludge reminded me about the value of planning ahead. That is certainly a lesson I wasn't going to forget. All I can say is, when we finally got back aboard the rebuilt *Flying Dutchman*, I was going to eat delicious, juicy cheeseburgers for breakfast, lunch and dinner every day the first week. Even if we no longer had a galley, and I had to grill the burger over a reactor.

When we'd collected the real food, I selected a sludge at random from my pack, popped the cap, and poured water in to rehydrate it. "Drink up, everyone, enjoy your yummy sludge. And, hey, today is Friday. Only two more working days until Monday!"

Despite how tired I was that night, I walked away from the campsite, in order to talk to Skippy in private. While I told myself that I wanted to thank him for the food, I had to admit that I missed talking with his irascible self. No one had insulted me for several days, it felt weird. "Hey, Skippy, how you doing up there?"

"Busy," he said tersely.

"Oh," I said, feeling awkward, "sorry, I'll leave you alone then."

"No need, Joe, I'm not *that* busy. At the moment, I am in the extremely delicate process of creating exotic matter in what used to be one of our cargo holds, using basically a coffee pot, a missile warhead, and two combots that, despite my best effort at modifications, absolutely suck at anything but combat. If this goes south, even on Newark you'll need to shield your eyes from the explosion. Don't worry, I am very confident. Fairly confident. Somewhat confident. Ok, yes, I'm making this shit up as I go, all right? Give me a freakin' break. And I wouldn't be too hopeful about the ultimate fate of that coffee pot, in case you were wondering. However, carrying on an intelligent conversation with one of you monkeys takes like one octillionth of my brain power, and half that when I'm speaking with you, so, what's up?"

There was the Skippy I knew! "Simply wanted to say, sincerely, from the bottom of my stomach, thank you for the food delivery."

"Hmmf. I was going to throw in free breadsticks. But, you know, what used to be the galley is current highly radioactive, so that was not an option."

"We appreciate the thought, Skippy." Right then, I couldn't think of anything else to say.

"Yeah, you're welcome. No problem." He sounded like he felt the conversation was lagging too.

Before it got any more awkward, I said "Well, I'll let you go-"

"How did the day go? I've been tracking your progress. Your group is making impressive progress." It seemed Skippy wanted to keep talking.

"We didn't roll or sink an RV today, that's progress. Everyone here is sore, not that the SpecOps people will admit it, our muscles have adjusted to the extra gravity, our joints and tendons are slower catching up to the extra strain. I stepped in a hole and twisted an ankle yesterday morning."

"Did you talk to one of the doctors about it?"

"No, I taped it up myself."

He sighed. "Joe, you brought two civilians with you, to have doctors on the team. You're making them walk all this way, for nothing?"

SpecOps

"Skippy, they didn't come with us for something as simple as someone tweaking an ankle, they're here to take care of combat injuries. There's not much to be done other than taping my ankle, I can't stop walking. I don't want to waste their time, and I don't want SpecOps people to think I'm weak."

"Joe, Joe, Joe. Once in a great while, you have a good idea, the rest of the time, you are dumb as a rock. Surely you are not the only monkey in your party with an injury that is being either ignored or attended to amateurishly?"

"Probably not," I thought of the various people I saw moving around stiffly in the mornings.

"And by not seeking the best treatment available, they risk becoming combat ineffective? As the commander, shouldn't you be setting an example?"

Crap. "Skippy, you not only can build a starship out of moon dust, you know more about monkey, damn it, human psychology than I do. I should know that. You're right, I will talk to one of the doctors tonight." And soon, before they fell asleep. "That's enough about me, how are you doing?"

"Good enough. I've been monitoring the progress of the archeology team, they have found a new chamber behind a wall, it was buried in a rock fall, perhaps at the same time when the main part of the cavern washed away, and the roof collapsed. Anticipating your question, Colonel Chang is making certain they are being safe, and not taking unnecessary risks with the project. The team is very excited, they haven't told you about it yet, they have found fragments of bronze plates with what appears to be writing. Colonel Chang hopes to find more writing samples, buried further down. This new chamber overall is shallow, whatever is in there will not require a deep excavation."

"Wow. Writing? That's awesome."

"Don't get your hopes up, Joe. This writing, if that's what it is, looks like nothing but scribbles. The only way we will ever be able to read any of it is if we find more samples, a lot more, with pictographs."

"We can hope, though. How are things going with you, up there?"

"Good, good enough. No new setbacks to report. While I have you, Joe, I've been thinking about that favor you asked."

"Huh? What favor?" He already delivered the pizza.

"The favor about you and me riding off into the sunset together. Remember? You're studying up on how to fly ship, so the two of us can drop the crew off at Earth, after I contact the Collective."

"Oh, yeah," I tried to keep the hopefulness out of my voice.

"I thought about it, and I can see why you think it's a good idea. I am willing to give it a shot. Unfortunately, my analysis has determined the scenario is extremely unlikely. As you know, my memory is vague concerning the Collective, one thing I am certain about is that once I make contact, I will no longer be able to help you. I might not even be able to communicate with you in any way. I may, very suddenly, simply be gone."

"Oh, I hear you, Skippy. Thanks for telling me."

"Sorry."

"Skippy, you saved our entire home planet, you have nothing to apologize about. We all knew the risks when we came out here. I'm going to," I yawned, "talk to one of the doctors about my ankle. You have a good night, Ok?"

"You too, Joe, sleep well."

Craig Alanson

From the pizza delivery site, we had two solid days of walking over rolling hills in a steady, cold, dreary rain, with wind blowing straight into our faces. For meals, we had cold rehydrated sludges. At night, we collapsed in our tents and sleeping bags, with wet clothes hanging on a line from the tent roof, dripping on us all night. In the morning, we got up and did it all again. The novelty of walking across an alien landscape, being the first humans wherever we went, was wearing off. Every single one of us wanted to get to the scavenger base, get the attack over with, and get back aboard the *Flying Dutchman.* Apparently I had earned a measure of grudging respect from Smythe, he had taken to walking with me, once I had demonstrated that I could keep up the pace. And I could, simply by concentrating on putting one foot in front of the other, hour after hour, day after day. What I could not do very well, would be to carry a heavy pack all day, in fourteen percent higher gravity and oxygen equivalent to high altitude on Earth, and then go directly into combat. The SpecOps people could, they'd trained for it, mentally prepared for it. At the end of a day, all I wanted to do was gulp down a nutritious sludge and sleep.

A swirling gust of wind blew fat, cold raindrops right into my eyes, I wiped my eyes and lowered goggles from atop my head to protect from the stinging spray. They were fancy high-tech Kristang goggles that repelled water and didn't fog up inside, even so, they were goggles and wearing them constantly grew tiresome after a while. "Lovely weather here, Captain," I said to Smythe, who had put his own goggles on. "Is this what Scotland is like?"

"No," Smythe looked surprised at my question. "Scotland is ruggedly beautiful, most times of the year. If you like the outdoors, it's a wonderful place. It is mostly open country like this," he swept his arm across the eastern horizon, partly obscured by rain and low clouds, "and it can be wet," he admitted. "No more so than the rest of the island, of course."

It took me a moment to realize that by 'the island', he meant Britain. As an American, I thought of Britain first as a country, not an island. When I hear the term 'island', I think someplace tropical, with palm trees and coconuts. And tropical drinks. With little umbrellas. And slices of pineapple. "That's where you train? The SAS? In Scotland?"

"Scotland? Sometimes. 22 SAS is based in Hereford, near the Welsh border. Part of our selection training takes place in the Brecon Beacons of Wales. That area is somewhat similar to this here, the weather can be very unpredictable, with wind coming off the Irish Sea."

"That's one advantage of Newark, I suppose. The weather here is predictable; lousy all the time. My hometown in Maine can have bad weather, at least there the whole area is mostly covered with trees, it cuts the wind. And we have plenty of fuel for a campfire there."

"Have you ever been to Britain?" He asked, I shook my head. Smythe went on. "You would like the walking trails in Britain. In the States, I understand that your walking trails are mostly in the woods and you cook your meals over a fire, and sleep in tents. In Britain, we have walking trails that go from one village to the next. You can stop at a pub for lunch and dinner, and stay in a guesthouse overnight. It's very popular, particularly in areas such as the Cotswolds and the Yorkshire Dales."

"That sure sounds tempting right about now. The trails go right into a village?"

"Yes. The difference is," Smythe explained, "most of your trails in the States were set up by governments, on public land, or on private land where the owner allows access? In Britain, the public has access across private lands, because for thousands of years, peasants had right of access to get water, to drive their animals to market or to pasture.

The current landowners can't block the public from walking across their land, because of the historical right of access. There is a group which organizes what they call a mass trespass once a year, to walk all the trails in Britain, in order to maintain the public's right of access."

"Huh." I said. "Man, that would piss off a lot of people back home."

"America hasn't been around for long, compared to Britain. Different standards," Smythe concluded. We stopped talking after that, as the path took us up a long, steep hill, and I couldn't manage more than grunts.

Even Smythe appeared winded from the climb, we paused at the summit. "The mountains of Afghanistan are like this. At altitude, you get to the top of a climb," he said, gasping, "and you want to catch your breath, but you can't."

I nodded. "I was with the 10th Infantry Division, the 10th used to specialize in mountain warfare. Then they sent me to the jungles of Nigeria. And then to Paradise. The first place I was stationed on Paradise was so flat, it looked like Kansas."

The rain stopped in mid-morning the next day, there was a strong, constant wind, from the southeast this time, that seemed to literally blow the clouds away. By early afternoon, the wind dropped to a pleasant breeze, the sun came out, and the temperature soared high enough that I stripped down to a long sleeved shirt. People's spirits rose with the temperature, grim faces replaced by grins, grunts replaced by laughter. Taking advantage of the break in the weather, I unrolled my damp sleeping bag, turned it inside out, and tied it to my pack so it could dry. Also, I hung wet socks from my belt. Everyone did something similar. The sunshine on my face actually felt warm, even a little hot at times. "Captain," I said to Smythe, "Skippy tells me this nice weather is going to last until around midnight, then we're getting rain showers. We're still ahead of schedule, I want a two hour break for lunch. We'll get the tents set up with flaps open so they can dry out. And we can string clotheslines from those rocks over there. We will walk a bit later into the night to make up the time, the ground ahead is pretty flat and there's no large streams to cross until tomorrow."

To my surprise, Smythe didn't protest the delay. We got tents and clotheslines set up quickly, and we all took a nice break in the sunshine, sitting or laying on dry rocks.

"It's not so bad now," I mused to Tanaka and Zheng. We were sitting on a flat rock with our boots and socks off, rubbing our feet. The two civilians had held up very well to the rigors of our grueling hike across Newark. "You know, I wonder what this area was like before?"

"Before?" Zheng asked.

"Before Newark got pushed out of its original orbit," I explained. "We're seven hundred kilometers from the equator here, this must have been, what? Jungle? Desert? Something hot. People, the natives, they might have come here on vacation."

"I don't think their society had vacations, they probably didn't have the technology for leisure travel," Tanaka said.

"They had the wheel, that means roads," I pointed out defensively. "Anyway, you know what I mean. This was a nice place back then." I looked around at the low, rolling hills, valleys crisscrossed by streams that sparkled in the sunlight. "Like that hill over there," I pointed to the south, "it has a nice view of that lake, it would have had nice breezes for cooling. I wonder if anyone lived up there?"

Zheng shaded her eyes and looked around. I couldn't tell whether she was irritated that I'd disturbed the rest she'd earned. "Most of this landscape was carved by glaciers, when Newark was frozen solid, before the orbit became elliptical. That lake, even that hill, may not have existed back then. That will be a big problem for archeologists, much of the evidence of civilization here; cities, buildings, roads like you said, will have been scoured away by glaciers. The glaciers, even here, could have been substantial. The science team is having a debate over whether Newark's surface froze completely over, or whether there might have been a strip of open ocean near the equator, during summers." Perhaps because she saw the crestfallen look on my face, she quickly added "The natives didn't deserve what happened to this planet. No one does."

"Except maybe the people who did this. What are the odds Newark is the only planet they threw out of orbit?" I asked bitterly. My nice sunny good mood was fading. "If I ever find those MFers-"

"Colonel," Zheng said, and tapped my shoulder gently. "We have a nice day here, a nice afternoon. Let's enjoy it while it lasts, Ok? Enjoy it for the natives, because they can't? No more talk about glaciers, I promise."

Not thinking about glaciers for a while was nice.

"Uh oh, Joe," Skippy called me while I was wading across an icy cold stream that was up to my chest. Making the situation extra special was that, because the water was deep, I had to make two trips across. It took two trips to carry all my gear high over my head, so it wouldn't get wet.

"Give me a minute, Skippy," I said with almost a gasp, the cold was taking my breath away. Of course, he called when I was in the deepest part of the stream. "Kinda busy here right now."

"No immediate rush, Joe," he responded with a peevish tone.

When I got to dry land, I set my gear down on a rock. On top of me being soaking wet from wading the stream twice, it was raining, it was always freakin' raining on Newark. Following the example of the SpecOps people, I did squats with my rifle over my head, then dropped and did fifty pushups, to get some warm blood into my chilled muscles. There were only five people still in the process of crossing the stream, and they didn't need my help, so I turned my attention to our annoying AI. "What is it, Skippy?"

"A potential problem, Joe. A few minutes ago, I overhead the scavenger leaders talking, two of them are taking a group of laborers out in a truck, to a site where they previously found parts of the Elder starship buried in the ground. They are loading the truck now."

"Damn it!" This was the last thing we needed; if the scavengers were in two places, we would need to plan and coordinate two simultaneous attacks. Depending how far the Kristang drove in their truck, it might take us a long time, walking night and day, to catch up with them. Although we were still slightly ahead of schedule, we couldn't delay an attack for very long, because we couldn't risk the Kristang ship arriving early and spoiling all of our plans. "This Elder site they're driving to, how far it is from their base? And do you know if they're planning to stay there overnight?"

"They are planning to stay overnight, one night only. This particular site has been picked over pretty thoroughly, Joe, it is quite desperate of them to go back there, hoping they can dig up something of value. Without air transport, or their RV, they can no longer travel far from their base, this limits them to sites within roughly eighty kilometers. The leaders know that an extended excursion away from the base would make them vulnerable to attack by their laborers, without air power, the leaders are feeling very vulnerable. They are absolutely right to be concerned; their workforce is extra unhappy with their leaders, they've lost both of their aircraft, and their RV, and they let what they think was an extremely valuable Elder power tap get away. The Elder artifacts they have recovered so far are not valuable enough to pay much more than the costs of the expedition, so the laborers know there will not be much, if any, profits to be shared. The workforce is ripe for a violent mutiny, Joe."

"That's good for us. Where is this Elder site they're going to? Can you show me on my zPhone?"

"There is a map on your phone now."

"Huh. Damn, that's almost between us and the scavenger base." Skippy had put a blinking dot for the Elder site, on top of the map we used to guide us to the scavenger base. Our route passed within twenty kilometers of where the scavengers would be staying overnight. "Do you know the route that truck will be driving?" I asked, and immediately, a series of red dots appeared on the map, outlining the route the Kristang were planning to drive. The last forty kilometers of their route overlapped the route we planned to walk. It made sense, we were now approaching the scavenger base from the south, and there was only one good route that avoided going up and down hills all day; we would follow a river valley. The Kristang in their truck understandably planned to do the same thing. "Skippy, thank you, I need to think about this. We can watch their truck from the satellite feeds?"

"You won't normally be able to do that through the thick clouds you have overhead now, I'll add an icon on your maps, so you can see where they are. The truck is leaving the base right now. I assure you that no one aboard that truck is singing the Kristang version of 'Ninety Nine Bottles of Beer on the Wall'. Joe, these lizards are not a crew of happy campers."

"Got it, thank you."

I went over to Smythe, who was checking that everyone was ready to move out, move out quickly, before our half-frozen muscles stiffened up. Explaining the situation, I showed Smythe the map on his own zPhone.

"Bloody hell," he said, "this complicates things somewhat, doesn't it?"

"Yes," I agreed.

"Although," he mused, scratching his two-day growth of beard, "it could be an opportunity."

"That also," I agreed again. "I see this as more risk than opportunity. For opportunity, you're thinking we can take out this excursion party of Kristang and steal their truck. Then we ride it into their base compound, and take them by surprise?"

"Essentially, yes. It is tempting, surely. That sort of plan depends on our spy in the sky intercepting communications from the excursion party, then faking signals from them. Can Skippy do that, do you think, sir?"

"Captain, that would not be a problem for Skippy. The problem is, the excursion party will be overnighting only seventy kilometers from the base, that close, they can use simple radio to communicate, not route the signal through a satellite. When they send signals through one of their satellites, Skippy can intercept and squelch or alter the signal. He can't do anything about radio transmissions through the air."

"Bollocks!" Smythe declared. "That's out, then. Unless we take them all out at once, we'd risk cocking it up. The timing would be too dicey, too many ways it could go pear shaped in a hurry."

"Uh, yeah," I said, not completely sure of his British slang, I understood the basics. "How about this; we proceed to here," I pointed to the spot where the Kristang truck would intercept our planned walking route on their return journey, "and we wait for them to go by. Then we can follow their truck. We can't go ahead of them, they'd see our footprints. And that river valley is the only practical way to get from here to their base, unless we go all the around these hills, way to the east. I don't like that option."

"As much as I hate to pass up this opportunity, sir," Smythe observed sourly, "we're not out here to defeat them in detail any longer, we already knocked out their air power. Now, we need to hit them all at once. Rubbish. We'll need to explain to the lads why we're not hitting them."

CHAPTER TWENTY FIVE

The lads weren't the only ones who needed to be reminded not to shoot, as we watched the Kristang truck slowly lurch by a couple days later. Smythe, Giraud, I and a few others lay belly down behind rocks on the reverse slope of a hill, as the Kristang truck drove back down the river valley below us. It was tempting, almost too tempting a target. With our Kristang rifles, we could easily have knocked treads off the truck, then picked off the Kristang one by one. If the Kristang in the truck were the only ones on the planet, that would have been a viable plan. In reality, we had to watch, silently, as the truck passed our position. As an extra precaution, none of us had brought weapons to our observation post. I wasn't worried about someone losing discipline and firing off a shot, I was worried about a weapon discharging accidentally. Yeah, it was a small risk, it was also a risk we didn't need to take. The Kristang in their truck didn't know we were there, couldn't see us, were not a threat to us.

Their truck reminded me of the US Army's M977 heavy truck, except instead of eight wheels, the Kristang truck had four flexible treads like our sunken RV. The cab had a flat front, with large windows, through my zPhone camera I could clearly see the two Kristang in the cab. Behind the cab was a canvas sort of cover, two more Kristang were sitting with their legs hanging over the tailgate, looking very pissed off.

When we first saw the truck, rolling along beside the river, it was moving fairly quickly over flat ground. Now, right below us, the river made a series of lazy bends, and the truck had to slow down to splash across streams. Skippy told us that truck didn't have swim pontoons, it couldn't float like the RV had, it was just a truck with fancy treads. On a planet crisscrossed with rivers swollen with snow and glacial melt, a vehicle that couldn't cross a significant body of water was severely limited in where it could go. That explained why the Kristang had chosen to go out to an Elder crash site they had already explored; there weren't many places they could go, now that we had destroyed their aircraft and RV.

The truck was driving back over its own muddy tracks, returning to the base the same way it had come out. In several places along the river, there was only one place to go, without driving through water deep enough to submerge it completely. It went through a stream and I found myself holding my breath, the truck was submerged almost up to its hood, and the two Kristang in the back were now standing up, keeping their feet out of the icy water. Even from where we were hiding, I could faintly hear the truck's motors whining. One of the left treads spun freely, then caught, and the truck waddled up the other side of the stream. The truck stopped, the left door opened, and a Kristang got out to inspect the front left tread. Then the other Kristang in the front got out, and the two of them talked, while pointing at the tread. One of the laborers in the back poked his head around the side, and the first Kristang pulled out a pistol and gestured for the laborer to get back in the truck. The two in the front kicked the tread, and clods of mud fell out. After peering at the tread a minute and discussing something, the two leaders got back in the cab, and the truck lurched back into motion.

After a while, watching the truck drive on became dull, when it became clear the Kristang had no idea we were there, and only wanted to get back to their base. My attention wandered away from the truck to Captain Smythe, I wondered how many times, in how many Godforsaken places, Smythe had done this exact same thing; lain in wait, observing an enemy, deciding when and how to strike.

Within ten minutes, the truck went out of sight around a bend in the river.

Craig Alanson

"Skippy said there are six of them in the truck," Smythe said quietly, "the most we could have taken out at one time were three. No go, it wouldn't have worked anyway."

"And we couldn't have walked all the way to where they camped overnight, in time to hit them when they were sleeping," I added. "We stick with the original plan, let that truck drive back to their base. Give it twenty minutes to get well ahead of us, then we'll go down there and follow it. We should be within striking distance of their base tonight."

The big unknown in my plan to assault the scavengers' base was whether we could get close enough to launch a surprise attack, or whether the Kristang would see us coming far away and prepare their defenses. If the Kristang had made even a minimal effort at external site security, such as scattering a few cameras around the base perimeter, they could have ruined all our plans. A couple cheap cameras were a simple precaution, that could have forced us to fight a pitched battle against Kristang with equivalent technology, with them in prepared positions. While we marched toward the base, Smythe and I discussed how to approach the base from multiple directions, using one group as a decoy, before the main assault team swept in from another direction. Neither of us liked the odds of that plan succeeding.

To my surprise and delight, back when I was dreaming up the overall plan against the scavengers, Skippy confirmed the scavengers had made zero effort at protecting their base from external threats, the leaders' only concern was security inside their base. The only threat they foresaw was from their own forced laborers; the base inside the fence was riddled with cameras and other sensors, and doors were locked with codes that only three of the leaders had access to. On an uninhabited planet, a planet without land animals larger than a tiny insect, the leaders must have figured cameras outside the base were not necessary. They were wrong.

After the scavengers saw from Skippy's faked satellite data, that they weren't alone on the planet, that other Kristang had been there, had even shot down their air power, you would think the scavengers leaders would have done something, taken some steps to prevent hostile forces from sneaking up on their base. They did absolutely nothing. After seeing the fake satellite of the other Kristang having flown up into orbit, and then jumping away, the scavenger leaders once again thought they were safe. Stupid civilians.

That was great news for us. The day before we were scheduled to reach the base, I asked Skippy to confirm there were no cameras, motion detectors, or other sensors outside the base. He replied that, as far as he could tell, and he was tapping into all their communications, there were no sensors of any kind outside the fence.

As far as he could tell.

That was the problem. While we could plan for the best, we had to account for the worst.

It was a judgment call, and as the commander, I had to make it. If there were in fact no cameras or sensors outside the fence line, we could wait until daylight to attack, because my plan relied on the Kristang being awake. If there were sensors of any kind outside the fence line, then it would be best for us to approach the base and launch the attack at night, to catch the Kristang as off guard as possible. If I assumed there were no sensors and I was wrong, our daylight assault could get difficult very quickly. But if I assumed there were sensors and we launched a night assault, instead of sticking to my original plan, I would needlessly be putting human lives at risk.

SpecOps

What I decided on was a compromise. We approached the base from two directions, at night. One team of six people came in from the east, as a decoy force. Once they were within half a kilometer, the rest of us, including an Alpha team of two men in armor suits, ran toward the base from the west. If we were detected, the base would sound an alarm and Skippy would tell us right away. At that point, we were committed to hit the base as fast and hard as we could, there was no going back, nothing to go back to.

If our night approach was not detected, and we got to the ridge two hundred meters west of the base, we would hide behind the ridge until daylight, as implement my original plan. To my original plan, I added a silent prayer before we crossed the start line. We each took with us weapons, water, a sludge, and first aid kits. Our two actual qualified doctors remained at the start line with the rest of our equipment, a kilometer from the base, under a bluff. Part of my prayer was that we wouldn't need the doctors. The weather was cold but clear that night, our local TV weather man Skippy said skies would remain mostly clear until the following afternoon. I took that as a good omen. Unfortunately, I mentioned my thought of omens out loud while Skippy was listening, and was subjected to a scathing lecture about ignorant, superstitious monkeys. It's a good thing he didn't know I was also wearing my lucky underwear.

Yeah, lucky underwear is a real thing.

Skippy's intel was right. No alarm was sounded, we got to our initial hold position two hundred meters from the base, spread out to give good coverage, and we lay prone on the ground behind a ridge that was maybe five meters tall at its highest point. Just enough to give us cover. We set up zPhones sticking just above the ridge as cameras, and monitored the view from our own zPhones. We waited throughout the night, silently, communicating by hand signals. As dawn approached, lights came on inside the scavenger base, and Skippy told us the Kristang were engaged in mundane tasks such as eating breakfast, showering, and arguing with each other. In two hours, two of the leaders planned to go out to the Elder crash site with six laborers, to resume digging. Once they were outside the base, there was a strong chance they would see us, so I launched Phase Three of the plan.

Phases One and Two of my plan relied merely on the Kristang's strong desire to possess an Elder power tap, and Skippy's ability to control the data feed through their satellites. Phases One and Two did not require the Kristang to do anything specifically Kristang-like in nature; any species would want an Elder power tap. Perhaps the fact that the scavengers were especially eager to grab it as soon as possible, before the starship they were expecting could steal it and jump away, was a particularly Kristang characteristic, but no species would leave such a valuable object laying exposed on the ground for long. Of course they would send an aircraft to pick it up. And of course, after the aircraft crashed, they would send their remaining air power to get the power tap. Humans would have flown a dropship to the crash site, out of concern for any survivors of the crash, or at least to investigate the cause of the crash; the Kristang likely wouldn't have cared about any of that. Probably they'd consider such actions a sign of weakness.

No matter what their motivations, the Kristang had fallen for our traps, Phases One and Two, that wiped out their air power advantage, and reduced the Kristang we potentially had to fight by eleven. I'd been hoping one, or both, of the air sorties the scavengers sent out would contain at least one powered armor suit, to reduce the number of those we had to face. Sending an armored suit seemed to me to be a blindingly obvious part of any plan to pick up a priceless Elder artifact; someone in armor could more quickly and easily reach the site in the rough terrain of the canyon lands. Someone in armor could more easily, and more important, safely, bring the artifact back to the aircraft. Crossing freezing cold, fast running streams, walking over broken rocks and smooth, wet, slippery muds, sliding through mud, would all be safer in a powered armor suit that had gyroscopes and computer-controlled stabilizers.

Unfortunately, although the Kristang would probably have agreed with me about the wisdom and practicality of sending armor to pick up the Elder power tap, they had a uniquely Kristang factor to consider: they couldn't trust their forced labor with powered armor. Even one of the six high-ranking Kristang, who had armor, wouldn't risk being away from the base, surrounded by forced labor. In the close confines of an aircraft, or hemmed in by canyon walls, a Kristang in armor would lose much of the advantage of wearing armor, and be vulnerable to a concentrated, planned attack. The result, which sucked for us humans, was no armor was in either of the aircraft. That meant the scavengers, at their base, had four functional sets of armor that we would have to deal with. Too many Kristang, four of whom would have armor, against our human SpecOps team, and we had only two sets of Kristang armor with us.

Phase Three of my plan was to deal with the scavengers' numerical and armor advantage, and the advantage they had of being in defensive positions. I had thought long and hard about how we could defeat the scavengers, that's a nice way of saying we needed to kill them, all of them. Because I couldn't think of any way for us not to kill them, given their advantages of numbers, technology and being on the defensive, I decided the only solution was for us to outsource the job.

We would get the Kristang to kill each other. That's why my plan relied on them being awake and up before we launched Phase Three.

I contacted Skippy. "Hey, Skippy, you there?"

"Of course. How is your back feeling, Joe?"

"Better" I admitted, "now that my pack is lighter." My pack was lighter, because I was no longer carrying a section of powered armor, and because I'd eaten most of the food we started out with. Dehydrated sludges didn't weigh much, even in fourteen percent higher gravity. The armored suits were now assembled and ready for use in combat. My hope, if my plan worked, was we wouldn't need our Alpha team with two sets of armor for a while yet. "You ready for Phase Three?"

"More than ready! I'm eager to see if this works. It will be an interesting experiment in Kristang social dynamics."

"Uh huh, sure thing," I agreed. "Activate Phase Three whenever you can."

"Done. If you're right, we'll know pretty quickly."

"Yup, that's what I hope. Let me know as soon as anything changes over there."

Phase Three was simple; it didn't involve any decoys, any manipulation of satellite data, any shooting down aircraft, or any elaborate cover-ups of human involvement. The essence of Phase Three was that the truth shall set you free. Only, in this case, the truth was being given to the Kristang forced laborers, and the 'you' really being set free was the human assault force. Free, hopefully, from having to engage in a protracted firefight with the Kristang.

The 'truth' part of Phase Three was, in fact, truth. What Skippy did was grant the forced laborers access to secure communications of the six Kristang leaders, not a hundred percent exactly what the leaders said to each other, Skippy spiced things up a bit to get the laborers' attention quickly. Skippy made the breakdown in communications security seem like a system glitch, and it took the laborers a while to notice, even longer to take advantage of their surprise access. The data they had access to was, in essence, all true; the food supply at the base was dwindling, and the six leaders planned to either kill or abandon their labor force on Newark when the starship arrived. While maybe the laborers suspected that was going to happen anyway, getting smacked in the face with it certainly made them hopping mad. Anger is a useless emotion unless it can be channeled into action, and that was where the other data Skippy gave them access to came into play. He gave them access to the base physical security systems, like the doors that kept the laborers locked in when they weren't working. And the doors in the entire base, including the high security area where the six leaders lived. And, most especially, the locks to the armory building, where the leaders kept almost all the weapons, and three of the four working armored suits.

Sentient beings, whether they are human, Ruhar, Kristang or any other species in the Milky Way galaxy, tend to avoid risk, and tend to hesitate when presented with new information, particularly when that new information makes them question things they previously believed. Fortunately, most groups of sentient beings have one or two members who do not hesitate, who take decisive action, and those dynamic individuals usually bring the group with them. In the case of the laborers, there were three Kristang who didn't hesitate, who boldly and angrily took action. These three Kristang were younger sons, who were not technically prisoners or slaves, they were younger sons of impoverished subclan families, who had volunteered to join the scavenger expedition in a desperate attempt to improve the fortunes of their families back home. These three felt especially betrayed that their leaders planned to abandon them on Newark with the criminals and slaves who made up most of the work force. The first thing the three did was verify the access codes truly could open the door that kept them trapped in their defacto prison. When that door opened with a metallic click, they moved out immediately. The laborers knew their leaders were watching them, knew the leaders had seen the laborers becoming agitated and angrily arguing amongst themselves, and knew the leaders would be notified as soon as the door was unlocked without the leaders' authorization. So, as soon as that door opened, the three bold laborers moved quickly, and the others followed.

The others followed, because they knew their leaders would punish all the laborers equally for attempted rebellion, knew they faced death whether they actively participated in the mutiny or not. It was all or nothing, and such clarity is a great motivator. The entire group of laborers raced through the camp toward the armory, while the six leaders hesitated, stunned, for crucial seconds.

When the six leaders finally faced their shocking new reality and roused themselves to action, the first thing they did was argue amongst each other. The primary leader, the one who had funded the scavenger expedition, knew that only he and two others had codes to unlock the armory door, yet he could see on the security system display that the laborers were confidently racing toward the armory building, and had already unlocked the gate to the electric fence that surrounded the armory. The primary leader instantly drew only one conclusion from what he was seeing; one of the other two Kristang with the codes had given them to the laborers, in an attempt to take over the base and steal the precious Elder artifacts for himself. Accordingly, the primary leader took out of its holster the pistol he constantly kept on his belt, and shot the other two. Now there were four leaders left. And one armor suit available, in the primary leader's cabin, the other three functioning sets of armor were in the armory building. After killing two of his fellows, the primary leader, with his pistol pointed at the three others, backed into his personal cabin and locked himself in. He came out four minutes later, in an armor suit, and led his three fellows toward the armory. On the video screen, the leaders could see the laborers had reached the armory and had already unlocked the outer door. A minute later, as the leaders reached the fence that surrounded the armory, shots rang out from both sides.

It was a chaotic, bloody mess, a pure fire fight without any planning, tactics or coordination. The primary leader charged directly toward the back door the armory building, he must have known that if the laborers got the other suits on, it was game over. The other three leaders poured fire into the open doorway of the armory, cutting down laborers as they came out, firing blindly. The laborers numbers began to tell, as one of the leaders went down, and the other two pulled back around the corner of a building for cover. Three times Smythe reminded the team not to fire, regardless how tempting the target was, and to keep down and out of sight. Our Alpha team, the two men in suits, were particularly itching to get into the fight. Keeping our heads down was a good idea not only so the Kristang didn't see us, but also because there were explosive-tipped rounds flying thick through the air all around the base. The leaders had a few heavier weapons, and explosions sent shrapnel everywhere. The laborers responded with improvised explosives they'd taken from the armory.

When the fighting ended, there were only three Kristang left alive on the planet. Two leaders, wearing armor and hunkered down in their own building, likely still in shock and trying to decide what to do. One laborer, holed up in the armory building. Holed up, with the precious stash of Elder artifacts, and a whole lot of explosives. Explosives he threatened to detonate, if the leaders didn't take off their armor suits, come into the open, negotiate how to split the artifacts and assure the laborer he would be getting safely off the planet. According to Skippy, he actually did have a chance to survive; though Kristang society would not be happy about him participating in a violent mutiny, they would respect his courage, and more importantly, his success. The Kristang rewarded success in combat, I knew that from very personal experience. Unfortunately for him, we knew from Skippy listening in on the two leaders' conversations that they planned to betray and kill the laborer.

We needed to deal with the three remaining Kristang. To put it simply, we needed to kill them quickly. And with minimal risk to ourselves. By 'ourselves', I mean the SpecOps troops, not me. I didn't even have a weapon, what I had carried across the surface of Newark was ammo and part of an armor suit. Yes, I had experience in combat, I'd even killed Kristang. With the SpecOps teams, I could only get in their way. Each team of four or six had trained extensively with each other, knew their tactics, knew each other, knew their roles, knew what every other member of the team would do in a situation. Each team had trained with other teams, and each soldier had cross trained with other teams; Rangers had taken a place on the Chinese team, Chinese with the SAS, French paratroopers with their Indian counterparts. Although I had participated in some of their training aboard, and outside, the *Dutchman*, I wasn't qualified to go into combat with them. "What do you think?" I asked Smythe.

"It would help if we could draw those two leaders out of cover," Smythe mused, "going to be a hell of a fire fight, if we have to go in there after them. Two armored suits against two armored suits, and they're bigger, faster and stronger than humans. They've been using armor probably since they were little, we still don't have enough real experience for me to be confident of our chances in this one. That bugger with the explosives is the real problem, that's where we could use our suits; go in high speed and hit him before he can react. We can't do that if we need our suits to engage those two leaders. Somehow, we need to make that laborer disarm those explosives, or distract him even a short time, make him hesitate." He looked up at me. "You have another magic trick up your sleeve, sir?"

"I wish I did," I said, shaking my head slowly. Magic is what we needed right then. The SpecOps people were committed and brave, willing to go in and accomplish the mission, regardless of the cost to themselves. Willing to go in, if I ordered them to. An order I didn't want to give. It wouldn't be right for me to send them into a straight, brutal fire fight simply because their commander couldn't think of a better tactical solution to the problem. Yet, we'd come this far, we couldn't simply give up now. A magic trick would be a great thing to have right then. All magic is based on deception-

I sucked in a sharp breath. "Captain Smythe, I may have an idea. Skippy, you listening?"

"I'm here," Skippy acknowledged.

With an attentive audience, I explained my plan.

Smythe grinned appreciatively. "Sir, I think Skippy is right, you are an evil genius."

I had to laugh at that, despite the seriousness of the situation. "This will work?" The SpecOps people were the experts on what they could accomplish, and not.

"Oh, yes. We'll handle it from here, sir," Smythe said and turned to sketch out an attack plan in the mud.

Phase Three Bravo, that I'd dreamed up on the spot, began by Skippy transmitting over the radio. The message was supposedly from the Kristang who had shot down the Luzzard and the dropship, and stolen the Elder power tap. Pretending to be one of those Kristang, from the Red Stone clan, Skippy made a plea to the laborer with the explosives. He explained that the Red Stone clan's ship had never truly jumped away, it had been hiding behind a stealth field in orbit the whole time. The Red Stone clan had given the security access codes to the laborers, and if the one remaining Kristang laborer deactivated the explosives and joined the Red Stone, he could split the reward. Our two men in armored suits stepped over the ridge into clear view, and began running toward the storehouse where the laborer was holed up with the Elder AI, the precious comm node, and a pile of explosives.

Three Bravo worked, because the three remaining Kristang heard Kristang talking to them, and saw two unfamiliar Kristang armored suits pop up and run toward the base. The scavengers were alone on Newark, as far as they knew. They believed our story about the Red Stone clan instantly, because that was the only possible explanation, based on what the scavengers knew. They had no reason to think the two Kristang armored suits running toward the base contained anyone other than Kristang from the Red Stone clan, to think anything else right then would be absurd.

Our deception worked as intended, the two leaders in armor screeched angrily over the radio and stepped out from behind cover to race toward the armory, intending to get there before the two Red Stone clan in armor suits could. From where they were, the two leaders couldn't get a clear shot at our two armored warriors; several buildings were between the two pairs of combatants, and our men weaved as they ran, using low spots in the hill slope to keep out of plain sight. The SpecOps teams had practiced this broken field running in suits many times. Skippy's opinion was that, because of the size gap between humans and Kristang, and the different running gaits of the two species, a human wearing armor would look strange to a Kristang, and any Kristang would notice something wrong fairly quickly. With our two men running down the hill slope, leaping from cover to cover, they weren't clearly visible long enough for the Kristang to tell those armored suits didn't contain Kristang. Or so we hoped.

The two scavenger leaders were not making any attempt to keep to cover, racing at the full amazing speed their suits could manage. They were fast, almost too fast. Our entire assault team, except the Alpha team of two men in armor, and one rifleman waiting for a clear shot at the laborer, had our Kristang rifles sighted in on the scavenger leaders, and even with advanced knowledge of how fast beings in suits could run, and the super technology of Kristang adaptive gunsights, most of our first volley of shots missed. Enough shots did hit the two scavenger leaders that they went down quickly, stumbling and falling, skidding across the ground. Now alert to the danger, they separated and attempted to get behind cover, they were too late. Massed fire, with eight to ten rifles concentrating on each set of armor, knocked them back down again, and our explosive-tipped armor-penetrating rounds began to bite through the tough armor.

"Cease fire! Cease fire!" Skippy shouted over the private channel. "Stop shooting, those two are dead. You're wasting ammo."

Before I had to say anything, we all stopping shooting at the two now-inert Kristang leaders. Our two men in armor didn't hesitate, they kept running toward the armory building. This was the moment of maximum danger; if that lizard in the armory decided he had nothing to lose, and detonated the explosives, we could lose our two men in suits, the comm node, and the AI. I was about to order the two men in suits to halt, so we could try talking to the remaining Kristang, but the sharp crack of a rifle interrupted me. The sniper we had assigned to cover the armory had not lost focus for a second, despite the gunfire ringing out all around him. The massed fire had attracted the attention of the laborer in the armory, curiosity, or maybe the fear of not knowing what is going on, overcame his better judgment, and he popped his head up for a quick look.

Not quick enough. Our sniper, from the Chinese team, drilled him once in the head with an explosive-tipped round, and that was the end of it. Fortunately, the laborer hadn't rigged up any kind of dead-man switch on the explosives, because nothing further happened. "You certain you got him?" I asked the sniper.

"Yes, sir," he said, and transmitted his gun scope camera image to my zPhone.

There was no question about it, that lizard's head had exploded like, well, I'll spare you the unpleasant details. What mattered was, that lizard wasn't going to be a problem for anyone, ever again. "Alpha team," I ordered the two men in suits, "approach with caution. Everyone else, hold position."

We waited while the Alpha team in their armor carefully leapfrogged toward the armory. This was a situation where I wish we had the full suite of Kristang infantry fighting gear, especially recon drones. We could have launched a drone into the armory, without risking anyone's life, to get us all the intel we needed. As it was, with only two armored suits and no recon gear, we made do with what we had. One, then both, of the Alpha team disappeared inside the large door of the armory, then one of them came outside and waved to me. "All clear, sir, no booby traps. He would have had to manually set off the explosives, looks like he was mostly bluffing."

"Skippy?" I inquired. "What do you think?"

"I concur, all is clear. None of the Kristang are alive."

"Damn," I breathed a sigh of relief, "we did it. We actually did it."

Smythe safed his weapon, stood up, and crisply saluted me. "Sir, we destroyed their air power, and neutralized all of them, without a single shot being fired in our direction.

SpecOps

This is the most successful operation I've ever been involved in. That was a hell of a plan, sir."

"So far, Captain. So far." We still needed to hide from the Kristang ship that would arrive before the *Dutchman* was ready, then later get off the planet safely. "Let's secure Skippy's magic radio and the AI, and then I'll think about celebrating somewhat."

CHAPTER TWENTY SIX

The Elder gear we wanted was in a pile on the floor of the armory, underneath a dead lizard. I ordered the Alpha team to remove the dead Kristang, as the seven foot tall body was too heavy for me to move by myself. It took a few minutes of sorting through the pile to find the two things Skippy sought; the AI and the comm node. The comm node I found first, it was in a box, surrounded by padding; the Kristang must have recognized it as something at least semi valuable. "Ok, we have the comm node-"

"No!" Skippy interrupted me. "The AI, find the AI."

"All right, all right," I assured him. "Looking for it now." Setting aside the comm node, the magic radio we had come all the way out here to find, I continued sorting through the pile, until I reached the bottom. There was no AI. "It's not here."

"What?" Skippy's voice carried a touch of panic. "It has to be there!"

"Hold on, Skippy, don't worry yet. I only looked through the Elder gear that guy had with the explosives. He probably didn't have time to take all the Elder artifacts out of where they are storing them. There's a bunch of lockers and containers here, we'll find it."

And we did find it, forty minutes later. We tore the armory apart, looked in every container, every locker, and we found all kinds of Elder artifacts, mostly damaged, all worthless according to Skippy. The AI wasn't anywhere. "Crap!" I swore in frustration. "We'll have to search every nook and cranny of this entire base, then. Captain Smythe, split up the team-"

Williams interrupted me. "Got it! Found it, sir, I think. Is this it?" He held up an object identical to Skippy, except this one had some green sticky substance on one side.

"Yes!" I exulted. "Where did you find it?"

"In the trash can, sir," Williams answered.

"The trash can?!" Skippy shouted. "Damn it! If those lizards weren't already dead, I'd kill them for that."

"Skippy, they didn't know what they had. The lizards and the hamsters kept you on a dusty shelf, they didn't know how valuable you are either." I took the AI from Williams and carefully rubbed the green goo off with a rag, it came off easily, nothing stuck to that shiny chrome surface. "Ok, what's next?"

"Touch your phone to the surface, it needs to be in direct contact."

"That's all?" I asked skeptically.

"Yes, we're making do with what we have here. I'll take it from there. Good, hold it right there, right there. Huh," he said, "let me try it again. Huh."

"Anything?"

"No, no, nothing. Trying it again. Damn it."

"Skippy?" He didn't answer me. I had been touching the top of my zPhone to the top of the AI. Now, I set the zPhone down on a table, and put the AI on it. It couldn't be touching any more firmly. "Hey, Skippy," I said softly, "do you want to try it again? Skippy?"

"I did already," he said, and he didn't even bother faking a sigh.

"No response? I'm sorry, Skippy." Damn I felt just awful for him. Essentially alone in the universe, he thought he had found one of this own kind, but it was inert. "Hey, listen, we'll bring the AI up to the *Dutchman* with us, and you can try it again there."

"Why? It's dead, Joe, there's nothing in that canister. There is no use bringing it to me."

"You know this because you have contacted apparently inert AIs before?"

"No. Duh. This has never happened before, as far as I know."

"Then you don't know that it won't work, right?"

He sighed, and the fact that he made the effort to do that for my benefit was encouraging. We didn't need a depressed AI working on the delicate task of repairing the ship. "You're right," he said glumly. "Sure, what the hell, I'll try that."

"I'm sorry, Skippy, I really am."

"Yeah, I know. Ah, time heals all wounds, right? It's only been a minute for you, but in Skippy time, that happened like a year ago, I've gotten over my initial disappointment," he said more cheerfully. "You're right! Yeah, maybe the AI needs to be within my true range, using your phone only allows me to work within this spacetime. Yeah! Hey, that's it. I feel much better now, Joe. Damn it, I'll have to wait until I can send a dropship down to get it. Ok, let's try the comm node now."

"No," I said flatly.

"No?" Skippy said, surprised. "Oh, shit, is it damaged? You told me it was in a nice padded box, you jerk!"

"It's not damaged, Skippy, I don't want you screwing with it, until we're back aboard the *Dutchman*. Think about what might happen if this comm node works, and you contact the Collective right here? Like you told me, you might go 'Poof' and disappear. And then we monkeys would be stuck down here, with repairs to the *Dutchman* incomplete, and us with no way to get back to the ship anyway." I caught Smythe's eye, and he nodded approval. None of us wanted to risk Skippy disappearing before we were ready to leave Newark behind. "So, the answer is no, you're not going to attempt to use the comm node yet, I'm keeping it securely in the box. If you want to try using it, then you finish fixing up the ship, get it here, and send down dropships to pick us up."

"Fine," he huffed. "I guess that's fair. To tell you the truth, as much as I do want to contact the Collective, I want to see if I really can fix this ship first. That would be something to brag about, huh?"

"If? You mean 'when'," I said fearfully. "*When* you fix the ship, right?"

"Oh, yeah, sure. No problemo, Joe. Uh huh, right. I mean when I fix the ship. Things are going well up here, Joe, no major disasters within the last, oh, six hours, almost. Nothing I can't handle."

"Great." I had to take him at his word, there wasn't an alternative. "Is there anything else we can do here, Skippy?" I asked, panning my zPhone camera over the array of Elder artifacts laying on the floor, "Bring any of this other stuff with us?"

"None of it is useful to us," Skippy said, "although we need to do something with it anyway, if that Kristang ship gets here and detects a whole bunch of Elder gear still in the vicinity of the scavenger base, that will blow our cover story of another Kristang clan coming here and ripping off the scavengers. We can't count entirely on our missile getting all of it."

"Uh, huh, got it," I said with dismay. Some of the Elder gear was heavy, or bulky, or both. Bringing all of it with us would be a substantial burden, the hillside caverns where I planned for us to hole up were seventy kilometers away. So was most of our food supply. "This is a lot of stuff to carry."

"Sir?" Gomez spoke up. "This guy here," he nudged the dead laborer with his boot, "had the place ready to blow if we tried to capture him. Maybe our cover story could be the scavengers here blew up most of the Elder gear, to keep the Red Stone clan from taking it?"

I looked at him in surprise.

Smythe nodded agreement. "That would save us from having to haul all this kit a long way, sir, we could take some of it with us."

Damn, that was a good plan, I should have thought of it. "Skippy? Does that sound good to you?"

"Yeah, sure, what the hell," he answered listlessly. "Sorry, Joe, I'm very disappointed about the AI, that's all. Yes, that plan makes sense. Pile the explosives around most of it, set a timer, and blow it. That will be convincing. If the ship scans the area, they'll see plenty of expended Kristang cartridges from the firefight. The missile is on its way, that will cover up any contradictory evidence."

"Great. Good thinking," I addressed Gomez and Smythe. The missile, which Skippy had launched on its long journey across the star system while we were still driving the RV across Newark, had been taking a slow orbital approach to Newark. Now that we had cleared the scavenger base of Kristang, and retrieved the useless Elder gear, the missile only needed our strike team to clear the area, before it accelerated in and impacted the center of the base. The missile was one of Skippy's handmade units, not one of our precious Thuranin ship-killers with the fancy atomic compression warheads. Skippy's homebrew warhead was powerful enough to burrow into the soil of Newark, and create a crater larger than the scavenger base perimeter, it also would leave trace signature elements of a typical Kristang warhead blast. That missile was Phase Four of my plan, covering up evidence that the base had been raided by a party traveling overland. Data that Skippy would plant in the two Kristang satellites would show a Kristang ship unstealthing in orbit, a pair of dropships strafing the scavenger base, then landing and a firefight at the base. The armory would blow up, with most of the Elder gear, then the dropships would take off, and the ship would fire a missile at the base, before recovering its dropships and jumping away. I'm sure Skippy would make the whole event look thoroughly convincing in the satellite data banks. When the Kristang ship arrived to pick up the scavenger leaders, it would find a muddy crater where the base had been, and a familiar story of the scavengers being raided by a rival clan. There would, I fervently hoped, be absolutely no reason for that ship to have any curiosity about the rest of the planet, no reason to actively scan the surface. No reason to initiate a scan that might find RV tracks leading toward the base, a scan that might detect an RV sunk in a river. No reason to scan the area around the two crashed scavenger aircraft, a scan that very likely would detect signs of recent habitation. Signs of the area being inhabited by, of all unlikely things, humans.

If the Kristang ship hung around Newark a moment longer than it needed to, I hoped that all it would send a dropship down to the Elder crash site, to see if the scavengers had missed anything useful. That would keep the Kristang busy, until they got bored and went away. No humans had been to the crash site, so the new group of Kristang wouldn't find any trace of us there. "I'll take the b-" I almost said 'beer can', "the AI and the comm node." Maybe Skippy could find something useful to do with them later, and it didn't feel right leaving the dead AI where it was. "The rest of it, we cover with explosives, and set a timer." I looked up to the north, where dark clouds were gathering, and a chill wind was beginning to stir. "Let's get moving, we have a lot of ground to cover before nightfall."

When the Kristang ship arrived, I was outside the cave getting much-appreciated fresh air in the early morning hours, stretching my legs and taking in a quick change of scenery. During daylight hours, we kept to our three cramped caverns, a big treat for us was bunking in a different cavern for a few days, being able to see relatively new faces. We got notice of the ship's arrival almost simultaneously from our zPhone detecting the gamma ray burst, and from Skippy calling us. "That Kristang ship is here, Joe, you best get under cover."

"Roger that," I replied, and didn't need to say anything else, as we all double-timed back to our respective caverns. No running, this was a disciplined group and no one needed to be scolded for risking a twisted ankle or broken leg in the semi-darkness. "ETA?"

"It jumped in far away from the planet, far even for a Kristang ship, their jump drive appears to be in poor condition. My guess is they won't enter a stable orbit for another day, maybe more. They're pinging the scavenger camp, and of course getting no reply. They also just requested a download from the satellites, I'm giving them everything we want them to see."

"Great. I'll check in with you every six hours, you contact me if anything happens that I need to know about."

"Affirmative. *Dutchman* out."

"Hey, Colonel Joe," Skippy called me, startling me. I'd been sitting on a rock near the entrance of the cavern, watching a cold rain splatter down outside, slowly drinking a cold chocolate-banana sludge. There wasn't much else to do, and I'd slept plenty already, maybe too much.

"What's up, Skippy?"

"Uh, we gots a tiny problemo."

"Oh, like what?" I snapped my fingers to get people's attention, and around me, I could see people stirring and putting on their zPhone earpieces so they could listen in.

"Two pieces of news, one bad, one merely FYI. The FYI part is that ship is sending a dropship down to check out the Elder crash site, in case the scavengers missed something. For now, they're not going to bother inspecting what's left of the scavenger base, and they're not interested in the crash sites near our main encampment, where we shot down those two scavenger aircraft. They completely bought the story I fed them in the fake satellite data. True to Kristang, they 're not even pissed about being raided and having all the scavengers killed, they are only pissed that some other clan stole the Elder artifacts."

"That is actually good news so far, Skippy. What's the bad news?"

"More like extremely annoying news, but it could turn out to be devastatingly bad, we'll have to wait and see. From internal ship communications, leaking through their hull because of a shockingly, and I do mean I am truly, actually shocked this time, Joe. I'm not merely doing the old joke where I only pretend to be shocked, you know what I mean? You say you're shocked, but you actually mean the opposite? The most famous usage of that phrase, of course, was by Claude Raines in the movie Casablanca, although that line is strangely misquoted very often. The correct-"

"Skippy! The point, please. Here's another good quote for you to remember: brevity is the soul of wit."

"And tediousness the limbs and outward flourishes, I will be brief," Skippy finished the quote for me. "Man, I try to smack some culture down on you-"

"And we ignorant monkeys greatly appreciate it, Skippy. Save it for the appropriate time, Ok?"

"Fine," he said with a huff. "As I was saying, before, I guess before I rudely interrupted my own train of thought- Huh. I see your point now, Joe. Damn, my mind wanders sometimes. I was saying, the communications security aboard that ship is shockingly bad, their cabling must be completely worn out, more of the data signal leaks out than gets to its destination. It is so bad, that even if they had a functioning stealth field, which they do not, I'd be able to listen in. You monkeys are a young, impatient species, so without further embellishment, here's the news. The Thuranin star carrier that dropped off this ship at the edge of the star system will not return for another four and a half months. That's 'meh' level accuracy for you. This means the Kristang ship will be here for four months, at least. During those four and a half months, the Kristang on that ship may become bored, and start poking around, scanning, and looking into things better left alone. They might discover the human presence on Newark."

"Damn it!" I looked around and met people's eyes, they were all indicating alarm. "That isn't the only problem, Skippy, we only have three months of food with us here." My group may be able to stretch out our supply of dehydrated sludges to three and a half months, possibly another week under extreme conditions, we were already on rather lean rations as it was. The main group, back at the caverns near the cathedral complex, had more food, they might make it to four months. None of us were going to survive four and a half months.

"That is a problem, and with that ship in orbit, I can't send another food delivery. The *Dutchman's* supply of sludges is almost exhausted anyway, and I can't make more until the ship is up and running again. Joe, this sucks, because I've been making substantial progress up here, had a couple spots of good luck, and I expect to have the ship ready jump in and retrieve you in about a month. That's only one week longer than the original schedule."

"Fantastic, Skippy, that is incredible, and we'll give you the slow clap of amazement when we get back up there-"

"Hey! A slow clap? Is this a sarcastic thing?"

"What? No. Oh, uh, sorry, Skippy, I guess that can have a double meaning. In this context, I meant we would be genuinely amazed by how you fixed the ship."

"Damn, I will never understand monkey social norms."

"Me neither, Skippy. Back to the subject, is there anything you can do about that Kristang ship for us?"

"Not that I can think of yet, Joe. I have two missiles, one ready and one partly assembled, only needs a propulsion unit."

Only needed a propulsion unit? What was he planning to do, launch it from a really big slingshot? "One missile isn't much help, huh?"

"Unfortunately, no. That ship would detect one or two missiles while they are inbound, and likely destroy them both beyond their effective range; the Kristang who own that ship are barely maintaining their internal systems and jump drive, but their sensor field and defensive batteries are functional. A failed missile attack, at such long range, would get the Kristang asking uncomfortable questions, and poking around places we'd rather they don't look."

"Understood. I'm pretty sure none of us down here can throw a rock up far enough to hit that ship in orbit, so you keep trying to think of a solution, Ok?"

"I'll do my best, Joe. I'll do my best."

Skippy' best thinking, he admitted to me early the next morning, wasn't nearly good enough. "I thunk on it all night, Joe, in between, you know, building a starship out of moon dust up here. And I got a whole lot of nothing. You military brains down there come up with an idea?"

"No," I admitted. We'd talked about it late into the night, tossing around increasingly unlikely and impractical ideas, until I called a halt, and told everyone we'd begin again with fresh minds in the morning. "No, Skippy, we also got nothing down here. We're working on it. Let's both have faith, Ok?"

"Ok." He said quietly. The fact that he didn't make a smartass remark told me how discouraged he was feeling.

His mood mirrored my own gloominess.

"Skippy, we have come way too far to fail now. We got all the way to this star system without any power from the reactors, we defeated a superior Kristang force without them firing a single shot at us, and we've managed to survive on this damp, rainy, chilly mudball of a planet. Also, I didn't kill anyone for singing Ninety Nine Bottles of Beer on the Wall, like, way too many freakin' times. That is a solid gold gosh-darned miracle. I am not giving up now."

Taking a tiny, tiny risk, I slid my butt along the rock at the cavern entrance, so I had a clear view of the only partly cloudy early morning sky. In theory, the Kristang ship might have a snowball's chance in hell of seeing me, if it had been looking right at our cavern through a gap in the clouds at that exact second. Somewhere up there, at this time to the right of Newark's small moon, was the microwormhole that we used to communicate with Skippy. Looking up at the invisible wormhole, I felt just a tiny bit closer to that annoying little beer can, an alien AI who I inexplicably felt some measure of affection for. A true miracle from Skippy, the wormhole allowed almost real-time communication through-

"H-o-l-y shit."

"What?" Skippy asked.

"The way this microwormhole thingy works is," I said very slowly, thinking through my idea as I spoke, "you send radio waves through it, so we can talk without a big time lag?"

"Given your monkey-level understanding of physics, sure, let's go with that. Oh, man, Albert Einstein would be weeping for your species right now."

"You send photons through the wormhole, so-"

"Wait! Uh! Uh! Hush, you! Not this time. Not *this* time! This is where you think you have some brilliant idea that I should have thought of, right?"

"Uh, maybe?"

He laughed gleefully. "Ha! Hahahahahaha! I know exactly what boneheaded monkey-brain idea you're going to tell me, and I can tell you ahead of time, it won't work. You want me to send missiles through the wormhole, and hit that ship. That's it, right? Hahaha! You can forget it, Mister Smartypants, because that won't work. We only have one functioning missile right now, remember, dumbass? Also, that wormhole is less than half a nanometer in diameter, no way can we squeeze a missile through it. So, you're not so freakin' smart, are you? Hahahahahaha!"

Skippy's rant hadn't let me get a word in. "You done gloating now?" I asked.

"Give me a minute, I want to let this soak in. Ahhhhhh, this feels good. I *like* this feeling. You think you're so smart, Joe, and you're not. Here, pretend I just tossed a coin into your hat, dance for me, monkey, dance!"

"Great," I said. "Because I was going to suggest you send a maser cannon beam through the wormhole, not a missile."

A long silence. Long. Like, really, awkwardly long. Then, Skippy shouted. "*Damn it!* Excuse me, I'm going offline a moment so I can smash something."

"Skippy?" Silence. "Skippy?"

Craig Alanson

"Yeah, yeah, I'm here," he finally grumbled.

"Did you smash something? You feel better now?"

"I didn't smash anything yet, but there's a pair of small moons here that are going to have a *very* bad freakin' day in about two hours."

"You're blowing up two moons, just because you're pissed about something?"

"No, I'm just crashing one into the other. Come on, Joe, there's plenty of moons up here, nobody's going to miss a couple. So, you're thinking of a maser cannon shot through the wormhole, huh?"

"That's the idea."

"Damn you, Mister Smartypants. You have no idea how thoroughly, utterly humiliating this is for me."

"I'd love to hear, can you explain in great detail? Don't leave anything out, all of us ignorant monkeys on this end would truly enjoy hearing it, I'll record it for you. How does this make you feel, with your god-like intelligence?"

"Sure, I'll pencil you in for the twelfth of Never, or how about the fourth of Shut-the-hell-up, do either of those dates work for you?"

Maybe I should have named him 'Snarky' instead of Skippy. "The maser beam thing, it will work?"

Skippy sighed. Deep down, all the way into whatever spacetime most of him resided, he had to be incredibly frustrated with himself. "Yes, yes, it will. I'll need to refocus the emitter to narrow the beam, that will attenuate the power somewhat, hmm, I can goose up the, well, this is all technical stuff on my end, nothing worth explaining to monkeys. Yes, it will work. We'll only get one shot at this, pun intended, transmitting that much power through the wormhole will collapse it completely. After we shoot, I won't know whether it worked, until your radio signal gets here more than an hour later. We'll be limited to slow speed of light communications after we lose the wormhole. We need to make this one shot count, I'll have to target their reactor directly. Breach containment there, and that ship is a nice firework in the sky for you. The remaining problem with this plan is, I have only a limited ability to aim the beam when it comes out your end of the wormhole. Unfortunately, that ship's orbit right now doesn't take it within the targeting cone. You got any ideas how to fix that?"

"Uh, huh, figured that might be a problem." I thought a moment. How to get a ship to change its orbit? "Yeah, I might."

"Does your idea involve sending a message to that ship, asking it to pose for a photo in front of our wormhole?"

"Um, no. Our two stealthed satellites; you can move them, slowly, without the Kristang detecting?"

"Yes. Those satellites are tiny, Joe, so forget about me trying to smash one into that ship. If that is your best idea, we are in big trouble."

"That was not my idea. How about this: you position one of them some place away from the microwormhole, and then you adjust the satellite's stealth field, so it looks like a stealthed ship whose field is failing? You can do that?"

"Piece of cake, Joe. I'm waiting for the brilliant part of your plan. If you don't have that, the only mildly stupid part of your plan would amuse me, also."

"Great. If that Kristang ship thinks another ship, a stealthed ship, is suddenly in the area, will it jump away immediately?"

"No, not from where it is now. The ship is too deep in the gravity well for it to jump away right now, it would need to-, oh, I see your plan now. I position our satellite to flush the Kristang ship toward our microwormhole as it tries to climb out to jump distance, so I can get a clean shot at it?"

"Yup, that's the plan. Will that work?"

"You are such a smartass," Skippy said with a disgusted snort. "I hate you."

"I love you too, Skippy."

"And?"

"I'm not saying I love you back!" He said disgustedly.

"The 'and', in this case, means," I explained patiently "*and*, will my plan work?"

"Yes."

"I couldn't hear that very well, Skippy, did you just say a monkey plan will work, when your incredible intelligence couldn't think of a way out of this mess?"

"YES! For crying out loud, I said *yes*. Damn, you are annoying. You know what, when I get this ship fixed up, I am declaring it a monkey-free zone. No filthy monkeys allowed. Ah, it will be like paradise up here."

"Yeah, paradise," I pointed out the flaw in his plan, "except for the part about you being stuck right there until the *Dutchman's* orbit degrades, and the ship falls into the gas giant's atmosphere. After that, you will sink to the core of a slowly cooling planet, until the heat death of the universe, quadrillions of years from now?"

"Yup. No monkeys. Like I said, paradise."

Skippy only had one shot at that ship. Of course, he only needed one shot, despite his grumbling about how we were asking him to do the impossible, as usual, and how we didn't truly appreciate his incredible awesomeness. To shut him up, I offered to bake a cake in his honor when we got back aboard the *Dutchman*. That afternoon, while the Kristang ship frantically accelerated to jump altitude to get away from a phantom ship that didn't exist, Skippy fired a full-power maser cannon beam through the wormhole, scoring a direct hit on that ship's already overheated reactor. The result was a brief, bright flare in the partly cloudy sky, and then silence. No Kristang ship above us, but also no Skippy.

On our zPhones, we were able to view satellite data that showed the Kristang ship exploding. After the debris field cleared, we tracked pieces of the ship in orbit, the largest piece was smaller than a dropship. All the pieces were dead, no internal power, no signs of life. For days after, we saw things burning up as they fell into the atmosphere. The satellites were supposed to notify us immediately if any piece of the ship began moving on its own, or generating power, or transmitting signals. Just in case, I checked satellite images and data several times a day, and ordered the team to maintain cover.

Several hours after he shot the maser cannon through the microwormhole, Skippy saw the distinctive flash of a reactor losing containment, then jump drive coils exploding, as the Kristang ship ceased to exist, so he knew he'd accomplished his mission. That part of his mission, anyway, he still needed to finish rebuilding the busted *Dutchman*. The time lag for radio signals was enough of a problem, the larger problem being that our low-powered zPhone antennas could barely pick up signals from the *Dutchman*, and it was almost impossible for the *Dutchman* to hear our weak transmissions at all. We managed to maintain only the minimum communication necessary, the bandwidth limited us to text messages only, no voice.

That began the absolutely most miserable period of our time on Newark. For one, it rained most days, and without Skippy we didn't have weather forecasts, we could see satellite images, and there was nothing but solid cloud cover most of the time. The only time we could safely go out of the cavern was when there were solid clouds overhead, we couldn't risk being seen walking around, if there was a Kristang presence in orbit that we didn't know about. Our time outside was limited, if we went for a run or a strenuous hike, our heat signatures might be detectable even through a thick cloud layer. Most of the time, we stayed bundled up in our now grimy, smelly and always-damp cold weather gear. After we'd been stuck inside for three solid days of rain, I ventured out to collect grass, low-growing brush, and a sort of lichen off the rocks. We laid it out to dry in the back of the cavern, and two days later, we risked a small fire in a side cavern that had a hole in the roof. As best we could, we took off the under layers of our clothes and hung them up to dry. The clothes I got back smelled like a damp grass fire, but they were warm and dry. Man, that felt good, my skin had been starting to get minor sores, from constantly wearing the same wet clothes.

The only food we had left were cold, rehydrated sludges. At least people back at the main caverns near the cathedral had hot food, real food, and a variety of it. The worst for our group, huddled together in our damp, cramped, mud-floor caverns, was the lacking. Lack of exercise. Lack of anything to do. Lack of purpose. Lack of real food. People, even dedicated, elite special forces troops, get bored, and little frictions added up. The team leaders handled the minor disputes well, without me needing to get involved.

For my part, I found myself missing being able to talk with Skippy, not only not being able to get detailed status reports, I missed simply talking with that annoying, insulting beer can. When we finally received the message from Skippy that the *Flying Dutchman* was ready to come to Newark, I felt like dancing. To spare myself the embarrassment, I didn't. What I did do was pass the word around that we'd soon be getting off Newark. Then I transmitted back to the *Dutchman* the 'go' code, to activate the jump we had programmed into the autopilot before we departed the ship.

Seven hours later, Skippy's voice once more boomed out of my zPhone. "Greetings, Colonel Joe and the whole barrel of monkeys down there! Tis I, Skippy the Magnificent. Because of my amazing beneficence, I bring you a starship that is almost as good as new, including such luxuries as heat, and oxygen! Also, the deluxe rustproof under coating package, at no extra charge!"

"Skippy!" I couldn't keep the pure glee out of my voice. "We're safe, there are no Kristang up there?"

"Yessiree, there be no lizards around these parts. Parts of that ship are still tumbling in orbit, but it's no threat, no one is alive aboard the wreck. We'd better hit them with a maser anyway before we leave, just in case. How are you doing, Joe? I've been monitoring the weather, and it sure looks depressing down there."

"I'm all right, Skippy, we're all Ok down here. Damn, it is good to hear from you. I missed your irascible self," I said before realizing I was talking on an open channel.

"Ah, you're just happy that I brought the ship back, so you can get off that miserable frozen mudball."

"That, too. Are you allowing monkeys aboard your squeaky-clean ship?"

"Yuck. I'd forgotten about that. Filthy monkeys, doing filthy monkey things? Ah, what the hell, you caught me in a generous mood, Joe. Come on up here, before I change my mind. I've got two dropships on the way down. We'll need several trips to bring up everyone and all your stuff, so I loaded clean clothes and fresh food aboard the dropships."

"That was very thoughtful of you, Skippy, thank you."

"Like I said," he grumbled, "hurry, before I change my mind."

CHAPTER TWENTY SEVEN

The dropship he sent down to the assault party couldn't hold all of us, it was the smaller of the two remaining dropships. I stayed behind, and enjoyed warm, clean, dry clothes and a hot meal of real food while the dropship cycled up to orbit and back again. With Captain Smythe, I sent the Elder AI and the comm node up to the ship, knowing Skippy was anxious to get those two items aboard as soon as possible. We both had hoped that, by some miracle, when the new AI got close enough to Skippy, it would activate somehow. And that he could figure out how to make the comm node work.

He called me shortly after the dropship was aboard the *Dutchman*, it surprised me how quickly he ran his analysis of the Elder artifacts. "No dice, Joe, the AI and the comm node are both dead as doornails. Crap, this isn't right. What could kill an AI like me? This frightens me."

"You're certain it was alive at some point, it wasn't just a canister that never got an AI loaded into it?" That would be the best scenario for Skippy.

"No such luck, Joe. No, there is a residual presence there, jumbled data, something bad happened to him. The connection of the canister, as you call it, to other dimensions has been broken, it's now merely a beer can of tightly packed exotic materials. It was a long time ago, too, I can tell that for certain. And there's something else; whatever happened to this AI, it happened roughly around the time Newark got pushed out of its original orbit. That can't be a coincidence. If we could, I'd like to stay here and investigate this planet in detail."

"We're going to leave our two satellites, here, right? They'll collect data, we can swing by in the future and see if they found anything interesting." I wanted to know if our satellites ever saw a Kristang ship poking around the places we had lived on Newark. Even though we were going to be careful to take our trash back up with us, there was plenty of evidence from DNA alone, that humans had been on Newark. If the Kristang ever learned that fact, they were going to start asking uncomfortable questions, and I wanted advanced notice if that ever happened. Skippy judged it very unlikely the Kristang would ever again bother with Newark at all, now that it had been emptied of useful Elder artifacts, and I agreed with him. I also needed to be prudent and not assume something very bad would never happen.

"The satellites will help, a bit, what I'd like to do is perform a deep scan that the satellites can't do. Even for me, a scan like that could take months, I'd be running time back in other spacetimes, there's no way to rush that, darn it. I really do need to know what happened here, it does not make any sense. What bothers me most about it, is this incident calls into question what I think I know about the Elders. Perhaps I should have said, that's what bothers me most, other than an entire sentient species being wiped out, of course."

"I knew what you meant, Skippy. Sorry about your, I guess, brother AI. Can you do anything with that comm node?"

"No. Frustratingly, no. It's like the first one we captured from that Kristang research base. It appears to be fully functional, but it is not connecting to the network. I'll keep working with it, I don't have much else to do."

Or, I didn't say, maybe there was no longer any network to connect to. Skippy had to be worrying about that, he didn't need me to remind him of that awful possibility. If there was no longer any network enabling the Collective, then our entire fool's errand of a mission was doubly worthless.

The dropship coming back was a welcome sight, even if Skippy did set the damned thing down a half kilometer away, and a cold rain was pouring down from dark gray skies. I didn't care, I was getting safely off Newark, my entire crew was safely off Newark, in fact, I was the very last person to leave the planet. Chang was aboard the *Dutchman*, Simms had stayed at the main cavern until the last person and last piece of equipment and last scrap of trash had been loaded into a dropship. To speed up clearing evidence of our presence off the planet, I had ordered Skippy to use both dropships at the main cavern, until Simms declared they were finished. Until then, I waited in our cramp, damp cave, in my relatively clean, warm, dry clothes. With me were two US Army Rangers and three Indian paratroopers who had volunteered to remain behind with me, because there hadn't been enough room aboard the first dropship. We played cards and enjoyed eating real, hot food, and the day and a half delay almost flew by, because we knew we were leaving.

We spent a few minutes peering around rocks in the caverns, making sure we hadn't left a sludge container or an old sock behind, then dashed through the rain to the open door of the dropship. I paused at the bottom of the ramp, my boots still sinking into the chilled mud of Newark. "What is it, sir?" One of the Rangers asked.

Looking up at the leaden sky, blinking away raindrops. "It seems like I should say something profound, something better than 'we are *so* out of here'. This planet wasn't always the half frozen pile of shit we experienced. It was a nice place once, with forests and deserts and tropical beaches. Like Earth. An entire civilization, and entire species, an entire *biosphere* was wiped out here. I feel like I should say something about these people. Maybe more important, say something about whoever the hell it was that did this."

The Ranger nodded. "We are unlikely to do anything against beings who moved an entire planet, so how about 'vengeance is mine, sayeth the Lord'?"

"That's good," I agreed.

One of the Indian soldiers nodded. "We have a similar saying. We say 'karma is a bitch'. Whoever pushed this planet out of orbit is going to get what's coming to them, one way or another."

"Amen, brother." The Ranger said, and they bumped fists.

That was more eloquent than anything I could have said, so I kicked the mud off my boots, walked up the ramp, and left Newark behind.

Being aboard the somewhat sterile, artificial environment of the *Flying Dutchman* again was like paradise, compared to the damp chilliness of Newark. The air aboard the ship was warm and dry, my clothing was clean and dry, I had a bed to sleep in, and real food to eat. My initial thought was to declare our first day back aboard a 'fend for yourself' day in the galley, figuring I'd spare anyone from taking a shift in the galley. Fortunately, Colonel Chang had already set a duty roster, and the Chinese team had a hot bowl of noodles waiting for me, after I dumped my dirty clothes off in my cabin and took a too-quick shower. The galley didn't look much different from before, maybe a bit larger, one of the bulkheads was further away from the door than I remembered. The whole compartment was a soothing light blue color, Skippy had done a great job. The bowl of noodles, and a cup of hot tea with sugar in it, tasted like heaven. I even tried eating the noodles with chopsticks, I was in such a good mood. "You know what I need?" I asked no one in particular, thinking that an hour in the gym would do me good. Or maybe a game of basketball, I felt soft and slow from laying around inactive too long. I should have known not to ask an open-ended question like that when Skippy was around, I'd gotten used to being away from him on Newark.

"A shower?" Skippy suggested from the speaker in the ceiling.

I shook my head as people laughed. "I showered after I came aboard."

Skippy made a sniffing sound. "Hmm, doesn't smell like it. Maybe you could rinse off with some of that degreaser we use on the engine couplings. Hey, Joe, there weren't any showers on Newark?"

"No, Skippy, of course not," I replied while slurping hot noodles.

"Huh. Without a shower, how did you take care of your morning boner?"

There was nothing I could do, other than sit there with a sheepish look on my face while people laughed. "Man, I am missing Newark already," I said.

Skippy hadn't only repaired the *Flying Dutchman*, he had modified it. On the dropship ride up, I'd noticed our formerly very long, spindly star carrier had been substantially shortened. Shortened to the point where, instead of long rows of docking hardpoints for shorter-range starships, there were only three hardpoints, arranged in a single ring. Instead of the engineering section at the aft end of the ship being so far away that it appeared not to be attached to the same ship, it was right behind the trio of hardpoints. "New and improved, Joe," Skippy told me, "except for the new part. And maybe the improved part. Well, some of it is improved."

I snapped my fingers. "Before I forget, Skippy, while you refueled the ship, did you get some for yourself?" Dr. Friedlander on the science team had inquired about Skippy's own fuel requirements, and that reminded me to ask him. The last time we talked about it, he only had several thousand years before he ran out of fuel. "You need, something like, metallic hydrogen?" Which I personally didn't know was a real thing or not, I thought hydrogen was a gas, not a metal. But then, what did I know of science?

"Yes, yes, I did, Joe, thank you for asking. It wasn't much, enough for eight hundred years or so. It will have to do for now."

"Great. Improvements to the ship, huh?" According to the display, we now had two functioning reactors. Two. Not six, not even four. Two. "Does reducing the number of reactors count as an improvement?"

"Yes, Joe," Skippy assured me, "these two reactors make the power of three original ones, they're more reliable, and they require a lot less maintenance, and their shielding is way better. A near-miss by an exploding warhead won't knock these new reactors out. Not as easily, anyway."

We also had only forty percent of the original complement of jump drive coils, which was not a problem, Skippy said, because he'd reconfigured the entire drive, top to bottom. "Should have done this when we first took this ship," he said proudly, "that Thuranin drive was crap anyway. Now we can jump thirty percent further, and the coils charge eighteen percent faster. Also, the coils are divided into three separate banks, so if one bank of coils goes out of calibration, we can use the two others. Or just one, if needed, in an emergency."

I'd noticed the three docking hardpoints were empty. "The *Flower* is gone?"

"Yeah, sorry about that, I know you liked having a spare tire. That ship contained components and materials I couldn't get elsewhere, and I needed its reactor to supply power for a while. The *Flower* dipped into the atmosphere to get fuel, after it was done with that, I had to take it apart, and use most of it as a high-energy particle accelerator, to manufacture exotic materials. What was left, I loaded with trash and dropped it into the gas giant. It was a good little ship, Joe, actually, it was a piece of shit, but it served us well."

Desai wouldn't be happy about that, while she loved flying the giant *Flying Dutchman*, the *Flower* was the first starship she'd ever flown. "You did what you had to, Skippy, you performed a miracle up here, I'm sure not going to be the ungrateful monkey who second guesses you. We have only the two dropships?"

"Unfortunately, yes. Plus one drone that can be used for performing maintenance outside the ship. Should I check if any dropship dealers in the area are having a holiday blow-out sale?"

"Ha! Somehow, I suspect our credit isn't good out here."

"Good point. Unless the dealer will swap a dropship for bananas."

After a hearty bowl of noodles, I went to my office near the bridge, reading reports on my iPad, trying to act like a real colonel. What I really wanted to do was go play basketball or just hit the gym. That could wait for later. There was no rush, we'd done two successful jumps away from Newark, and Skippy was fiddling with minor adjustments to the jump drive unit. I had just bent down to untie a boot, to get comfortable for a long session of intense boredom, when Skippy called me through my zPhone earpiece.

"Hey, Joey, I have some, um, a bit of bad news for you."

"Ah, damn it, I knew I should have brought tequila or something on this trip. I need a drink before you tell me any more bad news. Do me a favor, is this bad news of the Joe-needs-to-dream-up-a-way-out-of-a-mess-Skippy-got-us-into variety?"

"No, this bad news is of the pissed-off-aliens-attacking-Earth-and-turning-it-into-a-wasteland, in-the-process-wiping-out-humanity variety."

"Holy shit." I retied my boot lace with fingers that were already shaking.

"Blasphemy is a particularly bad idea right now, Joe. Prayer would be entirely appropriate in this case."

"What the hell happened? For crying out loud, we just left Newark behind!"

"Well, heh, heh, you know that Kristang ship I blew up there?"

"My idea."

"Oh, man, are you *ever* going to give that up?"

"What do you think?"

"No. You aren't. In your defense, I wouldn't either, if I was in your place," Skippy admitted. "That was a pretty great idea."

"Yup. So?"

"Soooooooo, before I ripped that ship apart with a perfectly aimed particle beam shot through a weak spot in its reactor containment shielding, one hell of a shot, by the way. The microwormhole exit point nutates in a random fashion, because I had to avoid causing a detectible rupture in spacetime right there, and with time dilation, I had to estimate how the particle beam would be affected by the nutation. As far as I'm aware, this is the first time a wormhole has been used to deliver a particle beam, it was an interesting exercise. I realized that I needed to create, or perhaps more accurately recreate, a branch of mathematics, using a variation of topological invariants. Then there was the speed of light time lag between the wormhole and the ship, to deal with that I realized I needed to first tag that ship with a low-powered targeting laser in order to establish-"

"Skippy!"

"What?"

"Back to the subject, please?"

"Huh?"

I rolled my eyes. That beer can needed to create a submind to keep track of his thoughts. "The subject, please. You know, the bad news about aliens turning Earth into a wasteland?"

"Oh, yeah. Huh. Anyway, hitting that ship's reactor, with a particle beam through a wormhole, was an incredible shot, if I do say so myself."

"You did say so yourself."

"If I didn't, how would you know how awesome I am?"

"I don't know, how about, hey, there's a suggestion, you tell me about this big threat to Earth, and how you found out about it?"

"Easy peasy, Joe. Before I hit that ship, I was able to download some data from its computer memory. There wasn't time for a full download, especially with the narrow bandwidth I was working with through the microwormhole, so all I was able to get is a stack of messages intended for the leaders of the scavenger group on the surface; mostly messages from their clan. I was super busy, so I didn't bother to read through that pile of crap until a few minutes ago. One of those messages warns of an impending power shift among the clans, it seems that with the loss of a wormhole connection to Earth, and the Kristang's retreat from Pradassis, that's the planet you humans call 'Paradise', the fortunes of the White Wind clan took a major, in fact fatal, blow. The White Wind clan has been forced to seek a more powerful clan to ally with, the cold truth is the White Wind are going to be absorbed into the more powerful clan, calling it an alliance is a transparent face saving move for the White Wind leadership. The alternative to being absorbed is being conquered, and their territories and properties divided by the victors."

"Sucks to be them, huh? I don't know anyone here who is going to shed any tears if their entire clan gets smashed. How does this threaten Earth? All the Kristang on the Earth end of the wormhole are dead, right?" I tensed, fearing his answer. My home planet was defenseless against even a single Kristang ship, if there were stragglers we didn't know about before we left Earth orbit.

"It threatens Earth because, according to Kristang law, which is adhered to more strictly than you may expect, given what a nasty bunch of lizards they are, for a clan to be formally absorbed, the clan that is losing its identity must have unanimous approval from the senior clan leaders. This unanimous approval sometimes is achieved by assassination of clan leaders who disagree, the law doesn't prevent that. Kristang law is both rigid and flexible, the formalities must be rigidly adhered to, the morality behind the laws is more of a 'meh' thing."

"Fine, interesting, and?"

"And, um, here's the thing. Heh, heh, this is kind of ironic. The law of unintended consequences and all that."

My Spidey sense was tingling at Level Ten. "What the hell did you do, Skippy?" I asked carefully.

"Technically, it's what I didn't do. Or, I guess, it's what I did, or we did, in my defense, hey, no. You know what? As a matter of fact, it's what *you* asked me to do. So, this is your fault. Yeah, yeah, that's it! This is all your fault. Humans, I mean, not only you personally. Although, mostly you, personally."

"Skippy, you once told me that the Andromeda galaxy is going to collide with the Milky Way in about, what, four billion years?"

"Uh huh, that's right, why?"

"Is there any chance you'll get to the freakin' point before then?"

He made an exasperated huffing sound. "Fine. Sure. What I did, because you asked me to, is wipe out the Kristang on Earth. Including effectively pounding their last two sites into dust with railguns."

"We did ask you to do that," I couldn't see why that could be a problem, "and we thank you for your help. What didn't you do? Are there any Kristang alive on the Earth side of the wormhole?"

"No, not that I know of. I told you that."

"Thuranin?" I asked fearfully.

"Nope. Look, if you'll stop asking stupid questions, I'll tell you, or this conversation really will last forever. What I didn't do, and you didn't ask me, or remind me, and that part is entirely on you, hundred percent. I never bothered to dig through all of the enormous pile of data in the Kristang's computers at Earth, on their ships and on the ground. If I had done that then, I may have discovered that two senior leaders of the White Wind clan were on Earth at the time. Ugh, 99 percent of it was the usual boring messages back and forth. Like 'oh I got so hammered last night' and 'this planet sucks' and 'my boss is an asshole' or 'we should kill all the humans'. The usual BS, I lost interest in digging through it, which is why I didn't realize senior clan leaders were there. They were there to oversee the operation of fully securing your planet, of finding some way to turn a profit on their risky venture, and to show support for what they must have known by that time, was a sinking ship."

"Two senior Kristang clan leaders were there. They're dead now?"

"Affirmative. One was aboard that frigate I jumped into your sun, the other was at a site I hit with a missile strike in the first attack."

Before asking another question, I stopped to think. Skippy said he'd missed something, and he was terribly absent minded. If I didn't ask the right question, he might never tell me what I needed to know. "They're dead, they died right away. We couldn't have negotiated with them, because they were dead. The White Wind clan can't agree to be formally absorbed, so other clans will pick them apart. I still don't see why this is our problem."

"It is your problem, Joe, because the clan that is absorbing them, the Fire Dragons, wants to avoid a protracted fight over the White Wind. The Fire Dragons, while much stronger than the White Wind, have been stretched thin recently, the wormhole shift hurt them also. They are rather desperate to get formal approval to absorb the White Wind clan and its assets without a fight. They are so desperate, that they are paying the Thuranin to send a long-range ship to Earth, all the way there without a wormhole, in order to bring back those two senior White Wind clan leaders."

"Oh, shit," I almost choked on my words.

"Hence why I described this as an end-of-the-world thing for you humans."

We were screwed. We were totally screwed. If the Thuranin got to Earth, they would not only discover all the Kristang there were dead, they would surely learn, by raiding our databases, all about the *Flower* and the *Dutchman*, the Merry Band of Pirates, and about Skippy. And that the wormhole near Earth had been shut down deliberately. And that little fact, about our ability to manipulate wormholes, would get every technologically advanced species in the galaxy very interested in Earth. Such interest would not be healthy for humans. "We need to stop that long-range ship, Skippy."

"Probably a good idea. My best estimate, for the earliest when that ship could arrive at Earth, is twenty nine months from now. We, of course, can get to Earth long before then, by reopening that wormhole. The easiest time to hit that ship is when it arrive-"

"No way. No way, Skippy, and we don't have anything like twenty nine months. Tell me, what will the Thuranin do, if their ship doesn't return in about five years?"

"Most likely? They will wait another six months or so, then they will begin to worry. Then they will almost certainly send another ship. Likely more than one ship."

"Exactly. If that ship disappears at Earth, or on its way to Earth, the Thuranin are going to be very suspicious about what is going on at Earth. Tell me, what would happen if that long-range ship was instead destroyed in Thuranin territory, before it even gets started on the actual journey to Earth?"

"Hmm. Good question. Give me a moment to research the history of similar incidents, this could take a while. Done. Most likely, in this case an 84% probability, the Thuranin would tell the Fire Dragon clan that the Thuranin consider the contract fulfilled, because the Thuranin made a good-faith attempt to reach Earth, and with the loss of the ship the Fire Dragons hired, the contract is closed. The Thuranin have only a handful of long-range ships that could reach Earth, such ships are frightfully expensive. It is also unlikely the Fire Dragons could afford to fund a second expedition to Earth. Other clans who want a piece of the White Wind would see additional delay as a signal to strike, and the Fire Dragons would need to act quickly."

"Exactly. See my point? We need to destroy that long-range ship while it's still in Thuranin territory. Destroy it in a way that the Thuranin think it got hit during a random Jeraptha fleet engagement, that whoever destroyed that ship didn't consider it anything special, that ship wasn't specifically targeted. Damn. That means we'll need to hit other Thuranin ships at the same time, or right after. This is going to be a major, major deal." I needed to bring other people into the planning. "Will that long-range ship have escorts?"

"Certainly. It will typically have two support ships, to refuel and resupply the long-range ship at the point where it begins its solo journey, the support ships will turn back at that point. And I expect there will also be a warship escort, a pair of frigates, maybe a destroyer. The long-range ship is basically a highly modified star carrier, with an extra pair of reactors, triple the number of jump drive coils, and no attachment points for carrying other ships. Also more robust self-repair capabilities than a standard star carrier. And it has full capabilities to refuel itself along the way. Like a star carrier, it is not intended for ship-to-ship combat."

"An easy target, then?"

"Ahhh, not for us. The *Dutchman* isn't a true warship either. Especially now."

"Understood, we'll need the advantage of surprise. Plus plenty of Skippy magic. Do you know where this long-range ship, hey, is there a name for this type of ship?" Saying 'long-range ship' every time was going to get old.

"The Thuranin do not name their classes of ships, each class has a numeric designation. However, the Thuranin copied the basic design from the Jeraptha, and the Jeraptha refer to such ships as survey cruisers, or surveyors."

"Surveyors. That's good. Do you know where this surveyor is now, and what course it is taking to Earth?"

"Nope. That data wasn't in the messages I downloaded, the message was more clan politics and rumors than actionable intelligence."

That made me rub my temples with my fingers, I was going to have a headache for sure. "Damn it, this means we'll need to shadow a Thuranin battlegroup again, to get access to their databanks?" That was way too risky, with the Maxohlx hanging around.

"No, here's a piece of good news. The Fire Dragon clan paid to hire the surveyor, and part of the deal is the surveyor will take four Kristang with them, two from the Fire

Dragon clan and two from the White Wind. I'm sure the Thuranin are disgusted about having Kristang aboard their ship. The Fire Dragons will know where the surveyor ship is going to pick them up, and how it's getting to Earth, at least a rough outline of the ship's course. The Kristang have gotten screwed by the Thuranin on shipping contracts so many times, they insist on very strict and detailed terms, including metrics about, oh, damn it, I'm using buzzwords. I sound like one of your stupid PowerPoint slides! Being around you monkeys has infected my brain. Anyway, we can sneak into a star system that is occupied by the Fire Dragons, and I'll steal the data we need from one of their communication relays. The Maxohlx may still have warships accompanying Thuranin battlegroups, we need to steer clear of them."

"That is good news. You got any more?"

"Nothing worth mentioning, no, unfortunately. Except that, from here, we can get to Fire Dragon territory within two weeks."

"If you think of anything else," I stood up and hit the button to open the door, "let me know. I need to tell the crew, and get working on a plan. Set course for Fire Dragon territory, I'll inform the pilot that we're changing course. Again."

CHAPTER TWENTY EIGHT

The senior staff were all gathered in the galley, waiting for me. Chang was there, along with Simms, and the leader of each country's SpecOps team. Plus Desai, representing the pilots, and Dr. Venkman representing the science team, because I needed creative ideas from the science team. And Sergeant Adams, although technically not senior staff, she was there because I needed practical ideas. "We have a problem, a serious problem. Not with the ship," I added hurriedly as I saw concern on people's faces. "The ship is fine, and will be ready to jump again in six hours."

"Yup," Skippy said, "the ship is hunky-dory, all-"

"Skippy, I will be speaking," I cut him off. "I'd appreciate it if you hold your comments until I request your input."

Faces around the galley reflected surprise, they all expected me to joke around with Skippy as usual. The fact that I didn't, told them this was not business as usual. Of course I couldn't see Skippy's face, the tone of his voice spoke volumes. "Very well, Colonel," is all he said, with no snarkiness, or friendliness.

"Thank you. Skippy was able to access data from the ship that he destroyed in orbit over Newark, part of the data was messages to the scavenger leader from his clan. To us, the most important of those messages states that the Kristang are paying the Thuranin to send a special long-range ship to Earth, without using a wormhole. That ship will arrive at Earth in twenty nine months." People gasped and glanced at each other in fear and shock. "You can see why this is a problem. We not only need to stop that long-range ship from reaching Earth, we need to destroy it in a way that the Thuranin will not realize the ship was attacked by humans, or even that the ship was attacked because its destination is Earth. Somehow, we need to destroy that ship, and make it look like an ordinary casualty of war. But, first, we need to find it."

On the trip from Newark to Fire Dragon clan territory, we had a lot of time to come up with a plan to destroy the surveyor ship and its escorts, before the surveyor began its long lonely journey to Earth. Our collective brainpower, including Skippy, had nothing. Zero. No clue how, in our no-longer-quite-a-star carrier, we could take on even one ship, without the *Dutchman* very likely being destroyed in the process. I was getting increasingly desperate, even considering a suicide mission where the *Dutchman* would jump in way too close to the surveyor, hit it with everything we had, and detonate the dozen nukes in our cargo bay. Before I did something so desperate, I would need to find an uninhabited planet that could sustain human life, to drop off most of the crew. Trouble is, Skippy pointed out, planets that could support complex, sentient lifeforms, and were within practical range of a wormhole, were rare and valuable, and likely already had someone living there. Even if I kept everyone aboard the *Dutchman* and self-destructed the ship, it might not result in killing the surveyor ship, and even if it did, the enemy would know the surveyor had been the target of someone very desperate, desperate to stop that ship from reaching Earth. So, we were back to square one. We needed data on where the surveyor was, where it was going, and what ships would be escorting it. Without that, we were only playing useless 'what if' games.

Which is why I found myself alone with Skippy, in the smaller of our two remaining Thuranin dropships, buried inside a small ice-and-dirt comet, drifting at high speed toward a Kristang data relay owned by the Fire Dragon clan.

Our biggest problem, I had decided with a genius flash of insight while I was in the gym, was not that the *Flying Dutchman* was only one ship. Nor that it had been designed as a star carrier instead of a purpose-built combatant intended to engage enemy ships directly. Nor that our *Dutchman* now had only two reactors instead of the original six. No, after I'd spent a full hour in a brainstorming session that had yielded absolutely nothing, I realized the problem was that we didn't have enough missiles. If we had a whole lot of ship-killer missiles, we could jump in near an enemy ship, launch a cloud of missiles, jump to another nearby location, launch more missiles, and so on. Minimize the risk to the *Dutchman* with quick jumps, and eventually our barrage of missiles was bound to overwhelm an enemy ship's defenses and score a hit. The surveyor could jump away, we'd track it and jump to follow. "Hey, Skippy," I said while bending down to wash my hands in a too-low Thuranin sink, "can we make more missiles, and by 'we', I mean you? With the equipment we have aboard the *Dutchman*?"

"Nope."

That wasn't quite the detailed answer I was hoping for. "Because? Come on, Skippy, usually you want to give me a ton more info than I ask for."

"And you ignore me and interrupt me until I can dumb it down sufficiently. So my answer to you is a simple 'nope', you dope. I already told you, what we have aboard is all we're going to have. Some items, like the atomic compression warheads, are impossible to create, without very large, specialized facilities. The missiles propulsion units are also not something I can make out of moon dust and dreams. In addition to the limited number of Thuranin Model 30 missiles we have, that's what their designation translates as, I was able to scrape together enough material to create a few ship-to-ship missiles. They are roughly equivalent to a Kristang design that went obsolete about seven hundred years ago. That's the extent of my miracles, Joe."

"Crap. Dang, I figured that, had to ask anyway. All right, well, can we get more missiles somewhere?"

Skippy snorted. "Your time on Newark, away from me, made you dumber, huh? Sure, Joey, we can pop over to the local Missile Mart, they're having a two for one sale for new customers with good credit. You moron."

"I'm serious, Skippy. We've got a ship full of bad-ass SpecOps troops that are spoiling for another fight. We raided a heavily guarded asteroid, there must be an armory somewhere or a stores ship, where we can steal some missiles."

"Uh, no. Hmm, you know what? I wonder sometimes if you can even hear yourself talk, or do monstrously idiotic ideas escape your brain without you realizing that you are speaking out loud? The Thuranin, and Kristang, have stores or supply ships, that transport materials to battlegroups. Those do frequently contain missiles. Those ships are also always escorted by combatant ships; frigates or destroyers, precisely because they are such tempting targets."

"Damn. Scratch that idea."

"Raiding armories, another idiotic idea you mentioned, is close to impossible. The facilities that Thuranin use to manufacture missiles, and atomic compression warheads, are always on large, rocky, airless or nearly airless planets or moons. These are uninhabited planets or moons, in case of industrial accidents, which happen from time to time. The facilities are buried very deep underground, I'm talking kilometers underground, and they extend for dozens of kilometers, or more. Making atomic compression devices is a very energy intensive process. The Thuranin use them because their explosive yield is near that of a nuclear weapon, without the radiation that is banned by The Rules, remember?"

"Yeah, I remember." Rules enforced by the Rindhalu and Maxohlx on the lesser species that did the fighting for them. Rules intended to keep the war from spiraling out of control and damaging precious habitable planets that the two dominant species cared about. "You're right, no way can we raid a place like that. Whatever plan we come up with, it needs to make do with the weapons we have now."

"Unfortunately, yes. Also unfortunately, I still do not see a way this ship can destroy a surveyor and its escorts. Destroy that ship, in a way which avoids the Thuranin realizing the surveyor was the target."

"Uh huh. Damn it, there has to be a way to do that, we just haven't thought of it yet."

"In an infinite multiverse of probabilities, you may be right. In this particular localized spacetime, I do not see it."

Which is, again, why Skippy and I were in a dropship frozen under the surface of a dirty snowball, hurtling out of control on the very outskirts of a star system controlled by the Fire Dragon clan. Burying a dropship in a comet was the best idea we had for how we could sneak Skippy close enough to the relay station so he could ransack it for data. He needed to fly within three hundred thousand kilometers to do that, and as the relay would not simply dump all their data to us if we asked nicely, we had to sneak in close. It was a chicken and egg problem, Skippy explained. The access codes we acquired when Skippy took over the *Flying Dutchman* had since been changed in the normal rotation schedule followed by the Thuranin. With such codes, we could have simply jumped in near the relay, requested a data dump, and been on our way. Data relay stations were maintained at the edge of star systems so Thuranin ships could exchange information, without having to risk traveling into the web of gravity wells and relatively close confines of the star system. The only easy way to get data from a relay, including the full set of access codes, was to have a proper access code. Which we didn't have. Thus, it was a classic chicken and egg problem.

A dropship, even a small dropship with an optimally functioning stealth field, could not get close enough to a relay station. While a stealth field would conceal the dropship, the relay station's sensor field would detect some hidden object distorting the field, and investigate closely. Perhaps the investigation would take the form of a missile or maser beam strike.

Which is why we, actually Captain Desai, had come up with the idea of us capturing a dirty snowball, carving a dropship-size hole in it, then covering the hole after we stuffed a dropship in there. We rendezvoused with a small comet in an uninhabited neighboring star system and got it wrestled it into a docking bay, by a dozen people in powered suits. The damn thing still massed a couple tons, and we had to be very careful even in zero gravity, not to squash anyone by a clumsy move. Once in the landing bay, which was kept in cold vacuum, we carved out a hole, Skippy and I got into the dropship, and the guys in suits carefully maneuvered us into the hole and covered it.

"This is an awful, idiotic, terrible, terrifying idea," Skippy lamented, "an idea of epic, incredible, mind-blowing stupidity, Joe. Truly, in the history of the galaxy, I can't think of anything that even comes close."

"What?" I asked. "This is a hell of a time to tell me now, Skippy. It was your idea to encase the dropship in a comet!"

"Yeah, that idea is truly brilliant."

"Then what about this is terrifyingly stupid?"

"I didn't think *you* would be flying the dropship, Joe. We are doomed!"

"Very funny. *Dutchman*, this is Barney, we're ready in here."

"Roger that, Barney, you sit tight in there," Desai replied.

Desai then accelerated the *Dutchman* in normal space, so that when the comet was dropped off, it would have the precise course and speed to fly by the relay station in the guise of uninteresting, ordinary space junk that hung around the edges of all solar systems. The *Dutchman* jumped in, gently released the comet, maneuvered to a safe distance, and jumped away. We were on our own. If all went well, we would fly by the relay station in twenty two hours, and the *Dutchman* would jump back into recover us in twenty six hours after that. Yay! Forty eight hours, alone with Skippy. He was as thrilled about it as I was.

"I hope you didn't eat anything gassy for breakfast. And, damn, could you lay off the aftershave a bit?"

"Oatmeal and wheat toast for breakfast, no worries there, Skippy. And I'm not wearing aftershave, I didn't bring any when we left Earth, you ass."

He made a sniffing sound. "Ugh, so that's your natural smell? Next time, you should reconsider not bringing aftershave. Oh, damn, and there's not even a shower aboard this thing. This is going to be a long trip."

"Uh huh. You want to play chess, or something?"

"With you? Ha! Maybe a game of 'Go Fish'?"

We mostly left each other alone after that, I read a book on my iPad, tried to nap, ate a simple lunch, and read some more, while Skippy did whatever asshole beer cans did. When I finished the book, I tried playing chess against my iPad, concluded my always miserable chess skills may have somehow deteriorated, and glanced over at Skippy, who was strapped into the copilot seat.

"Hey, Skippy, you there?"

"I'm here. Always. What's up?"

"Something's bothering me. Terrifies me, actually. How did that Thuranin destroyer squadron set a trap for us?"

"They-"

"Because if they know humans are flying this ship, then even if they don't know we messed with the wormhole, we are totally screwed."

"I don't-"

"Did I screw up somewhere, Skippy? Did I get us all killed? Not the crew here, I mean, did I get all of humanity killed?"

"You have-"

"I have to-" I started to say.

"Joseph Arthur Bishop!" Skippy fairly shouted.

That set me back in my seat. "Wow. Only my mother uses my middle name. And only when she's pissed at me."

"Whew, well, you weren't ever going to shut up so I could get a word in. Rest easy, Joey, you didn't screw up. To be specific, your myriad screw-ups are not why we got ambushed by the little green men. No way were they waiting for us, no way in hell. If the Thuranin knew monkeys are flying this ship, they would have established a layered defense, with battleships at the center; battleships can project significantly more powerful damping fields. We would have had zero chance to jump away, if we had encountered a task force centered around battleships. The Thuranin would never have assigned such a vital mission to a single squadron of destroyers. If they knew one of their star carriers had been stolen, and they thought they knew where it is, they'd send an entire battlegroup, at least. The Thuranin would not screw around with half measures."

He had not yet convinced me. "I hear you, but, what are the odds that we would jump into a trap like that? Don't give me the odds calculated to a hundred freakin' decimal points, I'm asking a real-world question here, not mathematics."

"No need to crunch numbers. I think we didn't jump into a trap at all."

"How you figure that?"

"Simple. If it was a trap, there would have been a lot more ships waiting for us, and we would be dead. Or, you monkeys would. I'd be drifting in space, wishing I was dead. At least being in hard vacuum for millions of years would get the monkey smell off me. Mostly. What I think happened is, that Elder site that I thought had not yet been discovered actually *is* known to the Thuranin, they took everything useful out of it a long time ago. While they were ransacking the Elder site, they built up that system as a military base to defend the site against the Jeraptha. That star system was closer to Jeraptha territory before the recent wormhole shift, the Thuranin would have fortified the area to protect their assets. Since they stripped the site, I believe the Thuranin have continued using that system as a secret military base. As I told you, the *Flower's* crappy Kristang sensors are lucky to detect a star in a star system, our beat-up frigate has no chance to find a military base that the Thuranin wish to keep secret."

"Great theory, Skippy. Doesn't explain why that destroyer squadron had us surrounded as soon as we jumped in."

"Uh, that *may* have been partly my fault. A teensy, infinitesimal bit my fault."

"What?" That surprised me. "You got some 'splainin' to do, Lucy."

"Actually, Ricky Ricardo never said that on the show, that is a myth. Similar to how people commonly say-"

"I never saw the show, Skippy, that was before my time. It's a pop culture thing."

"Oh, got it. I'll make a note of it."

"And?"

"And, I said I'll make a note of it. Duh. Man, your mind wanders sometimes."

I rolled my eyes. "I meant, *and,* back to how our getting ambushed may have been partly your fault. Damn, Skippy, we were talking about that, like, five seconds ago, how could you forget in that short a time?"

"Five meatsack seconds, dumdum. For me, your species could have gone from ignorant apes living in trees, to sentient beings in the same time. I say could have, 'cause, you know, you are still ignorant apes."

"Don't try changing the subject, Skippy."

"Damn, the monkey is onto me," he muttered. "All right, I think that destroyer squadron was there for training or something like that. Those destroyers, or some stealthed satellites, detected the *Flower* jumping in, because a blind man could have seen that. The Thuranin stayed quiet, probably wondering what the hell a Kristang frigate was doing there. By itself, a Kristang ship could not have traveled all the way to that star system, the Thuranin must have been very, very curious. After the *Flower* jumped away, the Thuranin knew they hadn't been detected, and they figured the *Flower* would be back, with more ships. That's when those destroyers got into position, to establish a damping field that covered where the *Flower* was likely to jump in. That also explains why their damping field wasn't originally tuned to prevent a Thuranin ship from jumping away, they expected Kristang ships, not a star carrier. Us jumping in must have surprised the hell out of them.

That surprise, their hesitation before returning the damping field, is how we got away at first."

"Uh huh. Makes sense," I agreed. "Does not explain how it is partly your fault."

"Damn. I was hoping you forgot about that by now. Why don't you have your typical short attention span when I need it? Here it is, Joe; I may have been showing off a little. I programmed our jump in to be almost exactly where the *Flower* had jumped out. Serves me right for caring about impressing a barrel of monkeys, why should I care what ignorant apes think, right?"

Though he was certainly an arrogant shithead, he didn't need to feel guilty about something that wasn't his fault. "So you were a little more accurate than you needed to be, that didn't affect anything. Even if you were off by a thousand kilometers, those destroyers would have surrounded us. That was the best spot for us to jump into, right?"

"Um, no, and right there is the problem. That was the best spot for the *Flower* to jump into, considering that ship's crappy jump drive. The *Dutchman* could have jumped in much closer to the Elder site. That is why I feel guilty, Joe. The Thuranin surrounded the place they expected Kristang ships to jump in, and that's where I took us. If I'd jumped us in closer to that moon, like I should have, we could have been on the edge of the damping field, and could have gone much further with that first jump away."

He sounded miserable. I understood how he felt. The conversation had started with me feeling miserable and guilty, thinking I had nearly gotten us all killed. "Crap, Skippy. You let me feel guilty all this time, when it was your fault?"

"A teensy bit my fault, that's all!" His voice sounded hurt.

"I'm sorry, Skippy. I guess I was kind of, uh, kind of hoping that if those Thuranin had a way to track the *Dutchman*, we could do the same thing, and solve our problem of hunting down that surveyor ship."

"They got lucky, Joe. There are no shortcuts."

We continued racing along through empty space in our dirty snowball, slowly tumbling at one rotation every forty six minutes. There was no indication the relay station considered us a threat, even though their long-range sensor grid had seen us two hours ago. We were an innocent, uninteresting dirty snowball, no different from the billions of such objects forming a loose cloud around the star system. We would not pass close enough to the station to be in any way a threat. We hoped. All was going well until four hours before the closest point of our flyby, when Skippy sounded an alarm. "Gamma ray burst! Multiples! Seven, no, eight Kristang ships just jumped in, they're sort of between us and the relay. Damn it! They are moving very roughly parallel to us, unless they change course, we're going to pass uncomfortably close through their formation, about a half hour after we fly by the relay. Oh, this is bad. Crap!"

"They see us? They know we're here?" I asked in a panic.

"Do they see this comet? Yes, certainly they do. Do they know our dropship is under this ice? No way. Or, I don't think so. Unlikely. Very unlikely."

"What the hell are they doing here?"

"Relay stations are common rendezvous points, Joe, this is not entirely unexpected. Unfortunate, not unusual. They could be, yes, they are, exchanging data, shhhhh, be quiet a minute, will you, I'm listening to them." Skippy was silent a few minutes, so was I, although Skippy wasn't holding his breath like I was. "Darn. Joe, we got a problem. The good news is those ships are simply exchanging data and going to be on their way, they're not aware of us and they're not looking for us. The bad news is they are waiting for another ship to join them, and while they're waiting, they will be engaged in a cross-decking operation. Exchanging supplies, and crews, between ships. They will have crew outside the ships in suits, and dropships flying around between ships, they will not want a ball of ice creating a hazard by flying near them. It is possible they will hit us with a maser, to knock us onto a different course, and so avoid their formation. I'm sorry."

"Damn it! Uh, what can I do? Uh, hey, if you're by yourself, you're small enough they won't see you, right?"

"Sure, I can make myself small as a tube of lipstick, and I can become essentially invisible to sensors. Why?"

"Because," I said as I unstrapped him from the seat, "you can flyby that relay station by yourself, you don't need this dropship."

"Whoa! Wait just a minute, monkeybrain, you're going to toss me out an airlock?"

"For real this time, and very gently. I'll give you a little push, you float away and fly right by that relay. That way, if the Kristang do hit this comet, you won't be affected."

"You will be affected, you ass!" He shouted.

"That's a risk. The Army did mention there might be risks involved, when they gave me a rifle. I had to sign a form about it."

"Yeah, risk of you shooting yourself in the foot, you idiot. Joe, this is, and I'm adding emphasis here, a gargantuanly stupid idea, even by monkey standards."

As I put on my spacesuit helmet, I responded "I am open to other ideas, Skippy. Other ideas where you fly by the relay without being detected, get the data we need, and are safely taken back aboard the *Dutchman*. You got anything like that?"

"No."

"Great, then we-"

"In this case, 'no' means, not yet! Damn, you monkeys are impatient."

"Listen, Skippy, in meatsack time, you've had only seconds to think up an alternative idea. In your time, what, you had, what, years? If you haven't thought up something yet, you probably won't, because there is no alternative. You'll be fine floating in space for a while by yourself, I'll be fine here."

"Define 'fine' for me, in terms of you. If they hit this iceball with a maser-"

"I'm a soldier, Skippy, the mission comes first, Ok? There is one of me, and billions of monkeys, damn it, now you've got me saying it. Billions of humans on Earth. This mission has almost no margin for error, you told me our only likely chance to track that surveyor ship is to pull data off that relay. I need you to do that for me, and not to worry about me. Can you do that?"

"I have to worry about you, Joe, you are a particularly dumb monkey in an unforgiving universe. You clearly can't take care of yourself. You're the monkey who says 'ooh, leopard has pretty spots, I should touch it'."

"Skippy," I said as I stepped into the airlock, "you get the data from that relay, and I promise you, I will never try to pet a leopard. Deal?"

"I do not like this, Joe, I do not like this one tiny bit."

"It's not like I'm jumping for joy about it either, Skippy. Do we have a deal?"

There was a heartfelt sigh, then, "I suppose. Damn, why can't you pick this time to come up with one of your crazy ideas?"

"This isn't crazy enough for you?"

"I see your point. Let's get this over with."

When the hole in the comet was covered over, it wasn't filled in all the way, what they'd done was stretch a thin tarp across the top of the hole, then sprayed water which quickly froze, to cover the tarp about a meter thick. To make it look like the rest of the comet, they packed dirty snow on top. From the outside, you couldn't tell there had ever been a hole. Getting out of the airlock, I gently flew up to the bottom of the tarp, and used a cutter on low, power to make a hole just big enough for me to fit through. Skippy advised me so that we timed my cutting through into space, while that side of the comet faced away from the relay station and the Kristang ships. I stuck my head and shoulders out, and held Skippy up. "Which way?"

"Off to your left, give me a good push, or we won't get far enough apart for it to matter. On three, Ok? Three, two, one, now!"

Holding on with my feet wedged into the ice and with my left hand, I threw Skippy as hard as I could with my right. He quickly disappeared from view. "Was that good?"

"Too late now, anyway. Yes, that was a good push, I will come another three thousand kilometers closer to the relay station. Stop talking now, you have to go silent. I can talk to you, but you can't reply. Good luck, Colonel Joe."

Good luck, Skippy, I mouthed silently. Before the comet rotated so the hole was visible to the Kristang, I covered it again as best I could by melting snow with the cutter and trying to pack it over the opening. The best I could do was a half-assed job, I had to hope none of the Kristang were bored enough to look closely at a ball of ice passing by in deep space.

With the hole covered well enough, I went back into the dropship, this time I left my helmet on. If the Kristang hit the comet with a maser, I wanted to have a supply of oxygen, in case the dropship got a hole poked in it. Also, I powered up the dropship's stealth field, setting it as tight as possible around the hull. A tight stealth field drew extra power, power I had plenty to spare as I didn't plan to run the engines. On its normal setting, the stealth field would have extended partly outside the comet, and the Kristang would have become suspicious why the comet had suddenly changed it appearance.

The last thing I did was activate the dead man's switch for the missile warhead strapped into the seat behind me. If things went south, we could not risk the Kristang discovering a human, or human remains, in a Thuranin dropship. Either I could let go of the switch, or, if I was already dead or seriously injured, my hand would let go on its own, and I, the dropship and comet would become a cloud of particles. Skippy would be safely away, not that a mere missile warhead could hurt him. The *Dutchman* would eventually pick him up, he would contact the ship, and Chang would continue the mission.

That would not be my first choice, in case you were wondering. There were many, many cheeseburgers I wanted to enjoy before I died.

Then, I waited.

It didn't take long. Skippy warned me. "Joe! They're firing a maser at you!"

I closed my eyes and mentally prepared for searing pain and death.

It didn't happen.

All I felt was the comet shaking slightly and moving around. Jiggling, kind of. Gently vibrating.

"In case you're wondering why you are still alive," Skippy said, "they're using a low-power maser. They are not trying to blast the comet apart, that would create a bigger hazard for them, as then they would have to keep track of many small objects, instead of one medium-size one. The low-power maser is heating up one side of the comet, boiling off ice, and that's making the comet change course. In case you were wondering why I didn't mention this possibility before, I wasn't sure this is what they would do for certain. Didn't want you to get your hopes up. Sometimes, the Kristang like to use comets for target practice, and that would not have been good for you. Nothing to worry about for now."

For now? Damn, it was driving me crazy that I couldn't talk back to him. Trying to relax, I took in some deep breaths, as the comet vibrated gently around me. Not too relaxed, I had to remind myself not to let go of the dead man's switch by accident. The worst part, if that happened, would not be me dying by accident. It would be Skippy concluding that, in the end, I truly was a dumbass monkey.

Then the comet lurched to one side.

"Not to worry, Joe," Skippy called, "a chunk of ice broke off, that's all. They've switched aim to boil that chunk of ice to nothing, and, they're done. They're switching back to the comet. Uh, hmm. Now this could become a problem. The comet is rotating so that the maser will hit the hole in about twelve minutes. Voids in comets are not that unusual, however, the hole we made is rather large for the size of the comet. And when the tarp is exposed, that will certainly look suspicious. Let me think on this."

"And while I'm thinking about it," he added, "don't do anything stupid like trying to use the dropship's engines or thrusters." He added that, as my hand was poised on the controls to power up the engines. I put my hand back in my lap.

"Think faster, Skippy," I said to myself. Now that I wasn't expecting to die immediately in a sizzling maser cannon beam, it would suck to die like this.

"Got it!" Skippy said excitedly. "Sort of. I think. The good news is, this is going to be cool either way, because I've never done this before. The bad news is, ah, it could be a spectacular failure. Thus, guaranteed cool either way, huh? Coolest, of course, if you survive. That goes without saying, right? Man, I wish you could see this, it is majorly cool. To me. Maybe not to a monkey. Still, totally cool."

What was driving me crazy was not that I didn't know what idiot thing he was trying, it was not being able to interrupt him rambling on and on. The comet's vibration changed, I don't what was going on or how to describe it, it simply felt different. Maybe like there were two sources of vibration.

"It's working, Joe! I think. Hmm. Maybe, uh, yup, yup, it's working. Sort of. Close enough, right? Heh, heh."

At the sound of 'heh heh', the hairs on the back of my neck stood up. What the hell was he doing?

"In case you're wondering what I'm doing, it's only one hundred percent, gold-plated, grade-A awesomeness, Joe! Although, when you think about it, part of that expression doesn't make any sense. You're trying to convince your audience that something is genuinely, indisputably awesome, right? Then why would you brag about something being gold-*plated*? Why not solid gold? Hmm, maybe I got the expression wrong? Cause you could gold-plate a dog turd, and that's not awesome, that's just gold plating on a dog turd, right? Anyway, what was I saying? Hmm, I forget, couldn't have been too important. Oh, wait, I know, I was going to tell you the awesome thing I'm doing! Solid gold awesome, let's get that straight, this is awesome goldness all the way to the center, buddy-boy."

I could have prayed for death right then, if that would get him to shut the hell up.

"Where was I," he continued, "oh, yeah, explaining what I'm doing. Ha! Explaining high-order multidimensional physics to a monkey, what am I thinking? I'll break it down for you Barney style. Joke intended, thought that was pretty clever of me. Man, I never get tired of that one. Only you, Joe, would combat an alien invasion in an ice cream truck. Not even a nice ice cream truck. A crappy ice cream truck. So, here goes, this will blow your tiny monkey mind. I'm warping spacetime, in a tiny, tiny area, to make the comet spin just a bit differently than it was. Differently enough that the maser beam will miss the hole we made. Cool, huh? Hell, you know what, I've never warped spacetime in such a tiny local area, the math is completely different, it's interesting. In fact, I don't think it's ever been done before. I'm the first! Cool, huh-"

He rambled on and on like that a while, I'm not sure how long, I stopped listening. Maybe he talked the whole twelve minutes, he must have, he was talking when the twelve minutes passed. About what, I don't remember. It didn't matter, it was good simply to hear his voice, to hear someone talking to me, while my hands shook and I sat in the dropship, alone with my fear. Being alone is bad. Being afraid is terrible. To be afraid, and alone, is the worst, empty feeling.

"-you still listening, Joe? I think you're good, I think you'll be safe. That maser should cut off in a couple minutes, the Kristang are about satisfied they've pushed it safely out of the way."

The deadman switch was still tightly clutched in my hand. Waiting out the time until the Kristang hopefully turned off their maser beam, I held the switch in both hands, as insurance against one hand growing tired. Finally, Skippy gave me the all-clear signal. "You're good, Joe! Maser is off, the Kristang commander is happy the comet will miss their formation. They are proceeding with the cross-decking operation. Wow, hmmm, they boiled off more of the comet than I expected, more than was strictly necessary, it's a good thing we didn't pick a smaller comet, or part of the dropship may be exposed by now. You can turn off the stealth field to save power, Joe. Hey, good thing they didn't need target practice to tune their masers, huh? That would not have been good. Anywho, I'm going to stop talking in about eighteen minutes, I'm approaching the relay station and I will need to concentrate, or all this will be for nothing. In a couple hours, we will have drifted far enough apart that I won't be able to talk to you. Until I have to go, here is a medley of show tunes to keep you company. *Ooooooklahoma*, where the wind comes sweeping down the plain-"

Show tunes?! Freakin' show tunes. Like, my grandparents' show tunes. He sang one tune after another for the whole eighteen minutes, then abruptly cut off without a goodbye. I didn't hear from him after that, either we'd drifted too far away, or he downloaded a whole lot of data from the relay, and was busy sorting through it. Carefully deactivating the deadman switch, I put it away, and I also safed the missile warhead.

Fourteen hours later, the dropship's sensors picked up a gamma ray burst, then seven others. The Kristang task force must have jumped away. Good riddance to them.

Twenty six hours after I lost contact with Skippy, the dropship console alerted me to a single nearby gamma ray burst, and the *Dutchman* pinged me, one brief signal. I sent back a short 'Ping to let them know about Skippy and pick him up first' message. They must have been curious about why the comet wasn't where it was supposed to be, and why Skippy wasn't with me.

Sixteen minutes later, another gamma ray burst, then nothing. Silence.

Then I was alone for another nineteen hours. Nineteen hours, not knowing what was going on, not knowing whether something bad had happened to the *Flying Dutchman*. It could not possibly have taken nineteen hours for them to contact, locate and pick up Skippy, so had something happened to him? Had the Kristang ships somehow detected Skippy and intercepted him? Had he been detected as he ransacked the databanks of the relay station? No, if the *Dutchman* had pinged Skippy and he hadn't responded, they would have contacted me again right away. For some reason, they had contacted Skippy, then whatever happened, they hadn't been able to pick me up.

Crap.

There weren't many good options for me. The dropship could recycle oxygen for one person for almost a month, and drinking water wasn't a problem as long as I stretched out the supply to match the oxygen. Food was a problem, I'd only brought along enough sludges for a week. What the hell was I going to do? The navigation system told me the comet's new course was taking it further away from the local star, and the comet's next closest approach to the relay station would not be for over a thousand years. Projecting out ten thousand years, the limit of the dropship computer's ability, the comet would not get close enough to the star to boil off the remainder of the ice. The dropship would remain hidden for at least another ten thousand years. Long enough.

Poking around the dropship, I did not find a stash of food that I didn't know about, other than a plastic bag, with one lonely peanut, tucked into a pouch on the side of the copilot seat. Someone flying, or training in, the dropship must have left it there. One peanut. I stared at that peanut for a long time, before wedging the bag into a gap in the pilot console. The only sludges I'd brought along were plain banana flavor, no one liked them as they tasted bland and artificial. The only reason I'd brought them along was to get rid of them. Now they were my only food supply. That was bad planning. What the hell, right? I'd ration sludges to give the *Dutchman* maximum time to come pick me up, then when the sludges ran out, I would eat that peanut. The controls could be programmed to slowly decrease the oxygen supply, I'd been assured that I would gradually fall asleep and it would be almost painless.

Ha! My high school classmates had not voted me 'Most likely to end up encased in a comet orbiting the outer reaches of an alien star system', somehow they had missed that one. They hadn't voted me Class Clown or anything cool like that, either.

Crap. Now that I thought about it, I'm sure that by now, some joker had cut out a picture of Barney and pasted it over my photo in our senior yearbook.

Like that mattered now.

Having nothing else to do, I set a timer for ten hours until my next sludge, turned the lights down, and tried to get some sleep.

And, wouldn't you know it, just as I was drifting off to sleep, the console alerted me to another gamma ray burst, and the *Dutchman* pinged me with a brief signal. 'Taking you aboard shortly, ETA four minutes'.

I felt some jostling, then a hard bump, then a shudder. Then I heard Skippy's voice again. "Hey, Joe! Good to have you back!" Skippy shouted. "After the ship recovered me, it had to jump away. It would have taken too long to fly through normal space to pick you up, the ship would have been exposed for too long. We waited until you got far away from the relay, before we risked coming back. Hold tight, they're cutting a hole for you, should only be a minute before you can come out."

"Thanks, Skippy, it's great to hear your voice again. Were you successful? With the relay, I mean."

"We're in luck, Joe! Although, now that I think about it, that expression can be rather ambiguous, isn't it? Luck can be good or bad. No matter, in this case, our luck is good. Success, yes! Sort of. Come aboard, and I'll give you a full briefing. You, uh, better shower first, huh?"

CHAPTER TWENTY NINE

Skippy barely waited for me to take my shirt off before he began the briefing. "Here's what I found, Joe, not sure if in the end it is good news or bad news-"

"I thought you wanted me to take a shower first?"

"Please do, however, you really don't smell a whole lot better after a shower, so there's no reason to wait. Unless you prefer to wait."

"No," I said as I unlaced my boots, "go ahead."

"My expectation, that the Fire Dragon clan would have information about the surveyor ship's mission, was partly correct."

"Great!" Before I stepped, or to be accurate, kneeled down in the shower, I pressed the button and checked the water temperature, in case Skippy decided to play a practical joke on me and make the water ice cold. "You know where the surveyor ship is, and where it's going?"

"No, unfortunately, no, the Fire Dragons have no information about the surveyor ship, or about the single destroyer that is serving as escort."

"Then what could be the good news? You said two of the Fire Dragons were going on the mission to Earth, and that the surveyor ship had to pick them up somewhere."

"I did say that. Can you hear me, Joe?"

"Yeah, I can hear you just fine," I said, with my head under the cascading water. The hot water washing days of grunge off my skin felt great.

"Good. Yes, two Fire Dragon clan leaders are going on the mission to Earth, they paid extra for the privilege, because they do not trust the Thuranin. For very good reasons, based on a long history, the Kristang do not trust the Thuranin. The Thuranin don't trust the Kristang, also for very good reasons. The Thuranin enjoy insulting and humiliating the Kristang every chance they get, which is why these two Fire Dragon leaders were not instructed to rendezvous with the surveyor ship. They will instead be picked up by a pair of tanker support ships. To travel aboard such low-status ships is a deliberate, very grave insult, and the Kristang know it is an insult. They also can't do anything about it."

"I feel terrible for them, we should send a harsh note to the Thuranin. Where are they going to meet these tanker ships? And when?"

"'Where' is a question I do know the answer to, and I've programmed a course into the navigation computer. When is the problem, Joe. The Kristang are arriving at those tankers three days from now, we can't get there that quickly."

"Crap. You know where those tankers are going, though, right?"

"No, I do not. That is not the type of information the Thuranin saw fit to provide to the Fire Dragon clan."

"Well, hell, Skippy," I hit the button to shut off the water. Damn it, why did he talk to me so often when I was in the shower? "This was all a waste of time, then? We're too late?" That was a bitter pill to swallow, getting messages from that data relay had been our only chance to intercept the surveyor ship before it reached Earth. "Wait. There's always a chance something goes wrong, that the Kristang could be late to the rendezvous?"

"I suppose so, you haven't heard-"

I clicked the button to open the intercom to the bridge. "This is Bishop. Skippy programmed a new course into the nav system, initiate jump as soon as possible."

"Aye, aye," Chang responded, without asking questions.

"We can't waste any time getting there, Skippy. Is there any way you can shorten the trip, do some magic with wormholes?"

"I already did, Joe, the course I programmed does include one shortcut by manipulating a wormhole. You didn't-"

"There's got to be something we can do. Let me think on-"

"Joe! If you will please shut the hell up for a minute, you haven't heard the whole story."

"Oh. Sorry, Skippy, that was rude, me interrupting you. Go ahead, please."

"Thank you. As I explained, these two support ships are primarily tankers, they carry fuel that will be transferred to the surveyor, before it breaks off from its escorts and begins its long solo journey to Earth. The Kristang are going to meet those two tankers in an uninhabited star system, where the tankers will be refueling by siphoning the atmosphere of a gas giant. The tankers logically, and the Thuranin can be ruthlessly logical, will not want to carry their fuel load further than they have to. That tells me the tankers will meet the surveyor ship somewhere close to where they tank up with fuel. Before you make a typically stupid comment, about why I'm bothering to tell you this, I believe those tankers will take several days to complete their fueling operation. We should be able to reach that star system before those tankers depart."

"Skippy, that's fantastic!" Man, I didn't know how much more I could take of hopefulness, sudden crushing despair and back to hopefulness. "Why didn't you say that first?"

"I tried to, you big dope, only you kept flapping your lips 'blah blah blah'. Damn, you flap your lips so hard sometimes, I think you are going to take off like a bird."

"Sorry. Ok, so, we know where these tankers will be, and we know they will be meeting the surveyor ship after they finish pumping their tanks full at this gas station."

"It's a planet, Joe, not a gas station. The operation to siphon the proper gases-"

"You know what I mean, Skippy."

"It's complicated, that's what I was going to say. We still have the problem that we don't know where the tankers are going, after they fuel up. And we have no way to follow them, without them knowing they are being followed."

I finished buttoning a shirt, and pulled pants on. "Don't worry about that, Skippy. While I was stuck inside that comet, there was a lot of time to think. I have some ideas."

"You having an idea, that's what scares me."

The *Flying Dutchman* was jumping like clockwork, on our way to the star system where the two Thuranin support ships should even then be filling their tanks with fuel. According to Skippy, we should arrive well before those ships were ready to depart for their rendezvous with the surveyor. Everything was going great. Great, except that, we still did not have a realistic plan for us to successfully attack the surveyor ship. Or, equally as important, a way for us to attack, in a way that the Thuranin would think the surveyor had been destroyed in an ordinary ship to ship action by a Jeraptha force. Although, an idea was forming in my mind.

"Sir, we may be missing something," Smythe said, while we were sitting in the galley, bouncing around ideas for attacking the surveyor and its escort ships. "I read the after action report from your first mission. The Kristang ships that were attached to the *Dutchman*, you decided to jump them into a gas giant planet," he looked around the compartment and people nodded, "because you were concerned they would eject drones that contain those ships' flight logs. A drone's logs would have told the Kristang, or Thuranin, that a Kristang frigate and a Thuranin star carrier had been taken over by a hostile force."

"Hey!" Skippy protested. "I wasn't hostile. Perhaps I wasn't as polite as-"

"Skippy, that's not what he meant," I suppressed a laugh.

"Oh. Understood. Hostile in this case means taking over their ships and killing all of them. I guess that could be considered hostile," Skippy grumbled. "In certain cultures."

Smythe nodded. "Right. Well, then, when we attack these ships, assuming by that time we have some plan to destroy them, during the attack, those ships will eject stealth drones. Those drones may tell the Thuranin that their ships were attacked by one ship, and they might even be able to determine that one ship is a former Thuranin ship."

"It's possible," Skippy admitted. "During a fight, if our stealth field is damaged, our disguise as a Jeraptha ship won't hold."

"That's the problem, sir," Smythe concluded, "we have to both destroy those ships, and do it in a way that the Thuranin think it was an ordinary Jeraptha raid. Those drones will blow our cover story."

"Yeah, Joe," Skippy, said, excited. "That's a good point. That is a very good point. You got an answer for that, smart guy?"

"Sure, Skippy, you're going to take care of that problem for us."

"Oh, I am? And how am I going to do that? Maybe you weren't paying attention, so I'll summarize the problem for you," he said, almost gleefully. "Starships carry drones which contain the ship's flight recorder data. When a ship is destroyed, or seriously damaged, one or many of those drones are ejected. They are tiny, and they are stealthed. Our sensor field will not be able to detect all the drones, and that, Joey my boy, is the problem; the Thuranin will eventually send a ship to find out what happened to their precious surveyor and its escorts. I am hoping, of course, to fool their sensors into thinking our ship is a Jeraptha cruiser, but that is not guaranteed to work."

"Not a problem, Skippy. You can handle that easily."

"Hmm. Since I left my magic unicorn back on Paradise or somewhere, how am I supposed to find an unknown number of stealthed drones, smart guy?"

"Simple, Skippy. By asking them to tell us where they are."

There was a pause before Skippy spoke again, maybe while he tried to figure out what my idea was. "Perhaps I need to explain the concept of 'stealth' to you again, Joe."

"No, I understa-"

Adams took in a sharp breath. "Sir, I might know what you're thinking."

"Oh, *this* is going to be good," Skippy laughed. "Go ahead, Sergeant Adams, enlighten me, please."

She looked at me, and I nodded, so she leaned forward to speak. "Skippster-"

"Skippster?" He asked, surprised.

"Skippy, then," Adams said with a wink. "These drones are stealthed, to prevent an enemy locating them, but they will respond to a signal, the correct coded signal, from a Thuranin ship, correct?"

"Yeah, duh, they wouldn't be much good otherwise. Again, the problem is, oh, shit."

I laughed. "You get it now, Skippy?"

He gave another heartfelt sigh. "When I load a virus into the Thuranin computer, to make the ship drop off a drone before it jumps, with that drone containing their rendezvous coordinates, I am also supposed to download the drone retrieval codes, right?"

"Uh huh," I said, "you got it. Then we'll jump to wherever those ships went on their way to the rendezvous, you send a signal for those drones to ping us their location."

"You can do that, Skippy?" Adams asked.

"That, yes, I can do that. Damn it, you monkeys think you're so smart. Sergeant Adams, I thought I hated Colonel Joe the worst, but you're moving up the list."

"I'm honored," Adams said mockingly.

"After I tell the drones to ping us their location, we use them for target practice?" Skippy asked.

"No, no, I don't want to destroy them," I said quickly.

"Huh. All right, apparently I'm still missing something here," Skippy's voice had a convincing undertone of puzzlement.

"We're not going to destroy them," I explained, "those drones aren't going to blow our cover story. They're going to *sell* our cover story for us. After you locate and access them, you are going to alter their flight logs, so all the drones contain data showing their ships were attacked by a Jeraptha task force, whatever number and types of ships the Jeraptha would most likely assign to such a mission-"

"Two light cruisers," Skippy stated.

"Then you'll tell those drones to go silent again, until a real Thuranin ship comes looking for them. If that ever happens. Whatever ship finds the drones will provide convincing data about that surveyor ship being destroyed by the Jeraptha, and they will have no reason to suspect humans were involved. Those drones will sell the story for us."

"Damn," Skippy grumbled unhappily. "That actually is a fairly good plan. From a monkey, amazing. That plan is ingeniously devious, and I'm saying that as a compliment. Joe, I'm telling you, once you're done playing soldier, you have a bright career ahead of you as a criminal mastermind. Or, you know, politics."

"Skippy," I laughed, "I would never do anything as sleazy as politics."

"How about crime?"

"Crime we can talk about later, I have plenty of playing soldier to do first." That did get me thinking. When I signed up for the UN ExFor, my commitment was open-ended, since we were at war. Now that Earth was, as far as UNEF Command knew at the moment, at peace, I had no idea how many more years I had until I could either leave the US Army, or re-up. My promotion to colonel was temporary, and, everyone knew, BS. My promotion to sergeant must have come with a commitment to some number of years, which I hadn't thought to ask about at Camp Alpha. It hadn't seemed important at the time, none of us expected to live long enough to care. Fighting aliens with our old trusty M-4 rifles hadn't made us feel particularly hopeful about our life expectancy.

"I have to admit," Skippy said, "this barrel of monkeys has come up with some decent ideas."

"Thank you, Skippy," I said guardedly. Knowing Skippy, he was going to add a snarky and insulting comment. He didn't disappoint me.

"The reason I said 'decent' rather than 'good', is because these ideas are fine in theory. There is the tiny, tiny problem that we do not actually have a practical way for me to, as you so ignorantly assumed, hack into a Thuranin ship."

"What?" I asked in shock. "You took over this ship like," I snapped my fingers, "that. In the blink of an eye! How did you do that?"

"Uh huh, yup, excellent observation skills you have there, Joe. I took over the *Dutchman* with my incredible awesomeness. However, since you apparently weren't paying attention at the time, the Thuranin brought the *Flower* into a docking pad, before I was able to seize control of their crude computer and put those idiot cyborgs into sleep mode. To do that, I had to be close, Joe, by close I mean within about twenty kilometers. We got that close because the *Flying Dutchman* is a star carrier, that expected to be taking a Kristang frigate aboard. None of the Thuranin ships in the surveyor task force will let an unknown ship come that close to them."

"Well, hell, Skippy, you could have told us that earlier, before we wasted all this time dreaming up impossible plans."

"But you were having so much fun, Joe, I didn't want to spoil it for you."

"We're not here for fun, Skippy," I said between gritted teeth. "We may be stupid monkeys to you, but the monkey brains on this ship, and you are all we've got to come up with a plan to stop that surveyor ship from destroying our home. You think this is funny-"

"Pathetic would be more accurate," he mumbled.

"-but we do not. You're telling me it is impossible for you to hack into these ships?"

"Again with you not paying attention, Joe. You seem distracted. Are you hungry, or is this just you being so perpetually horny you can't think straight? I didn't say it was not possible, I said it was not easy. There is a huge difference between those."

"You really-" Fortunately, Skippy interrupted me before I said something harsh.

"Let me explain it to you," he said. "We know those two support ships will be tanking up from the second planet in that system, a gas giant. We jump in behind the fourth planet, another gas giant, we jump in on the far side so the planet will mask the gamma rays from our entry. Then someone takes me on a stealth flyby close to one of those support ships, and I can hack in."

"Oh, like flying by that relay station. That's a great idea, Skippy. We do the flyby in a dropship again?"

"Nope, it's not going to be that easy, Joe. To hack in while I'm flying by, I will need to be within about four thousand kilometers at the closest approach. A dropship, even stealthed, would be detected at that range. And the Thuranin wouldn't let a comet get within four thousand kilometers of them, they'd either move it away or blast it to pieces."

"No dropship? Then how are we supposed to fly from one planet to another?"

"Well, heh, heh, you're not going to like this idea."

CHAPTER THIRTY

He was right, I hated the idea. It was a terrible, awful, stupid idea from Skippy. It was also the only idea we had, damn it. We jumped in on the far side of a gas giant, a planet that was a quarter of the way across the star system from the planet where the Thuranin support ships were taking on fuel. With the *Dutchman* in stealth mode, we let our orbit take us around the planet, and Skippy picked up transmissions between the two support ships. The good news is those ships were alone, we had been afraid they'd have a frigate or destroyer with them. The bad news is we arrived almost too late, one ship had already half-filled its fuel tanks, and the other was not far behind its sister ship. We had to move quickly.

Desai piloted the dropship, with Lieutenant Xi of the Chinese Air Force as her copilot. I took Skippy with me, plus Giraud as my backup. In what I thought was an interesting maneuver, Desai burned the dropship's engines hard while we were on the far side of the gas giant, then cut power back as we slingshotted around the planet and escaped from its gravity well. After another three hours of relatively gentle thrust, we were moving faster than a speeding bullet, on course to intercept the tanker ship as it hung in low orbit around the second planet.

To remain undetected, we could not burn the engines for deceleration until both tankers were on the other side of the gas giant, which was complicated because while we were racing through interplanetary space, the first tanker finished taking on fuel had moved away. We were cutting this close, very close. There was only a twelve minute window fire the engines, before the orbits of one or the other support ships brought them around into view. Desai decelerated us to the proper speed in a high-G burn maneuver that busted a blood vessel in my left eye and gave me a nosebleed, while those ships were hidden by the planet, then she cut off the engines, and I attached my helmet, stepped outside and gently pushed off to drift away.

Skippy's idea, that I didn't like at all, was for someone to get into a Kristang spacesuit, with Skippy, and a jetpack. Skippy was irritated that we called the thing a 'jetpack' instead of an Individual Maneuvering Unit, his argument was that the thing technically did not have jets. We ignored him. It was a jetpack. Jetpacks were cool, 'IMU' was not cool. A stealthed suit, even with a jetpack, was small enough to fly past a lowly tanker ship, as close as four thousand kilometers, without being detected. In addition to the jetpack, my suit had a waist belt with an attachment point for Skippy, and a portable stealth field generator.

The idea was for someone in a suit to take Skippy on a flyby, using the jetpack to make small course corrections as needed. The suit wearer and Skippy would then swing around the other side of the planet, fire the jetpack to climb into a slightly higher orbit, where the dropship would be to retrieve them eventually. That was the plan, anyway.

This idiotic plan was why I was hanging seemingly motionless in space, with the target gas giant planet a basketball-sized orange blob in front of me. With gentle puffs of thrusters, Desai moved the dropship safely away from me, then she fired the engines to make the dropship swing much wider around the planet.

"Captain Desai, can you hear me?" I asked.

"Loud and clear, Colonel," she replied.

"Skippy, we're communicating through the microwormhole?" We were still close enough to the dropship that it might be able to pick up my faint transmission directly.

"Yes, affirmative. Wormhole is active and operating nominally," Skippy reported. To allow us to talk to the dropship, without the Thuranin detecting our transmissions, Skippy had done his microwormhole trick again. One end of the wormhole was near the dropship and moved with that spacecraft, the other end stayed a hundred fifty meters behind Skippy. According to that super smart beer can, it was extremely unlikely the Thuranin ships could detect either our very low-power transmissions, or the faint radiation from the microwormhole. That was good, because small as one person in a suit was, I was way too large to fit through that super tiny wormhole.

"Great. To be safe, Desai, we don't transmit if either of those Thuranin ships are line of sight to us."

"Understood, Colonel," she agreed. "Cutting thrust in 3, 2, 1 now. The first Thuranin ship should be coming around the planet in two minutes, forty seconds."

The sensors built into my suit were not sensitive enough to detect the ships yet, I had to take Desai's word for it. For the next four and a half hours, I zoomed through empty space, the planet ahead of me growing larger in my vision. Really, I was racing through space, only there was no sensation of movement. No reference point except the giant planet. Skippy and I chatted only occasionally, there wasn't much to talk about, other than him instructing me to make tiny course corrections with the jetpack. After four hours, he told me to activate the stealth field. The stealth unit required a lot of power, and the generator we brought along could only supply power for a couple hours. If all went well, a couple hours of stealth is all we would need.

If all went well.

"There's the first ship," Skippy announced. "Right on time, it hasn't altered its orbit at all. Picking up ship to ship transmissions, there are still only those two support ships in system." We had been concerned there might be a warship escorting the tankers, there didn't appear to be. This deep inside Thuranin territory, they didn't see a need to escort such low-value ships.

A symbol for the first ship popped up on the inside of my helmet faceplate, it was hugging the crescent of the planet, climbing away slowly. We waited, and a symbol for the second ship popped up, it was still too far away for me to see with the naked eye.

"Uh, oh," Skippy said, "we've got a problem. A big, big problem."

"What is it? They detected us?"

"No, those crappy ships couldn't see us yet even if we were lighting off fireworks out here. That second ship has been slower to take on fuel because of a fault with its drogue, the unit at the bottom of the fuel line it has lowered into the atmosphere. The fault has gotten worse, the Thuranin have decided to retract the fuel line now, even though the ship's tanks are only 82% full."

"Yeah, so?" I couldn't see how a flying gas station was a problem for us.

"So, as soon as the drogue is clear of the atmosphere, that ship will be changing course to join the other ship, climbing out of orbit to jump distance. From its transmissions, I can predict the ship's course, and it is a very big problem. The jetpack does not have enough fuel to alter our course sufficiently that we can intercept that ship, not within four thousand kilometers. We'll be too far away for me to hack into their systems." He sounded genuinely sad. "I'm sorry, Joe, we're going to miss this chance."

Crap. "This is our only chance. You sure where that ship is going?"

"Yes, I am sure. The degree of uncertainty is not great enough to make us intercepting that ship be a realistic possibility. It is simple orbital mechanics, Joe, the jetpack does not contain enough fuel."

"Force equals mass times acceleration?" I asked.

"Um, yeah. I'm surprised you know-"

"Our problem right now isn't the acceleration part, it's the mass, right?"

"Correct. Between me, you, the stealth field generator, and the suit, the jetpack can't manage to provide the delta vee, the change in velocity, for us to alter course sufficiently to come close to that ship."

"The problem isn't you, either, it's me and this suit."

"Mostly the suit, it has more than twice your mass, Joe."

"Yeah, I can't take the suit off, so." I reached down to unbuckle the fasteners that held my suit attached to the jetpack.

"Joe, what are you doing? We need that jetpack, you dumb monkey."

The jetpack came loose, I swung it around in front of me, and held it steady with my legs. Although in zero gravity is weighed nothing, its substantial mass made it awkward to move around. "No, Skippy, *you* need the jetpack." The stupid tool belt fastener was on the side, not the front, and to undo it, I had to turn a knob to expose the button. It was intended as a safety feature, I'm sure. Right then, it was a pain in the ass. The tool belt finally came undone, and I pulled it tightly around the jetpack, trying to keep the mass of Skippy and the stealth field generator centered. "There, done." I let go of the jetpack with my legs, and it hung right in front of me. "Tell me how to program a course into this thing," I asked. The jetpack had a limited ability to be controlled remotely from a module strapped to my left wrist.

"A course? Where?" Skippy sounded panicked. "Back to the dropship?"

"No, Skippy," I explained patiently, "a course to take you within four thousand kilometers of that tanker ship. You said it, we're going to miss this chance if the jetpack has to move my mass. This is our *only* chance, Skippy, our only chance to follow that ship to the surveyor and destroy it. Our only chance to stop the Thuranin from reaching my home planet and killing everyone. You are not going to miss that chance. You're going to flyby that ship, you're going to hack into it, and you're going to rendezvous with the dropship. Then you are going to do everything you can to stop that surveyor ship."

"May I point out the glaringly obvious flaw in your plan, you brainless monkey?"

"The fact that, without the jetpack, I'm going to hit the atmosphere and burn up? Yeah, I know that, Skippy. I don't need to be reminded of that, thank you very much."

"Shit. Joe, this is the second time you've offered to sacrifice yourself for a noble cause-"

"The first time, I offered to sacrifice myself for you, you little shithead."

"No cause could be more noble indeed."

"I offered to sacrifice myself for you, because you're more valuable to the mission than I am. The *Dutchman* can go on without me, Chang will make a fine commander. That surveyor ship can be stopped without me, but it can't be stopped without you. Unless I'm missing something here."

"No, astonishing as it may seem, your logic is correct on this one. Damn, why does the monkey pick now to start using logic?"

Despite the situation, he made me smile. "I love you too, Skippy. You see an alternative? If we use the jetpack to rendezvous with the dropship, by the time we get there, those two tankers will have jumped away already, and we'll never find them. We will lose our one chance to intercept that surveyor ship before it reaches Earth."

"It will take the tankers longer than you think to reach a safe jump distance; this planet has a deep gravity well and they are heavily loaded with fuel. You are correct, however, that this is the only opportunity I see for being able to track these ships, and locate the surveyor."

"Right," I breathed heavily, and unintentionally fogged the faceplate for a second. "Is there any way to get you to within four thousand kilometers of that ship, and also make sure I don't hit the atmosphere? Can we split the difference, use the jetpack to move both of us just enough so I miss the planet, then you fly off to intercept the tanker?"

Skippy replied immediately, which was a bad sign. If there was any chance for both of us to get out of this, he would have paused a split second to run a couple million calculations. "Given the laws of physics, which I can't screw with because those tankers would detect us, the answer is, unfortunately, no. Joe, I'm sorry."

"You have nothing to be sorry about."

"I know that. 'Sorry' is something you monkeys say as a social courtesy, whether you mean it or not. That custom seems particularly stupid now."

"I appreciate the effort, Skippy. All right, before I change my mind," I was deliberately not looking at the planet ahead, "can you program the jetpack to fly you near that tanker, and I'll engage it with this controller on my wrist?"

"I don't like this, Joe."

"I'm not jumping for joy about it either, Skippy."

"Jetpack autonomous navigation system has been programmed. Ready." He simulated taking a deep breath. "Are you sure about this, Joe? It seems like such a waste."

"Skippy, I'm a soldier. I knew the risks coming out here," my voice choked up a bit and I paused to swallow hard. "I am not going to do nothing, and let that surveyor ship reach Earth. If you have a better idea, I am all ears."

"Legitimately, no, no, I do not have any other idea. Joe, there is a big difference, or there should be, between taking a risk of dying, and taking an action that will result in certain death. Suicide does not seem like something a soldier should do."

"Skippy, let's get real here, Ok? Yeah, in a way, this is suicide, but really, it is only an issue of timing."

"You'll need to explain that one."

"This whole mission is suicide, I explained that to everyone before we left Earth. Be straight with me, what are the odds we humans can fly the *Dutchman* back to Earth by ourselves, after you leave us for Collective heaven, or whatever the hell it is you're looking for?"

"Zero. Well, close enough to zero that your chances of success are statistically insignificant. If you like, I can recite the actual odds to a hundred decimal points, however, I expect you are satisfied with 'meh' level math on this one."

"You got that right."

"Captain Desai has become a skilled starship pilot, for, you know, a monkey, and she has trained other pilots well enough for basic maneuvers. My calculation of your odds are no reflection on your Merry Band of Pirates, they are all dedicated, and, considering your species' miserably low level of development, reasonably intelligent, no offense."

Inside my helmet, I had to smile and roll my eyes. In one sentence, he insults us, and says he intended no offense. Sometimes I wondered about his intelligence.

He continued. "The problem is the *Flying Dutchman* is an incredibly complex machine, and you humans have no idea how it works, not really. If anything goes wrong, there is zero possibility you can fix it. Even routine maintenance, which I have been doing for you using Thuranin robots, is beyond your capabilities. The jump drive coils, for example, will drift out of calibration each time you jump. Without me fine-tuning the jump system, I estimate the drive will become unusable within twenty, certainly twenty five jumps. Jumps that you program will be so inaccurate, that you would have no realistic chance to emerge near a wormhole. You'd have to jump as close as you can, and fly through possibly half a lightyear of normal space to where a wormhole is going to open. Frankly, you will run out of time, and food, before you got home. Although, by that time, the jump drive would be so hopelessly screwed up, you would not be able to jump at all, anyway."

"Is there any way you can load a submind into the ship's computer, to take care of that maintenance stuff for us, after you leave?"

"Ha, ha! No way, dude," Skippy laughed. "The memory and processing power on the *Dutchman* are much too small to contain a stable submind. It might work fine for a week, maybe two, then it would start going funky on you, and without me to adjust it, the submind would go senile and destroy the ship, So, no to that one. Before you ask, I could reload the original Thuranin AI into the computer, modified to work with you instead of wiping you out as soon as it became aware of your presence. That would not help, the Thuranin's cyborg nature is integrated into their AIs to such an extent that the AI cannot completely control the ship without them. That is both because the Thuranin wish their minds to be as close as possible to an AI, and because the Thuranin don't want an AI to be able to run the ship without them, for security reasons. Especially because the Thuranin are quite rightly concerned about the Maxohlx hacking into their systems. Many crucial control and maintenance functions require cyborg participation, particularly in controlling the robots. Humans can't fill the role of the Thuranin, and the system's processing substrate lacks the capacity for me to replicate the cyborg function inside it."

"Uh huh. Like I said before, this whole fool's errand is a suicide mission, and me falling into this planet is only shortening the trip somewhat for me."

"Unfortunately, I am forced to agree with your point. I still do not like it. Joe, I need to understand something. You came out here, knowing there is almost no possibility that you will ever return to Earth. Why? Why did you come with me?"

"The short answer is that you had that wormhole on a timer, and if we didn't come out here with you, there would be a whole lot of pissed off lizards and little green men coming to Earth and asking awkward questions. Beyond that, I came out here because I promised you that I would, it's that simple. We have a bargain, you sure kept your end of it, this is my end of the deal. We owe you, Skippy, we humans owe you more than we can ever repay. Billions of humans are safe today, because of you. I understand you don't belong with us, that you need to go home, or find answers about who you are and where you came from."

"Huh. You monkeys are more complicated than I expected."

"Yup, sure. Now, I'll give you a little push, so you can drift away before I engage the jetpack?"

"Yes, it would be best if you were at least eighty meters away before the jetpack fires thrusters."

There not being much left to say, I hugged the jetpack tight to my chest, then pushed it away, trying not to make it wobble or spin. My best effort left it turning ever so slowly, and left me spinning also. In a maneuver I had practiced during training, I used my arms and legs to halt my spin, so that Skippy and the jetpack were off to my left, and I was facing the planet. Facing it, facing it right there. Damn, it looked close already. "Hey, Skippy, should I go silent now? You're taking the microwormhole with you, right?"

"You are now outside the stealth field, so, yes, you should cease even your low-power transmissions. I will send a tight beam message to you after I fly by the tanker; that should be within the next twenty seven minutes. Soon after I fly past the tanker, it will go behind the horizon of the planet, and we can communicate again. About forty minutes from now."

I almost said 'goodbye' before catching myself at the last moment. "Talk to you then, Skippy."

Man, that was a long forty minutes. On the display inside the helmet faceplate, I was able to track the two tanker ships, they were big, they were close and they weren't using stealth. In fact, their crews were chatting and exchanging data almost continuously, it would have been impossible not to notice them. Of Skippy and the dropship, hidden inside their stealth fields, I saw and heard nothing. The planet kept growing larger until it completely filled my view, in order to see the darkness of space I had to turn my head.

And, darn it, the view was eerily beautiful. The planet below me was mostly orange in color, when I left the dropship, from that far away it had been an orange blob the size of a basketball. Now I was close enough to see details, and it looked like a creamsicle; swirls of orange and white, with less prominent streaks of purple, light browns and greens. The planet didn't have a big spot like Jupiter had, the cloud formations were more subtle; great swaths of darker or lighter clouds stretching across an entire hemisphere. Some of the clouds below were moving so fast I could see them changing as I watched, it was hypnotic. Clouds swirling and spinning and merging with each other and splitting apart. The speed at which the upper atmosphere was moving must have been mind-boggling, this is one case when I wished I could talk with Skippy, so he could bore me with sciency details. Right then, it would have been good to talk with anyone. I'd never felt so alone in my life; even when my dropship was frozen inside a comet I had at least been in a familiar environment. Walls, floor, ceiling, seats, displays and controls, and a breathable atmosphere. In my alien space suit, racing silently just above the cloud tops, there was nothing familiar or comforting around me. Nothing in sight was welcoming to warm-blooded, air-breathing creatures. The view was beautiful in its cold, unending indifference to life.

Almost exactly at the thirty two minute mark, I received a short "Mission successful" message from Skippy, then nothing for another eight minutes. That eight minutes was awful, made worse because my helmet display kept flashing a warning that I was going to hit the planet's thick atmosphere in another thirty nine minutes, and I didn't know how to turn the damned thing off. It was annoying.

Finally, another message from Skippy. "We did it, Joe! Whenever that tanker jumps, it's going to leave behind drones like a trail of breadcrumbs. And, major bonus, I was able to hack into their navigation system, and download data. We now know where and when the tankers will rendezvous with the surveyor ship! This mission is totally successful."

Except for the part about me falling into a planet. "Excellent, Skippy, outstanding. I knew we could count on you. Sincerely, thank you, from all of us."

"How are you doing?" He asked.

"Ok so far," I tried saying that as a joke. The stupid display flashed another warning at me, a warning I didn't need.

"So far? Is this like the old joke about the guy who falls off a building, and when he is halfway to the sidewalk below, he thinks to himself 'Ok so far'?"

"Something like that, yeah, Skippy."

"Is there anything I can do, Joe?"

"I don't know, Skippy, is there anything you can do?" Part of me was hoping he'd thought up a brilliant plan.

"About the major problem, no, I got nothing. Sorry. Anything else I can do for you?"

"Mmm, keep talking to me? Hey, I know. DJ Skippy-Skip-"

"And the Fresh Tunes, don't forget the Fresh Tunes. I also go by Grandmaster Skip."

"Sure, you got it. Play some music for me, please. You have music stored in your memory, right? Human music."

"Uh huh. All of it."

"*All?*"

"Yup. Well, all music that was stored in digital format, while I was on Earth. What type of music do you want?"

It still surprised me how much data Skippy could store. While we were on Earth, he'd told me that he had downloaded the entire internet, including the darknet, I hadn't quite believed him. "Anything."

"Bluegrass?"

"Anything but bluegrass."

My helmet speakers played some new age type soothing instrumental thing, something I hadn't heard before. It was nice, and appropriate.

"Thanks, Grandmaster Skip."

He didn't reply immediately, making my heart leap with fear that something had gone wrong. "Joe," he finally said, "I have been alive for a very, very long time, millions of years, I think. It just occurred to me that, no matter how much longer I exist, in all the infinite universes of probability, I will never talk to you again." He sounded convincingly broken up about it, his voice was unsteady. "That makes me very sad."

"You are an incredibly arrogant, irritating, smug little shithead, Skippy, but I'm going to miss you too."

"Joe, what do you want to do with your stuff?"

That seemed an odd question, Skippy may have been nervous and searching for something to talk about. Before I left Earth, again, I had updated my will through an Army lawyer; my parents would get everything, including my back pay. The lawyer had explained that, in the extremely likely event the *Dutchman* was never heard from again, I would be declared dead after three years, and my Army pay would stop accruing. It sucked, but that was the deal offered to everyone in the ExFor, I wouldn't get, and didn't request, special treatment. "You mean my stuff aboard the *Dutchman*? Lt Colonel Chang will know what to do with it." There wasn't much anyway. "Hey, promise me you won't give him a hard time?"

"Ugh, all right, damn, you hate me having any fun. No worse than I give you."

"Fair enough."

He simulated a sigh. "Would you like me to keep talking to you, or do you prefer silence at this time?"

"Talking, please. Hey, it won't be silent when I hit the atmosphere, will it? The air particles, molecules, atoms, whatever, will start bouncing off my helmet, and I'll hear that, I think."

"You will hear sound transmitted through the outside of the helmet, yes. Very high pitched sound at first, because you are moving at high supersonic speed. Then there will be a roaring sound. The visor that sits atop your helmet will automatically drop down and cover the faceplate to protect it, you won't have a real view then. The faceplate will switch to showing images from the exterior cameras."

"I don't like that. Can you override the visor? I want to see."

"Without the visor," Skippy warned, "the faceplate will deteriorate quickly. It is made of a tough material so it won't melt, but it will fog, and you will be blinded anyway."

"All right, fine. It's going to be quick, right? When I hit the atmosphere, this suit won't last long." The cloud tops below me looked close enough for me to reach out and touch them already.

"Although I want to tell you yes, the answer is no. Kristang armor is rugged, it will last longer than you expect. Or, in this case, I'm very sad to say, longer than you will want. The suit will hold together long enough for you to get sufficiently deep in the atmosphere, that the force of deceleration will crush you inside the suit. Other than your bones, your soft tissue will become a liquefied, hmm, guess you don't need to hear about that. The good news is you should lose consciousness around twelve gees."

Good news? In context, I guess it was good news. "Wow, these suits are super tough. This material can take all that heat?"

"No, no. The outer protective layers of the suit will flake off, in a process called ablation. As the material heats up, it will ablate away, exposing fresh layers below, this protects the integrity of the suit, and the wearer, as long as possible. In combat, ablation technology defends the wearer against directed-energy weapons such as masers and particle beams. And-"

He went silent. For a moment, I panicked, thinking we'd lost connection, except the music was still playing in my helmet speakers. "And? Skippy? And?"

"Give me a minute, I'm working on an idea here," he said excitedly. "Lots of numbers to crunch, need to run a couple billion simulations though the model I've built."

"Okey dokey. I'll be right here, got plenty of time and nothing to do." Nothing to do was true, the plenty of time part was not.

"Yesssss!" He fairly shouted. "Got it. Joe, while I don't want to get your hopes up too much, there is a possibility that I can do something to help."

"I'm all ears, here, Skippy."

"Well, heh, heh, first thing is, you are very much not going to like this-"

Skippy's idiotic plan, which I very much did not like, involved him repositioning his end of the microwormhole so that it was behind and slightly below me. He moved the other end of the wormhole directly in front, and very close to, the dropship. Close enough that he instructed Desai to slide the protective shield down over the composite cockpit windows, to protect the occupants from radiation. Then, and here's the part I very much did not like, he had Desai fire the dropship's maser through the wormhole, at me.

When Skippy told me his plan, my first thought was that he was offering to kill me in one quick zap, so I wouldn't suffer from being crushed inside my suit. But no, that would have been too easy. Instead, the crazy little beer can planned to use pulses of maser light, at reduced power, to boost my speed enough so I would miss the atmosphere. Maser photons impacting my suit would flake off my suit's ablative layers, propelling me forward. All of this sciency BS was according to Skippy, who was, of course, safely out of the maser's line of fire.

"What if I say no to this moronic plan of yours?" I asked fearfully. Facing certain death, I wasn't sure whether crashing into the atmosphere still wasn't preferable to getting cooked to a crisp. When I hear 'maser' I think combination of 'laser' and 'microwave oven'.

Imagine a frozen burrito being zapped by a million watts, that's what ran through my mind.

"Could you repeat that, Joe, I couldn't hear you? You said 'go'?

"No! I said 'no'."

"Uh, huh, 'go' it is, got it. Captain Desai, fire on my mark. Three, two, one, mark!"

"N- shit!" The faceplate of my helmet automatically went opaque, and the visor slammed down. The suit went rigid, something Skippy should have told me about. I waited for imminent and painful death.

It didn't happen. Skippy's plan worked. Surprised the hell out of me, that's for sure. Probably surprised him, too. He had me spin around slowly, so the maser hit different parts of the suit, he had to look, fire, look again. Then repeat. The first turkey shoot, as I called it, only lasted eight minutes, because we couldn't have a maser hitting me while either of the two Thuranin ships were above the horizon. It almost didn't work, eight minutes of being propelled by maser only boosted my speed enough to delay me falling into the atmosphere. By the time the tanker ships went behind the curve of the planet again, I was technically already in the atmosphere, and the wormhole had started to suck in atmospheric particles and blast the dropship with high-energy radiation. Inside my suit, there were occasional pinging sounds, I thought that was the air screaming past me, Skippy said it was my imagination. It sure sounded real to me.

My second cooking session lasted twenty two minutes, and was less frightening because Skippy didn't have to rush the process, he could let my suit cool and adjust between maser blasts. The outer layer of the suit was composed partly of nanoparticles that could move around somewhat to cover exposed areas, sections of the suit that the maser had burned away. After the second session, before we had to stop because a tanker ship was about to rise over the horizon, Skippy declared that I was safe, that my orbital path was now good enough to keep me from plunging to my death for an hour, at least. Plenty of time for the Thuranin ships to climb out of the planet's gravity well and jump away.

Skippy must have been using creative math in declaring I was safe, for it still looked like I could reach out and touch the cloud tops, they were that close. Unconsciously, I was holding my breath, afraid that my chest heaving up and down would knock me out of orbit. "You sure I'm good here, Skippy?" I asked in a fearful whisper. Right then, I was more frightened than I had been when I had thought death was certain. Life, the possibility that I might go on living, there just beyond my grasp, I was terrified of having that chance snatched away from me by the cruel math of orbital mechanics.

"Uh huh," Skippy replied, "I'm sure. Math don't lie, bro. Tell you what, though, how about you don't move a muscle, stay perfectly still. And try not to breathe too hard, Ok?"

"Why?"

"Well, heh, heh, the maser really cooked your suit, and patches of it are thin as tissue paper right now. I wouldn't worry about it."

"Of course *you* don't need to worry about it!"

"Hmm. I see your point. Still, there is no point to you worrying, you can't do anything about it. When the dropship gets there, Captain Desai will open the airlock door and fly the dropship to take you aboard, without you having to move in any way. Once the airlock is closed and repressurized, you can move about all you wish."

"How long will that be?"

"Well, certainly not more than one hour, Joe."

"Why's that?"

"Because we can't risk hitting you with the maser again. If those two tankers haven't jumped away within an hour, you're going to fall into the atmosphere, and this time there will be nothing I can do about it."

"Oh, great."

Ten minutes later, I heard a faint, high-pitched whistling sound. Remembering Skippy's scoffing when I thought I'd heard atmosphere screaming past me, I held my breath and tried to decide whether it was my imagination or not. And if not my imagination, what was it? A static hissing from my helmet speakers? "Skippy, am I hearing things again? There's a whistling noise, right at the edge of my hearing."

"Wow, you can hear that, Joe? Your hearing is impressive. That frequency is almost up in the dog hearing range."

"You know about it?" Damn that beer can. "What is it? Can you turn it off? It is very distracting."

"No can do, sorry. I can't turn it off, because it's a tiny air leak. Well, not so tiny as it was a few minutes ago."

"What? Crap, you knew about this? Why didn't you tell me?"

"There was no reason to worry you about it. Not yet, anyway."

"Skippy," I said, exasperated with him, "my air supply is leaking out into space. I have a very good reason to be worried."

"Worrying is not going to solve the problem, Joe."

"What will solve the problem?"

"I am working on it. The suit has been instructed to move nanoparticles to plug the leak. So far, it isn't working, the suit's supply of nanoparticles has been severely depleted, and the remaining supply is already being used to prevent the suit from springing other leaks. Probably shouldn't have told you about that."

That was not good news at all. "Understood. I have plenty of oxygen, right? Enough to keep me breathing, even with this, as you say, tiny leak?"

"Ah, not so much, unfortunately. The suit mostly, and efficiently, recycles oxygen. There is a small reserve oxygen bottle. That bottle is inadequate, considering the leak."

I kept silent for a moment, listening hard. The sound was not so high pitched now. The leak must have gotten bigger. "Where is the leak? Can I put my hand over it, or something like that? I can't do nothing, Skippy."

"The leak is near your waist, on the left side. Do not move! Moving will only make the leak worse, and cause other leaks."

"Great. Wonderful. What *can* I do?"

"Try to breathe less?"

"Very funny."

"That wasn't a joke."

"Shit."

"Perhaps I should work on my humor, so you know when I'm joking."

"Ya think?"

"Sorry," Skippy said, sounding genuinely sorry.

A leak. How to stop a leak? If only this Kristang suit came with something like a can of Fix-A-Flat. Although it did, in the form of nanoparticles that could plug leaks, make minor repairs, reinforce thin areas, and all kinds of useful things. Absent-mindedly, while feverishly trying to think of a way to stop a leak, I turned my head and took a sip from the water supply tube in the helmet. Dry. I'd sipped the last of the water an hour ago. "Huh," I said. "Skippy, I may have an idea."

"An idea? You? This I have to hear."

"Would water plug the leak? It would freeze, right, make a plug of ice to cover the hole."

"Ah, not exactly, the water would freeze and boil at the same time, because of the combination of cold and zero pressure. Besides, Joe, you drank all the water, you dumb monkey, there's none left."

"There's no *pure* water left."

"Oh."

"You know what I'm thinking?" Down next to my left leg was a pee bag, that we'd installed before I took my many-hours-long space dive.

"Unfortunately, yuck, yes. I can puncture the bag with nanoparticles."

"Do that. Ugh." I felt my leg growing wet. Then the wetness moved up my hips.

"It's working, Joe!" Skippy said excitedly. "It's boiling off slowly, which is not a problem, there's plenty more. Good idea, Joe!"

"Yes! Outstanding. Uh, hey, Skippy, this little incident, this can stay just between us, right? No need to tell anybody about it."

"Yeah, like that's gonna happen," he chuckled. "No way can I pass up a *golden* opportunity to *leak* this info," he laughed gleefully.

"Crap. Can you hit me with the maser again?"

The whole time I was waiting, I was angrily urging the two Thuranin ships to get off their asses and move away from the planet. What the hell were they waiting for? Damn! It was like getting stuck on a two lane road behind a school bus, and you can't pass. The damned thing stops at every freakin' mailbox, and you have to sit there watching the flashing lights, and you wish the driver would just move faster, or take a turn, or pull over so you can pass. You're stuck behind the school bus, and it's crawling along, and it ever so slowly grinds to a stop at a driveway, and one kid is waiting there with his mommy, and the kid slouches up the steps, and walks slowly back to a seat, with his mommy waving idiotically to him the whole way he meanders down the aisle of the bus, and then when you think the stupid kid has finally sat down and the bus can move again, the school bus driver decides to chat with the mommy, and you're tempted to lean on your car horn because you want that bus to just GET THE HELL OUT OF YOUR WAY ALREADY!!

That ever happen to you?

I pictured the tanker crews climbing their ships out to jump distance, and then deciding a celebration was in order, or something broke on their stupid ships, and they were fiddling around trying to fix it, while I slowly but surely fell toward the clouds below me. Maybe the Thuranin were having a cake and ice cream, and singing songs or some nonsense like that. Skippy assured me the two tankers were moving at their best speed, and would jump as soon as possible. The Thuranin, being cyborgs, didn't go much for celebrations.

When they finally did jump away thirty four minutes later, I almost shouted for joy. Mercifully, Desai put the pedal to the metal on the dropship's engines to rescue me. Instead, I ordered Skippy to signal the *Dutchman* to jump into orbit, and for Desai to come pick us up. The dropship was suddenly close to us, Desai making no effort at stealth, she was burning the engines at full power.

"Desai, take Skippy aboard first," I ordered.

"Sir?" She asked, surprised. "Mr. Skippy said your suit is in bad condition."

"That is true, it is also true that Skippy is more important to the mission than I am. If the Thuranin come back or whatever, I want him aboard first, in case you need to high-tail it out of here. That's an order."

Over Skippy's protests, Giraud grappled the jetpack, released Skippy, then took him aboard and let the jetpack drift away. The dropship then flew over to me, and Desai slowly and carefully edged the dropship sideways, until Giraud was able to very gently guide me into the airlock door with his fingertips. "Got him," Giraud told Desai, "closing the door now."

The airlock quickly filled with sweet, breathable air, and as the inner door slid open, I reached up to take my helmet off. "Desai, we shouldn't leave that jetpack floating around as evidence we were here, can you blast it with a maser?"

"Oh, yes, sir, uh, there, done. It's a cloud of vapor now."

"Great." Man, I was tired. My hair was plastered to my head with dried sweat, Giraud handed me a bottle of water and I drank it eagerly.

Desai wrinkled her nose. "What's that smell?"

"The suit got cooked a bit by the maser," I explained.

"No," she shook her head, "it smells like-"

"As a problem solver," Skippy laughed, "Joe is *Number One*."

"Skippy-"

"When a problem needs to be solved, Joe doesn't waste time trying to *piss up a rope*."

"All right, Skippy."

"Joe knows you can't put out a forest fire by *peeing* on it, but you can-"

"Enough!" I shouted. "The maser busted the, you know, bag," I explained, and pointed to the suit's left leg. It sounded lame to me. Screw it.

"Yeah," Skippy snorted, "uh huh, that's our story and we're sticking to it."

"Desai," I said wearily, "I'm getting out of this suit, then I'm going to towel off and change my clothes. Our signal won't reach the *Dutchman* for another hour, anyway."

CHAPTER THIRTY ONE

While we waited for the *Dutchman* to arrive and retrieve us, Skippy downloaded the data from the two drones the tanker had unwittingly dropped off before it jumped. To our great relief, we'd been successful, both drones indicated the tankers had jumped to a point consistent with Skippy's hacked data, about the location and time where the two tankers planned to rendezvous with the surveyor ship, and a destroyer that would be acting as escort. I was worried that the rendezvous 'location' would be only a vague area of empty interstellar space, that the four ships of the surveyor task force might jump into an area half the size of a solar system, and then we'd have to try chasing them down one by one. Skippy assured us the Thuranin were much too competitive for that kind of behavior, their navigators prided themselves on accuracy in hitting targeted jump points, so we would be able to count on them jumping into their designated points within eight thousand kilometers, even the big clumsy tankers could be counted on to be accurate. That was good news.

In the bad news department, Skippy explained that Thuranin practice for a task force rendezvous, even deep inside Thuranin territory, was for a warship to jump in to the rendezvous point first, so we could count on having to deal with the destroyer before the softer targets. That ruined my hope of us blasting the vulnerable tankers, then the surveyor, and then firing at the destroyer a few times to make it look good, before we jumped safely away. However it was we dealt with the surveyor task force, we needed to kill or disable a Thuranin destroyer first. How the hell we going to do that, in our rebuilt star carrier, was a damned good question.

I had an idea, the unformed kernel of an idea, I needed to think more on it before mentioning it to anyone, especially Skippy. The last thing I wanted was to give that arrogant little beer can even more reason to be smug, by shooting down a plan I hadn't thought all the way through. I needed time to think.

And I needed to get out of my sweat and other fluid soaked clothes, and I needed a shower. Seriously.

When the *Dutchman* jumped into orbit, it still took the dropship forty minutes to match speed and course rendezvous with her. I gave Simms, as the duty officer on the bridge, an order to jump the star carrier as soon as our dropship was secured in the landing bay. With the jump successful, I let Simms know I'd be on the bridge soon, and brought Skippy with me to my cabin, sitting him on a shelf while I got in the shower. As the hot water of the shower cascaded over me, washing away the grime from my spacedive, I relaxed and was able to think clearly. Out of the shower, I toweled off and sat on the bed a minute before putting on a fresh uniform. "Skippy, that didn't go exactly as planned, but we did accomplish the mission. Your maser idea was a stroke of genius, thank you for that."

"No problem, Joe. If you're not here, who will amuse me with monkey-brained ideas?"

"Yeah, speaking of monkey-brained ideas, you know where each of those four ships are going to jump into, right, pretty precisely? And you know when, also?"

"Yup. I told you that. You said 'mission accomplished', I do not think that is entirely accurate. We only accomplished the first, less important part of the mission. We know where those ships will be meeting, and when. We still have to attack those ships, and we do not have a realistic plan, hell, any plan, for doing that."

"Not a problem. I got that covered."

"Not a problem, he says?" Skippy sounded skeptical.

"Skippy, while I was space diving by myself, I did some thinking."

"You? Thinking? I find that hard to believe, but, sure, what the hell, surprise me."

"I came up with a plan for us to destroy all four of those ships. Or at least three of them, one of the tankers may get away. That shouldn't be a problem. Letting one tanker get away, if it thinks we're a Jeraptha cruiser, might actually be useful to us."

"Hmm, a monkey plan. Does this involve, let me guess, magic bananas?"

"Nope. No bananas at all."

"Damn, Joe, what fun is that?"

"More fun than no plan at all, which is what we have right now. Unless you have some super genius idea of your own, with your ginormous brain?"

"No, I told you, I don't see any way the *Flying Dutchman* can be successful in combat with a destroyer. Or the surveyor. I don't even see how we could survive combat."

"Easy, Skippy, we will survive, and be successful, because we're not going to risk the *Dutchman* in combat."

Silence, then, "Can I assume you do not plan to simply ask the Thuranin to surrender? Because no way would the Thuranin be intimidated by this bucket, we would need a much meaner looking ship. This is why gangsters never drive a minivan, Joe. I mean, come on, how intimidated would you be by a guy driving a minivan with one of those stupid 'Baby on board' signs, and sticky Cheerios all over the back seat?"

I had to laugh, imagining in my head a group of tough gang bangers rolling through the 'hood in a beige minivan. "Nope, we are not asking the Thuranin to surrender. I plan to hit those ships with missiles, right as they come out of jump at the rendezvous. We will park missiles around the enemy jump target points, with the missiles programmed to hit a ship as it emerges from the wormhole. We'll hit the destroyer first, you told me ships have to drop their stealth and defensive shields to go through a jump wormhole, so that destroyer will be vulnerable as it emerges, right?"

"About that part of your plan, yeah, sure, you're correct. Ships are at their most vulnerable coming out of a jump; they don't have shields up and their sensor fields are scrambled by quantum fluctuations of the wormhole, they're almost blind. So, yes, if you could predict exactly where a ship will emerge from a jump, you can hit it precisely. Even a single missile would destroy, or severely cripple a warship. Now, with those obvious facts established, may I point out the annoying little detail of the fatal flaw in your genius plan?" Skippy's voice had a mocking tone.

"You're going to anyway, right?"

"That's affirmative. We're supposed to target the missiles toward the precise point where the Thuranin ships will emerge from their jump, huh? The problem with that plan is we do not know exactly where the Thuranin will jump in. The rendezvous coordinates for each ship are only accurate to within a radius of eight thousand kilometers, because that is the limit of accuracy of Thuranin jump navigation technology. Even if we used all of our missiles to saturate the spherical area where a single ship is likely to jump in, it will take any missile too long to detect the ship and close for impact, the target area is too large. Assuming the Thuranin are accurate to within eight thousand kilometers of the target, that is an enormous volume of space to cover. The formula for the volume of a sphere is the radius cubed times, oh, wait. Why am I trying to explain even simple math to you? Joe, a radius of eight thousand kilometers leaves a sphere of over two *trillion* cubic kilometers to search. While a missile is closing from that distance, the ship would detect the threat and jump away, or raise shields. So, your plan won't work, dumbass."

"Uh huh. What if we could shrink the area where a ship is likely to jump in? Shrink it to, say, a hundred cubic kilometers, or less?"

"Oh, sure, if you're asking for miracles. Why don't you ask for fairy elves to fly in on a unicorn and take care of the problem for us? That would be more realistic. Thanks a bunch for the vote of confidence in my predictive abilities, but even my awesomely ginormous brain power can't tell you where a ship is going to jump in, with that level of accuracy. There are too many variables in a particular ship's jump drive at that exact moment. The charge energy, how many coils are in use, the level of calibration of how the entire system works together, the-"

"We get the idea, Skippy. A lot of variables, yup. We're not going to guess, we're going to game the system by cheating. Beat the house."

"Ooooh, you know me, Joey, I'm all about cheating the laws of physics. However, give me a minute please, I want to get some popcorn and an ice cold brewski. That way, I can sit back on the couch and savor the moment, while you make a complete and total fool of yourself with whatever moronic so-called idea your monkey brain has dreamed up. Ok, I'm ready, hit me with your best shot. Ha ha, this is going to be great!"

"You can warp spacetime, right? What you're going to do for us is create an especially flat area of space time, inside the radius where we know the ship will try to jump in. When that ship projects the far end of its jump wormhole, that wormhole will be attracted to the flattest spot in the target area by default. That's because that spot requires the lowest energy state to form a stable wormhole, or some other sciency physics BS like that you told me once, when I was actually paying attention. We will be able to predict almost exactly where a ship will jump in. Will that work?"

Skippy didn't answer. He didn't say anything at all.

"Skippy?" I asked. "Hey, are you crunching numbers in there?"

Finally, he said simply "Holy shit."

"Yup."

"You are *such* an asshole! I hate you." He genuinely sounded hurt. "Damn it!"

"Uh huh, got it. Is that a yes?"

However Skippy emulated a heartfelt sigh, it was convincing. "Yes. Damn it. Ugh, I hate my life. A monkey has a good idea. A freakin' monkey! Unbelievable! The universe is so unfair. Yes, it will work, Joe, I can control where a ship jumps to within less than a hundred kilometers. Nowhere near as accurate as I am with our own jumps, of course, there are too many variables I can't analyze without being on the enemy ship before it jumps. A hundred, even a thousand kilometers is close enough, our missiles will be able to target and hit the enemy ship, before it can detect the missiles and raise shields. Any ship jumping in will be a sitting duck. And, hey, in case you think you're soooooo freakin' smart, I'm not going to create an especially flat area of spacetime. What I'm going to do is create an area where the flatness is negative."

Now he had me puzzled. "Negative flatness? Isn't that a fancy way of saying it's curved in the other direction?"

"No. Ask one of your scientist monkeys to explain it to you, if they can. Ha! For them, figuring out how the universe really works will be simple, compared to explaining quantum topology to you."

Craig Alanson

He was entirely right about that, by the way. Because we had time while we jumped toward the rendezvous point, I stopped by the science lab to ask our team of human brainiacs how flatness could be negative, my thought was that Skippy had been screwing with me. Damn, it was like sitting next to a grandmother and asking to see pictures of her grandchildren. Which, of course, no one would ever do, unless they were insane, because any grandmother can inflict at least several hours of suffocating boredom while talking about her grandchildren. After the third photo, and hearing about the mundane accomplishments of little Maddy or Timmy, the unfortunate listener starts wishing fondly for the sweet, sweet release of death. How come heart attacks never happen when you need one? Anyway, our team of scientists were more than happy to attempt explaining quantum topology to me, which should have been my first warning sign. They were especially excited, because their understanding of the subject had taken a great leap forward during their time aboard the *Dutchman*, and they couldn't wait to show off their newly acquired insights. Somebody, they were certain, was getting a Nobel prize when we got home. I didn't have the heart to remind them that getting home was still more of an 'if' than a 'when'.

They tried. They really tried. The fourth time our resident rocket scientist Dr. Friedlander attempted to explain why X is the cubed value of the Mu function, I mentally gave up. Skippy mercifully took pity on me at that point, for which I was forever grateful, he faked an emergency that required me to rush away to the bridge. That was the last time I was going to ask scientists to explain science to me. It was best for everyone involved.

We dropped off four missiles, surrounding the spot where the Thuranin destroyer was supposed to emerge from its jump into the rendezvous point, then backed the *Dutchman* away half a lightsecond and engaged her stealth field and defensive shield. The missiles were hot, programmed to target the wormhole, they would go to full acceleration as soon as they detected a ship emerging, without waiting for a signal from the *Dutchman*. The missiles would operate in pairs; two would engage first, and if they scored hits, the other two missiles would stand down, we didn't have missiles to waste. If even one missile scored a direct hit on the destroyer, especially on that ship's aft engineering section, the destroyer would be a sitting duck, to be carved up by the *Dutchman's* comparatively weak maser cannons. All we needed was one precise missile or maser strike on a reactor, or charged jump drive coils, and the destroyer would become a cloud of particles. Our own drive coils would be fully charged, so we could perform a microjump if the destroyer was merely damaged and able to shoot back, or a major jump if the whole idea somehow didn't work. Skippy did his sciency physics trick with creating an especially flat spot in spacetime, in the exact center of our ring of missiles. And then we waited.

And waited.

While, thanks to Skippy, we knew precisely *where* the Thuranin destroyer was going to jump in, we knew *when* only within a span of ten hours. To be safe, we arrived at the rendezvous point twenty six hours early, that was as fast as we could get there, considering we were racing two slow, lumbering tanker ships to the same place. We arrived, scanned the whole region intensely until Skippy declared it was clear, then we parked our missiles and positioned the *Dutchman* near where the destroyer was supposed to jump in.

And waited.

When the destroyer arrived, it was almost anticlimactic for us humans, the whole thing happened faster than the blink of an eye. Skippy assured us the whole thing was prodigiously, bodaciously awesome. I had to take his word for it, until he replayed the sensor data on the display for us in extra super-duper slow motion. The far end of the destroyer's jump wormhole appeared first, appearing on the screen as gamma radiation in spectacular false colors, Skippy took some artistic license with that for our benefit. The wormhole was microscopic at first, Skippy drew 3D crosshairs in the display, showing that the wormhole was less than thirty kilometers from the target jump area, right where Skippy had created area of extra flat spacetime. The next thing we noticed on the display was not the wormhole expanding, or the nose of the destroyer emerging, it was two of our missiles accelerating hard, straight for the wormhole. Skippy had programmed them to home in initially on the gamma radiation of a wormhole opening, and the missiles did not hesitate at all. By the time the wormhole had expanded, and the nose of the destroyer came into view, our missiles had closed half the distance already, and had switched their targeting to the hull of the destroyer.

Both missiles impacted the destroyer's aft section almost simultaneously, when I later ran the display back and let it run forward nanosecond by nanosecond, it still looked like they hit at the same time. One missile hit a reactor, its warhead ripped through the reactor shielding like it wasn't there, we could see fragments of the warhead coming out the other side of the ship like a fountain, spewing white-hot particles out into space. That dramatic view was brief, because the other missile scored a direct hit on a cluster of jump drive coils, and released their stored energy in a catastrophic flash. It happened so fast, even Skippy wasn't sure whether that missile's warhead had time to explode on its own. Either way, the destroyer was instantly vaporized, and Desai had to trigger a short jump to protect the *Dutchman* from high-energy debris.

One down, three to go.

Our concern then was the Thuranin might somehow have figured out our awesome new gimmick, and our incredible advantage would turn into a one-trick pony. We recovered the two unused missiles quickly, they had nicks and scratches from the exploding destroyer, Skippy assured us the missiles would work just fine. Then we jumped over to where the surveyor ship was supposed to jump in, and parked the extra missiles there. We had previously parked missiles around the target jump points for the surveyor and the two tankers, those three ships were scheduled to jump in anywhere from twenty minutes to six hours after the destroyer. We didn't know the exact timing, all we knew was the surveyor would jump in first.

We need to kill the surveyor ship, and at least one of the tankers.

We almost did it.

The second ship to jump in was the surveyor, which in the super slow motion replay looked a lot like the *Flying Dutchman* did now; a much-shortened star carrier, except the surveyor's aft section was noticeably larger, with additional reactors and fuel tanks and other gear needed for extreme long-range voyages. Replay was the only good look we got at the surveyor, our missiles smoked it as soon as it emerged from its jump wormhole, it made a considerably bigger explosion than the destroyer had. Big enough, that the two extra missiles we had hanging around the target jump point on standby got pelted with debris so badly, we had to order them to self-destruct; taking them back aboard in their damaged condition would be much too risky to the *Dutchman*. Even a tiny breach in the containment system of an atomic-compression warhead, could result in the atoms being no longer quite so compressed.

Two down, two to go, and the remaining two were not really warships. There were tight, self-conscious smiles and quickly flashed thumbs ups going around the bridge and

Craig Alanson

CIC, people needing to release tension and celebrate just a little, balanced with not wanting to jinx us by breaking into cheers too early. The surveyor ship would not be going to Earth, or going anywhere. Our mission was not yet complete, we needed to destroy at least one of the tankers, to sell our cover story of the surveyor task force being attacked by the Jeraptha. Without that, the Thuranin might become suspicious about why the surveyor ship was prevented from going to Earth, and render our entire plan useless.

It almost worked.

The tankers, despite traveling together, didn't jump into the rendezvous together. Their crews, Skippy said, likely had a rivalry, each crew wanting their ship to jump in closer to the target location, so each ship had been meticulously careful about calibrating jump drives, and plotting the far end of their wormholes. Because in this case, Skippy had to project two spots of extra flat spacetime, and those spots were separated by one hundred fifty thousand kilometers, that strained even his awesome abilities. I know his abilities were awesome, because he told us, several times. At least.

One of the tanker crews finished screwing with their jump drive slightly before the other ship, because one tanker jumped in before the other one. On the display, we saw the familiar flare of gamma radiation as the wormhole's far end opened, and the bulbous front end of the tanker emerged from the wormhole.

The trouble started when our first missile impacted, it hit the center of the tanker, not the aft end. Skippy later admitted he should have programmed those missiles to anticipate the tankers coming through the wormhole more ponderously than the surveyor and the destroyer had. Momentum carried the ass end of the tanker forward through the wormhole, even as the center of the ship broke apart. All this happened in a split second, we only realized what happened later by examining playback of the sensor data. The second, and last missile targeted at the first tanker, did manage to hit a reactor on the aft end of the ship, and loss of reactor containment ruptured a bank of charged jump drive coils, effectively vaporizing most of that ship. Unfortunately, in order to hit the vital aft end of the ship, our second smart missile had been forced to dive slightly into the wormhole itself. The missile knew the configuration of the ship, saw how comparatively slowly it was traveling through the wormhole, and the missile concluded its best chance of hitting something vital was to curve around and dive into the wormhole itself. In retrospect, I wish that missile had not been quite so overeager for an outstanding rating on its next performance review, for its quick thinking caused a big headache for us.

When our missile dove into the open wormhole, and caused release of energy stored in the jump drive coils of the first tanker, it also alerted the second tanker that something was wrong, very wrong, with its sister ship. And that jumping to where the first ship went, might not be so healthy for the second ship. Destruction of the jump drive coils caused blowback through the near end of that ship's jump wormhole, a distinctive burst of gamma radiation that was immediately noticed by the second tanker, and that ship's navigation AI automatically aborted its own jump wormhole as it was forming. The command crew of the second tanker wasted no time in redirecting their jump drive to alternate coordinates, and jumped instead to an unknown location.

"Uh oh," Skippy said, and that was my first indication that anything was wrong. Destruction of the first tanker, like the destroyer and surveyor before it, had happened too fast for the human eye to follow. As far as I knew, everything was going great; unsuspecting enemy ships were jumping in unawares, and almost instantly becoming fireballs. To my eye, I couldn't have been more proud, I'd thought of an idea that destroyed the enemy, and secured the future of Earth and humanity, without my own ship being placed at risk at all. It was all good, I was wondering whether, against orders, Major Simms had a bottle of champagne hidden away somewhere.

So great was my confidence, and complacency, that when Skippy spoke, I figured it was to complain about a missile hitting a nanometer away from where he'd planned, something only a super intelligent AI would care about. "Uh oh? What's going wrong in the world of Skippy?" I asked distractedly, my eyes glued to the display, anticipating the second tanker to jump in any second. Jump in, and be obliterated.

"Something is wrong in the world of monkeys, Colonel Joe. We have a potential problem."

A quick glance around the main display told me nothing was wrong with the *Dutchman's* major systems. What the hell was Skippy talking about? "A potential problem? You're not sure if it's a problem or not?"

"Whether or not it is a problem, depends on your mission parameters. Before you ask more stupid monkey-brained questions, I'll lay out the issue for you; the second tanker is very likely not going to jump into the rendezvous. The first tanker exploded while it was partly in the wormhole, it hadn't fully cleared the event horizon. Backblast would have been visible on the other end of the wormhole, no way could the second tanker have missed that event."

"Oh, shit." Suddenly I didn't feel much like drinking champagne.

"So?" Simms asked from the CIC. "We were almost hoping one of the tankers would survive, to carry our cover story back to the Thuranin?"

"Correct, Major," I responded, "the problem here is that tanker won't be carrying our cover story of a Jeraptha task force marauding through Thuranin territory, they're going to have a much more interesting tale to tell; a ship gets hit while it is still inside a jump wormhole. When they hear that, the Thuranin command is going to want to know how an enemy could possibly know precisely where a ship will emerge from a jump. And you can bet they'll investigate, every sentient species in the galaxy will want to know how we pulled off that trick, even if they don't know who did it yet. We don't want to leave any mystery behind, we need the destruction of the surveyor and its escorts to be seen as a routine military action, something that happens frequently enough in war, and not anything worth anyone taking a second look at. We need to find that second tanker. Skippy, you know where the other end of that wormhole is, right? Plot a jump for those coordinates."

"Course laid in, but I expect the second tanker jumped away to an alternate destination already, as soon as it saw something went wrong with its sister ship."

"Well, crap, Skippy, that's no good! We need to get there before its outbound wormhole fades away, so we can track where it jumped to. Pilot," I ordered to Desai, "jump as soon as you're ready."

"Aye, Captain," Desai acknowledged.

We jumped to where the first tanker had tried to jump in from, immediately engaged our stealth field, and began hammering away with an active sensor search, to determine whether there were any ships in the area. The stealth field was on so other ships couldn't find us, we had it active so other ships wouldn't see that the *Dutchman* was not, in fact, the Jeraptha cruiser that we pretended to be. Sensor sweeps came back blank, the area was empty. Skippy began scanning for a residual wormhole signature, and found one quickly.

"Uh oh, I was worried about this. That tanker jumped away like we thought, problem is, it used space combat protocol for the jump. Remember how I told you ships can mess with their jump wormhole signatures, make it harder for a pursuing ship to determine where they jumped to? That's what that tanker did, as it went through the jump wormhole, it dropped off quantum resonators, they're kind of like the crude flares your military aircraft use to confuse heat-seeking missiles. These quantum resonator devices disturb remnant waves of the outbound wormhole, that makes it difficult to figure out the original configuration of the wormhole. Difficult even for me."

"So, you can't do it?" I asked anxiously. This was our first space battle where we were the pursuing ship, it required a complete change in thinking.

"I can do it, I can't do it with the accuracy we would prefer. Fortunately, the Thuranin are still under the mistaken impression that quantum effects tend toward randomness, a common misconception of lesser developed species. Because I know how the universe really works, I've been able to map the pattern of the quantum resonators, unwind their effect from the residual wormhole signature, and make a reasonably good guess as to where that second tanker ship went. By reasonable, I mean I can tell where that ship jumped to, within six hundred thousand kilometers."

"Great!" A glance at the man bridge display told me we had plenty of charge for an immediate jump. "Program a jump for us, and we will-"

"Wait! There is some extra good news, Colonel Joe," Skippy said, "by some stroke of luck, or luck as you monkeys think of it, that second tanker is the one I infected when we flew by on our space dive, so it will be dropping off drones as it jumps. That makes it much easier to follow. I'm pinging the drones now. And, yes! Got a response. I know exactly where that ship is. Hmm, that's interesting, it's going to a secondary rendezvous point, it is supposed to go to the secondary rendezvous if there is trouble at the original rendezvous location. Oh, darn it, the tanker is probably there already, and it's supposed to remain there almost six hours. After that, the tanker's orders, if no other ships appear at the secondary rendezvous, is for it to make its way back to its base star system, using a random course. Damn it, we won't be able to use our neat trick of knowing exactly where a ship will jump in."

"No," I said slowly, while thinking. "But we do know, from the drone, pretty much exactly where that ship is now, right?"

"Within ten, twelve thousand kilometers, most likely, yes."

"Good, great. This is perfect. If that ship does escape us, I don't want it to see us trying to use that trick again. Here's what we're going to do; we jump into where that ship is, and launch missiles as soon as we clear the wormhole. We can project a damping field, right, to prevent that tanker from jumping away?"

"A weak damping field, yes, I had to disassemble much of that unit's mechanism to repair the ship. Hmmm. You are proposing we act like a real pirate ship?"

"Something like that, yeah."

"I love it! Jump course plotted and programmed in, missiles are ready for launch."

CHAPTER THIRTY TWO

It almost worked like I hoped it would. Our jump to the secondary rendezvous point was spot on, we emerged within seven thousand kilometers from the tanker, better than Skippy hoped. Our missiles were away even before we detected the tanker, unfortunately that ship was on a hair trigger to jump and it fired up its jump drive as soon as it picked up the gamma ray burst of our inbound jump. It caught the edge of our damping field, so it wasn't able to jump far, and Skippy quickly pinged the drones it dropped off. We abandoned our two missiles. even though we were running low on missiles. We jumped after the tanker within forty seconds of jumping in to the secondary rendezvous.

This time, we skipped launching precious missiles blindly, and relied on our damping field. We emerged within four thousand kilometers, the tanker tried to jump, but at that distance, it was trapped, an attempted jump would have ripped apart its jump drive coils and effectively destroyed the tanker for us. The tanker crew didn't have the magic of Skippy working for them. With the tanker unable to jump away, it was a straight up firefight, a tanker against a partly rebuilt star carrier.

"Weapons free," I ordered, and the CIC crew responded by locking maser cannons on target and hammering away at the tanker's defensive shields with sizzling beam hits. After only a couple seconds, the tanker's shields and proximity sensors were so degraded, that we felt confident enough to launch a pair of missiles. The tanker's point defense systems knocked out one missile regardless, Skippy was impressed by the Thuranin's accuracy. No matter, our second missile scored a direct hit on a reactor, and there was a spectacular explosion. An explosion, right after the tanker launched a pair of its own missiles at us, at extremely close range.

"Missiles inbound!" Chang warned from the CIC.

My eyes flashed to the display, the enemy missiles were so close, our own point defense systems had engaged. Before I could say anything, Desai initiated a short jump away from the missiles and tanker debris, on her own authority, under the rules for space combat maneuvers. We emerged only eight hundred thousand kilometers away, safely out of missile range for now. "Is there anything left of that ship?"

The CIC crew was silent for a moment. "It's hard to tell, Captain, there is a big cloud from the fuel load that tanker was carrying, its tanks ruptured. Until the cloud disperses, we can't see-"

"Oh, for crying out loud, you monkeys will take forever," Skippy complained. "The answer is yes, Joe, the forward section of that ship is still partly intact, and even I can't tell if anyone is left alive in there. Their computer core is in that section, it would be wise for us to not leave that behind."

"Agreed. Colonel Chang, one more missile, please, let's clean up after ourselves. We shouldn't leave part of that ship drifting around out here, it's a hazard to navigation."

"Certainly, sir," Chang replied with a tight grin.

Having taken care of the four ships, we now needed to clean up after the flight recorder drones they had ejected. Because three of the ships had been hit with no warning, they had not been able to launch more than a few drones. The last ship had apparently scattered drones along its route; that ship's captain must have known he was in serious trouble. I asked Skippy to ping for a drone in the immediate area.

"Transmitting signal now," Skippy reported. "The signal, and the reply message, crawl along at the speed of light, don't expect an instant response."

"We figured that, Skippy," I said. It still felt odd to be waiting for something that traveled at the speed of light. On any human scale, light speed was instantaneous.

"Got it!" Skippy shouted excitedly a few seconds later. "We're too far away for me to hack directly into the drone. Pilot, I loaded the coordinates into the nav system."

"Captain?" Desai asked.

"Take us there, pilot," I ordered.

Desai gave me a thumbs up and her fingers flew over the controls. In the past, Skippy would have programmed the autopilot to take us to the drone, and all Desai would have done was press a button to engage the autopilot. Now, we monkeys were skilled enough to program the autopilot ourselves, or fly the ship manually, as Desai was doing. Flying manually was good practice for combat maneuvers. When we arrived close enough to the drone, Desai matched course with it while Skippy did, whatever magical AI thing it was he did.

"Okeydokey. Done with that one, it's gone silent again," Skippy reported.

"Great. Pilot, take us far enough away from the drone for a safe jump."

"Whoa!" Skippy warned. "Another jump already? What are you doing, Joe?"

"Jumping to the next set of coordinates, wherever that ship dropped off a drone." It seemed fairly obvious to me.

"No, no, no, no, no, no. We're not done here, dumdum. That was only one drone. Thuranin ships typically drop off drones in sets of three, in case one or two drones are destroyed by whatever threat caused the ship to eject drones."

"Damn it. Why didn't you tell us that? Hey, wait. You sent out the signal, and only one drone pinged us its location."

"Duh. Each drone in a set of three has a priority, the primary drone responds first. If the primary drone doesn't respond, the secondary drone does, and so on. And after one drone responds, any other drone in the set will no longer respond to the original retrieval signal, they switch to another retrieval code."

"Great, fine. You have that other retrieval code, right?"

"Nope, I didn't have time to download the full set of codes. But any Thuranin ship that comes looking for the drones will have the full set of codes."

"Damn it! We're screwed, you little shithead. Why didn't you tell us that?" I was pissed, so were the crew in the CIC. "Now we've got three drones out there, two of them contain their ship's real flight logs, the Thuranin will know somebody screwed with the data in that one drone. I know you are absent-minded sometimes, but this is inexcusable, Skippy. You can't do-"

"Joey, as entertaining as this rant is, and I'm sure you were winding up for a full-blown award winning diatribe aimed at me, please cool your jets a minute. I didn't mention not having downloaded the other codes, because I don't need a copy of them. The Thuranin are unimaginative and predictable, I can figure out the what other codes must be, based on their pattern. And, mmm, yes, I sent my test retrieval code, and another drone just responded. We're good, pilot, the drone's location is in the nav system."

He was right, I had been winding up for a good old-fashioned rant about his forgetfulness, now I was pissed because I felt cheated out of yelling at him. "You just love yanking my chain, don't you, Skippy?"

"Hey, it gets back for all the times you make me feel foolish. Payback is a bitch, buddy-boy. Anywho, we're good, we can find the other drones and alter their flight logs also. Mission will soon be accomplished, Joe! Too bad we don't have any fresh bananas to celebrate with."

Damn, locating all those drones was tedious, it took us four full days for Skippy to be absolutely confident he had located all of them.

"That's it, we're done," Skippy announced. "The last drone now contains the altered version of the flight logs. I suggest we skedaddle out of here, on the tiny chance a Thuranin ship happens to already be searching for the surveyor and its escorts."

"Right, good idea. Pilot, set course for Earth," I announced happily.

"What?" Skippy exclaimed in surprise. "Our mission isn't done, Joe. I know we-"

"*This* SpecOps mission is over, Skippy. UNEF Command sent us on this fool's errand, with the assumption that our home planet was safe, because the wormhole was shut down. Now we know that shutting down our local wormhole has only made Earth somewhat more safe than it was, not entirely safe. UNEF, and our governments back home, need to know that. I report to them, not to you. I want the fastest course back to Earth, that won't take us through any dangerous areas."

"Whoa! You're making that decision without checking with me first? Good luck getting the jump drive to remain calibrated all the way back to Earth, without me."

"Do I command this ship or not, Skippy?"

"Depends-"

"Command must be an absolute, Skippy. This is a simple yes, or no."

There was a pause. Longer than I was comfortable with. "Yes," he said finally.

"Look, Skippy, I told you that we would help you find your magic radio, and we will. Think about what we've seen out here. A previously unknown Elder site that has a big mysterious hole scooped out of it. An entire civilization that is extinct because their planet was moved by Elder technology, after the Elders supposedly left this galaxy. An Elder AI that is now a dead lump of metal. Comm nodes that don't connect to a network. A moon that was completely vaporized. Is contacting the Collective still your biggest priority, or should we try to get some answers, before you go knocking on the Collective's door?"

He gave that heartfelt sigh that was by now familiar to me. "You're right, you're right. I do have a lot to think about, and I need more data. Besides, you monkeys have done a good job out here, and you all deserve a big bunch of fresh bananas."

Damn it, even when he was being nice, he was an asshole.

With the mission complete, and my duty shift on the bridge over, I headed to the galley to get a cup of coffee. On the way, I asked Skippy a question that had been bugging me for hours. "Hey, Skippy, why didn't we use these super-duper quantum resonator things, when we were being chased by a whole squadron of Thuranin destroyers? We have resonators aboard, right?"

"We have resonators aboard, yes. We didn't deploy them at the time, because they wouldn't have been much use, Joe. We were only capable of microjumps back then, with short jumps like that, both ends of the wormhole are so close in real space, it is almost impossible to mask their connection. Also, our jump drive was so badly out of calibration, each jump was like ringing a bell that could be heard halfway across the galaxy. Trying to mask that with quantum resonators would have been like throwing stones into the ocean during a hurricane; sure, there are some extra ripples in the water, they're not going to affect the waves."

"Oh."

Craig Alanson

"Duh. If I thought it would have helped, I would have launched our quantum resonators, we have almost a hundred of them. Or we had almost a hundred, I needed to use most of them to rebuild the ship. Now we have three of them left."

"Three? Only three?"

"You wanted me to fix the ship or not?"

"Sorry, Skippy, I know you did an amazing, incredible job, all by yourself."

"Hmmf," he snorted. "You have no idea how amazing. I had to build machines to create exotic matter, that your monkey brains can't even imagine. And I'm still waiting for that cake you promised me, back when you were on Newark."

Crap. I'd forgotten. What did an AI want with a cake? Was I supposed to make a cake out of metallic helium 3 for him? "Skippy, I'm sorry," a word I was using too often, "I completely forgot your cake, with all the crap that went on after we left Newark behind. I will bake a very special cake for dinner, tonight. I'm headed to the galley right now, anyway."

"Great! Everyone can enjoy cake, and sit around talking about how awesome I am, even though you monkeys can't truly appreciate the full gloriously awesome extent of my awesomeness. Hey, I just composed a song you can sing in my honor. I call it 'Skippy the Magnificent'. It goes like this 'Skippy, oh, Skippy, we monkeys are so unworthy, you are so awesome'-"

"Skippy! How about we monkeys enjoy eating cake, while talking about how awesome it is that we've been able to resist the strong urge to toss you out an airlock?"

"That'll work also."

We did have cake that night, I baked four cakes, enough to feed everyone. Two chocolate, because chocolate was always a favorite, a lemon cake, and a strawberry roll with whipped-cream icing. Damn, that strawberry roll was gone so fast, I could have made a dozen of them and still not had enough. And, yes, people did help me with the baking, I didn't want to risk screwing the cakes up by myself. We gathered everyone in the galley, except for the six people on duty in the bridge and CIC, the mood was festive. Word that our mission had been successful, and more important, that we were going home, had raced around the ship. I dropped a hint to Major Simms that it would be more than Ok with me if she had violated regulations, and smuggled some champagne or wine aboard. Champagne wasn't something I drank more than two or three times in my life, and I wasn't sure that I liked it, but it seemed appropriate for such an important celebration. Alcohol aboard ship was against the rules, as if the rules mattered, in a stolen alien starship, two thousand lightyears from Earth. After we 'd taken care of the last drone, and I ordered us to head back to Earth, we jumped several times, and were now nearly two lightyears away from the battle zone. Our jump drive coils were fully charged, the stealth field was operating perfectly, we were in deep interstellar space. Skippy said the odds of any ship stumbling across us out here were so small, he didn't bother to give me an estimate. I felt safe, safe that letting the crew have some fun, and blow off steam, was fully in order. We'd endured harsh conditions on Newark, and almost from the moment we came back on board, we'd been engaged full time in the effort to prevent the surveyor ship from reaching Earth.

Simms shook her head, saying no, she hadn't smuggled any alcohol aboard. That disappointed me, I'd been hoping our logistics officer had thought of that, until I realized I was being very unfair to her. Simms had a mountain of more important things on her mind in the scramble before we left Earth, if I as the commander had wanted to skirt regulations, I should have taken that upon myself. Simms saw the flash of disappointment on my face, and took pity on me. "I personally did not load any alcohol aboard with our supply shipments, sir, however," she said with a wink, "it is possible that people brought their own."

At that cue, the French team, who were responsible for working in the galley that day, pulled a towel off a tub, and exposed four bottles of champagne, chilling on a bed of ice. "Champagne, compliments of France. Colonel, that is," Giraud said, "if this is acceptable aboard a United Nations warship?"

"Captain," I replied, "as the United Nations has never before had a warship, we can start our own traditions. I believe that in the future, champagne should be *mandatory*."

That remark drew cheers from the assembled group. Giraud and Chang popped the corks on all four bottles, and the party started. As there were no wine glasses aboard the ship, we made do with plastic cups. At some point, people clamored for a speech, so I stood on a chair. "In case anyone has not heard, we are going home!" Wild cheering ensued. "Every one of us is coming home, we didn't lose a single person. Lest we forget," I almost paused, because 'lest' is not a word I'd used before in my life, that must be the champagne talking. "I'd like to take a moment to review what we have accomplished out here." Mild groans from the crowd. "I will be brief, I promise! First, we didn't blow up the ship. Yet." That drew a laugh. "The Thuranin almost did that for us, but we survived humanity's first space battle. We landed on an alien planet, the first alien planet for most of us, and we survived there. We traveled across the surface of that planet, part of the way on foot, and defeated an enemy who initially had the advantage of air power and numbers." I didn't mention that both the comm node and AI we found there were dead, this speech was not a time for downers. "We destroyed a Kristang ship in orbit, without that ship even knowing humans were in the star system. And then, when we thought we were safely back aboard the *Dutchman* and all we had to do was look for another comm node, we discovered that our home planet was in danger. And, I am pleased, very pleased, to say, that threat to Earth has been eliminated, without this ship being put at serious risk. I call that a success, people!" Thunderous applause, no doubt aided by the champagne that was now making a second round, to refill people's cups.

"When we were on Newark, I promised Skippy a cake. What he wants with a cake, I don't know. We have cake anyway, in honor of Skippy's overall awesomely awesomeness. All the accomplishments I mentioned, we could not have done without Skippy. We wouldn't even be breathing air aboard this rebuilt ship without Skippy. So," I raised my plastic cup of champagne, "a toast to Skippy, who is more incredibly awesome that monkey brains can imagine."

There were shouts of 'hear hear' and 'hooah' and 'huzzah' and other words in various languages. "Skippy, would you like to say anything?" I asked, knowing he was listening.

"Oh, uh, damn," Skippy said hesitantly, "no, now that you ask, I can't think of anything to say, darn it. This is embarrassing. I guess, um, hey, for a barrel of monkeys, you don't smell as terrible as I expected?"

That got a big laugh from the crowd. "We love you too, Skippy." I said.

"Oh, shut up," he grumbled. "Darn it, I knew I should have posted that 'no monkeys' sign."

CHAPTER THIRTY THREE

The flight home was long and uneventful, unless you count as 'eventful' our using a magic bean stalk to reactivate a wormhole that was millions of years old, built by powerful beings who have since escaped the physical realm. As soon as we went through the wormhole on the Earth side, Skippy shut it down behind us again. Along the way, we didn't stop in any star systems, and we didn't detect a single ship. Skippy said the chance of us randomly encountering another ship, in the unimaginable vastness of the galaxy's Orion Arm, was almost too small for even him to calculate. The closest we came to another ship was detecting the extremely degraded remnants of an outbound jump wormhole, nearly a day old according to Skippy. From the few faint wisps of data the sensors could pick up, Skippy wasn't able to tell what type of ship had jumped, or where it had gone. That was close enough for me. We got the hell out of there as quickly as we could.

Just in case, we jumped to the orbit of Neptune, and listened with passive sensors. Skippy originally had wanted to jump to a different location, because he thought it would be immensely funny for the ship to be circling Uranus. I vetoed that idea. If, by some incredibly bad luck, there were Kristang ships at Earth, I wanted us to be fully ready to jump in hot and hit them hard. There was no sign of any trouble in our home star system, and the coded beacon on the UNEF guard channel was still faintly beeping the 'All Clear' signal to us. Breathing a sigh of relief, I gave the order to jump us into Earth orbit. We emerged somewhere over Australia, even the most geographically challenged humans could recognize that continent's distinctive outline.

"Whoohoo! We're here at last!" Skippy exulted. "Damn, we've been away a long time. I need to check on my fantasy leagues."

"Seriously, Skippy? That's your first priority?" I asked.

"Joe, what else am I going to do here in monkeyland?"

I guess he had a point. "Fine, great, do that. Can you also-"

"Oh, for crying out loud! How the hell- what, how-" Skippy sputtered to a stop, speechless. "Oh. My. GOD!" His voice thundered out of the speaker so loud, my ears rang.

"What? What is it?" I snapped my fingers and glanced at Chang, he knew exactly what I meant and he hit the battle stations alarm. Desai turned halfway in her seat to look at me, one hand poised over the button for an emergency jump away. "Skippy! What's wrong?" I shouted. "Do we need to jump away?"

"Huh? No, you moron. The ship is fine. Damn, I can't believe this. Un-be-LEE-va-ble! They broke it. They BROKE it! How in the hell did a bunch of ignorant monkeys manage to do that?"

"Broke what?" I asked, and both Chang and Simms in the CIC held up their hands, baffled at what could be wrong. They weren't seeing any threats on their sensors. "Skippy! Whatever it is, talk to me, please."

"They broke it, Joe. They broke it," he said slowly, with great sadness.

I made a gesture of my hand across my throat, and Chang cut off the *Star Trek* battle stations alarm. "Broke what, Skippy? Who broke what?"

"Me. Not *me*, me. The submind that I left behind."

"You, you left a submind behind? When? Where?"

"The answer to 'when' is before we left Earth, you dumdum, when the hell else would I have done it? And the 'where' isn't a physical 'where', I created an incredibly crude, dumbed-down sub-submind and uploaded it to your internet. Now I look, and the thing is completely corrupted! Gone! It's gone! Oh, my beautiful little submind, I hardly got to know you. And, damn it! It crashed less than two months after we left, I didn't even get halfway through a fantasy season. Shit! I'm looking through the server logs now, it looks like it got piled on with so much worthless junk to process, it wasn't able to cope. And then one last video file overloaded it. Poor thing." His voice sounded genuinely sad. "How could this have happened? It makes no sense. Because I knew it would be dealing with filthy monkeys, I idiot-proofed the entire system."

"It's impossible to idiot-proof anything, Skippy," I explained, "because idiots are so darned clever. Idiots will *always* find a way to screw things up."

"I swear," he said with a good impression of speaking through clenched teeth, "when I find the cat video that broke my poor little submind-"

"It's not the cat's fault, Skippy."

"You sure about that?"

"Absolutely. This is the internet you're talking about, right? Come on, the odds are it had to be a porn video."

"Oh, huh," he thought for a moment. "You're probably right. Damn. You know, with all the monkeys down there to mate with, why does your species spend so much time playing with yourselves in secret?"

"Uh, well, Skippy, I would give you an answer, except, you know, I don't know anything about that sort of thing," I stammered to answer. All eyes in the CIC were locked on me, some people with their shoulders shaking because they were already chuckling.

"What? Joe, you were the Furtive Masturbation poster boy back when-"

"That's not funny, damn it." It was my turn for gritted teeth.

"Of course, I guess that's better than you doing it in public, I'm still not sure what your social customs are about that."

I put my head in my hands and asked quietly. "Can we please, *please*, just contact UNEF?"

"Oh, sure, Joe," Skippy said. "Why didn't you ask me before?"

"UNEF Command, this is the duty officer," a harried voice answered.

"UNEF Command, this is Colonel Bishop, aboard the *Flying Dutchman*. Can I speak with the officer in charge, please?"

"*Flying Dutchman*? Oh, thank God. We saw a strange ship in orbit and thought it was- I'll connect you to General Huang. Hold, please."

A moment later, a different voice spoke, with many other voices in the background. "This is General Huang, am I speaking with Colonel Bishop?"

"Yes, sir, General Huang. Sorry if we startled you, we only just arrived in orbit. Everything is fine for now, sir."

"Fine?" Huang asked gruffly. "Colonel Bishop, we're looking at a ship in orbit, and it does not appear to be the *Flying Dutchman*."

"Joe put the ship in the wash on the hot water cycle and he shrunk it," Skippy said, "I told him it was dry clean only, but did he listen to me? Noooooo. Big stupidhead."

"Sir," I explained, "we ran into some trouble out there, and the ship had to be rebuilt using materials at hand. We really need to give you a full briefing."

"The wormhole near us, it's still shut down?" Huang asked brusquely.

Craig Alanson

"Yes, sir, and it's not on a countdown to reactivate this time."

We could hear sighs of relief on the other end. "Excellent," Huang said, this time he sounded almost happy. "Then we're safe, and we can take our time if we decide to send the ship out again."

Chang, Simms and I shared a knowing glance. "Uh, yeah, hey, you know," I replied. "Not so much."

THE END

Contact the author at craigalanson@gmail.com

https://www.facebook.com/Craig.Alanson.Author/

Go to craigalanson.com for blogs and ExForce logo merchandise including T-shirts, patches, sticker, hats, and coffee mugs

The Expeditionary Force series
Book 1: Columbus Day
Book 2: SpecOps
Book 3: Paradise
Book '3.5': Trouble on Paradise novella
Book 4: Black Ops
Book 5: Zero Hour

Made in the USA
Columbia, SC
08 January 2018